The Accidental
Salvation
of
Gracie Lee

The Accidental Salvation of Gracie Lee

Talya Tate Boerner

Talya Tate Boerner

Published by:
Southern Yellow Pine (SYP) Publishing
4351 Natural Bridge Rd.
Tallahassee, FL 32305

www.syppublishing.com

This is a work of fiction. Names, characters, places, and events that occur either are the products of the author's imagination or are used fictitiously. Any resemblance to actual persons, places, or events is purely coincidental.

The contents and opinions expressed in this book do not necessarily reflect the views and opinions of Southern Yellow Pine Publishing, nor does the mention of brands or trade names constitute endorsement.

ISBN-10: 1940869617 Trade Paperback
ISBN-13: 13: 978-1-940869-61-2 Trade Paperback
ISBN-13: 978-1-940869-63-6 Hardcover
ISBN-13: 978-1-940869-62-9 ePub
ISBN-13: 978-1-940869-64-3 Adobe eBook
Library of Congress Control Number: 2015959264

Front Cover Design: James C. Hamer
Author photo: Jerry McClure, Jmac Images

Printed in the United States of America
First Edition January 2016

To Momma, who taught me to love books, and to my father-in-law, Eugene Boerner, who once reminded me that I wasn't getting any younger.

Chapter One

Daddy was in a bad mood. I could tell by the slow, drawn-out crunch of gravel on the driveway. He'd parked by the old plum tree and was taking forever to walk through the back door. He was predictable. Just like my life so far.

One Mississippi, Two Mississippi...

The truck engine fell quiet, leaving only the sound of tree frogs. Lucky's ears perked. I rubbed the white spot on the back of his neck, and he relaxed back onto the floor beside me.

Three Mississippi, Four Mississippi...

Tucking Barbie underneath the throw pillow on my lap, I traced my finger over the red blooms that covered my library book. Abby, my little sister, lay dozing on the opposite end of the couch, sprawled flat on her back. She had a way of sleeping through anything—a loud television show, or even one of Momma and Daddy's late-night arguments. As I watched, her long eyelashes fluttered, just slightly. Then she giggled in her sleep, rolled over onto her belly, and continued snoozing.

Seven Mississippi, Eight Mississippi...

Slipping my hands under the pillow, I twirled Barbie's silky hair and stroked the bumpy fabric of her pin-dot skirt. Momma sewed most all of Barbie's clothes from scrap material, and sometimes we even dressed alike. Barbie and me, not Momma and me.

Nine Mississippi, Ten Mississippi...

I stared at the back door for a good long time.

What was Daddy doing? Resting, thinking, deciding whether or not to turn around and leave for good?

Twelve Mississippi...

From my spot on the couch, I listened to the nightly sounds of our house, as familiar as the hymns we sang every Sunday morning at Boon Chapel. The crack of the ice tray. The opening of the silverware drawer with its earsplitting creak. As Momma reheated Daddy's supper, the smell of fried potatoes and salt pork filled the air. Abby and I had eaten hours ago.

When Daddy worked extra late, Momma didn't make us wait to eat. Those were the best nights, especially when she let us eat hot dogs and macaroni and cheese in front of the television.

The screen door slapped shut, its echo vibrating through our house and inside my head. I jolted even though I had expected the rattle.

Fifteen Mississippi.

Daddy tossed his grimy thermos and a stack of ledger papers on the side table near his favorite recliner and then wiped his brow with a handkerchief he pulled from his back pocket. When he nodded and grunted in my direction, I half-smiled back and reminded myself to breathe. As though allowed only so many syllables per day, Daddy made sure not to use too many at once. His bronzed face and creased forehead made him appear older than some of my friends' fathers, but I realized that wasn't the case. When I grew up, I was not going to be a farmer. This much I knew.

Daddy disappeared into the kitchen. He grumbled about something, his words low and dull. I was unable to make them out. Momma answered, sounding cheerful, but in a forced way. Momma had the hardest job of all.

Eventually, after Daddy vanished into the bathroom, Momma swept the kitchen floor. That was always her last chore before everything repeated in the morning. I considered it curious, the amount of filth and food and odd things that ended up in the dustpan after supper. One day's worth of leftover life tossed into the trash.

"Gracie, time for bed," Momma called out to me from the kitchen. Tugging Barbie from beneath the pillow, I smoothed her hair and poked my still-sleeping sister with Barbie's feet, frozen in tiptoe position.

"Let's go to bed, Abby," I said. She rubbed her eyes, muttered okay and followed me through the kitchen and along the hallway into our bedroom, dragging her feet without fully waking up. Abby changed into her nightgown and tumbled into bed without saying a word. Tomorrow, she wouldn't remember how she had gotten there.

No matter how tired I was, I refused to go to bed without first brushing my teeth. No way. Not since Mrs. Barns, the school nurse, took all the girls into the home economics room for a special health class and made us chew tablets that dyed our teeth bright red. When my best friend, Janice, saw her flaming scarlet gums in the bathroom mirror, she started crying. I clasped my hand over my mouth, certain I'd soon be wearing false teeth like Papa Pete. Later on the playground, Bubba, who is my friend even though he's a boy, told me that Coach Greene forced the boys to chew the same red tablets; their lesson was in the gym. Bubba told me not to worry. "The dye comes off. Momma makes me chew those things once a month." Bubba knew a lot about health sort of things because Mrs. Barns was his mother.

I squirted a length of toothpaste on my brush, trying to make it curl on the end like the pictures in Momma's magazines. It never did. While I brushed, I sang all the words to "The Star-Spangled Banner" in my head, a little trick I taught myself to make sure I brushed long enough. I stared at myself through toothpaste splatters that dotted the mirror. My aunts and uncles always said I looked just like Momma. I couldn't see it, except maybe in the shape of my face, which was thin like hers, but certainly not in my eyes. Momma had movie-star eyes—that's how Daddy described them—because hers were an unusual blue color that changed from icy to slate, depending upon the color shirt she wore or the mood she was in. My eyes were the same uninteresting color as Daddy's. Hazel. With sixty-four shades in the largest crayon box, not a single one was named Hazel. Hazel was a non-color.

Although the weather had not turned hot yet, the freckles across my cheeks had begun to darken and multiply, and my wavy, brown hair, normally a drab shade during winter, had brightened. Momma said women would pay good money for natural blonde highlights like mine, but she never said any such thing about my freckles. Or my hazel eyes.

My sister and I shared a tiny bedroom that barely had enough space for twin beds, a dresser, and the nightstand Daddy made in high-school shop class. Sometimes sharing a room was annoying, but mostly it was okay. I found my favorite nightgown in the top dresser drawer, pulled it over my head, and dropped my dirty clothes in a heap on the floor at the foot of my bed. I'd pick them up tomorrow.

As I climbed into bed, Lucky was already waiting for me, his head on my pillow like a human instead of a dog. Abby made a faint noise and rolled onto her back. The fan oscillated back and forth, pushing a breeze through our bedroom that lifted and moved wisps of her dark hair. The blinds behind our pink ruffled curtain tap-tap-tapped against the pane. Outside, trucks on the nearby interstate hummed, driving someplace else. Thunder rumbled. Rain would come before morning.

While Abby slept and the house was dark and silent, I struggled to quiet the ideas swirling in my head. Sometimes my thoughts were silly and amounted to nothing, like why I favored strawberry ice cream over chocolate. But often I wondered about bottomless things like what happened when old people died, or why I was born to Lee and Anne Abbott instead of Elvis and Priscilla Presley.

Last week, I heard Momma tell her best friend Maggie about some man who jumped from the Memphis Bridge into the Mississippi River. His body was never found. I haven't been able to erase the picture from my mind, especially at night. I imagine that man's dead body floating around all bloated and exaggerated in the Gulf of Mexico. Things don't just disappear.

In our corner of Arkansas, the Mississippi River provided the only nearby place of interest. It was our very own natural wonder, the spot we took out-of-town guests. "Let's go look at the river," Momma had said to her college roommate when she visited in October. We drove behind the levee at Savage Crossing, parked near the concrete embankment used for backing fishing boats into the river, and watched the muddy water roil by. When a barge moved past, Momma's friend took a picture with her camera and seemed impressed. Everyone always was. Last summer, Nana and Papa Pete mailed Abby and me a postcard from St. Louis. I wondered what the Mississippi River looked like from the top of the St. Louis arch. Sometimes a change of perspective made the world more interesting. Savage Crossing could have used an arch overlooking its river port. Or maybe a lookout tower for kids to climb and to toss paper airplanes from.

As I lay motionless, I stared at the dark space above my bed until I floated through the ceiling and into the black sky. I imagined the view of our farmhouse from high above—the rock chimney, the back porch, a good supply of shade trees, and the yard filled with more clover than grass. Surrounding our house, rows of cotton spread to the ditch bank at the far edge of our property. We lived in the Delta, also known as the middle of nowhere, where dirt roads divided farmland like sections of an old quilt, and most every bend in the road had a name. Our house was only two miles from Cottonwood Corner, an exit on the interstate, a place where travelers gassed up cars and maybe bought a cup of coffee or used the bathroom. That was it. The only semi-exciting thing that ever happened occurred the first Friday of the month when the old building next to the gas station became the site of a live auction selling mostly junk. Not that an auction was all that exciting.

A crack of lightning flashed and brightened the bedroom. Lucky moved to the foot of my bed, circling and circling before curling into a knot at my feet.

I gave some thought to my upcoming birthday on August twenty-first. Even though it sounded like a long time away, it wasn't. Summer days always went by faster than school days, so I knew my birthday would come quickly. I lay tree-trunk still and tried to imagine being ten, feeling older and different. Ten would be better than nine. It had to be. Double digits stood for something, I was sure of it.

Every year, just before my big day, Momma would retell the story of my birth like it was as interesting as baby Jesus's manger tale. On a steamy morning, seven days past my due date, Dr. Fairley tugged me from Momma's stomach with stainless-steel forceps. I knew it was true because he left a pale scar on my lower back that turned bright white every time I cried or stayed out in the sun too long. I considered that birthmark proof I had never wished to be born into my crazy family. From the very beginning, my life was tainted. Momma saw to that by giving me a long, ridiculous name—Grace Lee Eudora Abbott. Four names instead of three, which right away set me on a complicated path. And Eudora? I had never heard such an ugly name, even considering all the strange names in the Old Testament.

I spent years trying to decipher a reason for my horrid name. I had studied my baby pictures and knew I had been cute, so that couldn't have been it. My cheeks glowed rosy, and my pale-blonde hair made a perfect curl on top, like the Gerber baby whose face was plastered on rice cereal boxes at the grocery store. When I eventually asked Momma about my long name, she gave me an equally long explanation: Grace, because I was born on a Tuesday morning, and Tuesday's child was full of grace—whatever that meant; Lee, because that was Daddy's first name; and, Eudora, after his favorite author Eudora Welty. No matter how famous an author she might have been, I thought Eudora was a terrible baby girl name. Daddy thought otherwise. He kept a book of Eudora Welty's short stories on his bedside table next to the Vicks VapoRub. His favorite, "Death of a Traveling Salesman," was marked with a Cardinals baseball ticket stub. What a gloomy sounding story.

Two years, nine months, and seven days later, when the stork brought another baby to our house, Momma wised up and gave my sister a normal name—Abigail Anne, after herself and Nana. Abby's chubby cheeks and naturally pouty lips fascinated everyone. "She doesn't look anything like Gracie. I just want to eat her up." That's what Momma's friend Maggie said when she brought over a vase of pink carnations and a silver rattle and then left with half a cup of oleo. Maggie never left our house without borrowing Momma's food.

Most everyone called me Grace or Gracie Lee, except on the first day of school when teachers insisted on calling students by their God-given names. Even though school had just let out for summer break, I was already worrying about the fall. That was how my mind worked. I worried about things so far in advance of the bad that I never enjoyed the good. Nana said I was an old soul like her. Momma always told me not to stew so much about silly things, but believe me, when kids knew your name was Eudora, there was plenty to worry about at Savage Crossing Elementary School.

Chapter Two

Some days felt different right from the start, as though something special had been planned, but my brain wasn't awake enough to remember exactly what. Other than the hum of the fan, the house lay still and quiet. Even the blackbirds had forgotten their early crowing.

I stood on my pillow, stretched my arms to grip the window ledge above my bed, and hoisted myself onto the edge of my iron headboard. Balancing on tiptoes, I pushed aside the shade and peeked outside the high narrow window. From house to horizon, mucky water covered Daddy's cotton crop—a crop that had only just sprouted from the soil. The ditches, which normally divided fields into neat squares, had completely disappeared beneath a brown sea. Next to our playhouse, my favorite willow tree looked squatty with a partially submerged trunk and weeping branches that skimmed the water.

"Oh, my God! Abby, wake up! There's a lake."

Abby scrambled from underneath her quilt and joined me, her fat toes gripping the rim of the headboard. She was barely able to peer above the window ledge. "Oh wow," she gasped as her eyes scanned from left to right. "Let's go swimming, Gracie!"

Tossing our matching nightgowns to the floor, we dressed in cutoffs and T-shirts, the ones we were allowed to wear when we played in the mud. I pulled my hair back into a long ponytail to keep it out of my face and then helped my sister with her hair. Hers was tricky. She had a wad of bubble gum matted in the curls near her ear, but I worked around it, raking strands up and over the sticky part and securing it with a pink plastic hairband, the same color as the gum. Momma would have to deal with that later.

I grabbed Barbie and Ken, knowing they would enjoy a swim too. Ken got a neat boat last Christmas, but so far, the only water it had seen was in the boring bathtub. "Why is Ken naked?" Abby asked. I had stripped him of his fancy suit and placed him at the helm of his boat.

"I don't want his good clothes to get stained in the muddy water." Barbie had a red bathing suit, but Ken only had work clothes and a tuxedo for fancy affairs. What did it matter, anyway? Ken didn't have real boy parts. I knew all about those weird boy parts because my friend Janice accidentally found a picture of Michelangelo's naked *David* statue in the *World Book Encyclopedia*. Sometimes interesting things like that happened when nothing much was expected from the day. The first time we saw it, we gawked and whispered. I felt dirty and bad but later decided if the picture was in the encyclopedia, it must have been educational and that was okay, even encouraged. Plus, the naked statue was considered art by some. From then on, each time we went to the library, we sneaked looks at his "thing" while Mrs. Penny, the school librarian, tried to keep the boys quiet.

Once Abby and I dressed and gathered up Barbie and Ken, we tiptoed down the hallway careful not to wake Momma and Daddy. "Step exactly where I step, Abby," I whispered. The worn hardwood floors creaked in certain places, especially across the span of flooring between the bedrooms. Lucky darted past us, but I counted my footsteps, which helped me remember where to place my feet. Surprisingly, Abby did as instructed, and we pushed open the back door, undetected.

On a regular day, our backyard appeared level, but I had come to realize nothing was as it appeared. Instead, the ground was uneven, filled with dips and peaks and a low spot in the center where rainwater pooled. The same held true for the cotton fields in our county. When I drove my bicycle on the road in front of our house, the land in every direction looked flat enough to walk between two rows of cotton and off the edge of the planet. Living in the Mississippi Delta made it hard to believe the Earth was round.

As I stepped off the back patio into cold water, the grass felt strange and squishy between my bare toes. My feet sank into the spongy earth, and my ankles disappeared beneath coffee-colored water. Lucky forged ahead, swimming fast as though I had thrown something for him to fetch. He held his head high above the water, but the black and tan splotches on his back were barely visible. Abby giggled as we held hands and waded toward the middle of the backyard, the lowest spot behind the house. Water reached the edge of my shorts and almost to Abby's waist. To the far right, Daddy's truck sat parked atop a gravel driveway higher than the yard. Water reached the top of his truck tires and lapped at the bark of the nearby plum tree. I squeezed my eyes tight, flopped down, dunked my head, and reappeared after swimming underwater a few strokes. The water felt gritty and thick, completely different from the clean, cold water at the swimming pool in town or even the water at Lake Norfork where Nana and Papa had a fishing cabin. Plunging under again, I swam straight, keeping my body taut and holding my breath as long as possible. I was Jane, swimming with Tarzan in a hippo-infested African river. Surfacing, I smeared the water from around my eyes. Abby made motorboat sounds while pulling Barbie and Ken in my muddy wake. She showed no concern for the menacing crocodiles lurking all around.

Our playhouse stood on higher ground in the back corner of the yard near a row of cherry trees. Daddy and his farm hands built the small house last winter, when there wasn't much farm work to do. "They're on the payroll. I may as well put them to work," Daddy had said. Momma moved most of our games and toys into the playhouse so our bedroom would stay neater, but I wouldn't let her move Barbie. Barbie and her friends lived inside the real house, with us. Pushing open the door, I saw that everything remained as we had left it. Our pink plastic cups and saucers were set out on the kitchen table, yesterday's undisturbed tea party.

"Gracie, let's make a raft!" Sometimes Abby had good ideas. Our wooden toy box lid was the perfect size to support both of us lying flat on our bellies. Plus, it floated, which was a raft requirement. We kicked and paddled around the yard, exploring the water and grabbing sticks that we found drifting around like water moccasins. Lucky found a stick too. He swam with it in his mouth until he discovered a grassy spot near the house. Then he lay with it between his paws and chewed it like a bone. I liked how some days turned out to be okay and good, days worth remembering for a long time.

"Abby-Grace! Get in the house this minute!" Momma screeched from the back door, blending our names together as she was prone to do when she became overly excited. Along the sides of Momma's face, bobby pins held her dark, twisty curls in place, but the top of her hair was crazy messy like she had been turning somersaults in her sleep. She wore gold house slippers that turned up at the toes like genie shoes, and her pale blue robe was wrapped tight at her slender waist. I felt pretty sure Momma was naked underneath because she didn't sleep in pajamas. I discovered that late one night after rushing into her bedroom when something scary moved underneath my bed. I never made that mistake again.

"Momma, look at all this water. Isn't it cool!" I said. Abby and I splashed toward her, riding our toy box raft and making waves with our cupped fingers. Lucky raced toward her and jumped up, nearly getting her bathrobe muddy. She shoved him away just in time.

"Don't you dare let Daddy hear you say that! His cotton is floating down the Mississippi River." She slammed the door, rattling the windowpane. Hundreds of blackbirds rose from the willow in one dazzling cloud, flying over the playhouse before changing direction and swarming over the pump house on the opposite side of our yard. Once Momma went back inside, they returned to the same willow branches. Lucky barked and barked and barked. I thought he was making up for not having noticed them before. Abby and I kept right on playing in the water until Momma made us come inside and wash our hair.

Daddy wasn't always a farmer. Before I knew him, he was a regular person who played on the football team at Savage Crossing High School and liked to fish for trout at White River. Momma has a whole photo album with pictures of him smiling and looking happy, back when he wore white T-shirts with the sleeves rolled up. Momma said they had been childhood sweethearts since he stole her heart the first day she saw him at Savage Crossing Junior High. Now that he was a grouch, I had a hard time picturing them young or being mushy in love. Most of the time, I didn't know why she put up with Daddy. I was never getting married, that was for sure. Barbie got the last good man.

One thing I could say about Daddy is that he had always been a hard worker and smart too. As a kid, he never missed a day of school, and he made perfect grades in both high school and college. Before I was born, Daddy worked as an accountant in town. Momma said he wore a suit to work and even carried a leather briefcase. I often wondered how life would have turned out if Daddy had kept his desk job instead of becoming a farmer. Maybe he wouldn't have gotten sick, anyway.

The word sick has lots of different meanings. There is "throwing up sick," like the time I had the flu. Dr. Fairley poked a stick down my throat and gave me a shot in my rear end. There was also "sick and tired," like when Abby and I grated on Momma's nerves, whining or begging to go to Sterling's. And then there was Daddy's kind of sick, from drinking too much beer and whiskey. Momma believed it really was a sickness, but I thought it was a lame excuse for pure meanness. Nana said our bodies were temples, and if Daddy didn't stop poisoning his, one of these days it would kill him. I was waiting for that time, which made me feel a little sick inside. But not like flu-sick, more like I-did-something-bad sick.

After Momma washed my hair and rolled it in pink brush curlers, I lay back in the tub with the nape of my neck on a towel rolled as a pillow. I stared at my flat chest. There was no change from yesterday. My friend Janice started wearing a training bra last month even though she was as flat as me. Her mother was cool that way. Plus, since she had two older sisters, she always did things earlier than I did. My thirteen-year-old cousin, Candi, who lived with Mamaw Pearl, had been wearing a bra forever. She told me the whole growing titties thing happened fast. Overnight even. One day she was as flat as a piece of plywood, and the next day, there they were, big and round enough that Mamaw Pearl took her to Sterling's to buy a three-pack of real bras, skipping the training kind altogether.

Maybe tomorrow, I thought.

The curlers poked my head and made my scalp itch, but Momma said we girls had to suffer to be beautiful. "Church hair," as she called it, should be shiny and bouncy and certainly squeaky clean. The agony seemed pointless to me since there was no one to impress at Boon Chapel. Plus, no matter how long the curlers stayed in my hair, it still went dull and stringy before Brother Brown finished preaching. The worst part of the hair-washing routine was after Momma rolled our hair, Abby and I couldn't play outside or do anything rowdy. Instead, we passed the time playing jacks on the kitchen floor and coloring in our bedroom. Just before lunch, Momma turned on the television so we could all watch the weather in case Daddy quizzed us. Sometimes he did that.

Except in the coldest, deadest time of winter when nothing was growing, Daddy rarely took a day off. And even in winter, he found jobs to do like work on his equipment or unstop a ditch where the water wouldn't drain. Rain or shine, he drove to each of his fields at least twice a day to see what had changed since the last trip over. Since our land was spread around the county—a cotton field here, a soybean field over by town, a wheat field by the levee—there was always something going on. A section needed plowing. A crop had bugs chomping on it. A field, like the one behind our house, got too much rain. Papa Pete said buying land scattered around the area helped spread the risk of farming. To me, it spread the driving time.

"What's for lunch?" Daddy asked as he walked in the door, tracking mud all over Momma's clean kitchen floor. She stared at the mess but didn't say anything. Daddy sat in his regular chair closest to the icebox and opened the newspaper to the business and farm section. Janice thought he was the handsomest man around. He had straight teeth and wasn't fat anywhere that I could see. And he had plenty of brown hair, unlike Janice's dad who had a slick, shiny head. I reckoned those were all positive traits.

"Soup and sandwiches," Momma said, placing his plate in front of him. Momma's dishes were always carefully arranged, even plain grilled-cheese sandwiches cut into triangles and tomato soup from a can. Daddy scooped up the crackers circling his soup bowl, squeezed them in the palm of his hand and dumped them on top of his soup. The crumbs mounded like an anthill and didn't sink. With a stir of his spoon, his soup became thick and goopy and no longer watery. He ate with deliberate motions, moving one heaping spoonful at a time to his mouth, slow and steady, his throat shifting with each swallow.

"I'll have to replant most of the cotton. At least here around the house," he grumbled. "It'll cost a fortune." For the first time, I noticed a few gray hairs scattered in his dark sideburns.

"I'm so sorry, Lee," Momma said as she untied her apron, hung it on the back of her chair, and sat down. "But maybe not. Maybe it's not as bad as you think."

And that was all it took to rile him—the wrong word or tone of voice, a certain facial expression. Daddy dropped his spoon into his bowl and stared at her. Momma touched his wrist right above his watch, but he yanked back his arm. She began apologizing over and over. For what, I had no idea. I didn't think she knew either.

Daddy pushed his bowl aside and rubbed his forehead. Gathering the newspaper into a messy bundle, he tossed it to the countertop. It fell to the floor, separated, and glided across the linoleum. "Just shut the hell up, Anne. I'm doing the best I can."

Momma glanced at me and then averted her eyes toward the ceiling. "Does anyone want potato chips? I bought a new kind." She jumped to her feet and pulled opened the high cabinet where chips and crackers and breakfast cereal were stored. Pretending nothing was wrong—that was one of her specialties. She fussed and messed with the hard to open chip bag and finally ripped open the corner with her teeth.

"You act like I don't know what I'm doing. How 'bout you farm all day and I'll sit around thinking of ways to spend money?" Daddy yelled.

And he kept yelling.

I couldn't understand how she stayed quiet and allowed Daddy to be so mean to her. To all of us. The knot that lived in the bottom of my stomach twisted and tightened until my eyes began to burn. Somewhere in the distance, I heard a small, clear voice ask, "Why do you have to yell at Momma all the time?"

It was my voice.

Me.

No one blinked. A stony silence filled the kitchen, a silence so loud my ears rang.

"Gracie, it's okay," Momma said. "Let's all settle down and eat." Her eyes, a watery pale color, matched her blouse, and the thin band on her finger hung loose as she dumped chips into a bowl.

Daddy exploded from his chair, shoving it backward into the icebox door. It clattered onto the floor. He said lots of bad words and the vein on his neck stuck out so far I was afraid it might pop. Abby held her hands over her ears and began to cry.

I was a rock, a boulder, unable to move or speak or feel anything. A cold, hard rock. I clinched my jaw, grasped my hands in my lap and pressed my fingers into my palms until my fingernails bit into my skin. Daddy gripped the edge of his soup bowl and lobbed it into the sink like a Frisbee. A million shards of glass scattered through the air like buckshot and bounced across the linoleum floor.

It was one of Momma's favorite bowls, the ones she'd bought with Quality Stamps. She'd saved those stamps for a year. After each trip to the grocery store, she'd let Abby and me stick them in the stamp book. On the day we finally filled enough books, we made a special trip to Memphis and proudly handed them over to the lady behind the counter in exchange for eight matching bowls. As soon as we got home, we celebrated with scoops of ice cream.

Daddy slammed the back door, vibrating the entire house. A glob of soppy crackers slid off the edge of the sink and down the cabinet into a puddle at the baseboard. I didn't breathe until I heard his truck peel onto the highway, slinging gravel.

Momma slumped her shoulders, looking as tired as I'd ever seen her. Her hands trembled, and her face was drawn and tight. "My God, Gracie, what were you thinking? You can't talk to your dad that way. He's tired and worried about all the rain, and when he comes home, you need to apologize."

"I hope he never comes home!" A giant moan escaped from deep inside me. I held my head inside my hands and felt the weight of those heavy curlers shift. I hated my stupid hair. I hated Daddy. I hated my entire pointless life.

Our kitchen was a scene from one of the scary movies Janice and I watched when I spent the night with her. Momma picked up the largest pieces of glass then began sweeping the slivers we couldn't see. I offered to help, but she told Abby and me to go sit on the couch and watch television and not mess up our curlers. I went to my bedroom and read a book instead. After only a few pages, I forgot about the

14

craziness in our house, at least until it was time for me to practice piano. "Practice until Mae gets here," Momma said.

"Mae's still coming?" Mae came to stay with us most Saturday nights so Momma and Daddy could go out. I couldn't believe Momma would agree to go anywhere with Daddy after his lunchtime mood.

"It's Saturday night."

I snorted. "Daddy would have to beg me on his hands and knees to go out with him and bring me a huge box of chocolate. I still probably wouldn't go."

"Go practice your piano lesson."

Abby and I agreed that spending time with Mae was one of our favorite things about weekends. On Saturday nights, while Momma and Daddy were out doing whatever it was that they did, we laughed about nothing, talked about everything, and ate giant bowls of popcorn. Mae never got upset if our pink curlers fell out. She snapped them back into place without yanking our hair, and Momma was never the wiser. Mae was like our very own Mary Poppins, only she was a large, black woman who lived in town with a whole bunch of her own kids. It was nice of her to leave her real children at home while taking care of Abby and me when our own parents didn't feel like it.

"I don't hear you practicing, Grace," Momma yelled from her bedroom.

"*Oui, maman.*" Last summer, Momma decided Abby and I should learn to play the piano. She said it would make us better rounded and even bought a metronome to help keep proper rhythm for practice. The tick-tick-ticking bored into my brain right along with those pink curlers. Abby was excited about the whole thing, but since I never planned to be in the Miss America pageant and wouldn't need such a talent, I saw no point. What I really wanted to do was learn to speak French. I wanted to be that girl who, when invited to the White House for an important state dinner, would be the only person in the room who could speak with the French prime minister in his native language. I would help solve international problems while sipping champagne and wearing a black ball gown like Audrey Hepburn. President Nixon would be impressed to learn I started out as a farm girl from Arkansas. Last fall, I bought an old French lesson book at the library's used book sale. Momma thought it was a silly waste. Besides English, Momma

15

said the only practical language to learn was Spanish, because of our Mexican cotton choppers. Since I used my own money, she really didn't have a say.

"Now, Grace!" She was relentless about piano practice.

"Hold your horses," I said, but not so she could hear.

Foreign notes and bars flowed across the sheet music, still open to where I left it last week. Even though Mrs. Allard didn't teach piano lessons during summer break, she had assigned a difficult song and expected me to master it by the time school started back in September. Momma saw to it that I practiced so the summer sun wouldn't erase my brain. I warmed up my fingers with major and minor scales then played a few measures of my homework before moving on to "Frère Jacques" just for fun. At least it was a French song.

Mae and Daddy pulled into the driveway at the same time. Abby and I ran to the back door and pulled Mae inside in a flurry of smiles and hugs and easy laughter. We ignored Daddy. He talked with Mae and behaved as though nothing unusual had happened at lunch. I wasn't surprised. Usually after he acted like the meanest man in the United States of America, he did something nice and stunned all of us, or at least acted like a regular person for a few days.

That's how Lucky had come to live with us. A few months back, when Daddy got really drunk and ran Momma's car into a ditch at Cottonwood Corner, he bought his way out of the doghouse with an actual dog. Abby and I had been begging for a pet forever—a dog or cat or even a fish. Until Momma's car had to be towed into town, Daddy had refused.

While Daddy showered, Momma went over last-minute instructions with Mae, the same instructions each week about where they'd be and when they would be home. "Supper's on the stove, and there's enough for you too, Mae. I made hamburgers," Momma said. A few minutes later, Daddy walked through the kitchen with his hair slicked back, still wet. He wore a fresh shirt and his clean cowboy boots with the pointy toes. Momma fastened a necklace around her neck and fluffed her wavy hair in the mirror over the dining room buffet. With a stern reminder to "be good," they were out the door, Daddy with his arm around Momma's shoulder, and Momma smiling and laughing.

16

Finally. It had taken them forever to leave.

I had gotten into the habit of counting the beer bottles lining the shelf of the icebox. Sometimes lots more beer had been added, which messed up my math. When Mae asked me to fetch a jar of mustard, I glanced to the place where the beer was always kept and made a mental note of how many had disappeared since the last time I'd checked. Only two beers had disappeared since the day before. Not as many as normal.

Mae said she wasn't hungry, so while Abby and I ate supper, she added another coat of fuchsia polish to her curved, talon-like fingernails.

"Mae, I need to ask you a serious question," I said.

"Okay, child. Go ahead." With the polish wand hovering over the bottle, she paused and stared right into my eyes as though whatever I had to discuss was the most important thing in her world.

"Do you think our Daddy will go to Hell because he never goes to church?" I took another bite of my hamburger.

Mae looked at me sharply, with marble-hard eyes. "I'm sure I don't know anything about that, Gracie." She dipped the wand back into the polish and pulled it out, wiping the excess on the rim. Her nails were thick and strong like concrete because she never removed her polish. Instead, she added more color. I wondered if her age could be determined by peeling back the layers of paint on her nails, much like the rings on a tree.

"Well, I think so, and I may be going to Hell right along with him. Sometimes I hate him. I really do." I swirled a french fry in my puddle of ketchup but didn't eat it. They had turned soggy.

"Child, don't be talking nonsense. Of course you don't hate Mr. Lee."

"Oh yes, I do. He's mean, he never plays with us and sometimes calls me names. Momma says he's sick and can't help it."

Last week, Daddy had made fun of me and called me Baby-Grace, all because I was playing with Barbie. I didn't tell Mae because I couldn't stand to say the words out loud. To make fun of your own kid was horrible and something I would never do.

"Honey, your Daddy is too busy to be playing. He's an important farmer around these parts. What do you expect him to do, play with dolls? You need to wash out your mouth, and don't let me hear you talking like that again." Mae shook her head so forcefully I felt the air move around me. Her plaits swung from side to side and the multicolored beads attached to the ends of each tiny braid made a clinking noise as they collided then fell back into place across her shoulders. She gave me a serious look and stared into my eyes just long enough to make me uncomfortable.

"It's just like I tell my own kids," she continued, "you girls need to remember how good you got it with a nice house and food to eat and clothes on your back. They's plenty of young people fighting for our freedom and getting killed every day over in the war. You remember that when you gets so upset about your doll playing. Now, let's talk about something more pleasant." She puckered her full lips and blew air across her wet nails. Her lips were a lighter shade of fuchsia than her nails, but she never wore lipstick. That was her natural lip color. I wanted to ask Mae how she washed her hair, but I didn't. I didn't say anything more about hating Daddy either, but decided I would think more about it before I fell asleep, and maybe even discuss it with Brother Brown tomorrow at church.

Chapter Three

There must have been a rule that country churches should be plain and ordinary, because most of those around Mississippi County were that way. As Momma pulled into the circle drive, which was filled with more dandelions than gravel, I stared at the Boon Chapel Baptist Church sign out front. A few weeks ago, someone had painted over the "n" in Boon. "Just for meanness," Nana had said.

"Why hasn't someone fixed the sign yet?" I asked. "It just looks pitiful, and everyone who drives by will think we changed the name to Boo Chapel." I could barely stand to even get out of the car and walk inside.

"I doubt it," Momma said as she checked her lipstick in the rearview mirror.

The front porch had begun to lean to the right. The twisty vines wrapped along the columns and over the roof likely kept the building from collapsing. Over to the side, tombstones poked up through a carpet of clover, but it was the mound of fresh, black dirt that caught my eye.

"Who died?"

"A man from Sugar Ditch. No one you know," Momma said.

"Momma, if I die, don't bury me at 'Boo' Chapel." I said "boo" with extra emphasis.

Momma laughed as we walked together up the front porch steps, carrying our Bibles and wearing our Sunday best. "Where would you like me to bury you, Gracie Lee?"

"I don't know, but not out there."

"Me neither!" Abby, who was the biggest copycat in the history of copycats, echoed me. I rolled my eyes at her.

Beyond the graveyard, cotton and soybean fields splayed out like a fan, the view broken only by weeds and wildflowers growing on the ditch banks. All around the church, pecan trees kept watch, whether we were there or not.

But we were there.

Everyone but Daddy, anyway.

For as far back as I could remember, each Sunday morning at nine a.m. sharp, Mr. Donaldson, the official Boon Chapel church secretary, called service to order by saying a prayer and leading the congregation in the singing of a hymn. After everyone was good and awake, we went to our designated Sunday school classes, which were determined mostly by age. People like Aunt Fannie and Mrs. Donaldson went across the hall to the young married class even though they weren't young and had all been married long enough to have kids at least Abby's age. The largest class belonged to the old ladies—Nana, Mrs. Sweet, Aunt Clara, and a few other women—who all wore sweaters draped on their shoulders even in the summer. Since they were closest to dying, they took their Sunday school lesson as serious as anything. On any given day, Nana's lesson book could be found rolled up in her pocketbook like a treasure map.

Lumped together in a separate class away from the women, the Boon Chapel men stood around outside and leaned against Uncle Will's truck, drinking coffee from paper cups. During the summer, when Momma opened our classroom window to let the hot air escape, we could hear them talking about farming. Farming was the only topic of interest to men in our corner of Arkansas.

I was in the youth class with Abby, our cousin, Dian, and the Donaldson twins, who were girls too. There had never been any boys in our class, which seemed a little strange when I really stopped to think about it. But I wasn't complaining. The thing I did complain about was having Momma for our Sunday school teacher. What sort of sense did it make for Abby and me to get up early every Sunday morning so that our own Momma could teach to us from the Bible?

"Today's lesson is about the importance of church," Momma said. "I know sometimes it would be nice to sleep late on Sunday morning, but God commands us to attend. If you knew Jesus was planning to walk into the doors of Boon Chapel and listen to Brother Brown's sermon today, I bet you wouldn't think twice about coming. Right?" A tractor passed by on the road in front of the church, rumbling louder and louder until it faded away in the distance.

"I'd wear my Easter dress," Abby said as she glanced down at her shirt that was already stained with a dribble of orange juice.

Momma's example was a good one, and I understood what she was saying, but still I didn't think it was fair that Daddy never had to go to church. And Momma never bugged him about it, either. In some ways, she lived as two different people. At church, Momma talked about Jesus and reminded us to be kind and to do unto others, but where Daddy was concerned, she did whatever it took to survive. We all did.

After Sunday school class when Mr. Donaldson rang the hall bell, everyone gathered back into the sanctuary for the reading of announcements and other important church information. Mr. Donaldson had all the best church jobs, including changing out the paper numbers on the wooden tote board that hung above the piano. It was a board much like the baseball scoreboard at school, only smaller. This week's numbers didn't look very different from last week's numbers. Or the week before. "Attendance this Sunday thirty-nine, Bibles brought twenty-five, and offering fifty-two dollars and forty-three cents."

After we dragged through a few too-slow hymns, Brother Brown walked up to the pulpit. "Good Sunday morning," he said, while opening his Bible and paging through to the Book he wanted. Slowly, slowly, he licked his thumb and continued turning pages. Why, oh, why didn't he know about bookmarks? "Ah, here we are." He paused, looked at the congregation, and nodded. I glanced at my Cinderella watch. Brother Brown was allotted exactly twenty-five minutes. He'd best get on with it.

Brother Brown's sermon drifted over the congregation like crop defoliant, settling on the faithful Baptist like a fog. Week after week, the same tired tone, the same woeful words about Hell and sin and Satan. The pew beneath my rear end became rock hard, my eyelids heavy. Everyone, even the devout old ladies, seemed to have difficulty listening. Nana sat with her Bible open to the day's passages, her

21

normally attentive eyes glazed over. Every few minutes, she pushed the short curls around her face behind her ears and sat a little taller as though trying her best to pay attention. Uncle Will snored from the back row. Brother Brown's words rarely reached my ears. I counted ceiling tiles to stay awake, *un, deux, trois*. I carefully peeled the silver lining away from my spearmint gum wrapper and made a tiny ball. I imagined the pot roast Momma left simmering in the oven. When my stomach yowled like a cat, Abby giggled.

"Nana, draw a duck," I whispered, hoping for a distraction. Pulling an offering envelope from the wooden pew in front of me, I handed it to her. In a pinch, offering envelopes made good scrap paper.

Nana nodded and slipped a pencil from inside her Bible. In one graceful hand movement, she drew her own unique version of a duck, more of a one-legged flamingo or strange swan.

"That doesn't look like a duck," Abby muttered, stifling her laugh. Then she hiccupped, and we teetered headfirst into a fit of silent, shoulder-shaking giggles, the sort easily mistaken for sobbing. Momma shot us the stink eye from her place at the piano bench. Since Momma was stuck sitting up front as the Boon Chapel piano player, Nana was tasked with keeping us quiet during preaching. It rarely worked. Nana had the biggest giggle box of all.

Sunday service always ended with Brother Brown's invitation to join Boon Chapel Baptist Church, followed by five, long stanzas of "Just as I Am." Momma played a few chords of the introduction while Brother Brown reminded everyone to bow their heads and close their eyes. I saw no point in closing my eyes, so I lowered my head but watched the whole time. As I suspected, nothing much happened.

"Just as I am, without one plea, but that thy blood was shed for me."

While the congregation sang, Brother Brown shut his hymnal, clasped his Bible in the crook of his arm, and walked from the pulpit to the front of the sanctuary. Stooping toward the empty front pew, he picked up his hat then stood ready to greet all the potential new church members moved by his message. Once again, there were none. The invitational hymn was a waste of time. Boon Chapel membership had been stuck at forty-four since I was in the nursery.

By the end of the second verse, I felt sorry for him. No one ever went up there. Not since Aunt Clara had pretended to rededicate her life.

If anyone had her life straightened out, it was Aunt Clara. Everyone knew she was only trying to be supportive.

Well, today would be different. After doing some serious thinking last night, I decided to walk up during the invitational hymn and visit with Brother Brown. Even though I questioned whether or not Brother Brown had a direct link to Jesus, or if Jesus existed at all, I thought it would be a nice gesture and give me something to do during all those tedious stanzas. Plus, maybe Brother Brown could help Daddy or, at the very least, become inspired for future sermons.

"Just as I am, though tossed about with many a conflict, many a doubt."

Squeezing between Abby and the pew in front of us, I placed one foot onto the red aisle carpet. "Where are you going?" she whispered, tugging the back of my blouse. I ignored her and took another step forward, hardly feeling my feet. The untied lace on my right shoe flopped with each step. I wished I had worn my black Mary Janes instead of my saddle Oxfords, even though they pinched my toes.

In the back of the church, the air conditioner kicked on with a sudden whooshing sound, making the floor pulsate and the walls groan. I was thankful for the timing, certain the racket would conceal the loud thump of my heartbeat. The lights hanging from the ceiling, dimmed for an instant, and maybe even swayed before returning to normal. I continued to stare at my slow-moving feet. *Just keep walking.*

"O Lamb of God, I come, I come."

Glancing toward Brother Brown, I noticed an upraised bushy eyebrow, a hint of excitement at having a customer. I didn't look at Momma but felt her smile in my direction. When I reached the front of the church, he took my hand in his cold, clammy one and draped an arm around my shoulder, which felt surprisingly nice. His breath smelled of coffee and peppermints, and tufts of white hair protruded from inside each nostril.

"Hello, Miss Grace." He smoothed the top of his deeply parted hair and smiled like I had made his day perfect.

"Hi, Brother Brown." I smiled back but felt nervous. He had never really spoken to me before, and I was surprised he knew my name. Since I didn't know what to do with my hands, I crossed my arms over my chest, but when that didn't feel right, I dropped them to my side and let them hang, doing nothing.

"Are you ready to turn your life over to Jesus?" he asked in a low, soothing voice that moved my hair and tickled my ear.

"No sir, I just came up to say hello and ask you to pray for my Daddy. He's mean to Momma, he drinks too much beer, and I think he's probably going to Hell. In fact, I'm sure of it." I tugged on the hem of my dress and couldn't take my eyes from his amazing crop of nose hair. I had never before noticed how much he looked like the walrus at the Memphis Zoo.

With his hand firmly planted on my back, he guided me to the front pew and we knelt there, because Boon Chapel had no proper altar. Around us, the music swelled as though my walk to the pulpit had energized the church members. Brother Brown mumbled a few words that I could barely hear and read from the book of Matthew, something about all things being possible. The congregation continued singing and even started over with the first verse. That made me feel bad, because I knew everyone wanted to go home for lunch. My mind blanked out, like it sometimes did during history class when the teacher went over something for the tenth time. My stomach growled and even cramped up from hunger. Hurry up, hurry up, hurry up, I concentrated as hard as I could, hoping he might hear me with his mind. Yet, on he droned. A different sort of sermon especially for me.

Why did I ever walk up here?

My foot was asleep.

Tingling. Tingling. I shifted my balance and almost fell.

I never heard Brother Brown actually pray for Daddy, but I knew Mae would be proud that I made the effort. From my spot kneeling at the first pew, Momma's piano playing sounded louder than normal and vibrated the floor beneath my knees. Finally, we stood. I stomped my dead foot to wake it up, but not too loud. He shook my hand as though we made some sort of deal, and the whole thing was over.

***

After the torture of church, Momma's pot roast was pure deliverance. Loading my fork with a piece of meat and a wedge of potato, I savored the flavor of Sunday afternoon.

"Grace, don't you have some good news to share with Daddy?" Momma jolted me from my perfect pot roast moment. That was what Momma always did, and I hated it. She tried to force Abby and me to chit-chat with Daddy, the man who would have rather pulled weeds with his teeth than make small talk. Daddy stabbed a chunk of meat, looked up from his plate, and waited for me to say something. My face flushed. I hated that too.

"Not really," I said through clinched teeth. I didn't look at Daddy, but from the corner of my eye, I saw him shake his head like I was impossible.

"Gracie got saved today," Abby blurted out and flashed a gigantic smile showing lots of rosy gum between several missing teeth.

Daddy shot me a knowing look, like he could see right through me, as though he knew there was more to the story.

"I just went up to talk to Brother Brown. It's no big deal." I hid behind my glass of tea. When I attempted a gulp, the ice cubes moved in one giant mass to the front of my glass. Tea poured down the sides of my chin and onto my favorite T-shirt. Abby clasped her hand over her mouth to hold back a giggle.

"Of course it's a big deal. It's a huge deal," Momma said, handing me a dishtowel. "Right, Lee?" She tried once again to drag Daddy into the conversation.

"If you say so," he mumbled. "Do we have any of those hot peppers left?"

Momma popped up from her chair, opened the icebox door, grabbed a handful of jalapenos from the bottom drawer and rinsed them. "She'll be getting baptized in a few weeks," Momma beamed. She placed the peppers on a saucer beside Daddy's plate.

"What?" I stared at Momma. She looked as pleased as the time I won first prize in the countywide essay contest and received a certificate of achievement signed by Governor Bumpers. My essay entitled "What Makes Arkansas Special to Me" was printed in the local *Savage Crossing Crier*, and my picture appeared on the front page of the gossip section. Today, I don't remember a word of what I wrote.

"Maybe we should have a big baptism party to celebrate, invite the whole family over, Mamaw Pearl, Nana and Papa, Aunt Fannie. What do you think, Lee? It's been forever since we had a family party. I can make that chocolate cake you like, the one with the coconut." Momma grinned at Daddy. Her eyes flitted around as though ideas churned in her head.

Daddy glared at me, his stare so sharp and cutting I could feel it inside my chest.

Abby wiggled in her chair like she had to pee. She cheered, "Yes, a party!"

I dropped my fork. It skipped off the edge of my plate and bounced to the floor.

This was the sort of thing that happened when I didn't mind my own business. My one and only attempt to be social with Brother Brown and to possibly help Daddy had resulted in a complete misunderstanding. And I had known something was up too. When the service was finally over, most of the church members, including every old lady, formed a line and walked to the front to shake my hand and congratulate me like I was a celebrity or something. It was the craziest thing.

"Do I have to get in that water with Brother Brown?" I asked. As soon as the words left my mouth, I felt bad. Not thirty minutes before, Brother Brown talked with me and held my hand, and I smelled his coffee breath and all.

"Yes, Grace. That's the only way to Heaven. You know that. We talked about it in Sunday school just this morning," Momma said.

I didn't remember any such thing.

"Shit. That's the whole problem with religion," Daddy said in a mocking tone. Momma cut her eyes at him. She hated when he said bad words at the kitchen table and especially on Sunday. "And we aren't wasting a red cent on any damn party. In case you've all forgotten, our cotton is still underwater."

No one had forgotten.

After yesterday's firestorm, no one dared blink or breathe or swallow or speak another word until Daddy left the table. But I agreed with him about the whole religion problem, and that worried me a little.

26

Later that night as I tried to fall asleep, I stared at the shadowy space between our twin beds. The weatherman had forecasted more rain, and in the distance, I heard thunder. If God really and truly existed, he wouldn't let it rain again so soon. What had started out as a fun, pretend, backyard swimming pool turned bad all around, especially in the way our cotton was ruined. According to Daddy, we would probably end up in the poor house, wherever that was.

"Abby, are you still awake?"

"A little." Her sheet shifted as she turned toward me. Most of our best conversations happened in the dark just before we fell asleep.

"If something ever happened to Momma, and Nana and Mamaw Pearl weren't around anymore, I would go live with Mae."

"Where would Nana and Mamaw Pearl be?" Her words sounded thick and dreamy.

"Dead. If all our grandmothers were dead and something happened to Momma, I would go live with Mae. There's no way I'd stay and take care of Daddy." I explained it extra slowly because she was only seven years old and sometimes didn't understand things.

"Me too. I'm going wherever you go." She turned the opposite direction from me. Her breathing became steady and even.

Chapter Four

After nearly a week, the floodwaters seeped into the ground and evaporated into the skies. When the sun finally came out, Daddy's cotton seedlings turned brown and withered away. Papa Pete, who was a farmer before he got too old to work, always said it was better to get too much rain in the spring than not enough. As I stared out the dining room window at the dark, black field, I didn't see how that could be true.

Since Daddy had to replant his cotton anyway, Momma decided we should use a corner of the field for a vegetable garden. She brought up the idea at supper on Friday night. A garden sounded like fun, but Daddy wasn't going along with it. He drained his beer and cracked open another. "I don't have time to worry with a garden. I have a cotton crop to replant."

"No, Lee. You don't have to do anything other than say it's okay." Daddy skimmed the business section of the newspaper and occasionally cut his eyes at Momma as she continued to nag.

"We'll do all the work, buying the seeds, planting, watering, weeding." Momma sounded like the Little Red Hen. She was willing to do all the work while Daddy, the ornery pig, would reap the benefit of fresh salads all summer. Ornery pigs loved green salads with garden onions and juicy tomatoes. "I know you can spare a few rows," Momma said.

Daddy shook his head and turned the page of his newspaper. "Not a good idea," he mumbled.

"Lee, it's the perfect idea. Think of all the money we'll save this summer with our own garden." I couldn't believe how Momma continued to push him. *Very risky,* I thought. I continued eating my baked chicken, but without anyone noticing, I scattered a handful of green peas on the floor for Lucky. I hated green peas.

After smirking and grumbling, Daddy finally agreed we could use a small section of field next to the driveway for our garden. Since that spot was closest to the kitchen, it would make for easier vegetable harvesting. Plus, if we hooked two hoses together and dragged them across the side yard without getting any knots, we could water our garden when the plants got dry in the summer. I was surprised he went along with it, but he pointed out that we would probably abandon the project before morning. That only made Momma more determined to get a garden in the ground.

The next morning, just before lunch, we drove to town to buy seeds. As we passed into the city limits, I read the population sign for the millionth time. SAVAGE CROSSING—POPULATION 5,253. I always checked the population number to see if anyone new had moved into town or if anyone old had died. The numbers never changed. Momma said even though we lived five miles away, our family was included in the Savage Crossing population number because we had to be counted somewhere.

"What numbers are we?" I asked Momma as we turned on Main Street.

"What do you mean?" Momma glanced in the rearview mirror at me.

"Of the five thousand two hundred and fifty-three people, which four numbers are we? I'm sure we aren't the first four or the last four, but hopefully we have good numbers like maybe two hundred, two hundred and one, two hundred and two, and two hundred and three."

"Gracie, sometimes I don't understand how your mind works." She shook her head.

"Do you think the first person on the population list is the oldest person in town?"

"I really have no idea." Momma shook her head. I had given her something to think about. I wondered if the town librarian knew.

Even though Savage Crossing was only a one stoplight town, most everything important could be found along the square—Savage Groceries, Savage Supply & Hardware, First Bank, the library, and

Sterling's Five and Dime. And across the street from First Baptist Church, the red brick school building sat beneath a group of tall cottonwood trees. HOME OF THE SAVAGE CROSSING MIGHTY YELLOW JACKETS, the sign out front said. As we drove past, I noticed rows of yellow school buses filled the parking lot near the gym. They were parked so close together their dirty wheels almost touched. Even though our car windows were rolled up tight, the smell of the freshly cut grass on the playground saturated the air. I stared at the steep, concrete steps leading up to the glass doors in front of the main building. Come September, those steps would be crowded with squirmy students waiting for the first bell to ring, but, as of now, they were empty. School didn't seem so horrible during summer.

The courthouse where Momma paid farm taxes served as the centerpiece of town with a copper dome that reflected light on a sunny day. Catty corner from that, the Yellow Jacket Café served hamburgers with buns smashed flat and just the perfect amount of grease on top. Burgers came with fries or onion rings, a difficult choice because both were delicious. Junior high kids were allowed to walk to the Yellow Jacket for lunch instead of being forced to eat in the cafeteria. Looking forward to a pile of deep fried onion rings for lunch everyday probably made kids work extra hard to graduate sixth grade.

After circling the square, Momma pulled into a parking spot in front of the hardware store. Abby and I piled out of the back seat and into the warm day just as the noon siren blasted through town. Momma said most small towns had noon sirens to test the tornado warning equipment and to remind people about lunchtime. The sirens never went off on Sunday though, because of church.

"So, since it's noon, can we eat lunch at the Yellow Jacket?" I asked.

"No, we'll eat at home."

"I'm hungry," Abby said. Momma gave me a see-what-you-started look and shoved open the door to the hardware store. A silver bell hanging overhead made a tinkling sound to let everyone know we were there.

Just inside the door, a display contained American flags of all sizes. There were big ones on wooden poles for mounting and other small ones for poking into flowerpots or waving in a parade. A sign on the wall said, SUPPORT OUR FIGHTING MEN IN VIETNAM.

"Can we get a flag?" I asked. "Pleeeee-ase?"

"Let's just get what we came for, Gracie." I could tell I was wearing on her nerves, but I couldn't keep from talking.

"But, Momma, it would be the patriotic thing to do." Momma shook her head and steered Abby and me toward the section with gardening supplies.

Spanning half an aisle, seed packets were displayed on a rack much like the birthday cards at Sterling's. The bottom section contained vegetable seeds, and the top half contained rows and rows of neatly aligned flower seed envelopes. Those packets with the brightest flowers on the covers lured me closer. I began grabbing the prettiest ones—orange marigolds and petunias with candy cane stripes and something called evening primrose, which sounded fancy. Abby took some too.

"We're only getting vegetables," Momma reminded.

"Why?" Abby blurted and stomped her foot.

"Don't start, Abby, or we'll go straight home with nothing," Momma said. I stared at the seed packets in my hand and began putting them back into the appropriate slots. I could tell by Momma's hard face that she meant it, and I hoped we weren't in for one of Abby's full-out tantrums. Instead, her pout dissolved and she said, "Okay," in a deflated voice. That was a huge improvement compared to the tantrum she had thrown a few months ago when Momma refused to buy the new cereal Abby begged for. She had only wanted the "kite fun kit" mentioned on the front of the box. When I explained there was no real kite inside, and that she'd have to send money to get it, Abby flung herself onto the dirty floor, screaming and pounding her fists. People stared. Momma ignored her and pushed her grocery basket right on down the aisle. I hid behind the toilet paper display and watched to make sure no one kidnapped her. Of course, someone would have to want a kid really bad to steal a shrieking child. After only a few minutes of being ignored, Abby stopped crying and ran to find Momma one aisle over. I worried that Abby had a bit of Daddy's temper inside her but considered maybe she was outgrowing it.

31

Picking up a package of patty pan squash seeds, I studied the picture on the front. The name sounded silly, like something from a nursery rhyme, and the round white squash looked like a flying saucer. "Can I get this one?" I was more curious about how it would grow than taste. I never planned to eat it for supper.

Momma nodded and placed it inside our shopping basket with the other packets. Seeds didn't cost very much, so we selected a variety. Momma chose two kinds of eggplant and yellow squash with crooked necks. She inspected green onion sets tied with a length of twine that were lying in a big bin. She took two bundles to put with our seeds. Abby chose watermelon seeds. Nana once told me that watermelons were tricky to grow in our Delta soil, but I kept quiet about it. I didn't want Abby to get upset again.

"Momma, there's Roy Henry," I said, pointing to the front door.

"Maybe he won't see us," she said.

I ran toward him before Momma could stop me, weaving around Mr. Turpin, the hardware store manager, who restocked bags of charcoal in the middle aisle. Roy Henry was a celebrity in Savage Crossing, like the town's mascot. Even though he was a full-grown man, he had the mind of a little kid. All the children and most of the adults around town loved him. Those who avoided him were probably just afraid.

"Did you-you-you-you see my hor-hor-horse?" Roy Henry asked me.

"*Oui*, I did."

"His name is Trig-Trig-Trig-ger," he said, trying to spit the thick words from his mouth. Silver whiskers poked from his chin, and dried snot circled the bottom of his bony nose.

"I know. I've met Trigger before," I said. During the school year, Roy Henry usually came around during recess, riding his "horse" which was really a blue bicycle with a ripped black seat. He stuttered and stammered and laughed with all the students until Mr. Mooney, the school principal, ran him off with a harsh look and a wave of his hand. I always felt a bit sorry for Roy Henry, yet knew he had no worries, not about a job, or money, or whether or not the crops needed rain. He lived with his momma, not too far from my friend Janice, and most of the people in town helped take care of him in one way or another.

"Grace!" Momma motioned for me to return, so I walked back over to our shopping cart and waited for her to pay. As Mr. Turpin loaded the sacks into our car, I saw Roy Henry standing in the middle of Main Street, across from the Yellow Jacket Café. After securing his horse to a tree, he stomped several paces back, spun on his boots, and with the skill of Roy Rogers, pulled imaginary cavalry revolvers from his invisible holsters. *Bam-bam-bam-bam-bam*! Roy Henry fired his bullets down the street toward the water tower.

"Oh, good Lord, he's at it again. What's he doing with his bicycle?" Momma asked as she shoved us into the car. There was no reason for us to be in such a hurry. Roy Henry had stopped traffic in both directions, not that Savage Crossing ever had more than three or four cars driving through at a time.

"Momma, that's not a bicycle. That's Trigger, Roy Henry's horse." Abby said.

"Well, he's sick. Something needs to be done with him," she said.

"Like what?" I asked.

Momma never said.

***

Abby and I couldn't wait to plant the garden, but like many things, the preparation took much of the fun out of it. While we ate lunch— leftover tuna fish that I didn't like—Momma drew a garden plan on a piece of notebook paper. She said it was important to know exactly where every vegetable would be planted before we started sowing seeds. "Gardening is like farming," she said. "It doesn't magically happen." Based on all the drawing and planning going on around our kitchen table, I didn't think it would ever happen.

"Why can't we just decide as we go?" I asked.

"Because we want our garden to look nice and organized, Gracie. Small plants that need afternoon shade will do better planted next to stronger, taller plants. See, if we put squash here and peppers here…" She wrote squash and peppers on her diagram. "One will shade the other. Understand?"

"Yes," I answered in a "can-we-please-get-on-with-it tone."

Abby sat beside me without moving, possibly in a trance. Eventually, she murmured, "Yes," but her face said, "No," according to the crinkles between her confused eyes. Tons of planning and talking and drawing carrots on a diagram only seemed to translate into a convenient stalling tactic.

A long lunch turned into an even longer afternoon. Although we had a garden "plan," there was much work to do before we could drop the first seeds into their assigned holes. After the big rain, weeds had sprouted in the field. They even seemed to multiply between furrows while we were eating lunch. Abby and I pulled the ones growing along the first row, while Momma chopped with a hoe. When the ground was finally ready for planting, Abby ripped open a package of spinach with too much excitement. Tiny seeds scattered through the air like black pepper. So much for Momma's careful garden plan. Momma smiled and laughed and didn't seem upset that soon we would have spinach growing everywhere, maybe even in the grass beside the driveway. I found it amazing that such small seeds could produce an entire salad.

The sun moved overhead as we worked. It took us the better part of the afternoon, and I knew that by nighttime my shoulders would be marked with a sunburn line where my tank top was. After we planted the last seed and put away all our tools, Momma leaned against the mimosa tree to survey our handiwork. Stakes stapled with seed packets poked up at intervals to identify each plant.

"Later in the summer, I'll teach you girls to can sweet pickles," Momma told us. "This is gonna be our best garden ever."

We toasted to our success with Dixie cups filled with sweet tea. It was the only garden I ever remembered planting, but I agreed it was *très* exciting, especially my row of spaceship squash near the back.

That night as I brushed my teeth, my cheeks were flushed from the sun, and my body felt tired from all the hard gardening work. I wondered if Daddy felt the same way after a day working in the fields. It was a happy sort of tired, the type that made me feel like I had done something important. By the time I climbed into bed, Abby had already fallen asleep. I closed my eyes and wondered about those seeds buried in the field and whether or not they had stirred at all in the soil. The fan blew a calm breeze across my face. I floated to another place where gardens grew lush and the sweet-scented air felt cool on my arms.

Chapter Five

When Momma woke us for church on Sunday morning, I thought for sure she was confused. A crack of yellow sunlight streamed through the space between our curtains, making the morning feel more like a barefoot sort of day rather than one spent wearing hard-soled shoes. "How can it already be Sunday again?" I moaned, rolled back over and pulled the covers over my head.

"Gracie Lee, yesterday was Saturday. Remember? We planted the garden." Momma snatched my pink bedspread away, leaving me lying there in my cotton shorty pajamas. Lucky didn't appreciate the abrupt awakening either, and he howled.

"Momma!" I tugged the bedspread back. "I don't feel good. I need to stay home."

"Me too," Abby piped up, ruining my only chance of faking sick. There was no way Momma would buy it, especially with my little sister trying to skip out too. I lay in bed as long as possible, thinking it was starting out to be a strange Sunday, because Mae hadn't come last night, and Momma forgot to roll our hair. Momma never forgot to roll our hair for church.

***

Nana was an early bird wherever she went and always got to church before us. Right off, I saw her sitting in our regular spots in the third pew. She stood, waved us over, and suddenly I was glad to be there.

"Are y'all wearing new dresses?" she asked, hugging us at the same time.

"Nana, we wear these dresses all the time," I shook my head and smoothed the skirt of the blue dress Momma made a while back. Abby's was identical, only smaller.

"We're so proud of you Gracie Lee," Aunt Clara said, giving me a hug. Aunt Clara was a wisp of a lady, not much taller than me, but her hands were strong from a life spent urging vegetables from her patch of earth and washing clothes by hand on her back porch. When she drew me to her, her body felt fragile and bird-like, but her fingertips pressed into my shoulder blades with force. Aunt Clara was Nana's oldest sister, but they didn't look very much alike.

"Thank you, Aunt Clara," I said. I had hoped the events of last Sunday had been forgotten so I could return to being a non-person at Boon Chapel, a regular kid going about my business. Instead, people began walking over and patting me on the back, offering congratulations, even a few of the back-row farmers who had never spoken to me before. I wanted to melt into the floor and disappear into the secret hiding place beneath the church house.

Boon Chapel was an old building that balanced on cinderblocks. The adults didn't know about the crawlspace beneath the floor, or if they knew, they didn't give it a thought. Adults preferred to sit inside with air-conditioning. The dark space beneath the building stayed cave-cool, even in the hottest part of summer, and nothing grew because the sun couldn't touch it. Last August, when Arkansas was blistering hot, Boon Chapel hosted a weeklong revival with a visiting preacher from Tennessee. Lots of people came from all over the county to hear his sermons. He was a short, round man who got excited and sweaty and talked on and on, mostly about hellfire. Afterwards, the adults all sat around talking forever while the kids played outside, running through the graveyard and crawling underneath the church building. That's when I found a magical marble partially buried in the sandy dirt beneath Boon Chapel. It looked like a miniature Earth, deep blue and bright white with a green swirl in the center like a flame. I hid it inside my jewelry box and considered it valuable and a sign of good luck.

Aunt Clara always sat at the end of the pew, and Nana sat beside her. Abby and I took turns sitting beside Nana, and today was my turn.

Nana draped her arm around my shoulder and kept it there until we stood to sing the first hymn. Occasionally, she gave me a light pat on the arm, and then sometimes she reached further and patted Abby too.

After Sunday school class, we returned to the same seats. I stared at the tote board while Mr. Donaldson read attendance numbers to us. "Attendance this Sunday, thirty-eight; Bibles brought, twenty-four; and Offering, forty-nine dollars and twenty-five cents."

When Momma played the introduction to "Blessed Assurance," I watched for Nana's expression. It was her most favorite song, even including all the songs on the radio. We all knew the words by heart, but Nana passed the hymnal to me, and I held it low so Abby could see. There was something good and right about following along with the musical notes in the hymnal. Nana sang with an enthusiasm that was contagious, but Aunt Clara, who was tone deaf, drowned out our entire pew.

Then the singing was over.

Clutching my hands in my lap to keep from fidgeting, I stared at Brother Brown and focused on the words drifting from his lips. Right away, I became disappointed. In the one week since our conversation, nothing had changed. Not at home or at church. When he mentioned something about growing your garden, he caught my attention for half a second until I realized he wasn't talking about squash or tomatoes or dirt. Instead, he meant developing your faith. I flipped through the colorful pictures in my Bible, stopping at the one of Noah. Now, that was a flood.

Brother Brown got worked up toward the end of his sermon, worked up for him, anyway, and invited the lost to come up and turn their lives over to Jesus. He spoke more quickly than normal, with a raised voice, and after a while his vocal chords began to sound strained. Removing a handkerchief from inside his suit pocket, he pressed it to his forehead twice, then folded it and placed it back in his pocket. Based on the number of stanzas he made us sing, he must have thought I started a new trend the week before, but this week no one seemed willing to follow my lead.

I pulled an offering envelope from inside my Bible and began writing my name, over and over. "Grace Lee Abbott." I slanted my cursive to the right and then the left, which looked more French. I even got bored enough to write my second middle name, Eudora.

Grace Lee Eudora Abbott

GRACIE EUDORA ABBOTT

Gracie-Le… What? I heard my name called from the pulpit. My full name. Grace Lee Eudora Abbott. I looked up to see Brother Brown smiling at me, a big smile, showing the space between his front teeth. Abby poked me in the ribs with her sharp elbow. The air conditioner fell silent as a sanctuary of faces stared at me.

"Huh?" I said automatically. Uncle Will snickered from the back row. Brother Brown's wife, Mrs. Brown, who as far as I knew had never smiled in her life, turned and looked at me, wearing a sour expression. My cheeks flamed. I sat there in the third row, with dirty hair pulled into two long pigtails because Momma forgot to wash and roll it, and I had no idea why Brother Brown had said my full name to the Boon Chapel congregation.

I soon discovered the reason.

"Next Sunday night, be sure to come back and see Grace Lee Eudora Abbott officially join the church with a full immersion baptism right here behind me." He stepped back and with a sweep of his arm motioned to the area behind the pulpit reserved for rare Boon Chapel baptisms. The baptismal tank, built into the back wall, had a partial glass front, which allowed the congregation to watch without leaving their pews. Red velvet curtains draped both sides of the small space, giving the whole area an important feel. Usually the curtains were closed, but today they were halfway open as though the water welcomed me. Only there was no water inside the tank yet.

"And there will be refreshments afterwards. Cookies and orange sherbet punch?" He looked to Momma who sat perched on the piano bench, her posture perfect. She smiled and nodded. I accidentally swallowed my spearmint gum.

***

The only patch of woods in our flat world of cotton and soybean fields passed the window in a dark blur.

"There's the woods," Abby said.

I ignored her. Usually on the way home from church, we made up silly stories about black bears and hobos living in the woods, but I didn't feel like talking. I sat beside her in the back seat, thinking and twirling Barbie's hair.

"Momma, why doesn't Daddy ever go to church?" I asked.

"He has to farm."

"But he didn't go last week when it was too wet to farm."

"He was thinking about the farm," she said.

"What about Uncle Will?" I asked. Uncle Will, who was Nana's baby brother and Dian's Daddy, was a farmer too. Although he slept a lot in church, he must have been able to think about farming from his pew. Momma always made excuses for Daddy.

"Grace, you're making me tired." She spoke slowly, spitting out each word separately like it tasted bad in her mouth.

In the distance, the sky had begun to darken toward home. "Is it supposed to rain again?" I asked.

"Lord, I hope not. We'll have to bury Daddy if we get another heavy rain," Momma said. "Our new garden doesn't need a downpour either," she added as she stared toward the flat horizon.

We had almost made it home, when Momma pulled to the shoulder of the road to let a huge tractor pass. I stared at the gray house sitting off the highway. It was the closest house to ours and my favorite turning-around-place when I rode my bicycle. Even though shrubs and trees hid much of it, a wide porch wrapped around the front and clung to the sides, making it seem extra-large and special. No one had lived there since old man Burton died two years ago. It was much too pretty of a house to have no life inside it. As the tractor rumbled beside us, I felt the ground tremble, almost like an earthquake. Lots of earthquakes struck our area of Arkansas, but I knew the difference between an earthquake tremor and a tractor rumble.

"I think that's one of Daddy's tractors," Momma said as she waved at the driver. I couldn't tell. Every tractor looked the same to me.

I felt the bump of gravel as Momma pulled into the driveway. "Are we having pot roast?" I asked. "I'm starved to death." Brother Brown had kept us longer than normal talking about my upcoming baptism, and then Momma talked to Nana forever while we stood outside in the parking lot. But before Momma answered my question or even drove into the carport, she slammed on the brakes and stared at the field to the right of the driveway.

"Shit. Shit. Shit! I can't believe this." She bolted from the car leaving the door wide open, something that aggravated her when we did it. Momma ran straight to the field.

"What?" Abby whispered. Too afraid to move, we watched from the back seat as Momma picked up a splintered garden stake that was half buried in the dirt. Shaking her head, she released the shredded paper. I watched the torn seed packet float to her feet. The freshly plowed field that spread rich and dark, from our driveway to the horizon, was ready for a second planting of cottonseed. There was no sign of our garden.

"Our garden's gone!" I yelled. Yesterday's hard work had been plowed under.

Momma started marching toward the house while Abby and I sat stunned in the back seat. As she reached the edge of the carport, we chased after her. For a moment, I completely forgot about Brother Brown and how I had gotten myself into this whole baptism mess. Momma opened the screen door with such force that she smacked the side of the carport wall and knocked over the shovel and hoe we had used only yesterday to plant our garden. Abby covered her ears.

Daddy looked up from the kitchen table where he sat hunched over, working on his transistor radio. Tiny electronic parts were spread across Momma's placemat. In one hand, he held a screwdriver. With the other, he removed the glasses that had been perched on the tip of his nose. "Anne, what the hell's gotten into you?"

"I'll tell you what the hell's gotten into me. You. You and your stupid, idiot tractor driver. Or did you tell him to plow up our garden? You probably think it's hilarious after we slaved all day yesterday." Momma's tears cut pale tracks in the rouge on her cheeks. I didn't want to watch her cry, but just like when someone threw up at school, I couldn't look away either. Abby clung to the folds of Momma's skirt and began bawling.

"You need to calm down, Anne." Daddy returned his glasses to his nose, tilted his head just so and tightened a screw, gripping the screwdriver with steady fingers.

"Don't talk to me!" Momma screamed. She snatched a package of Daddy's cigarettes from the kitchen drawer and stormed through the den, slamming the back door on her way out. Abby raced after her, tripped down the step between the kitchen and den, and wailed even louder. The entire house seemed to shudder and sink a few inches into the ground.

I stood in the kitchen, unable to move.

Daddy continued fiddling with his radio. "Grace, your Momma is completely overreacting," he said, without looking up from his work. "I'm sure my tractor driver didn't notice your little garden."

I glared at him, not because I thought he was lying, but because he had made Momma cry and he didn't care.

For the next several hours, Momma sat in the backyard smoking cigarettes, one after another, while staring at a crumpled paperback. Every few minutes, I peeped out the bedroom window to make sure she was still there. Smashed cigarette butts stained with rosy lipstick filled the ashtray next to her chair. With the flick of a lighter, she lit another. Pushing a lock of hair behind her ear, she took a long pull, closed her eyes and sank deeper into the vinyl straps of her chair. I never saw Momma turn a page of her book. Once, she noticed me watching her, but even then she only sighed and looked off toward Savage Crossing where rainclouds gathered over the water tower.

Chapter Six

Although there was no further mention of our short-lived garden or the prior day's argument, a dull feeling spread over Monday morning and hung around like fog that wouldn't clear. When the gloominess became too much to stomach, Momma announced Abby and I would spend the afternoon with Nana and Papa Pete. "I need a break from my normal life," she said, while washing the last of the lunch dishes.

"So do we," I said. Abby nodded in agreement. My job was to dry the plates and pass them over to Abby, who did nothing more than place them on the kitchen table for Momma to put away later. But that was something.

During the short drive to Nana and Papa's house, I sat in the back seat, twirling Barbie's hair and watching Momma's reflection in the rearview mirror. She stared hard at the gravel road. I watched her eyes and wondered what she was thinking about. I blinked when she blinked.

"I'm so proud of you for getting saved, Gracie," she said and turned to look at me in the back seat.

I smiled but didn't say anything. I had only walked to the front to talk to Brother Brown about Daddy. He was the one who needed saving, not me. It wasn't that I didn't want to go to Heaven, I just figured I had plenty of time to worry about such things later. Instead, I was forced to think about it during the summer, when life should have been worry-free.

Nana and Papa Pete live in a farmhouse on the home place, not too far from Boon Chapel. We call it the home place because it's the first home our family had in Arkansas, and it had been in the family now for generations. Papa Pete's grandmother bought the land a long, long time ago, before televisions, telephones, or anything fun had been invented, back when Mississippi County was swampy and not fit for much. I knew Grandma Lily through old faded photographs and stories re-told by Papa Pete. She seemed nothing like the flower she was named after. Instead, her face looked hard and tough as though she had sprouted like a weed on the ditch dump. Since she was the original farmer in our family, I blamed her for the whole predicament of Momma's plowed-up garden.

Momma honked as we pulled into the driveway. Nana was stooped over, tending to the flowerbeds planted along the stone pathway leading to her back porch. She waved and grinned with her whole face, her cheeks as pink as the roses climbing beneath the kitchen window. Instantly, everything seemed okay again.

"Can we please walk down to the ditch dump?" I asked the moment my feet touched the ground.

Nana said, "Yes," so without even a goodbye wave to Momma, Abby and I raced toward the cotton field. We knew Nana would follow us, because she loved to walk to the ditch too. It was one of our regular things to do, especially in spring and fall when the weather was best.

Daddy stored cotton pickers, combines, and farm tools in the barn behind the home place, and behind the barn, a row of silos divided the yard from the cotton field. When Momma was a kid, Papa Pete raised hogs in a pen back there. Sometimes, I swore I could hear squeals and cries echoing around the silos, but Momma said it was only my imagination. I wasn't so sure. Standing a safe distance away from the grain bins, Abby and I waited at the edge of the field while Nana caught up with us.

"Hurry, Nana!" Abby shouted. Even though the wind caught Abby's words, and I didn't think Nana could hear her, she waved back, laughing the whole time. Why Nana always chose to wear dresses, even while gardening or walking to the ditch dump, made no sense to me. As her circle-tailed skirt whipped around her legs, she almost stumbled trying to keep it from flying above her head. But her hair didn't move at all. The headscarf tied beneath her chin kept it in place.

When Nana reached us, we set off together toward the mass of trees at the end of the cotton field, walking between furrows, careful not to upset the ankle-high cotton plants poking from the ground. The ground was mostly dry, and I was relieved to see the cotton at the home place had survived the flood. Almost halfway there, Abby stopped to take off her shoe. A tiny pebble, no bigger than a grass seed, had sneaked inside. Even something that teeny could drive a person crazy and make the ditch dump not so fun, so I understood why we had stopped. While Abby retied her shoe, I stared back at the home place. From our vantage point in the middle of the cotton field, everything looked different, the silos squatty and the house completely swallowed by trees. Distance was an interesting thing and something to think about.

Continuing on, I dragged my feet through the loamy soil, hoping to uncover an arrowhead or shards of Indian pottery. Daddy's collection of arrowheads filled an entire shelf on his office bookcase, but I never found anything on our field walks except pearly shells. Last year in science class, we learned how the Mississippi River once covered half of Arkansas, but the whole idea was hard to believe. I couldn't picture Indians weaving baskets and making pottery in Nana and Papa Pete's yard.

"Nana, what was your baptism like?" I asked.

"Oh, goodness. I remember it like yesterday. We were just kids. Will and Clara and I were all baptized together in Little River." She smiled and stared off to the left toward Uncle Will's house on Little River. "There was a Baptist church down the road. That's where the whole family attended church. All twelve of my brothers and sisters were eventually baptized in that river." Her eyes had a faraway look as though she thought about something romantic.

I couldn't think of a single thing from my boring past that would give me such a dreamy expression. Maybe those feelings were only felt by grown-ups, something to make being old not so depressing.

"Weren't you afraid to be dunked in Little River?" I asked. "The water is gross, plus, Uncle Will always warns us about huge snakes living in that water. I can't believe he would have agreed to that."

She grinned. "Oh, no. We grew up swimming in Little River. We even learned to ski there behind Daddy's fishing boat. A hundred years ago, we didn't know any better. Plus, the important thing was to be baptized."

I tried to imagine her skiing on Little River or at the lake or anywhere. She was exaggerating when she said "a hundred years ago" because she had turned fifty-five on her last birthday. With Momma's help, Abby and I had made her a heart-shaped strawberry cake and put lots of pink candles on it, but not fifty-five because we didn't want to melt the icing.

"I'm happy you're getting baptized, Gracie. It's the first step in your salvation."

First step?

First step meant future steps. I didn't want to know about future steps, so I didn't say anything else about it.

The ditch at the end of the field was deep and wide, more like a river than the shallow trenches surrounding our house. It was an important ditch because it had an official name. "How do you say it again, Nana?" I asked.

"Koe-tis-ski," Nana said, pronouncing each syllable slowly.

"Koe-tis-ski," I repeated. Abby echoed me.

The water of the Kochtitzki Ditch didn't churn like the Mississippi River or even Little River after a big storm. If I stood still in one spot long enough and stared through the jumble of brush growing tall on the bank, I saw turtles break the surface of the water before dipping back below. While Nana watched for rattlesnakes, Abby and I explored the hollowed-out gullies surrounding the ditch.

"Why is there an icebox down there?" I pointed.

"Some people don't have any respect for the land. They dump trash in the ditch instead of burning it or hauling it away," Nana said.

Along with the icebox, I counted two old tires, a faded orange couch with stuffing poking out of its stained cushions, and a stove with the oven door standing open. Johnson grass grew thick, and vines covered the icebox like Christmas garland.

"I bet when the Indians lived here, they weren't litterbugs," I said.

"Mercy, no," Nana agreed. In the distance, thunder boomed as murky clouds gathered. The wind kicked up dirt across the field, and the earthy smell of rain saturated the air. Nana retied her headscarf and said we'd best get back before the storm blew up. We made it to the back porch just as the skies opened. I watched from the dining room window as leaves blew across the yard and rain fell in silver sheets.

45

Even though the storm was short-lived, rain was something we didn't need.

***

"Abby-Grace!" Momma cracked open the back door and yelled at us. We were busy coloring at Nana's dining room table, so we pretended not to hear her. "Abigail! Gracieeeeeeee!" The second time she hollered, we ran to the door.

"Help me unload the car." As we walked to the car, we told her about the ditch and seeing junk in the bottom.

"We barely made it back before the storm. Did Daddy get more rain at home?" I asked.

"Yes." That was all she said.

"What is all this stuff?" I asked. Grocery sacks lined Momma's back seat, but instead of food, they were filled with fabric and blue jeans and old shoes.

"Material for the quilt Nana's making and old clothes for church. I cleaned out your closet this afternoon." Momma passed me a sack and handed another to Abby. Outfits that had been hanging in our closet just yesterday looked worn out now that they were piled up in Savage Crossing grocery bags.

"Just put them there," Nana said looking up from her quilting and motioning to the dining room table where Abby and I had been coloring. We plopped the bags down and returned to the car for another load while Momma made a pot of coffee.

Nana's wooden quilting frame was the size of my twin bed, a long contraption with material stretched from one end to the other. I studied the quilt design—small squares of fabric sewn together to make larger squares. Each large square formed a colorful turtle pattern. It was the most unique quilt I'd ever seen. I traced my finger over a section of the soft fabric and recognized the material from one of my play dresses.

"Nana, who's this quilt for?" I asked.

"Someone special, you'll see," Nana said, stretching her lower back, removing the half-glasses from her nose and rubbing her eyes.

"*C'est* cool," I said.

46

Each time I asked if Abby and I could go back outside to play, Momma said, "No, we're leaving in just a minute." Then she continued drinking coffee and yakking and sewing with Nana. Abby and I kept coloring.

While Nana sewed even, white stitches, she whistled. I watched her, the way she pursed her lips, the way she stopped and smiled or laughed when Momma said something funny, then returned to whistling as automatically as blinking. They talked about regular things—the cotton crop, Sunday school lessons, Lona Barns's new coconut cream pie recipe. Conversations that might have seemed boring to most people felt soothing to a worrywart like me. Momma flipped off her shoes and leaned back into the chair, wearing a more relaxed expression than the one we saw at home.

"How's Lee?" Nana asked quietly. With one question, a haze drifted over our afternoon and the mood shifted.

Momma glanced up then returned to her sewing. I kept my head down and colored, but opened my ears.

"Better today," Momma whispered. "Some days are better than others. He has an appointment next Wednesday."

An appointment?

Chapter Seven

I always got in trouble for being nosy, so I didn't ask about Daddy's appointment, even though I almost had to lock myself in the bedroom for three days to keep from saying anything. Like Nancy Drew, I searched for clues and eavesdropped on the adults, especially the adult with the best gossip—Momma's friend Maggie.

Most afternoons, after Momma watched her favorite soap opera, Momma and Maggie lit up the party line that connected our farmhouse to the wider world. From Maggie's kitchen table in nearby Cottonwood Corner, she yammered through a pinched mouth of crowded teeth into the twisty-green cord glued to Momma's ear. If I listened from my spot on the linoleum where I played jacks, Momma would eventually mention Daddy's appointment to her best friend. I felt sure of it.

"I think someone picked up the line." Momma paused long enough to inhale. "Is someone there? I can hear you breathing."

Slinging my jacks, I ran through the dining room and picked up the hallway extension outside Momma and Daddy's bedroom.

"Please…call an ambulance. I've shot myself." The man on the line gasped and sputtered. Although he sounded far away, I knew only a handful of distant neighbors talked on our party line. I clamped my hand over my mouth, thinking this was just the sort of drama we needed to add some excitement to our boring farm.

"I don't know what you're up to but hang up this phone right away! Prank calls are not funny." Momma scolded the man in her most annoyed and serious voice, the one she used when Daddy forgot to come home one night.

"This is a private conversation!" Maggie added. "Can you believe the nerve of some people?"

"I live in the old Burton house down from Cottonwood Corner. Call an ambulance…please…" His voice faded, and I heard a muffled crash that made me sick to my stomach. There was a rattling sound in my ear, followed by silence.

The gray house?

As the seriousness of the situation sank in, Momma stopped talking to Maggie so she could call for help. I slammed down the extension and ran back into the kitchen to see what would happen. Momma's finger shook as she turned the dial on the phone. In no time, an ambulance screamed down the highway. I watched from the porch as it turned into the driveway of my favorite house.

"Oh, my God, Momma. It's the pretty gray house, the one we thought was empty." Momma stared at the phone and looked a little pale. "Do you think that man is dead?" I asked. The idea that a dead man laid just across the cotton field from us was one of the most interesting things I could imagine.

"Gracie Lee Eudora, stop being a spy and do something productive with your time." Momma seemed in a bad mood now that our neighbor had tried to kill himself—and nervous too, probably because she had been the one to call the police.

"Do you think you'll have to give a statement to the cops?"

"Young lady, you've been watching too much *Ironside*."

I hated that television show, but kept my mouth shut.

When Momma ran her hand through the top of her hair, I knew I was getting on her last nerve. One more wrong move and I wouldn't get to watch television after supper. Slipping out the back door, I sneaked around to the front yard. My tennis shoes sank into the soggy grass. After last night's rain, our world was wet again. Not flooded, just a regular soaking that left water standing between rows and filled low spots on the driveway. As I climbed the mimosa tree, overhead branches sprinkled me with water. My best sitting limb felt wet through the seat of my shorts.

From the tree, I had a better view of the ambulance stopped in front of the gray house. Even though we hadn't realized anyone lived there, I felt a tinge of responsibility, as though we should have known, as though our lack of neighborliness played a part in the man's problems.

A police car sped by our house, splashing water along the side of the road. It turned into the dead man's driveway. Or maybe he wasn't dead. I had no way of knowing, but the thought of possibly hearing a man's last spoken words gave me something to think about.

I tried to imagine why he would shoot himself. Maybe he was insane like one of those scary people in the late-late movies Mae sometimes let us watch. He may have just found out he had an incurable disease that would make him bleed from his eyeballs, and he wanted to die on his own terms. Maybe the whole thing was an accident. An accident was the only decent explanation. Otherwise, he pulled the trigger on purpose, and I couldn't imagine such a thing. After all, if he had really wanted to kill himself, why would he cut in on Momma and Maggie's phone call to ask for help?

Accidents do sometimes happen.

I climbed higher, hoping for a better view, but the house was too far away to see anything other than flashing lights from the ambulance parked in the driveway. Next Christmas, I would ask Santa for binoculars.

Right then, hidden inside the mimosa tree, I said a prayer for him, a man I'd never met and, until minutes ago, didn't know existed. It was nothing fancy like the prayers I'd heard spoken at Boon Chapel with words that flowed like poetry. Mine was a simple one. A prayer that if he died, he wouldn't go to Hell. And if he did go to Hell, that it wasn't the fiery place Brother Brown described every Sunday.

Soon, the ambulance flashed back by our house in the direction of the interstate. The noise pierced my eardrums, and I poked my fingers in my ears until it was a good ways down the road. It was only right that something so traumatic hurt my ears. From my spot in the tree, I stared at the gray house for a long time. I had driven by on my bike many times, yet I had never imagined anything bad happening within those walls.

Sleuthing made me thirsty. I went back inside to pour a glass of tea. I wondered if that man liked tea, or if he was one of those people who drank whiskey all day.

"Wanna play jacks again?" Abby asked. Even with all the excitement, she had not moved from the kitchen floor.

"No. I'm busy."

"Doing what?"

"Worrying about our neighbor, of course." I stepped over Abby's jacks and toward the dining room.

Momma was strumming her nails on the dining room table and staring out the large picture window toward the cotton field while holding the phone to her ear. Occasionally, she mumbled, "Uh-huh." When I walked beneath the curly phone cord that was stretched taut from the kitchen wall to her ear, she paid me no mind. I listened in on the extension, as I sipped my tea.

"Lucille at the beauty shop said he moved in over Memorial Day weekend. He's a grandson of old man Burton. You know, Lucille always did have a soft spot for old man Burton even though he was a strange duck." Maggie laughed, and I jerked the extension from my ear. When the screeching died down, I continued listening. "I heard the young man was odd, just like his grandfather, an actor or artist, or maybe a writer. They're a strange bunch, those artist types. I bet he died, don't you, Anne?" Maggie rattled on, but Momma didn't say much. I couldn't believe how much information Maggie had learned in such a short amount of time.

When Momma hung up the phone, I called my friend Janice to tell her about the man in the gray house. She said he probably stuck the gun in his mouth and pulled the trigger, because her next-door neighbor's uncle who lived in Chicago did that. "Killed him instantly," she said, "but they never washed all the blood stains off the walls and had to move."

"No, that's not what happened. I heard him talking on the phone. There's no way he could talk or do anything with his head blown to smithereens." I stretched the phone as far as I could into my bedroom and closed the door, smashing the cord in the doorway. Someday I would have my own telephone, maybe a princess phone like the one my cousin Candi had in her bedroom.

"He's probably a lunatic or an axe murderer or something worse," she said.

I wondered what could be worse than an axe murderer.

***

Our Easy Bake Oven, which sat next to the real oven, kept us out of Momma's hair while she cooked supper. Abby pulled cake mixes from the cabinet, and I looked around the kitchen and really saw it for the first time, dull and plain, filled with the same smells and routine every day. The whole room would look better if Momma painted her oven turquoise, like our Easy Bake. She said it didn't work that way.

"Momma, why would that man want to kill himself?" I asked.

"Grace, we don't know anything about that man or his situation. Stop worrying about it."

"I'm not worried. Just curious. Aren't you curious about why a man lucky enough to live in that pretty house would kill himself?" Momma was strange not to wonder. "If I could live in a house like that, I'd be over the moon," I said.

"Grace, help your sister with the cake." Momma was good at changing the subject.

"He was probably depressed from having to live in this gloomy area of the country. When I grow up, I plan to live in a big city and work for the company that makes Easy Bake cake mix. Kenner—that's the name of the company. See, it's written here." I pointed to the front of the oven. Even though the notion had just come to me, it was a good one. "I have lots of ideas for foods other than desserts, like pizza," I explained to Momma, while she diced potatoes into tiny squares.

"That sounds like an interesting plan," Momma said. "But maybe by then you'll want to live on the farm." She poured buttermilk into cornmeal and whipped a batter together without measuring any of the ingredients.

"Nope. That would be a sad conclusion to my life. My future plans do not include Arkansas or farming."

"Such drama, Grace. Maybe you should be an actress." Momma chuckled at me, but I was serious. She never took me seriously.

"Maybe I will," I said.

Abby spread out the cake mix packages on the kitchen table like playing cards, picked each one up, looked at the picture, then flipped over the back and studied the list of ingredients. Since it was her turn to pick, she treated the whole process like it was the most important thing ever. Eventually, she held up a yellow cake mix with chocolate frosting, grinning as though she had solved the world's hardest math problem. As she ripped open the top, a poof of powder escaped and disappeared into the greasy kitchen air. Abby couldn't reach the faucet without a chair, so I measured a tablespoon of water and poured it into the tin pie pan that Santa gave us with our oven. Abby stirred until enough of the lumps dissolved so that the cake would bake right. Nana always said over-stirred cake batter would be as tough as a brickbat.

I leaned down and watched as the tiny pan moved through the insides of the oven. I felt the heat from the light bulb inside. "Grace, don't sit so close. You're gonna burn off your eyelashes," Momma said.

I almost said, "Now who's being dramatic," but I stopped the words from coming out right before they spewed off the end of my tongue.

"Momma, is Daddy sick?" I asked instead. "I don't mean beer-drinking sick, but sick-sick?"

"Why would you think that?" she asked.

"You told Nana he had an appointment."

"Gracie, what have I told you about eavesdropping? You shouldn't be so nosy. People have appointments all the time." I knew that was true, but thought her eyes looked worried. Regular appointments didn't usually call for worrying.

Our cake came out looking like a miniature pan of cornbread but smelled sweet, like vanilla. I poked a toothpick in the center the way Momma taught me, and it came out clean. Abby swirled icing on top and licked the spoon, leaving a chocolate outline around her mouth. Daddy turned into the driveway just as Momma pulled the skillet of cornbread from the oven. She cut a wedge and placed it on his supper plate. When she added a pat of butter to the top, it instantly melted and dripped into his fried potatoes. I scooped out a piece of yellow cake and plopped it on Daddy's napkin.

After all that work, it looked disappointing—small and crumbly, and the icing was messy because we forgot to let the cake cool first. Daddy would say it was ugly, because it was. I wanted to remove it from the table, but there was no time. The screen door slammed shut, and Daddy walked into the kitchen before I even had time to count one Mississippi.

"Daddy, guess what?" I began to tell him about our excitement with the man in the gray house. It felt good to have something real to talk about with him.

"Damn, Grace. Can't you give me one minute to breathe?" He held up his hand like a stop sign.

"Sor-reeeey." I clamped my lips shut and took my usual seat at the table, feeling as though I'd been hit in the stomach with a dodge ball.

"What's all that?" He motioned at the table, while slinging his sweaty cap across the kitchen countertop next to the coffeepot. His khaki shirt had a grease spot down the front, and his jeans hung loose and tired.

"Supper. We made your favorites. The girls even made a cake."

Daddy picked up the napkin holding our Easy Bake cake, sniffed it and slung the whole thing into the sink. "Not hungry," he mumbled as he began to fix himself a drink. I ran to the sink to rescue our cake, but it had soaked up dishwater like a sponge.

"You have to eat something." Momma began wiping down the already clean countertops.

"I'll eat when I'm good and ready and not when you've served up the same old mess." After taking a long drink from his glass, Daddy began scrubbing his hands underneath the kitchen faucet, scrubbing and scrubbing as steam rose from the sink, the water too hot for a normal person to withstand. The day's dirt would wash off, but the yellow chemical stains were permanent. He dried his hands on a kitchen towel and barked, "Come here. All of you. Family meeting." Even though our kitchen was tiny and we were all within steps from one another, he waved the towel as though rounding us up with a lasso.

At first, I didn't move. When Momma gave me a pleading look and nodded to the spot beside her, I stood against the cabinet, my shoulder next to her arm, and waited. Daddy's eyes filled with rage, a tired rage I recognized. I stared at my hands and noticed that the shapes of my fingernails were identical to his, more square than round. "All of you better start understanding, if this rain doesn't stop, none of us will ever eat again. No money, no food, no damn toys all over this messy house." He kicked Barbie's boat, which we'd been playing with earlier,

54

and it sailed underneath the kitchen table. Momma had told us to put it away, but we had forgotten.

"I know, Lee," Momma said. "We all know."

Abby and I kept quiet, but I wanted to ask him why, if he was so worried about not having money for food, he threw our cake away and refused to eat supper. My chest squeezed like something inside might shatter. Lucky sat at the kitchen door, staring and not moving.

"Grace, since you and Jesus are best friends now, maybe you should start praying for more sunshine and a few dry days, so we don't go broke." He stared at me stony-faced.

"Yes, sir," I whispered. Daddy didn't realize I already prayed for sunshine, or rain, or whatever it was he griped about from one night to the next. For the most part, my prayers were never answered.

As we stood in a line, he continued ranting about the energy crisis and price controls on food and other things I didn't understand nor care about. Eventually, I tuned him out to think about the man in the gray house. I imagined him lying on stark hospital sheets, connected to tubes and equipment that kept his heart pumping, his head wrapped like a mummy. Then I saw him cold and dead and stuffed in a black bag. I wasn't sure which scenario was worse.

Daddy and his whiskey disappeared into his office. Momma covered his food with foil and left it on the stove in case he wanted it later. He wouldn't want it later. I had the urge to sling the plate at the icebox door and make a big scene, but I didn't. Instead, I took three pieces of chocolate candy from Daddy's secret stash and hid it in my Barbie satchel underneath my bed, in case we never ate again.

Chapter Eight

Momma tricked me into getting my hair cut off. I thought I was going to Lucille's to get a stylish new hairdo, and I was excited about the possibility. Instead, in the matter of a few minutes, my life was ruined.

Everything started out well enough. "Just relax, Grace," Lucille had said as she reclined my chair and laid my head back in the sink. I stared at a stain on the ceiling, a rectangular splotch in the shape of Tennessee. As Lucille massaged my scalp, the suds grew thick and tingly on my head. The shampoo smelled like the honeysuckle growing near our playhouse. It was no wonder Momma loved to go to the beauty shop.

After she rinsed my hair and set me back up in my chair, I barely felt her comb the tangles from my hair. Lucille was a professional, all right. She squirted a special spray that made the snarls disappear. But after that, things turned bad. Lucille began to snip, snip, snip with her scissors, and with my back to the mirror, I couldn't see what she was doing. Since hair was flying around the room, I closed my eyes so I wouldn't go blind. It would be fun to be surprised, anyway.

"Okay, sweetie. All done," she said.

I opened my eyes and stared at the dark-blonde waves piled in my lap, hair that swirled and curled and twisted, a mass of still damp hair that was glued to the arms of the chair, mounded on the floor, and stuck on the toes of my white tennis shoes. Abby sat across from me with eyes the size of powdered doughnuts. She didn't say a word but shook her head slowly.

Lucille quickly brushed the hair from my lap and shoulders and spun my chair to face the mirror.

"Voila!" she beamed.

A complete stranger stared back at me, a drab, dull-haired, unremarkable urchin child. My sun-streaked locks were gone, and my neck itched.

"Momma, I look like Bubba!" I felt the tears build and hang in my eyelashes. Exposed with no hair to hide behind, I covered my eyes with my palms. All the old ladies sitting under hair dryers stared at me.

"Don't be silly. You look cute. It's the latest style." Momma ran her hand through the back of my hair. She said it was called a Buster Brown haircut, which in my opinion sounded too much like our preacher's name to be even a tiny bit stylish. Lucille rushed around with her hand mirror, showing me how it looked from different angles and saying it enhanced my eyes.

"I hate it! *Je déteste! Je ressemble un stinky garçon.*" The more upset I became, the better my French flowed.

Lucille apologized over and over, saying annoying things like, "Give it a week, and it'll look better." That just made me madder, because even she didn't think it looked good. I couldn't imagine one week would make any difference.

There was nothing to be done.

I plopped in a vacant chair, crossed my hands over my flat chest, and waited to go home and die. After my disastrous results, I couldn't believe Abby agreed to take her turn in the chair and get the exact haircut. She copied every single thing I did, even when it was the worst sort of idea.

"Would you girls like to stop at Sterling's on the way home?" Momma asked as we climbed into the back seat of the car.

"Yes!" Abby cheered. I glared at her and for a nickel would have punched her in the arm.

"No way!" I said. Tears waited behind my eyelids, stinging and smarting, until they freely flowed down my cheeks. Sterling's was my favorite store, but there was no way I would parade around town with a scalped head. "I'll sit in the car. Maybe for the rest of my no-good days."

Momma said I had a bad attitude and took us straight home. Abby pouted about missing a trip to Sterling's, but I didn't care. I slunk low in the seat so no one would see me as we drove around the square and past the hardware store. Once safely in the house, I ran to my room, dug through my bottom drawer reserved for winter clothes, pulled out my black knit cap and wore it low over my eyebrows like a cat burglar. Hiding, I played in the bedroom with Lucky until he had to go outside to pee, and even then we stayed in the backyard.

Later, when it was time to eat lunch, Momma forced me to remove my hat at the table. "Bad manners," she said. I yanked it off and felt what was left of my hair stick straight up.

"That hairstyle looks adorable. I don't know why you're so upset, Gracie. Wait till Daddy sees," Momma said as she tamed it with her fingers. I studied my reflection in the mirror over the buffet. It was the first time I realized how crazy Momma was for mirrors. A mirror hung in almost every room of our house.

***

Watching Momma dress for a date with Daddy was one of my favorite things to do—helping her select an outfit, standing on the bed to zip up the back of her dress, and giving input on which necklace to wear. Even though I would be staying home with Abby, having a say made me feel part of the night. Momma had decided to wear white sandals that showed her toes and a bright green dress that was short. Too short. If she bent over, everyone in town would see her panties. I told her so, but she was wearing it anyway.

Momma had a certain calm way of smoothing lipstick onto her lips, starting in the center of her top lip, moving across one side then the other and covering the bottom in one motion. Smacking both lips together over a tissue, she left a trail of frosted pink kisses in all our wastebaskets. When she began teasing and ratting her hair on top, I picked up the Eudora Welty book from Daddy's nightstand. My namesake's book. The cover was mostly yellow and in the center, a sketch drawn in heavy-black ink showed a house with white columns and steps leading up to it. It looked like the gray house. I thumbed through the pages and read a few lines from the story. Right off, it was uninteresting. I read the entire first page and part of the second, but it didn't get any better. As far as I could tell, it was about a man driving around, lost in the country and sick with a fever.

I returned the book to the bedside table and stared at myself in the mirror above Momma's dresser. I still didn't recognize the plain face looking back. I tried to push my hair behind my ears, but it stuck up, all weird-like. When Daddy walked in to get a clean shirt from his closet, he didn't say anything about my new look. At the very least, I expected him to think I was a guest visiting from out of town.

Finally, just when it seemed Mae would never arrive, I heard her car turn onto the driveway. Abby and I nearly collided in the hallway as we ran to greet her at the back door. Lucky chased after us.

"Oooohhhhh, look at my babies! Y'all got all your hair cut off!"

Abby and I stood statue still while Mae circled us, looking at our new hairdos. I held my breath and waited for her assessment. She was the first real person to see my new look. "It's so sophisticated! You girls is gonna be movie stars for sure now," she said.

"You really like it, Mae? Cause I don't know if I do. I look like Bubba Barns," I said, falling to my knees and hugging Lucky, who didn't care how bad my hair looked.

"Honey child, you don't look nothing like Bubba. You look like a little angel with that new 'do. Miss Lucille should style hair for the stars. You think she'd fix 'ole Mae's hair?" She made a big to-do over our hair, making it seem less of a catastrophe.

Daddy walked into the kitchen, wearing the blue plaid shirt Momma bought him last week in town. It was a nice switch from his regular khaki work shirt, but he still looked like an Arkansas farmer. When Mae asked what he thought of our new hairstyles, he said, "A huge improvement." Then he pulled a bottle of whiskey from beneath the counter and mixed a drink at the kitchen table. He looked at me and almost smiled, more of a smirk than a smile, a don't-mess-with-me-smile, then stirred his drink with a little stick that looked like a black straw. Daddy had always compared my long hair to a dirty mop. He was to blame for my haircut. I knew it.

Momma and Daddy left instructions about where they were going and when they would return, but I didn't care. I just wanted them to hurry up and leave so I could breathe for a while and maybe even forget about my hair for ten minutes. When Momma walked out the back door, she looked thin and cool, like Twiggy. I couldn't see her panties either, so that was good. Lately, Momma had started doing jumping jacks in front of the television with *Jack LaLanne* while Abby and I ate cereal. All her exercising was paying off, and I hoped I could remember to tell her later.

"Guess what? Marvin Gaye is on *Soul Train* tonight. I read all about it in the *TV Guide*," I said, knowing Mae loved both Marvin Gaye and Soul Train.

"Oh, Lordy. That man is sexy with a capital S!" Mae did a little jig in the kitchen and fanned herself with a potholder."

Abby looked at me, and we both snickered.

"Mae, I need to ask you something serious before we start having too much fun," I said. "I wanted to ask you for two weeks now, but last Saturday you didn't come over, and now it's almost too late."

"Child, you know you can always call me on the telephone. Anytime, day or night. My number is in the book." Mae pointed to the telephone book on the counter beside the notepad Momma used to make out her grocery list.

I had never considered calling Mae on the telephone. Besides, what I needed to discuss seemed like an in-person conversation anyway.

"Gracie's getting baptized tomorrow night!" Abby blurted out my news then sunk into her chair when I glared at her.

"Jesus, Abby can't you let me tell anything?"

Abby stuck her tongue out at me. I tried to kick her underneath the table but smacked my bare foot on a chair instead, which hurt like the devil.

"Praise be! Child, I've been praying for this." Mae exclaimed. She did another little jig, just like the Marvin Gaye dance, and then gave me one of her bear hugs, smothering my nose in her huge bosom, where there was never any oxygen.

"You have?" I asked.

"My Lord, yes! All my babies needs to be baptized, black and white."

While eating supper, we discussed my fear of baptism, mainly getting in that water with Brother Brown dunking my head.

60

"Gracie, you is practically a fish. Why you so worried 'bout a little water?"

"I'm not afraid of water, Mae, I'm afraid Brother Brown might hold me down and not let me up in time, and I'll drown right there at Boon Chapel in front of Nana and Mamaw Pearl and Candi and everyone." Just thinking about it made my heart pound faster.

"Honey, you is the most dramatic child I ever heard talk. Don't you think if you was to get in trouble, Brother Brown would pull you out of the water? He's in the business of saving people, not killing folks."

"I guess so. But I don't think I want to be saved. Not yet anyway."

Mae gave me a look and shook her head.

"What, you done changed your mind and decided to spend eternity in Hell with all the murderers?"

Abby's eyes grew huge, and she looked back to me for my answer.

"It's just that this has all happened because of a lie. I went up to the front to pray for Daddy, and now my hair is ruined, and tomorrow I'm getting baptized without really thinking it through. I don't think it'll do any good. I'll still be just as bad. I'll be the same."

"Child, you do beat all. The whole point is you won't be the same. You'll be forgiven."

Later that night, I fell asleep on the den floor, waiting to hear Marvin Gaye sing. Mae woke me just in time to save me from drowning in the Mississippi River. I was spinning in a fast-moving current filled with logs and litter and swollen bodies that trapped and tugged me under. I tried to scream and call for help, but water filled my mouth and lungs, and I sank down, down, down into the dark churning water.

"Gracie, you must have been having a bad dream." She rubbed my back and then helped me to my feet. I nodded yes and was thankful to be home instead of floating in the Mississippi. After brushing my teeth, I lay in bed, wide-eyed and worried. I almost called Janice to ask if she'd ever been baptized, but I knew it was too late to talk on the phone. I wondered about the man in the gray house, and whether or not he was alive or dead or awake or asleep. When Lucky jumped up to my bed and curled at my feet, I finally fell asleep.

Chapter Nine

I stared at my shoes. Between my feet, a perfect circle was imprinted on the wooden floor. It was a faint outline, but definitely a circle. A knothole. Although I'd noticed it before, today it seemed more obvious. When I pressed my foot against it, the knothole jiggled a little. I began grinding my heel into it, hoping to pop it out or push it down underneath the church. It would be neat to see the dirt beneath the building from my third-row pew. Although it never popped out, I may have loosened it a bit. It gave me something to do, anyway.

The baptismal booth looked just like it did every other Sunday—an empty, concrete box painted a sickly green color like the girls' bathroom at school. I tried to picture myself on the other side of that glass partition, standing in water with Brother Brown, but I couldn't. I wondered how the water got inside.

Earlier, when we had arrived at church, Nana and Aunt Clara had made a big fuss over our new short hairstyles, which I had expected. My cousin Dian still had long, dark hair, a mane so thick that Aunt Fannie always used extra-large plastic bands to hold it in a high ponytail. She wore a lavender ribbon in her hair too. Her ribbon caught the light spilling in from the side window, and I wanted to yank it from her hair and strangle her with it. Not really, but kind of, I did. I stared at that ribbon all during Sunday school class and paid no attention to the lesson Momma shared with us.

Brother Brown's sermon was as stale and dry as a turkey sandwich without a drop of mayonnaise or a slice of tomato or anything. Dull. Dull. Dull. I stared at the scripture engraved across the wooden communion table and read it over and over again. "This Do in Remembrance of Me." Something about that sentence bothered me.

This time tomorrow, I wondered if I would really be different.

I went back to working on the knothole, but grinding my foot into the floor without squirming was tricky. Nana patted me on the shoulder, like I was bugging her, so I stopped messing with it.

I'd only witnessed one baptism at Boon Chapel, Mrs. Sweet's nephew who'd come to stay the summer. He was a high-school boy who liked to play the guitar and had a huge, brown mole on his neck that stuck out like a pencil eraser. During his last week in Arkansas, Brother Brown baptized him in the baptismal font where I would be later tonight. Even though the whole thing went off without any problem, I had felt nervous for him, like I had been watching something personal and private and not for my eyes.

Brother Brown read from Proverbs. By the time I found Proverbs, he had moved on to Acts, so I closed my Bible and tried to listen. He talked about marriage and how it was like a vine that had to be nurtured and watered and provided plenty of sunshine to grow thick and dense along a garden trellis. Too bad Daddy wasn't here to listen to this sermon.

Abby drew a bunch of dots evenly on a piece of paper, poked me, and raised her eyebrows, which meant do you want to play connect-the-dots? So we did.

At last, Brother Brown ended his sermon by saying, "The last point I'd like to make..." Right on cue, he nodded at Momma, and she played a few introductory chords to the invitational hymn. I noticed an added flourish in her fingers and a slight lilt in her wrists. Abby and I shared a hymnal, but I sang the first verse by heart.

When the second stanza began, I walked right up to the front to talk to Brother Brown. I didn't stare at my feet or feel my heart banging inside my chest. I wasn't nervous at all, since I'd already done it once before.

"I'm surprised to see you back up here, Grace," he said. This time his breath didn't smell like coffee or peppermint, but more like strong mouthwash, so I scooted back a bit, to where the air was plain.

"I need to tell you something, Brother Brown." I spoke in my library voice. Just like before, he motioned toward the first empty pew, we knelt together, and he draped his arm around my shoulder.

"What's on your mind?"

"Remember how last time we talked, I was worried about Daddy? I'm still worried about him, and I think you should keep praying because so far it's not working too good. Plus, I don't think Momma and Daddy have a very strong marriage vine." He smiled and seemed impressed that I had listened to his sermon. "But also, if you have time, I hope you could pray for my neighbor who lives in the gray house not too far from us. He shot himself the other day. Momma called an ambulance, and they hauled him off to the hospital. Probably in Memphis. For all I know he may be dead, but if he isn't, I figure he could use some prayers."

Brother Brown's eyes got huge when I said the words "shot himself" and he said "oh my" sort of in a whisper to himself. "I'll sure pray for him too."

"I don't know his name, but I figure if you just say 'the man in the gray house,' God will know who you're talking about, right?"

"I feel certain he will. Thanks for letting me know. And Grace, are you looking forward to tonight?"

"Not really. I'm a little nervous about the whole thing, and I may be getting a headache above my eyebrows." He smiled, gave me a pat on the arm, and said I'd be fine.

***

I rested my head on the back seat and stared out the window. Telephone poles passed by, one after another, leaning slightly toward the ditch. They looked like a line of old wooden crosses, and for a while, I counted them.

Once home, I put on my play clothes and crawled back into bed. Lucky joined me, burrowing under the covers to my feet. The things on my mind made me feel a little sick, and I told Momma I would eat lunch later. Sunlight streamed through the curtains above the bed. The birds chirping outside in the willow tree reminded me of the whole perfect play day I was missing, but I couldn't bring myself to move.

I must have fallen asleep, because when I woke up Abby was hovering over me like a weirdo, with her nose only an inch from my face. "What are you doing, trying to scare me to death?" I bolted upright, and we banged heads.

"Just making sure you were breathing. I don't think you were breathing," she said. "And I can't find Lucky." Lucky leaped from underneath the covers.

"Of course I was breathing." Sometimes Abby was so ridiculous that I wished I were an only child, like Dian.

Since I was awake, and my head didn't hurt anymore except for where my forehead had smacked into Abby's cheek, we went outside to play with Lucky. If he didn't exercise in the backyard, he got into mischief, chewing Momma's shoes. While I tossed his ball toward the row of cherry trees, Lucky fetched, sometimes even catching the ball in the air. Abby played in the sandbox with her Matchbox cars. Momma had built the sandbox right beside our playhouse, using lumber she bought at the hardware store in town. She had nailed the boards together herself and painted it red because she got tired of begging Daddy to do it. Now that he knew Momma could build those sorts of things, he probably would never do anything for her again. Sometimes things like that backfired.

Lucky became bored with the ball and began digging a deep hole beside Abby, slinging sand and dirt and messing up the roadway she was building. "Fetch, Lucky!" I threw his ball again, accidentally hitting the back of the house, leaving a brown smudge on the white siding. Lucky abandoned his hole and chased after it.

"What was that noise?" Daddy staggered around the corner, dragging his boots and slurring his words, a sure sign he had already been drinking.

"I accidentally threw Lucky's ball against the house," I said. I waited for his reaction, feeling dread creep through my body.

Instead of yelling or cussing he laughed and laughed. "Fetch, boy," Daddy said, throwing the ball against the house over and over again. Lucky jumped for it—he was a fantastic jumper—but he couldn't catch the wild bounces Daddy threw.

"Look at this mess!" Momma said. Hearing the ball bounce off the house, she had come outside to see about the racket. Dirty brown spots dotted the back of our white house.

"We're just having fun, right girls?" Daddy said. His words were slow and thick, and when he took a step, he stumbled over his feet and fell onto the lounge chair. Lucky bounded over to him and stood with his front paws on Daddy's legs. "You love me, don't you, boy?" Daddy grabbed Lucky by the collar and held him in his lap. He rubbed his head and face and squeezed him tight.

"Lee, you better stop," Momma warned.

"Oh no, Lucky and I are like this." Daddy crossed his fingers as though they were best friends. "We're buddies, aren't we?" He squeezed Lucky around the neck and pulled him closer and closer with his face right in his, nose to nose. I had a bad feeling and thought if we were watching a movie, this is where the gloomy music would start.

"He doesn't like that," Momma warned again. A low growl came from deep inside Lucky's belly, and he flared large fang-like teeth we had never seen before.

"Don't you growl at me." Daddy pressed Lucky in a headlock like I'd seen the Saturday morning wrestlers do. "I'll take you right back to the mud hole where I found you," he threatened.

When Lucky snapped at Daddy's nose, Daddy slung him to the concrete and Lucky made a horrible yelping noise. "I'm gonna kill that son-of-a-bitch dog." Daddy knocked the chair over and stomped around the house.

"Momma, stop him!" Abby screamed.

I screamed too. "Run, Lucky!" And he did. He darted across the patio and disappeared behind the playhouse.

"Girls, go to your bedroom," Momma said as she picked up the chair Daddy had knocked over. But we didn't. We ran inside the playhouse, slammed the door, hunkered down and watched everything unfold through the window draped in white eyelet.

"Lee, don't do anything stupid," Momma pleaded when Daddy came back around the house, swinging the shovel. But she kept her distance. I wanted to run outside and jump on Daddy's back and snatch the shovel from him, but I knew there was no use. His eyes flashed a crazed look. Lucky had been too good to be true.

Abby sat in the corner of the playhouse, rolled into a tight ball. She hugged her knees and held her face in her hands. I heard a banging. Once. Twice. I held my hands over my eyes and ears. A great pain, the worst of pains, blasted inside my chest and heart, and I never wanted another dog for as long as I lived. My stomach seized into my throat and unraveled into a sob.

"Lucky, dammit, where are you?" Daddy yelled, his words thick and sluggish.

Lucky was still alive?

I peeped out the window and saw Daddy walking around the pump house, beside the cherry trees and around to the other side of the yard. "You better come when I call!" he yelled.

That's when I saw Lucky.

"Abby, look," I whispered. "It's okay. Come look." Abby crawled over and peeked out the playhouse window, her cheeks mottled and wet from crying. While Daddy had been getting the shovel, Lucky climbed the weeping willow tree and sat perched four feet off the ground inside a cradle-like spot next to the trunk.

Daddy continued walking around the house—he must have walked around four or five times. Please, God, if I could only have one answered prayer my whole life, let this be it—that Lucky would stay in the tree and not be discovered. Daddy yelled for Lucky and swung the shovel through the air like a sickle, occasionally banging it against the house. Momma told him to go inside and calm down. He called her a bad name but eventually staggered through the door and into the house. Daddy never noticed Lucky hiding in the bend of the tree.

***

Being in the back room of the church while everyone else sat in the sanctuary felt strange. Since Momma had to play the piano, Aunt Fannie helped me get ready, a good thing because Momma made me nervous during the drive to church. She had lots of last-minute baptism tips, advice about paying attention while Brother Brown spoke, how to properly hold my hand over my nose, and a reminder to not holler if the water was freezing cold. Mostly, I worried about Lucky and wanted to hurry up and get saved so we could rush home. Momma said Lucky was a survivor and that he'd be fine while we were at church, but I wasn't so sure. Just before we left, I gave him a big hug, told him to hide under the bed if Daddy woke up, and promised I'd be home soon. He looked at me hard like he understood what I was saying. Daddy lay passed out on the couch, flat on his back with his shirt unbuttoned to the waist. Compared to his suntanned arms and face, his flat stomach shined albino white. The weird snores and mumbling noises coming from his mouth would have been funny had I not hated him so much.

I wore a regular play dress for my baptism. Momma said since I would be wearing a white robe no one would notice what clothes hid underneath. "Then why can't I wear my new bathing suit?" I asked.

"Don't be a smart aleck," Momma said. But I wasn't trying to be.

Turned out my white robe wasn't a white robe at all. It was a long white T-shirt with a tag on the back that said Hanes. Aunt Fannie pulled it over my head like I was helpless, and since the whole thing felt so odd, I stood there and let her. "Aunt Fannie, I thought I was supposed to wear a robe. Like a choir robe. Something nicer than this man's undershirt."

She patted me on the shoulder. "Oh, we just always use these old T-shirts. Plain and simple like Jesus. We don't want to wear anything flashy to take away from the true meaning of baptism." Aunt Fannie knew a lot about the Bible, so I didn't say anything more about my missing robe, but I felt somewhat disappointed.

When Momma began playing the piano, Aunt Fannie took my elbow and nudged me toward the opening of the dunking booth. Then she held my arm to keep me from walking in too soon, and we stood there listening to the congregation sing. "Shall we gather at the river, where bright angel feet have trod..." After only one verse, Momma paused so Brother Brown could talk. His voice echoed and bounced off the water as though he stood in a cave.

I thought I might throw up.

The baptismal font was basically a big bathtub with concrete steps leading down into the water. Aunt Fannie nodded. I put one bare foot in the water. It felt cold, but not ice cold like Momma had warned. I took another step. Brother Brown reached both hands out to me, and right away, I noticed he was wearing a fancy white robe with gold and purple rickrack around the collar. That made me suspicious, but when I looked back to see if Aunt Fannie noticed, she had already disappeared from the top of the steps. I kept walking.

The floor of the baptismal font felt rough against my toes, like maybe the paint was peeling. Brother Brown spewed out a few Bible verses and spoke about being born of water and entering the Kingdom of Heaven. For the first time, I noticed a microphone suspended by a wire over the baptismal font. Everyone knew water and electricity didn't mix.

I stared at it then tried to signal to Mr. Donaldson with my eyes, but he didn't notice.

When Brother Brown formally introduced me, he spoke my name into the microphone, enunciating every syllable. "Grace-Lee-Eu-dor-a-Ab-BOTT." That last "Bott" made the microphone sway. Yes, it definitely swayed, and next it would fall straight into the baptismal water, electrocute both of us, and that would be it. I tried to put this from my mind, because I felt close to calling the whole thing off. I remembered how Momma had spent all afternoon making raisin cookies and cutting the crust off homemade pimento cheese sandwiches for my baptism reception. Daddy hated pimento cheese. If she had to drag all that food home, I'd be in big trouble.

During the last two weeks, I'd thought a lot about the course my life had taken. Mae always said a good way to decide something important is to make a list of pros and cons. I tried that but didn't come up with much on either side of the baptism issue. Even without having a clear answer, I decided not getting baptized was the biggest negative of all because of the whole Hell thing. That was before electrocution entered into the equation.

Like a magician, Brother Brown pulled a white handkerchief from thin air, positioned it over my nose, and held it tightly in place. It was too late for me to back out. My heart raced. I felt terror grow in my stomach until I remembered I could still breathe out of my mouth, like when my nose was stopped up with allergies. He mentioned something about Peter and the Holy Ghost and how the Word was God. Then he nodded at me. I clamped my lips together and held my breath as he pushed me back into the coolness. My gigantic T-shirt billowed out around me. My left foot involuntarily jerked above the water and splashed back down. *One Mississippi..., Two Mississippi...*

It all happened real fast, but while he held me beneath the water, my eyes shot open, and I saw my sin evaporate in a kaleidoscope of color. Or maybe the color explosion simply came from the reflection of light against the water. I wasn't sure. I spluttered, gasped, smeared the water from my eyes, and looked at the microphone still hanging above our heads. If it fell now, I would go to Heaven.

Brother Brown's fancy white robe was now wet to his neck. His thin strands of hair, normally glued in place, looked damp and lopsided. In that split second, he seemed a bit more human, but then he said something that sounded like, "Go ye into the world and preach the gospel to every creature." I hoped he wasn't expecting me to become a preacher, because I was still planning to work for the Easy Bake Oven Company.

The lights were woozy bright, the congregation a blur of people. I heard a few "Amens" from the back of the sanctuary, and someone near the front clapped. I smiled and waved, more from relief than being freed from sin, and searched beyond the water spots on the glass partition, trying to find Abby or Nana or Mamaw Pearl. I knew they were there somewhere. The congregation sang the last verse of the baptism hymn with more enthusiasm than I'd ever heard. And there in the very front pew, clapping and cheering and wearing the swankiest hat ever to grace Boon Chapel, sat Mae.

Some things fit right together, like pieces of a jigsaw puzzle. Although Mae had never been inside Boon Chapel, because black folks had their own church over by the river, she was completely at ease and seemed to be my biggest fan. Daddy, on the other hand, would never have been comfortable, even on the back farmer row. Momma begged Daddy to do many things, but coming to my baptism wasn't one of them. I didn't bother looking for him, and not having him there wasn't odd at all. What did turn out to be odd was, once we finished stuffing ourselves with cookies and pimento cheese sandwiches and went home, Daddy's truck wasn't in the driveway.

Lucky greeted us at the door, barking, jumping, and turning circles around the kitchen floor. I was relieved to see him, and based on the speed of his tail wagging, he was happy to see us too. With Lucky underfoot, we made several trips to the car, carrying in dirty platters and the glass punch bowl with ice cream scum around the rim. I put my wet clothes on top of the washing machine, like Momma said, and pretended not to notice Daddy's empty bottle of whiskey beside the coffeepot.

Momma picked up the notepad beside the phone and dropped it when she saw there was nothing written. "Girls, get back in the car. We're going to find your daddy." When Momma got mad, she referred to him as "Your daddy," as though we had had some choice in the matter or had hand selected him from all the farmers at Savage Supply and Hardware.

"Where are we going?" I asked. Momma didn't say, but she let Lucky ride along. As we drove back down the highway, Boon Chapel stood dark and abandoned after being filled with church people only minutes ago. We passed a solitary cottonwood tree growing in the middle of a soybean field. Struck by lightning during the last storm, it looked scary now, like something from an evil forest that might walk across the street, waving its charred limbs and branches through the sky. Momma drove a few minutes longer, to Sugar Ditch, a rumor of a place, with abandoned farmhouses and a barn leaning close to the earth, pulled by a snarl of vines. The only attraction was the bar. Vera's Bar. A windowless place where nameless, faceless people did God only knew what. Even on Sunday.

"There's Daddy's truck!" I said. "He parked crooked." Daddy's brown Chevy was parked sideways, opposite the other trucks lining the gravel parking lot, as though he'd spun into the driveway and ducked out in a hurry.

"Where?" Abby asked. She crawled over my lap to see from my side of the backseat window. "I bet someone was chasing him," she added. Lucky raced back and forth from one side of the back seat to the other. He didn't have much experience riding in a car.

Momma apparently wasn't too worried about someone chasing Daddy. She slowed down, turned around in the old cotton gin lot, and headed back home. She didn't say anything while driving down the dark highway. When a certain song came on the radio, she flipped it off like it hurt her heart to hear it. I tried to think of something other than Daddy to talk about. "Momma, I was thinking today about the man in the gray house. Have you heard anything about him? Is he ever coming home?" I asked.

"He doesn't concern you." She sounded mad, so I hushed about him.

As soon as we got home, I brushed my teeth and got into bed, tired from the events of the day. Still, I couldn't sleep. While I had stood dripping wet in the baptismal booth, Brother Brown reintroduced me to the Boon Chapel congregation like I was a brand new person. "Washed in the blood of the Lamb," he called it. But as I lay quiet and still, staring at the bedroom ceiling, I felt no different. No calmer. No closer to understanding anything. Every time I almost dozed off, my body startled with a violent, intense spasm that rocked and nearly threw me from the edge of my bed. I decided it was God's way of telling me to stay awake and listen for Daddy to come home. I listened until I heard the dining room clock strike eleven o'clock. Then I could listen no longer.

Chapter Ten

Momma yanked open drawers, pulled out Daddy's white underwear and the jeans she had starched and pressed just last week, and stuffed everything into a black garbage bag. I watched as she lugged the bag across the carport and heaved it over the bed of irises. When she dragged it along the side yard, dandelion seed heads scattered and floated, then disappeared, a thousand wishes wasted. I expected Momma to haul the bag to the trash barrels behind the pump house where she burned broken tree limbs and garbage. Instead, she walked to Daddy's parking spot near the plum tree, dumped the clothes into a twisted heap on the gravel, dusted her hands together as though she had rid herself of a messy chore, and then calmly walked back to the porch, stopping first to knock down a spider web from the corner of the carport.

Daddy had been missing for three days. Last night, when I suggested maybe something bad happened to him and she should file a missing person report like they did on television, Momma shook her head.

"If something happened to your Daddy, everyone in this gossipy county would be talking about it." She did have a point.

I ran to the back porch and gaped at Daddy's clothes piled in the bright sunshine. Momma said nothing as she brushed past me. Even her sandals on the linoleum made no sound. I stared as she calmly opened her address book to a page marked with a paper clip. Using the eraser end of a No. 2 pencil, she phoned someone, the whirling sound of the dial the only noise in the room.

"Yes, I'm calling to cancel Lee Abbott's appointment. He won't be able to make it today." She paused and then added, "I have no idea. He'll need to call back later to reschedule." She placed the receiver back on the base of the phone and turned to me. "Gracie, have you practiced piano lately?"

"Momma, are you feeling okay? Are you sure you want to leave Daddy's underwear in the driveway for everyone in the world to see?"

Momma stuck a cigarette between her lips, leaned over the stove, and turned the knob until the gas made a whooshing sound. The tip of her cigarette glowed orange. "This doesn't concern you, Gracie." While she smoked, she made out a grocery list. I watched her hand as she lightly gripped the same pencil she had used to dial the phone. Tuna. Eggs. Aspirin.

"It'll be my business all right when Daddy murders us in our sleep."

Momma pursed her lips and blew a smoke ring toward the ceiling, a perfect circle that hovered above her head before widening and vanishing.

Nothing concerned me.

I went to my bedroom.

I sat on the bed and looked around for something to do. After stewing for a few minutes about how the whole world had gone mad, I decided to take action about the one thing I was most curious about. I yanked open my notebook with a pop of the tight binder rings and removed a clean sheet of paper. In my best cursive handwriting, I began to write.

Gracie Abbott
Rt. 1, Box 468A
Savage Crossing, Arkansas 72351
May 30, 1972

Dear Man Who Lives in the Pretty Gray House,

My name is Gracie Abbott. Even though we are practically neighbors, you don't know me. I am almost ten years old. My birthday is August 21. In September, I will be in the fourth grade at Savage Crossing

Elementary School. My daddy—who seems to have run away from home—is a farmer. We live in the plain, one-story, white house just down the road from you. I'm sure you've seen it on your way to town. There's a big mimosa tree in the front yard that's blooming right now. The bees love it.

I heard you talking on the party line the day you shot yourself. My momma is the person who called the ambulance. Ever since that day, I've watched your house—not all the time, but sometimes—to see if you are back home yet. Your house looks lonely. No one will tell me exactly what happened or if you are okay, but I hope you are visiting relatives and not dead.

I would like to invite you to my church. I am the newest member of Boon Chapel Baptist. Boon Chapel isn't too far down the highway past Savage Crossing, before you get to Sugar Ditch. Do you know it? (Someone messed up the sign, so you might think it's Boo Chapel, but it's really Boon Chapel.) Sunday school starts at 9:30—I wouldn't bother with that unless you are really looking for something to do—but preaching is at 11:00. You are welcome to sit on the third pew with my Nana and me. Even though the sermons are usually boring, you might want to think about attending. If you went to church, you probably wouldn't have tried to kill yourself—if that's what happened. The Bible believes that's a one-way ticket to you-know-where.

Anyway, I hope you are feeling better. I don't know for sure why you shot yourself, but I understand how hopeless life can be around here. Write back soon.

Your neighbor,
Gracie Lee Abbott

P.S. If you want to save yourself a stamp, you can leave a letter in the mailbox in front of our house. That would be fine by me. Momma checks the mail every day.

P.P.S. I have one sister, Abby, who is seven years old and a dog named Lucky. Maybe you should get a dog.

I re-read my letter to make sure everything was spelled correctly. Then I folded it into a tight little square, stuck it in my pocket, and ran out the back door without Abby noticing. That was a miracle, for sure. "Momma, I'm going to ride my bicycle," I yelled as the screen door smacked shut. She didn't say anything, or if she did, I didn't hear her.

I looked both ways, quickly crossed the road, and peddled toward the gray house. Lucky followed me, but stayed mostly in the field, barking and running after birds. The asphalt was smooth for bicycle riding, much better than our chunky gravel driveway. I stretched my arms to both sides for balance and rode with no hands for a few yards. Fast. Free. In the distance, an eighteen-wheeler barreled in my direction, so I pulled to the side of the road and waited. When I saw the driver's face in the bug-splattered window, I motioned my arm up and down, the signal for horn blowing. As he blasted by in a wave of hot air, he honked and waved. There was something exciting about hearing a huge truck honk and knowing, that in a way, I caused it to happen.

I parked my bike on the side of the road and pulled open the mailbox door to peep inside. The box overflowed with letters and magazines and some of the identical junk mail we received. I slammed it shut and began walking along the circle driveway leading to the house. An old tree shaded much of the front yard with sweeping branches and rugged, braided bark. The grass, filled with shaggy dandelions and bell-shaped flowers, looked more like a meadow than a yard. I stopped to pick a handful.

The house was even bigger up close. Gray paint peeled around the porch railing, but otherwise the home looked well cared for and clean. I knocked on the door and waited ten Mississippis, but nobody answered. I knocked a second time in case he was upstairs or using the bathroom or maybe napping on the couch. Still no answer.

I poked my fat letter into the brass mail slot and heard it fall to the floor on the other side. When I peeked back through the opening, it lay there on the hardwood. I wondered if the mailman knew about the cool mail slot.

On both sides of the door, big windows allowed for easing spying. A humongous dining-room table sat beneath a sparkly chandelier that filled the ceiling. There must have been twelve chairs circling the table, with room for more. Books laying in all different directions crammed shelves on both sides of the fireplace, serious looking books with thick spines. On top of the mantle, an ivory sculpture of a man's head seemed to watch over the room with scooped out eyes. It was a creepy thing, especially since he looked a little like Mr. Mooney, the school principal.

Chapter Eleven

We survived sloppy-wet spring, and although planting season was later than usual, Daddy managed to grow a perfect stand of cotton, "His best yet," according to Momma. All my praying had paid off. June and July, the best months for catching lightning bugs and swimming at the pool in town, passed in a dizzy, green blur. Now August was nearly here, a month filled with hot, motionless days. The month of my birthday.

Abby and I lay flat on our backs, staring at the late afternoon sky. The dry grass itched and stuck to our sweaty legs, but we didn't care. We did our best cloud-gazing that way.

"That one looks like Lucky!" I pointed to a fluffy cloud moving overhead. Lucky barked upon hearing his name then ran toward a flock of birds underneath the pecan tree.

"I see a rabbit!" Abby pointed. We continued shouting out shapes of animals and objects, like a game of I Spy.

"There's a doughnut. See?" I cupped my hand above my eyes to block the glare of the sun. It was one of those perfect summer days when white clumps of clouds drifted across a sky of pure blue. Abby was motionless, her eyes shut, but fluttering, as though she was watching a dream. "Are you asleep?" I asked.

"No, just thinking." Freckles splattered her nose and cheeks like chocolate chips. Dark lashes, lusher than my sparse, paler ones, fringed her eyes.

"About what?"

"Nothing." She looked away from me.

On the night of my baptism, when Daddy ran away to Vera's Bar, he stayed gone for five whole days and nights. As abruptly as he had left, he walked back through the door while we were eating leftover spaghetti.

"I have something for you," he had said, as he pulled new coloring books from a bag, like he'd been away on a business trip.

I thanked him for mine but, weeks later, still hadn't used it. Thinking back on it, I'm shocked that he knew where to buy such a thing. Momma had spent the next two days washing and drying the clothes she'd thrown out the back door. After nearly a week, the mound of underwear and khaki shirts had spread and settled into the gravel, beaten down by rain and wind, and coated with pollen that tinted our world pea green. By the time she finished scrubbing and bleaching and ironing, his cotton T-shirts were folded into tight stacks and returned to his drawer, arranged as neat as the ones for sale in town.

After that, Daddy tried to get on our good side by being a bit nicer. For the most part, he did a decent job, even taking us on a weekend trip to Hot Springs with the Barns family. Our families rented tiny cabins side-by-side on the shore of a pretty lake and spent the days swimming and hiking and the nights eating hot dogs and hamburgers beneath the picnic pavilion. But the weekend didn't end so well. Daddy got sick and puked all night. Mrs. Barns, who's not only the school nurse but also one of those always-prepared women, gave Daddy some medicine from her emergency kit. Momma drove us home while Daddy lay in the back seat of the car, moaning. She had to pull over three times for him to throw up on the side of the interstate.

As Abby and I continued watching the sky, Abby turned toward me and asked, "Gracie, where do you think the clouds go after they drift over our house?"

"I'm not sure, maybe Memphis." I pictured a trail of clouds evenly spaced and floating over the country, beginning in California and ending in Florida, where they would evaporate—as though other countries had their own clouds.

"I bet Elvis sees the same clouds we do!" She propped on her elbow and waited for my reaction. Sometimes Abby was clever beyond her seven years.

79

"I bet so too!" The idea of an Elvis connection was interesting, and I wished I'd thought of it. We both lay back down, our feet almost touching, and stared overhead without saying anything for a long time.

"Do you think Daddy's gonna die?" Abby asked.

"Yes. Everyone will die sooner or later," I said, but I knew that wasn't what she meant. After off and on bouts of the flu, Daddy finally went to his appointment in Memphis. Later, there were lots of whispered conversations we weren't meant to hear. Eventually, Momma called a family meeting at the backyard picnic table to officially tell us Daddy was sick. Really sick, not just drunk-sick.

"That's not what I mean, Gracie," Abby said.

"I know." As the sun dropped lower in the sky, the clouds began to spread further and further apart, like cotton being stretched into thin threads.

"So, what's your answer? About Daddy?" she asked.

I didn't have an answer. On the afternoon of our family meeting, Momma had said his condition was serious, but the doctors caught it early. "He'll be good as new after his procedure in a few days," she had said with a slight tremble in her voice. Daddy sat with us at the picnic table but never spoke a word, as though opening his mouth and talking would make the whole thing true. I'd picked at a loose splinter on the edge of the picnic table, thankful for a simple distraction and not knowing what to say to Daddy. He wasn't one of those people to hug or offer comforts. Abby's bottom lip quivered as a single, fat tear rolled down her cheek. Daddy kept chewing on the end of a toothpick and staring off toward the cotton field.

"I think he'll be fine, Abby," I said, to fill the silence. As dusk stretched over our yard, bugs began circling the carport light, drawn there without knowing why.

"Gracie, what do you think happened to the man who lived in the house down the road?"

"I think he went somewhere exciting to get well. Don't you?"

"I don't know," she said.

During the past two months, I had written three more letters to the man in the gray house. I thought he'd want to keep up to date with the non-goings-on around Savage Crossing. Although I had not yet received a response from him, last week someone mowed his grass, which had to be a good sign.

After supper, I decided to write him another letter. I intended to tell him about how I made a red and blue, construction paper chain to count down the days until my birthday, and how it drapes over the headboard of my bed, and how it looks festive, and how each morning when I remove a link, I feel excited to be one day closer to ten years old. But I didn't. As I began to write and words flowed from my brain, none of those thoughts made it to paper. Instead, I told him about Daddy, and how he would soon go to the hospital for a procedure I didn't understand, and how even though he was grumpy and mean and most of the time he hated me, I worried about him anyway. I hoped when Daddy got well, he would be nicer like my friend Janice's dad. When I re-read my letter, my own words surprised me as though they had come from a secret place I didn't know about.

I signed my name Gracie, and dotted my "i" with a heart the way my cousin Candi always did. But that one silly, tiny heart ruined the entire letter. Word for word, I re-wrote the letter on another piece of notebook paper. After signing Gracie the normal way, I ripped the first letter into teeny pieces so a nosy person couldn't tape it together.

Daddy was already asleep. Momma and Abby watched a television show. "I'm taking Lucky out to pee and to play fetch for a while," I yelled.

"Stay in the back yard," Momma said.

"*Oui*," I said, crossing my fingers to cancel out my fib.

The half-moon and a dark sky of dazzling stars provided just enough light. I propped my bike against the wooden railing and stepped onto the porch of the gray house. The floor creaked. My face felt sticky, and the hair along my neck felt damp. I wiped my forehead with the back of my hand. Lucky followed beside me, panting. Nearby, something somewhere bloomed, saturating the heavy air with a too strong scent. In the distance, an owl hooted. Once. Twice.

I pushed my letter into the front-door, brass mail slot, and heard its thud on the hardwood floor. It was too dark to see inside the house, but I knew it lay there, waiting. I poked the opening of the mail slot once more just to hear the clanging noise. When I got back home, no one had moved.

Chapter Twelve

Silly Putty was one of the best things ever invented. As long as I returned the blob to its plastic egg, it stayed soft and stretchy and ready to play with at the breakfast table. And the best way to play with it was to press it against a comic-strip picture, and, like magic, the newspaper print transferred onto the putty. Momma always saved the Sunday newspaper because that was the only day the funnies were in color. Bright pictures worked best.

I pressed the rubbery putty against a picture of Snoopy sitting on his doghouse. While counting to three Mississippi—to let the picture stick really tight—I glanced at the front page of the newspaper so my eyes would have something to do. And there was Elvis looking right at me. He wore a white jumpsuit slit open to a wide, jeweled belt. His black hair was bushy and sweaty, and his thick sideburns swept almost to his chin. He didn't look as handsome as some of the other pictures I'd seen of him. Fat and puffy, that's how he looked. The headline read "ELVIS TREATED FOR HYPERTENSION."

"Momma, what's hy-per-ten-sion?" I slowly sounded out the word.

"High blood pressure," she said. Momma crawled on her hands and knees, wiping the cabinet baseboards. Sometimes she dreamed up extra work for herself.

"Elvis has it."

"I'm not surprised."

I peeled back the putty and showed Abby the colorful image of Snoopy and Woodstock. She smiled because it turned out good. I sensed a calmness never felt when Daddy was home. I didn't admit it to anyone, not even Abby, but while Daddy was in the hospital, it was a relief not to always worry about saying the wrong thing. And I could play with Barbie right out in the open without anyone making fun of me.

"Momma, what hospital is Daddy in?" While reading the first few lines of the newspaper article, I erased the Snoopy picture with a squeeze of my palm and flattened the putty over Elvis's face.

"Baptist."

"Are you kidding me? That's where Elvis is!" I yanked the putty off Elvis's nose and shoved the paper toward Momma. When Elvis was home in Memphis, he was often spotted at the iron gates of Graceland, chatting with crazed fans and handing out diamond rings like sticks of gum. When he was sick, which seemed to happen often, news of his hospital stays always made the headlines. Where we lived, even President Nixon was forced to share news coverage with Elvis.

Momma's blue eyes danced side to side as she read the article. "I guess with all the craziness going on, I missed this. Maybe we'll see Elvis this afternoon when we pick up your Daddy," Momma laughed and handed the paper back to me.

Daddy had been in the hospital the entire first week of August. Momma never said much about his surgery other than, "They think they got it all." I didn't really know what "it" meant, but later I overheard her tell Maggie that Daddy's stomach tumor had been the size of a grapefruit. All week, Momma had been staying up late and calling Daddy after ten o'clock when a long distance phone call didn't cost so much. I lay in bed and listened, while she made each piece of news sound exciting, from the daily mail to the weather report. Momma even talked Daddy into letting Abby and me go to church camp next week. Maybe his sickness was making him more agreeable.

"Do you really think we'll see Elvis today?" I asked as I stretched and stretched the putty into a long thin strand. It broke with a snap.

"Gracie, I'm kidding," she said.

I wasn't. I felt certain I would meet Elvis later that day, so I planned to wear a nice dress to the hospital just in case.

***

The hospital was shaped like a building with wings—two towers connected in the center with a fountain out front. All around it, the grounds looked park-like with benches scattered under tall shade trees. I didn't think those benches were for regular picnicking or having fun, but were for taking a break from the sickness inside the hospital. Momma turned at the corner and drove around to the other side of the building. "They want an arm and a leg for parking," she said. A man walked by, chattering away to himself, wearing only his nightgown and black socks pulled up to his knees. Nana, who had ridden along with us, said the man was crazy. I waited until we were a safe distance away from him then rolled down the window.

"There it is!" I stretched my arm toward the sky and pointed, straining to see Elvis's hospital window. Elvis's top floor window was easy to spot, because it was covered with aluminum foil. According to the newspaper, the foil made his hospital room extra dark. I imagined the whole idea was to keep people from scaling up the building to look at Elvis in his pajamas.

"Where?" Abby yelled and jumped over to my side of the back seat. She leaned out the window.

"Stop hanging out the window like a couple of dogs!" Momma slowed the car to yell at us. A police officer blew his whistle and motioned us on down the highway.

We found a place to park two blocks away underneath a light pole. "Remember our spot beside the streetlight," Momma said, "or we'll never find our car later."

I looked at it hard and snapped a picture with my mind.

Sunshine beat down from every direction, reflecting from glass buildings, bouncing from cars, and glaring off parking meters lining the street. Heat sprung from the sidewalk like a living, breathing thing. I walked lightly, avoiding the cracks. According to the "step on a crack, break your Momma's back" saying, she could end up in the hospital too. I didn't really believe that rhyme to be true but wouldn't risk it. Lots of true things made no sense.

The hospital world with its pristine nurses and medicine smells was different than any place I'd ever seen. A doctor walked by, writing on a clipboard. His shoes made no sound on the smooth, clean floor. I wondered if they let Daddy wear his dirty farm boots into this place.

"Listen to me." Momma stopped us just outside the waiting room, grabbed our chins with her hands, and made us look right into her face. "There are sick people here. You can't be loud. Think of it like the library. Sit with Nana and read the books you brought. Mind what she says." We both promised before Momma disappeared behind the elevator doors.

I flipped a page in my book, but even Nancy Drew couldn't hold my attention. Sitting in an uncomfortable waiting room chair, while Elvis lay somewhere above me, proved to be harder than sitting on the rigid pews at Boon Chapel. I stared at the ceiling. Abby started reading her book aloud to Nana. Since there were no other people in the waiting room, I moved to an empty chair across the room where I couldn't hear Abby right in my ear. My new chair was uncomfortable too.

"Nana, can I get something to drink? I saw a machine by the elevator."

"I want a drink too," Abby chimed in.

Nana unzipped her change purse and handed me a quarter. "I only have twenty-five cents. You'll have to share." I grabbed the coin before Abby could pout or follow me. She continued reading to Nana.

I slipped the quarter into the slot, opened the glass door and yanked a Coca-Cola from the vending machine. I had a nickel left over, which was just enough for one package of peanuts. I floated the peanuts inside the syrupy drink. Then I stepped inside the empty elevator, poked the Close button over and over to make the door shut faster, and set off to find Elvis.

When I pushed the white button for floor eighteen, the highest floor in the hospital, nothing happened. So, I pushed seventeen. Instantly, the light glowed red, and the floor beneath me bumped as I traveled up. My ears popped. I swallowed hard. When the door opened, I stepped into the hallway. The seventeenth floor looked the same as the first floor, with a visitor waiting room to the left and a door with an Exit sign above it. I shoved open the heavy door and stepped into the stairwell.

The air smelled stale, unlike the sterile space of the hospital corridors. I took the stairs two at a time, then, when I reached the next landing, stopped and stared at the door marked floor eighteen. Act casual, I told myself. My heart thumped as I peeped into another identical beige corridor. Only this one lead to Elvis's hospital room.

"Can I help you?" a stern voice boomed off the wall.

"Oh my goodness, you scared me," I said, clutching my chest with the hand not carrying my cola. A bald man with white, bushy eyebrows stood blocking my entrance into the hallway. His hands were clamped behind his back, and his feet were planted wide against the shiny floor. He wore a white hospital outfit, like an orderly, but seemed more like a security guard.

His round face lowered toward me, and he looked like the man on the bottle of Momma's kitchen cleaner. "Are you lost?"

"No, I came to visit Elvis." I tried to sound friendly, like I had received a personal invitation.

He stepped closer to me. "Mr. Presley isn't receiving fans, and no one under twelve is allowed outside waiting rooms. Where are your parents?" He glowered.

"My Daddy's dead, and my Momma used to date Elvis," I stammered and rushed back out the door, letting it slam behind me. Even though I didn't think the man was following me, I ran as fast as I could and didn't stop until I reached the first floor. When I pushed open the door at the bottom of the stairwell, there stood Nana and Abby pacing around the elevators. "Here's your drink," I thrust it at Abby and doubled over, trying to catch my breath.

"Where have you been?" Abby asked.

"Grace, you're going to get both of us in big trouble." Nana pulled me back into the waiting room to give me a proper lecture.

"I thought I might be able to see Elvis, but I didn't. I was only gone a minute." I didn't tell them about the man yelling at me. Nana seemed more worried she would be in trouble for allowing me to escape inside the hospital. Abby pouted, because she had missed out on the excitement of almost seeing Elvis. I felt bad for upsetting Nana but not for leaving Abby behind.

Nana decided, since no harm had been done, the whole thing would be our secret. "Your mother has too much to worry about," she said. I didn't think we could trust Abby to keep quiet, but I had no choice.

When the elevator dinged, a nurse came out pushing Daddy in a wheelchair. Momma walked beside him, carrying a vase of white and red flowers. He sort of smiled, but looked pale and tired and not like his regular strong self. The collar of his shirt gaped, and his neck looked as thin as a chicken's. I wondered if he couldn't walk anymore.

Nana gave him a hug around the shoulders. I walked up and patted his arm. Daddy wore his regular farmer clothes—jeans and a khaki work shirt—but instead of his boots, he wore his house slippers. He yanked at a plastic bracelet wrapped around his wrist.

"Who gave you the pretty flowers?" I asked.

"You and your sister." That was strange. I wondered how many other unknown things we had done.

"Daddy, Elvis is in this exact same hospital!" Abby said. "Grace saw it in the paper this morning, and his room is covered in aluminum foil. We saw it from the street." She said nothing about my attempt to find him, and I wondered if that would cost me later.

"Hmmmm," was all he said. He shoved back his thick hair with an open palm.

"Have you seen him?" I asked.

"I haven't seen anyone but these nurses who won't let me sleep more than ten minutes at a time." The nurse in charge of pushing his chair smiled nervously like she wasn't sure if he was making a joke or really upset. He tugged at the bracelet again and then dropped his arm back into his lap.

"Can I see your bracelet?" Daddy held out his arm, and I read the words wrapped around his wrist—Lee Abbott, followed by our address and his doctor's name and some numbers I didn't understand. "Is this so you don't escape?" I asked.

"Something like that." He laughed but then coughed and winced as though something hurt deep inside.

"Can I have it when you're through with it?"

"You can have it now, if you can get it off." Even though there was a plastic snap on the end of it, I couldn't remove it from Daddy's arm either.

"If you'll just be patient, I'll cut it off when we pass by the admissions desk," the nurse said. And she did. Daddy rubbed his arm like it had been too tight and handed it to me.

"Can you not walk anymore?" Abby asked.

"She won't let me." He tilted his head toward the nurse.

"Hospital regulation," she said. While Momma went to get the car, we waited on one of those nice park benches we had driven by earlier. I had forgotten to remind her that the car was parked underneath a streetlight, so I worried she might not find it, and we'd never see her again.

"What kind of food did they give you?" I asked. The hospital bracelet wouldn't stay around my wrist, so I held it in place with my other hand.

"Sick people food. Like chicken broth and tea."

"You look skinny," Abby said. I rolled my eyes at her and didn't think it was nice to draw attention to his sick appearance.

He nodded while fumbling for a cigarette from the package in his front pocket. He took a long pull, held his breath for a few seconds, then dropped his head and closed his eyes against the sun. He exhaled long and steady, releasing a long stream of smoke and smiling like it was the best thing he'd done in ages. Nana, who hated cigarette smoke, moved a few steps away underneath a tree.

Chapter Thirteen

Sunday night, I ran around like a wild and crazy person making lists and trying to decide what to take to camp. Finally, I threw everything in my suitcase and announced myself packed. I couldn't wait!

By sunrise on Monday morning, after sleeping very little, I decided to stay home. Although the adventurous and brave side of me had always wanted to go to camp, the scaredy-cat side thought of a billion reasons to forget all about it.

What if I had to shower in front of a bunch of strangers?

What if the man in the gray house returned during the one week I was gone?

And worst of all, what if Daddy got mad and tried to kill Lucky again?

I rolled back over, pulled the covers over my head and fell asleep, content in my decision. When Momma woke us up, she didn't see it the same way. "It's a done deal," she said. "Daddy's already paid for you to go." And that was that.

Abby and I had thirty minutes to dress, eat breakfast, and get to Savage Crossing where we would catch the church bus and ride to camp. If the church bus was anything like the regular school bus I rode during fall, it was another good reason not to go.

During our short drive to town, Abby chatted non-stop, asking question after question, her animated eyes flashing. If words were visible, hers would have gushed from her lips in puffy pink letters with lots of exclamation points. She shifted her red baseball cap so that the bill faced sideways then grinned at her reflection in the rearview mirror.

I stared at the waist-high cotton flashing by the window and worried about not being able to sleep without my fan.

"What if I don't know anyone on the bus?" I said.

"You know that's not going to happen. Dian's going," Momma assured me. Besides, that's the great thing about having a sister. You'll always have a friend with you."

"Yeah!" Abby said and bounced in the seat like she had to pee.

My stomach hurt.

"Will you promise to take good care of Lucky and make sure Daddy doesn't go after him again?"

"Grace, your Daddy can barely get off the couch."

A man loaded suitcases into the back of a long, white bus. Along the side of the bus the words "Savage Crossing Hallelujah Bus" were printed in black-block letters. "Oh, brother," I said. Momma cut her eyes at me. Inside the bus, heads bobbed and moved, already filling the space. Parents waved from the gravel parking lot, some already beginning to pull away in their cars.

Abby gave Momma a quick hug goodbye and hopped onto the bus without looking back. I forced myself out of the car and across the gravel lot. As soon as I stepped into the bus, I realized Momma had been right. Friends from school filled the seats, mostly older kids, but familiar faces. Dian was saving seats for us. Even though I had no idea what to expect, when the bus pulled from the church parking lot, I felt a thrill, more excitement than fear, and I expected I'd survive and maybe even have a good time. Five whole days of something new—anything new—had to be better than being stuck at home. From the open window, I waved at Momma. She waved back.

As we drove down Main Street, the town was not fully awake. Mr. Turpin swept the sidewalk in front of the hardware store, yet the sign on the door still said, "Closed, Please Come Again." An important-looking man unlocked the front door of the bank. We made it almost to the stoplight when our driver pulled the bus into the gas station and jerked to a halt. As the doors burst open, in popped Bubba and his best friend, Mitchell, carrying duffle bags and pillows and looking like they were half-asleep. Everyone laughed. "One more minute and you boys would've had to walk," the driver said. I saw Mrs. Barns pull away in her car.

90

The landscape gradually changed from flat, delta fields to rolling hills to an honest-to-goodness forest, not like the woods near Boon Chapel, but dense trees that held the sun from the ground. Four hours after we left Savage Crossing, we drove through the main gate and passed an official sign welcoming us to church camp. "Keep your seats," the bus driver barked, but everyone piled into the aisles anyway. When the bus doors finally pushed open, we spilled into the warm day, stretching and jumping. We were surrounded by nothing but nature. I had five whole days to be different and do different things. Five days of possibility.

The girls from the Savage Crossing bus were assigned to Cabin Esther. We dragged our bags to the last cabin in a row of eight, completely hidden in the forest and farthest from the cafeteria. I couldn't remember exactly what role Esther played in the Bible, but I thought she was a queen and an overall good person. Inside Cabin Esther, the air was hot, and the walls were lined with wooden bunk beds that creaked as kids plopped down, claiming bottom or top. Since I had never slept on a top bunk, I scrambled to make sure I snagged one. Abby took the one beneath me, a good thing since she often fell off the bed while sleeping.

***

Had Momma warned me about all the actual "church" at church camp, I would have flat refused to go. Preaching happened twice a day. Outside. Underneath a pavilion with stuffy air. And instead of canoeing and crafts, there was singing. Lots of singing. We sang before and after preaching, after supper, while sitting around the campfire, and before bedtime. A few of the girls seemed to sing themselves to sleep.

Preaching and singing.

Singing and preaching.

After three and a half days, six sermons, and a million songs, I couldn't bear the thought of one more second of preaching under that stifling-hot pavilion. "Let's skip church this afternoon," I said to Abby. The other girls from Cabin Esther had already headed over to the pavilion to get a good seat for preaching, but we lagged behind, waiting while Dian used the bathroom. She always had trouble using the bathroom away from home.

"Can we?" Abby asked, yanking the headband from her hair and slinging it across her bed. Her bangs stuck straight up on top, and I wondered how many days she had gone without washing it with anything more than pool chlorine. With all the camp rules, there were none about hygiene, so that was nice.

"We can do whatever we want to do," I said, somehow summoning the courage to be a rule-breaker.

"I hope we get in trouble, and they call Momma to come get me," Dian yelled from the toilet stall. While I knew with one phone call Aunt Fannie would immediately come get Dian, Abby and I were stuck until Saturday. Momma would make us see the whole week through.

We watched from the windows of Cabin Esther until campers and counselors were settled in a mass beneath the pavilion. After a few minutes of seeing no one, we sneaked into the woods behind our cabin, with no plan other than to talk about something other than Jesus. The sound of singing trailed behind us, becoming fainter and fainter the deeper into the woods we walked. Eventually, the only sounds we heard, were those of the chirping birds and leaves rustling in the trees. Once we found the hiking trail through the gorge, we headed to Devil's Bathtub, a supposedly bottomless pool filled with stagnant water and topped with a layer of algae as thick as pudding. We knew about it because on Tuesday, between singing and preaching, Cabin Esther had gone on an official hike. What could have been exciting had become just another closely supervised activity as counselors warned us to stay on the trail and not touch anything.

"Be careful where you step, the moss is slippery," the lead counselor had repeated, over and over. He had even tried to scare all the little kids by saying no one could survive a fall into Devil's Bathtub because there was no bottom.

"How do you know there's no bottom? Besides, if you can swim, what does that matter? Couldn't someone be pulled out with a rope?" I had challenged him.

He shook his head no, and yelled at me, again, "Watch your step!"

"But why not?" I persisted.

He ignored me.

92

I said a bad word in my head. There was something about church camp that made me want to say bad words all the time.

Church camp made me want to do bad things too, like skip out on preaching. Now that we were finally away from the counselors, I felt as free as a weed. Trees soared overhead, swaying with a slight summer breeze. We'd barely been able to notice these same trees earlier in the week, when we weren't allowed to move our eyes from the narrow pathway. Church camp would have been loads better if the counselors talked more about how God made the trees and less about going to Hell where there were no trees.

When we got to Devil's Bathtub, we sat in a row on the sheer edge and dropped rocks into the dark green water. "Do you think there's a bottom?" Dian asked.

"Yes, unless it really is the opening to Hell. But somehow I doubt the door to Hell is at a church camp in the Ozark Mountains," I said. I dropped a small stick into the pool, and it floated along the surface, supported by a spinach-like layer of scum.

We talked about all sorts of things, like why Mr. Mooney, the school principal, had one leg longer than the other, and why Roy Henry was born retarded. Trees veiled the afternoon sun, making the temperature more tolerable than underneath the pavilion at camp. On the way back, we sang songs, not "Kumbaya," but David Cassidy songs. We talked about how we could get our bangs to feather back like his.

That night, I decided to eat with Bubba since he was sitting alone at the end of a table. After the constant yakking and laughing that happened around girls, I appreciated that, although Bubba could be annoying, he didn't talk all the time. Abby and Dian joined a group of girls on the opposite end of the mess hall. I reminded them not to breathe a word of our afternoon adventure, and they promised to keep their mouths shut about it.

"Hi, Bubba," I said as I placed my tray of food opposite him.

"Hey, Gracie."

"Can I sit with you?"

"If you promise not to talk too much."

"I promise. Where's Mitchell?"

He pointed toward the end of the line. "Way back there. He was being slow so I ran off and left him. Are you gonna eat your roll?"

"No, you can have it." I handed it across the table. Even though it was soggy and gross from sitting in green bean juice, he wolfed it down. There wasn't enough food at church camp, especially for boys, and I could tell he was starving by the intensity in his eyes and the way he ate too fast to taste the bread. He pushed hair away from his eyes with the back of his hand and drank his milk in one long guzzle.

"Do you like camp, Bubba?"

"No." He squinted his small eyes and shook his head back and forth rapidly, swinging the curls framing his face. "Momma only sent me here to get some peace and quiet before school starts. We don't even go to church. What about you? Do you like it?"

"Not really. There's too much preaching and singing, but I like being in the woods away from home, especially Daddy. He's always in a bad mood. Is your Daddy that way?"

"Yeah. Most of the time." Somehow I didn't think Mr. Barns's moods were as bad as my Daddy's. I wondered whether Daddy was feeling better since his surgery, and if he was, would I even be able to tell?

Bubba and I talked for a few minutes about nothing much, and I asked him about his cabin. The Savage Crossing boys had been assigned to Cabin Cain. I couldn't figure out why a cabin had been named for Cain, since he was the jealous, murdering brother of Abel. Bubba said his cabin was old and smelled like dirty socks, so I knew it was just like Cabin Esther.

"Hey, why didn't you sit with Mitchell and me during preaching today?" He slurped up his spaghetti noodles in big clumps, splattering red sauce on his chin. I twisted a forkful and stuck it into my mouth, feeling the dangling pieces stain my chin too. There was no clean way to eat spaghetti.

"We came in late and sat in the back. I didn't see you," I said. Mitchell was inching his way toward the buffet line. He waved at me and shrugged his shoulders, probably famished by now.

"But we always sit in the same place," he said. He squinted and gave me a funny look, like he could tell there was more to the story. "Gracie, you're lying. You always look guilty when you lie." For a boy, Bubba was sometimes perceptive.

94

I looked around to make sure no one was spying, then whispered, "If I tell you, you can't breathe a word. Promise."

He nodded yes and stuck his hand across the table. I reached out and clasped my little finger with his and we shook. By doing a pinkie swear, I knew he would keep his mouth shut for the rest of our lives.

"We skipped preaching and hiked to Devil's Bathtub. Abby, Dian, and me. We spent the whole afternoon exploring the woods."

His eyes popped, and he smiled showing something green stuck between his teeth. "Really?" he asked.

"Uh-huh," I nodded. "I don't believe that whole story about how it has no bottom, do you?"

"No, that's stupid."

"Yeah, I think so too. We threw rocks and sticks in it and had a great day away from all the church talk. I might go back tomorrow," I said.

"Let's go tonight. Just you and me." Bubba sat straight in his chair, excited about the prospect. "I have a flashlight I can bring." Mitchell had finally reached the stack of plastic trays. He slid one onto the railing around the buffet and pulled utensils from the rack.

"Are you sure? We'll get in big trouble if anyone finds us roaming around after curfew." But I had already decided it was a fantastic idea.

"Yeah," he said with a crooked, spaghetti-stained smile. "But no one will catch us." Even though there was no need, we did another pinkie swear before Mitchell sat down, to cement our plans. I told him about the food stuck between his teeth too.

***

At exactly eleven-fifteen, our agreed-upon time, I climbed down from my top bunk, pulled on my tennis shoes, and tiptoed across the rough concrete floor of Cabin Esther. Since sunset, the night had cooled considerably. A box fan in the corner near the bathrooms was humming and stirring the mountain air. My bunkmates slept soundly underneath sleeping bags and quilts brought from home. Easy, I thought, as I pressed the screen door shut, careful not to let it slam, and slung my pillowcase over my shoulder like a backpack. Inside, I had replaced my pillow with things we might need for late-night exploring—bug spray, a Hershey's bar, and an extra T-shirt, just in case.

An almost full moon lit the hillside. Beyond the pavilion, a shadow approached, moving across the dry grass. It was Bubba. We met at the edge of the woods, and neither of us spoke as we eased into the protection of the trees. Once we were safely hidden, Bubba flipped on his flashlight, held it beneath his chin, and smiled. "We made it." His hair curled around the edges of his Savage Crossing baseball cap, and his eyelashes gleamed in the glow of the light.

I pulled the can of bug spray from my pillowcase-duffel bag and misted my legs and arms. "You want some?" I asked.

He nodded and held out his arms. The hiss of spray mingled with the steady buzz of the night forest. "You lead the way. I don't remember," he said.

As we walked deeper into the darkness, I mocked the counselors and their warnings. "Stay on the path. Don't touch anything or you'll surely die."

Bubba laughed. Abby and Dian, still sleeping on their bunk beds, were missing all the fun. I felt a pang of guilt that we had not included them. Mitchell too. There was a different sort of excitement in the woods at night.

The nearby leaves rustled. I heard a stick snap. Goosebumps popped out on my arms. "What was that noise?"

"Probably a squirrel," he said. *Or Bigfoot.* I moved the flashlight toward the direction of the noise, but even with the light, I couldn't see past a tunnel of low-hanging branches.

Neither of us spoke the rest of the way. The night felt trapped within the trees, and I concentrated on each footstep, thankful to be carrying the flashlight. When we reached a narrower section of the path, small twigs brushed my legs and stung my arms. Everything looked different in the dark, and I worried we had wandered off the trail. Then the familiar rock outcropping towered ahead.

"Here it is," I said, waving the light around the sides of the deep, black pool. Carefully, we inched our way to the edge and sat down side-by-side.

"It looks weird, like the water is gurgling," Bubba said. He took the flashlight and aimed it below our feet. Bubbles skimmed the surface of the water, inflating then popping and leaving circles before disappearing.

"Yuck. That water really is creepy, but I'd still like to know how deep it is, wouldn't you?" I asked.

"I could dive in and touch the bottom." He lurched closer to the edge and jerked like he might jump. Even though I was pretty sure he was teasing, I grabbed his arm and yelled at him to stop, just in case.

"I have a better idea. Follow me." During the day, I'd noticed a fallen pine on the opposite side of Devil's Bathtub, long and straight and empty of other branches. Carefully, I made my way toward it and Bubba followed. "I think this tree was struck by lightning," I said, touching my fingertips to the charred bark. "Maybe we can find the bottom with it."

Bubba kicked the tree like it was an old truck tire. "Okay, you pick up that end," he said, nodding to the section of trunk nearest the clearing. I held the flashlight while Bubba found the other end, further back in the trees. The tree was over ten feet tall and heavier than it looked. At first, we couldn't move it at all. Bubba stood on top, rocking back and forth, extending his arms for balance. Eventually, he loosened a section that had been partially buried in dirt and leaves.

We shimmied and moved the trunk into the path, stopping once for me to re-adjust my grip. "Let's push that end over the edge, then slowly drop it and try to make it stand up in the water," he suggested. I admired how quickly he had developed a plan.

Together, we pulled one end of the tree to the edge, then went to the other end and started pushing as we walked toward the drop down to Devil's Bathtub. The trunk moved out over the pool, slow and steady, its center of balance beginning to shift. When the weight of the tree pulled against our hands, it flipped upright and tore from my grip. Bubba kept holding on and was swung up in the air.

"Let go!" I yelled, panicked.

Bubba fell and slid, almost in slow motion, as the tree cartwheeled off the edge. Gravel loosened beneath his feet as the rocky lip began to crumble. With a gulping noise, Devil's Bathtub swallowed the tree, and Bubba's body disappeared over the edge. His baseball cap popped into the air and vanished.

My scream echoed across the Ozark Mountains.

I rushed forward to find Bubba dangling above the pool, his arms and hands clinging to the sharp edge. In one movement, I dove to my belly and grabbed his shoulders. Indian-style, I braced my arms around his, like in a game of Red Rover. I felt him slip and heard rocks hit the water below. I squeezed tighter and so did he.

His shoulders tensed.

I felt his breath against my face.

My grip weakened. I knew if I reached down further for him or pulled harder, we'd both fall.

With a grunt and a moan, he heaved a leg over the side. Then he swung his other leg over to safety. We both lay on our backs in the dirt, gulping air and trembling. A million stars twinkled overhead, yet I knew they had burned out an eternity ago.

Bubba was silent.

"Are you okay?" I pressed the space where my heart hammered against my chest. Although we didn't prove that Devil's Bathtub wasn't really bottomless, we understood how deep and dangerous it was. It was rightly named too.

"I lost a shoe," he finally said. His voice sounded faint and breathless, and when I looked at him, his chest heaved as much as mine.

"God, that was scary. You could have died." I glanced at Bubba, this friend I had never not known. I didn't want to think of what would have happened if he had fallen in. I swallowed hard to keep from crying.

"Nah. You would have saved me, Gracie. Somehow." He nudged me with his elbow but continued staring overhead.

Above us, stars flickered and winked as though trying to tell me something.

Me.

A nobody, barely a blip on this mountainside. I was filled with questions I didn't understand, surrounded by answers I couldn't hear. Overhead, the sky was a glass bowl I could reach out to, yet never touch, endless because that's what I believed. Although I would never find the bottom of Devil's Bathtub, I knew it was there, somewhere beneath the murky surface.

My heart fluttered as something inside me shifted, just slightly.

"Bubba, do you believe in God?"

"Sometimes. Do you?"

"Sometimes. Like right now, I do. But other times, I can't believe in anything."

We twisted over onto our stomachs and peered over the edge, shining the flashlight at the inky surface of the water. There was no sign of Bubba's shoe, or baseball cap, or the ten-foot pine tree. Backing away from the rim, we sat up. I pulled out the Hershey's bar to share, and we ate it silently, in small pieces, to make it last.

Chapter Fourteen

"I just got back from church camp," I told Brother Brown who stood in front of the pulpit, practically waiting for me. He wore the same brown suit, brown tie, and brown shoes that he always wore. I wondered if he did it to match his name or if it was his favorite color.

"Yes, I heard. How was it, Grace?" he asked. Sweat covered his forehead, and his gray hair, deeply parted over the top of his head, looked damp. He glanced to Mrs. Brown in the far corner of the second pew, and I wondered if he would rather say a final amen and rush to his air-conditioned car than talk with me.

"It was okay. A lot of people got saved, but since I am already baptized, most of it was a waste of time for me. I did have an experience I wanted to talk to you about. Something weird that made me feel closer to God. Something that made me think he really does exist."

His eyes widened, his eyebrows shifted together, and the skin on his forehead scrunched into rolls. "Of course he exists, Grace."

"Well, what I mean is, when my friend Bubba fell over the edge of Devil's Bathtub and hung by his fingertips, I felt like maybe God pressed down on my body and gave me strength enough to grip Bubba's shoulders so he could crawl over the rim, instead of plunging over the side."

Brother Brown moved in a little closer and cocked his head like Lucky always did when I made a funny noise. "Is this a true story, Grace?"

"Yes, sir, and afterwards the stars were shining and it seemed like God was all around. Do you know what I mean?"

"God is all around," he said. With the palm of his wide hand across my back, Brother Brown guided me to the front pew, and we knelt at our regular place. My dress felt too short and tight around the shoulders, but I tried to ignore it while he talked about Satan. "Grace, the devil will get into your head and make you doubt your faith." He pointed his finger to my ear as though my earhole was the exact opening the devil used to sneak into my brain. "You have to stand strong in your faith, believe in your salvation." He grabbed my hand and squeezed hard. His hand was sweaty, and I had to concentrate not to jerk mine away.

"But do you ever think the whole thing may only be something to make us feel better and give us hope? Like a fairy tale?"

Brother Brown coughed and shook his head. His face flushed bright red. I wondered if he swallowed a piece of gum and if someone would have to do mouth-to-mouth, because I wouldn't and didn't know how anyway. After clearing his throat, he said, "No, Grace. You mustn't think that way." Then he recited a couple of verses about fighting the fight and being a good and faithful servant.

"Brother Brown, could you maybe speak English?"

He stared blankly, pulled an offering envelope from inside his coat pocket, and scribbled something across it. "Gracie, when you get home, look these verses up in your Bible. See if they don't help answer your questions," he said.

I nodded and thought it was interesting that he used offering envelopes for scrap paper too. I walked back to my seat, thinking maybe we believe what we want to believe.

Chapter Fifteen

The hands of my Cinderella watch glowed in the dark. I held the round face in front of my nose and watched as both hands pointed straight up. Midnight. I placed the watch on the nightstand, extended my arms overhead, stretched my toes toward the footboard, and stared up at the ceiling I knew was there but couldn't see. I felt older. Definitely.

My birthday had officially arrived. For ten years, I had lived on this farm down the road from Cottonwood Corner and slept in this pale pink room. My grandest ideas and worst worries had been conjured up within this square space beneath the dark ceiling of our bedroom. And for much of that time, Abby lay in the twin bed next to me. That was an amazing thing.

With the excitement of my birthday party only a few hours away, falling asleep was harder than normal. There would be presents and cake, but instead of a regular party in the backyard, Momma and Nana planned a special day for me in Memphis. We were going to Shakey's Pizza for lunch and to the Pink Palace Museum. I was allowed to invite a friend, so I asked Dian. Janice was away on vacation with her family, and in a way, I was glad, because I wouldn't have to choose between them. Of course, Abby would be going too. She was like a freebie, a built-in friend who was sometimes a pest. At supper, when I asked Daddy if he would be coming, he said he missed too much work and needed to farm. That was only an excuse, but it was nice of him to lie instead of gripe about the cost and say I was too old for birthday parties. I knew birthday parties weren't his thing and never remembered him attending one. Not one for Abby or me, anyway.

Abby and I hadn't missed anything exciting during our week at church camp. Momma said she'd almost hogtied Daddy to keep him from overdoing it, but he felt better by the end of the week and got a good report from his doctor on Friday. While Daddy rested, Papa Pete did all the farming. I'd expected by the time I returned from camp, there would be a letter or postcard waiting for me from the man in the gray house. But there was nothing.

I picked up my watch from the nightstand and looked at the time again. I had been ten years old for ten whole minutes. Lucky, who slept next to me with his head on my pillow, rolled over and poked me with a paw in the process. I didn't mind, I'd missed him more than I had realized. Underneath my pillow, the sheet was extra cool. I pulled Barbie out, smoothed her hair, and placed her on the pillow near the edge of the bed. Barbie had spent her first week at church camp too. She stayed hidden in the bottom of my suitcase the whole time.

I thought about the verses Brother Brown had given me to look up. I read them after church and again before I went to bed. The first one said something like, "Watch, stand fast in the faith, quit acting like a man and be strong." And there was a "ye" in there somewhere because King James said ye a lot. I liked the one in Psalms best, because in my opinion, Psalms was the happiest book of the Bible. That verse was worded something like, "Be strong and take heart and have hope in the Lord." It fit exactly what I was trying to say to Brother Brown. The Bible gives us something to hope for. Something to make us feel better about. Like a fairy tale.

I closed my eyes and imagined the silver stars shining over Devil's Bathtub. Bubba's tennis shoe would be somewhere underneath the surface of that stagnant water until the end of time or until it disintegrated and disappeared. I wondered if he threw the other shoe in the trash at Cabin Cain, or if it was sitting in his closet without a match.

***

Our waiter at Shakey's Pizza was very short—like one of the munchkins on *The Wizard of Oz.* I'd never seen such a small adult before. When he brought our large pepperoni pizza with extra cheese to the table, he barely stood as tall as the back of my chair. His head looked adult-sized, but his arms and legs were the size of a child. I tried not to stare but found myself watching him more than once. When he found out it was my birthday, he said, "That's groovy," and brought us a free pitcher of grape soda. He seemed nice, maybe nicer than most people I knew. I thought maybe his size made him try harder.

After eating our pizza, I blew out all eleven candles, ten years plus one to grow on, in one steady breath of air, and Momma passed around slices of the strawberry cake she had brought from home. Everyone, including the waiter, sang "Happy Birthday," which was embarrassing and nice at the same time. When Momma offered him a piece of cake, he said, "Thank you, ma'am, but I'm not allowed to eat during my shift." He really was a polite little guy.

My gifts were piled in the center of the table, a stack of gifts, all sizes and shapes, wrapped in shades of pink and yellow and orange polka dot, and tied in ribbons of every color. I opened them right there at the pizza restaurant too. People I didn't know watched as though everyone at Shakey's had come for me. The birthday present wrapped in pink balloon paper looked to be a book. Imagine my surprise when I unwrapped a Cinderella diary. I thumbed through the blank pages and couldn't wait to write something secret and lock away my words with the tiny gold key that came with the diary. The funny thing about the gift was that it came from Abby, the person who wanted to know my secrets most of all. Momma actually bought the diary and wrote Abby's name on the gift tag. I knew when Abby learned how it worked, she would regret being part of such a gift.

Dian bought me the new Sonny and Cher album, with "I Got You Babe" on it. I could tell by the shape of the package that it was an album, but I didn't know which one, so it was still a surprise.

Nana's present was the turtle quilt she had been working on for months. Made from scraps of fabric identical to the outfits in my closet, the material looked better shaped like turtles. Nana signed her name in the corner like it was a painting.

"*J'adore!*" I gave her a huge hug.

The biggest surprise of the day—something Momma kept secret until the last minute—was riding a real riverboat on the Mississippi River. Momma took lots of pictures so later we could remember all the details of churning along the muddy water like Huckleberry Finn with sweat dripping into our eyes. The boat went underneath the same bridge that carried us to Memphis. I'd never seen a bridge from that point of view and hoped the next big earthquake wouldn't happen while cars drove over us.

The grand finale of my birthday trip was driving past Graceland. Momma slowed down so we could get a better look, but Elvis wasn't outside. Neither was Lisa Marie. I wondered which window was her bedroom.

***

After we returned from a full day in Memphis, Mamaw Pearl and Candi were waiting in the driveway. Momma said, "Oh, great," and then "What in the world?" when Candi lugged a gigantic birthday present to the back door. It was wrapped in purple and orange paper and topped with curly-cue ribbons. Once we got inside, Candi stood it up in the corner of the kitchen. It was taller than the washing machine.

I stared at it while Momma sliced up strawberry cake for Mamaw and Candi and second helpings for the rest of us. After carrying the cake to Memphis and back, it was sticky and half-melted from being cooped up in our hot car all day. Even so, it was still delicious. When Candi noticed me staring at my gift, she swung her stick-straight hair over her shoulder and said, "Open it, Gracie." So I did.

It was a girl.

Not a real girl, but she looked real. Her light brown hair hung to her waist, and her emerald eyes were rimmed in black eyelashes that felt soft and real. When I touched her face, her eyelids shut then popped back open.

"Do you like her?" Candi asked. "Her name is Patti."

I stared, not sure what to think. She was the most life-like doll I'd ever seen. "Yes, I do. Thank you," I said, hoping my voice didn't give me away. I had expected something a bit more grown-up, especially from Candi.

"Wow," Abby said. She ran over and stood back-to-back with Patti. She was only a little taller.

"Oh, and there's one more thing," Candi said, as she reached for her shoulder bag hanging from the back of her chair. At first I thought she was going to give me her purse which would have been neat, because it was tan leather with long fringe hanging from the bottom and a peace sign imprinted on the side like a cattle brand. She dug inside and pulled out a small paper sack. "Sorry I didn't wrap it," she said, handing it across the table to me.

It was a bottle of self-tanning lotion, something Candi always used that only seemed to make her skin orange instead of tan. I thanked Candi and placed it in the large gift sack containing my turtle quilt and other gifts from the day. Momma gave me a look and shook her head, just slightly, but there was no need for her to worry. I never planned to use it.

Usually when Mamaw Pearl visited, she hung around as long as possible, hoping to still be at our house when Daddy got home for supper. But not this time. Since Candi had a friend coming over, she bugged and bugged Mamaw to leave until finally they did.

I stared at that doll standing in the corner. She stared back at me. "What are we gonna do with Patti?" I asked Momma.

"What do you mean?"

"She will be impossible to hide from Daddy."

"I love her," Abby said, running up to Patti and squeezing her around the shoulders.

"Great. You can have her," I said.

"I can?" Abby grabbed her around the neck and dragged her away to the bedroom while Momma stared at me like she didn't understand anything I'd said.

"You don't like Mamaw's gift?" Momma asked as she placed a strip of salt pork into the skillet. The grease sizzled and popped. She pulled her hand back quickly.

"Momma, don't you think I'm too old to be adding new dolls to my collection, especially ones as big as real people?" Already I'd been keeping my doll playing a secret from Daddy as best I could. "Look at Baby-Grace playing with dolls," he'd said a few months back. Being called Baby-Grace was worse than Eudora.

Just before supper, Abby scooted an extra chair up to the kitchen table so Patti could eat with us. Momma even set a place for her and spooned mashed potatoes onto her plate. "I bet she's starving after being wrapped in birthday paper all day," Abby said, sweeping the doll's bangs from her eyes.

"Oh, brother," I said. For my tenth birthday, I gained another annoying sister.

When Daddy turned into the driveway, I began counting Mississippis while staring at the back door, waiting for it to open. Daddy took forever, which only added to the force of the explosion when he walked into the kitchen.

"What in God's name is that?"

"My new sister," I said.

"Jesus H. Christ."

"Yeah," I said hoping he would sense right away the whole thing was not my idea. "Mamaw Pearl bought me a ridiculous doll for my birthday like I'm five years old instead of ten. I gave her to Abby. What else could I do?"

"I think she's beautiful." Abby hugged her around the shoulders.

Daddy shook his head, hung his cap on the hook behind the door, and dropped his thermos to the floor. The kitchen went from smelling of fried potatoes to smelling of the farm—dust and sweat and a day's hard work. "So now we have to eat with that thing staring at us?" he asked, as he dropped ice cubes into a glass and poured whiskey to the top.

Abby placed her hands over Patti's ears. "You hurt her feelings!" she yelled and thrust out her bottom lip.

"Lee, can't you play along? She's only a doll. And besides, your mother brought it." Daddy grumbled but couldn't say much. "And by the way, you might want to let her in on what's going on with you before she hears it on the street. It was awkward having her here and not being able to tell her about your surgery." Since Daddy had first gotten sick, Momma and Daddy had both reminded us a million times not to mention anything about it to Mamaw. She got hysterical easily, and when she did, she phoned the house several times a day, which drove Momma nuts, or she came over which put Daddy in a worse mood.

Daddy shook his head but said nothing.

I could see both sides to the Mamaw Pearl problem. So many people around her had died—Grandpa Abbott, Candi's momma, and her twin sister I'd never met—plus, Daddy was her only son. The way he avoided her, she probably felt like she'd lost him too. Daddy on the other hand, got tired of listening to her pester him about working too hard and never going to church.

We finished supper with Momma still talking about Mamaw Pearl and Daddy complaining about the farm. Daddy forgot to wish me a happy birthday and never even asked about our trip to Memphis. I didn't bother reminding him. He'd had too much to drink and was extra grumpy. I stayed up late listening to my new album while Abby pretended Patti was a friend visiting from New York. She dressed her in her favorite pajamas and read her a book. I thought about writing in my new diary, but decided to wait.

The next morning at the breakfast table, Daddy looked over the top of the newspaper and handed me a birthday card. "Do you feel any older, Grace?" he asked.

"No. Do I look older?"

He told me I didn't. "Be glad of it," he said. "You'll be old, soon enough."

I wasn't glad of it. I wanted to blink my eyes and be grown and living somewhere other than in our house. As I opened the card, two five-dollar bills floated out and landed on my toast. I held the money in my hand and was happy to have it but felt disappointed that he hadn't given it to me on the actual day. When I read the card, it didn't say much other than "Happy Birthday, Daddy."

"Thank you," I said, even though I figured Momma pulled the card from her stash in the desk drawer and handed him a pen to sign it.

Chapter Sixteen

After my birthday trip to Memphis, the rest of the week was so long and drab my brain turned to nothing, and any simmering ideas dried up like dust. So far, even though I was a year older, nothing about me was different. My hair, my face, my flat chest—everything was exactly the same. Janice finally returned from her summer vacation, so we talked on the phone twice. She chattered non-stop about all the fun things she did in Texas at her aunt's house. When she asked me what I did during the summer, I couldn't remember a single thing. Later, I told her about my birthday trip and riding on the Mississippi in a riverboat. "That sounds cool," she said, but I didn't think she meant it.

On Saturday, I convinced Momma to drop Abby and me off at the library while she bought groceries. She gave us exactly thirty minutes to check out books and meet her on the corner. When we got back in the car, a big bag of potatoes lay on the floorboard and the front seat was crowded with sacks of groceries. Same old food, I would have bet my ten dollars on it.

Summer was nearing an end. Without looking at the calendar, I could feel it in the afternoon breeze that somehow felt slightly different by sunset. Even more obvious was the glaring message on the sign in front of the school. "Welcome Back Students. School Starts September 5." Only ten more days. I didn't want to go back to school, yet there was no real reason for me to sit around the house.

I spent the remainder of the afternoon reading a Nancy Drew book from beginning to end, and just before supper, I decided to write another letter to the man in the gray house. I told him about my birthday trip to Memphis and made a list of the gifts I had gotten—everything other than Patti, who now belonged to my sister. I didn't tell him about Daddy forgetting my birthday, either. Although it wasn't my longest letter to him, I believed sometimes not saying much said a lot. I folded the letter into a square and slipped it underneath my pillow with Barbie. I'd take it to his house later. Momma was yelling at me to set the table.

At supper, Daddy was quiet, like he had a lot on his mind—not what I considered a good mood, but not a bad mood either. A neutral mood. Sometimes, that was all we could hope for. Momma asked him about going to the lake for Labor Day weekend. Nana and Papa Pete had a small fishing cabin right on the water and a ski boat too. We hadn't been all summer, which was unusual. Daddy said there was no time with all the things he needed to do on the farm. Being sick had made him behind. It seemed to me, he was behind no matter. Momma must have been enjoying his neutral mood too, because she didn't mention it again. After supper, Daddy fell asleep on the couch while Momma helped Abby bake a cake in the Easy Bake Oven.

"I'm going to ride my bike for a while," I said.

With a reminder from Momma to "Look both ways and come home before dark," I was out the door with Lucky following me.

There was no traffic in either direction on the road in front of our house. I raced to the gray house with Lucky barking and chasing me. The early evening was warm, and a blood-red sun hung over the distant Savage Crossing water tower. The days were getting shorter. As usual, there was no car in the driveway. I propped my bike against the front porch railing, wiped my forehead with the bottom of my T-shirt, and walked up the wooden steps. Squatting at the front door, I poked open the mail slot and looked inside. My last letter wasn't there. Lucky panted beside me, the heat from his body radiating all around. Just as I pushed my letter through the hole, a cat raced across the porch and into the surrounding bushes. Lucky tore after her.

He was easy to find, lying on the ground with his nose pressed to the place where the cat had vanished underneath the side of the house. Staring and whining, he treed the spot and wouldn't come when I called.

I walked around back and threw a stick so that he'd see it. "Lucky, fetch!" He continued to ignore me.

110

There was a porch across the back of the house, and the screen door wasn't shut all the way. I walked over and tried to close it, but the door sprung back open a few inches. I tried again with the same results. The wood around the bottom edge looked warped like maybe it had gotten wet. The paint was peeling too.

Come on in, the porch seemed to say to me.

It was only a porch. A back porch was no different than a front porch, except for the screens in place to keep mosquitoes out. So I stepped inside.

In the corner, clay pots partially filled with dirt were stacked three and four high. A fern sitting on a plant stand was so dry the fronds turned to powder when I passed by. Empty soda bottles filled wooden crates along the wall. I couldn't believe anyone would leave all those unclaimed nickels lying around. A small, square window in the back door provided a clear view of the kitchen. So I peeped inside. When I touched the tarnished doorknob, it felt loose in my hand.

I took a deep breath and turned it.

I was standing inside the pretty gray house.

"Hello?"

No one answered.

The room was tidy and sparse with red and white checkerboard floor tiles. The stove looked more like a television or a piece of furniture than a place to bake cornbread. Above the sink, coffee cups hung in a row from tiny hooks. I opened the icebox and looked inside. Other than a box of baking soda, it was empty. A black telephone, much like the one in our kitchen, hung on the wall next to the icebox. Was it *the* telephone? I walked over and looked carefully at it, but didn't see blood anywhere, not even inside the dial holes, which would have been hard to clean.

According to the long shadows and fading light, I had only a few minutes to walk through the house looking for clues. There had to be clues. Clues about what happened to the man and where he'd gone. As I took one step into the hallway, the shrill ring of the nearby telephone pierced the silence as though my snooping tripped an alarm. I raced from the kitchen, slammed the warped screen door and could still hear the phone ringing inside my head when I got home. Lucky ran the whole way with me.

That night I lay in bed, thinking about the gray house and all the things I saw inside it. I would go back. Definitely. I stared at Abby who slept in her bed next to me. She made little noises and occasionally giggled in her dreams. She would love to know about the gray house, but I couldn't tell her. Maybe when she was older.

As I stared at the ceiling, the thought of school returned to me. I wondered if my classmates would think I changed at all since classes let out in May. Other than my new hairstyle, which had grown out a bit and looked decent when I pulled the sides back into barrettes, most of my changes happened inside. I got baptized, and I was a year older. But I didn't feel any different. Not really. Changes probably happened so gradually no one noticed any small thing, until suddenly, everything caught up.

I felt sleepy, but couldn't sleep.

My mind raced.

The fan hummed.

I twirled Barbie's hair.

I tried to count sheep, but I'd never understood how the whole sheep thing worked. Instead of falling asleep, I began to question whether or not sheep were truly capable of jumping over fences at all. Maybe I would research that in the library the next time I went.

I thought about Nana and Papa Pete and their little house at the lake. I wanted to go there so bad my whole body ached. We hadn't been since Easter, and it was too cold to swim then. I imagined the clear water and the sound of doves in the trees outside the bedroom window. At some point, I slept.

Chapter Seventeen

I stared out the car window. The blue sky held not a single cloud. A row of blackbirds sat on a telephone line as though watching for rain. Already I regretted my choice of dress for church. It was too short, and my knees looked knobbier than normal.

"There's the woods!" Abby announced. The patch of trees passed on her side of the car so I didn't bother looking.

"Uh-huh." I stretched my knee socks up over my knees, but still they looked sharp and bony.

"I see Bigfoot!" Abby shouted and smacked her hand against the glass, leaving her sticky fingerprints behind. Since we'd overslept and had no time for breakfast, Momma agreed she could eat in the car. I hadn't been hungry, so I skipped.

"There's no such thing," Momma said. She pressed an eight-track into the car stereo, and Elvis began to croon. Abby dusted crumbs from her lap onto the floor of the back seat. Momma would regret allowing that piece of buttered toast in the car.

"Momma, can I invite a friend over for supper Friday night?" I asked.

"Sure. Janice? Let me know what you'd like me to cook," Momma said.

As we pulled into the church lot, I saw all the normal cars were lined along the circle gravel drive, and Brother Brown's car was parked in its regular spot next to the front porch. Although there was no sign with his name on it, everyone understood that place was his, and no one parked there. Momma parked closest to the highway so our car wouldn't get trapped if people stayed and visited. Another full house at Boon Chapel Baptist Church.

Our Sunday school lesson was about friendship. Momma talked about the parables of the Lost Sheep and the Lost Coin. There were lots of sheep stories in the Bible, but I had never heard the Lost Coin tale, so I learned something new, not that I would remember it later. When Momma asked, "What makes a good friendship?" everyone blurted out different ideas, like helping each other, not being two-faced at school, and sharing notebook paper when classmates forgot theirs. Momma said all of our answers were correct.

After Sunday school class, I returned to my regular spot on the third pew and positioned my feet on either side of the knothole. It stared at me like it did every Sunday, a small circle that looked like it had been drawn with a charcoal pencil. I pressed it with the ball of my shoe and felt it move. Again, I pressed down and smashed my shoe the way Daddy did when he crushed out a cigarette on the carport. When I moved my foot, a hole stared back at me, a perfectly round hole.

Wow.

I bent down and pretended to mess with my sock. There was room enough for me to stick two fingers into the empty space and wiggle them around in the cool air beneath the church. I poked Abby and pointed. She pretended to mess with her sock too.

Throughout the sermon, I tried to listen to Brother Brown, but mostly I stared at the hole. When the invitational hymn began, I abandoned the hole and walked to the front.

"How are you today, Grace?" Brother Brown asked.

"*Très bien, merci.* That means very well, thank you in French, in case you don't know," I said.

He smiled. I'm sure he had no idea I spoke French, because even though I had been baptized, and we talked in this very spot quite often, he hadn't taken the time to get to know me yet.

"What's on your mind today?" he asked. Brother Brown seemed in a hurry and didn't offer to kneel at the front pew with me. Instead, we walked over to the side near the humongous furnace and chatted.

"I wanted to invite you for supper at our house Friday night," I said. "Momma is a really good cook most of the time, and if you tell me what you like, I'll see if she can make it special for you."

"Well, that's a very nice invitation, but you should probably ask your parents first."

"I already did. She said sure, and to find out what you like to eat so she can cook it. I hope it's not liver, though."

Brother Brown chuckled and glanced over at Momma. "I'm sure anything she cooks will be just fine. I don't much like liver either," he added with a big smile.

As the third stanza ended, I turned to walk back to my pew, but stopped to add one more thing. "Mrs. Brown can come too if you want to bring her."

"I'm sure she'd be delighted," he said. I doubted that. She didn't seem the type.

"What was that all about?" Momma asked when we got situated in the car.

"*Quoi*?" I asked.

"What were you talking about with Brother Brown? He stared right at me like you were talking about me. Grace, you better not be telling him our personal family business."

"Momma, don't worry. It's a good thing. You'll see." I smoothed Barbie's hair and sat her on the armrest. Barbie still wore her nightgown, but that was okay. She was lucky to stay in the car during church.

***

When we turned into the driveway, Momma heaved a big sigh. She came to an abrupt stop in the carport, grabbed her pocketbook and Bible, and marched into the house, slamming the screen door behind her. Right away, I knew she was upset because Daddy was mowing the ditch on Sunday. Everyone who drove down the highway would see Daddy violating the "keeping Sabbath Holy" rule with his riding lawn mower.

I slipped Barbie underneath the pillow on my bed and told her to take a nap. When I finally yanked that too short dress off, which for a while felt stuck on my shoulders forever, I hung it on Abby's side of the closet. Her side was becoming fuller every day, and mine was thinning out. Hopefully, Daddy would let us go shopping for new school clothes soon. When I grew up, I would have my own money instead of a husband who was in charge of that sort of thing.

Momma filled our plates with pot roast as Daddy stomped his boots on the back porch to loosen the grass and dirt.

"Pour the tea, Gracie," Momma said. She ignored Daddy.

My stomach no longer felt hungry. Abby pulled an extra chair up and plopped Patti down at the table. "Patti needs a plate," she said.

"Not this time," Momma said. "She can sit there quietly."

Abby sulked a little but went along with it.

Daddy washed his hands and was the first to start eating. He repeated something funny his tractor driver had said, and Momma grinned. Maybe she wouldn't make a federal case out of Daddy mowing the grass on Sunday.

"When does school start, Grace?" he asked.

"Right after Labor Day," I said, surprised that Daddy was talking like a regular person, even if it was about school. "And I could really use some new school clothes. Everything I have is too little."

Daddy nodded like he was thinking about it, but everything was ruined when Momma remembered about the ditch.

"Lee, I wish you wouldn't mow on Sunday. Everyone can see you out there, plus you still need to take it easy." Momma pulled the rolls out of the oven and dropped the pan with a clatter on the stove. On Sunday, Momma usually forgot the rolls until they were almost burnt, and we were halfway through eating. Today, she remembered on time.

He glared at her. So did I. Everything had been going so well.

"Let's see if I can help you understand," Daddy said. "Number one, someone has to mow it, and you sure won't. Number two, I feel fine, so stop nagging my ass. And, number three, why you give a shit what anyone around here thinks is beyond me."

Momma drank a sip of tea. She didn't respond and ate not one bite of pot roast.

"Well, I have some news," I said, after a period of prickly silence. I almost forgot my announcement. Daddy stopped chewing and slanted one eyebrow in my direction. In that instant, as I stared at the miniscule dab of butter on his bottom lip, I realized he wouldn't appreciate my newsflash. Not in the least.

"What, Gracie? Tell us!" Abby asked. At least she was interested.

116

"Brother Brown is coming for supper Friday night." I spoke in my most upbeat tone, hoping my enthusiasm would be contagious. Instead, my words hung over the table, almost echoing.

"Cool," Abby said. She offered a sliver of meat to Lucky, who was trolling underneath the table.

"What?" Momma said, emphasizing the "t" like it was an extra syllable. I imagined she of all people would be excited. She was always talking to her friend Maggie about dinner parties and new recipes, and how she wished she had a reason to use the good china. "There was a time Lee and I used to have friends over every weekend," she had said to her just last week. "He would dress nice and bring me flowers for the table, and it was all very elegant and romantic." Apparently, Brother Brown wasn't the guest she had in mind.

Daddy's nostrils flared. He held his fork above his plate, and I worried he might stab me with it. The skin between his cheeks and jaws pulsed as he swallowed.

I began to blabber. To dance around my announcement. To say anything to stall the explosion sure to come. "You said I could invite a friend, so I asked Brother Brown. He eats with the Davidsons all the time, and even Nana has invited him over before. I thought we should do it. It's our turn."

"Well, you can damn well un-invite him." Daddy spat each word through clenched teeth. He barely moved his lips. If he hadn't been a farmer, he could have worked as a ventriloquist, although ventriloquists probably needed to be happy.

"That would be rude!" I yelled.

"Gracie, I said you could invite a friend. Brother Brown is not a friend. He's our preacher." Momma spoke scary-quiet and shoved her pot roast away. She dug into her bowl of vanilla pudding, skipping her healthy food altogether.

"He said you can cook whatever you want. He isn't a picky eater, but he doesn't like liver. Isn't that interesting? He's the only adult I've ever known who doesn't like liver. I think that's so curious." I couldn't stop the vomit of nervous words gushing from my mouth.

Momma rubbed the space between her eyes. Daddy flushed ruddy and speared his fork into his dinner roll. It stood straight up.

"Lee, don't worry, I'll take care of it," Momma said, touching his wrist. "Gracie. Go to your room," she said.

"Why?"

"Just go!"

"Now!" they both yelled at the same time.

I ran to my room and crawled underneath the bed, shoving aside board games and books and other junk that, over time, got pushed under there. Flat on my back, I lay and stared at the wooden slats holding my mattress in place. One slat was split, a deep crack running half the length of the board. It was my fault, the crack, because I liked to jump on the bed even though Momma told me not to. That crack was mine. No one in the world, not even Abby or Momma, knew it existed. I knew if I kept jumping on the bed, the slat would eventually break, and my bed would be saggy and lumpy. But I didn't care. I didn't care about anything.

A pencil practically jumped into my hand, so I wrote "Gracie was here" on the slat. My handwriting looked a little sloppy upside down, but it was readable. I jammed the pencil into the deep split in the wood and bent it, snapping it firmly to the side. The splintering-shattering-cracking feeling felt good in my hand, but then I felt bad to have ruined a perfectly good pencil with a like-new eraser.

In the kitchen on the other side of the bedroom wall, I heard the muffled sounds of Momma and Daddy talking, not really yelling, but using louder than regular voices. I shut my eyes and imagined breathing in the musty particles that had lived under my bed for years, a whole nasty world of molecules that floated into my nose and settled into my lungs, giving me an instant and horrible disease. Incurable even.

"Can we come under there with you?" Abby poked her head underneath my bed. She dragged Patti with her, so her face appeared too, like a real person. Patti's hard marble eyes blinked but not in sync. God, I hated that creepy doll.

"Go away. I need to be alone." Abby crawled underneath her own bed but left Patti lying in the middle of the room.

Abby was the only person who really knew what life was like in our house, and I shouldn't have been mean to her. But I couldn't take it back. Words could never be taken back. As hard as I tried, thoughts could never be un-thought. "I'm sorry, Abby. I didn't mean to yell at you," I said.

"It's okay," she said, but she sounded sad.

What little pot roast I managed to eat swam in a lump all the way from my stomach to the back of my throat. I felt feverish and chilled all at the same time. I closed my eyes and waited to die. Momma and Daddy would be sorry then.

I could barely breathe. There was no real reason for me to suffocate, other than the overall unfairness of life that strangled me in my own home.

I stared at the crack in the wooden slat above me and waited.

I never died, but I stayed under there a long time.

Chapter Eighteen

Before Momma had the chance to cancel supper with Brother Brown, Mrs. Brown called our house to gush over the invitation. Momma stammered and said, "You're so welcome" and never got up the courage to un-invite them.

I was listening on the hallway extension, and if I hadn't heard Mrs. Brown say, "This is Velveeta Brown calling," I would not have recognized her voice. She sounded like she was smiling a big toothy smile, the sort that could transform someone's entire spirit from a sourpuss to happy-go-lucky.

Daddy was none too pleased about the whole thing and announced he wouldn't be home on Friday in time for supper with Brother Brown. Momma threw a hissy fit and said it wouldn't kill him to be sober and pleasant for one night. She didn't take a stand often, but when she did, Daddy usually went along with it. I was skeptical that he would join us and had a bad feeling in my stomach.

Even though I originally got in trouble for inviting Brother Brown, as Friday approached, Momma grew more and more excited. She cleaned and wiped down the cabinets with soapy water and made Abby and me pick up our bedrooms.

"Momma, you act like the President of the United States is coming for supper. It's only Brother Brown," I said when she told me to sweep the back porch.

"We want to make a nice impression."

After poring over recipe books for three days, Momma announced her menu—pepper steak, twice-baked potatoes, and green beans almondine. Thursday afternoon, she drove all the way to the big grocery store in West Memphis for a special loaf of bread, and instead of our regular lettuce salad, this morning she made a strange concoction with lime gelatin, whipped cream, apples, and pecans.

"You aren't going to make Brother Brown eat that, are you?" I asked. It didn't look very appetizing.

"Gracie, don't be so negative. It will be delicious, you'll see." Momma called it "Pecan Delight Whipped Salad," but it didn't look like a salad at all. She partially redeemed herself by making Maggie's famous pineapple upside-down cake for dessert. The cake looked delicious and filled the whole house with a sugary smell. I felt certain dessert would be the best part of the meal. With a warning not to touch the cake, Momma left it to cool on the side buffet while she changed clothes.

The dining room table looked like it had been set for Christmas dinner. She had used the good dishes and fancy glasses, and the forks and knives were placed like the diagram in her cookbook. As I walked around the table and thought about the fancy meal that was soon to happen, a brilliant idea came to me. That's how my most excellent ideas always happened, when my mind wasn't trying to come up with any notions at all.

I walked into the kitchen and opened the special cabinet where Daddy kept his whiskey.

"What are you doing, Gracie?" Abby asked. She sat at the kitchen table coloring.

"Shhhh. Helping Daddy. He just doesn't know it," I said. "Keep a lookout for me, okay?" One by one, I pulled out the bottles, unscrewed lids, poured smelly liquid into the kitchen sink and replenished each bottle with tap water, making sure to refill to the same level. I left a bit of whiskey in the bottom of each to add color. Then I found Daddy's beer in the side door of the icebox, beside the ketchup and mustard. I poured seven bottles of beer down the sink drain too, and buried the empties in the bottom of the trashcan on the back porch. A squirt of dishwashing liquid mixed with hot water cleared the sink of any lingering odor. This simple solution would solve all our problems. I couldn't believe I hadn't thought of it sooner.

***

Brother Brown looked different, wearing street clothes and no church hat. Mrs. Brown wore a bright orange dress that tied at the waist. It was the first time I'd ever seen her wear a color, something other than gray or brown or navy blue. Momma offered iced tea and made excuses for Daddy, saying he was still working. "I'm sure he'll be along soon," she said.

"Oh, I've been looking forward to meeting him," Mrs. Brown nodded and smiled, and I noticed her straight teeth. She should show her teeth more often.

"I've heard a lot about Lee," Brother Brown said. I didn't think he meant anything bad by it, but Momma gave me a dirty look as she placed the cheese log on the dining room table. I sat quietly in my chair and listened while the adults talked about all sorts of topics, including how nice the new housing development looked on the other side of town. Mrs. Brown said her sister lived in one of those houses. I didn't know she had a sister.

They discussed the Olympics, which had only started a few days ago. "You should wait and talk about this when Daddy gets here," I said. "He loves the Olympics. Right, Momma?" I wasn't telling a joke, but everyone laughed like I had said the funniest thing ever and then kept right on talking as though I had said nothing at all. They'd understand later when Daddy came home and talked non-stop about cotton farming. Brother Brown bragged on a swimmer who had won a bunch of gold medals. I was shocked to learn that Brother Brown had interests beyond Boon Chapel. In fact, Boon Chapel never came up.

After an hour of making small talk and trying to stall for Daddy, Momma declared we would go ahead and eat without him. "I can't imagine what's keeping Lee," she said, looking out the dining room window.

I could, but I kept quiet.

"I hope he hasn't gotten sick again," Momma said.

Oh, brother.

"How's he doing since his surgery?" Mrs. Brown asked. She added a bunch of salt to her food without tasting it first. Momma didn't like it when we salted without tasting, but she didn't seem to notice what Mrs. Brown was doing.

"He's much better. The doctor got it all," Momma said. She spoke in a hushed tone, almost whispering it, but not quite. I didn't know why everything had to be a secret.

"Thank the Lord," Mrs. Brown said.

"Gracie, would you like to bless the food?" Momma asked.

"Me?" Unless it was Christmas, we never blessed the food at our house, and even then, Nana or Papa Pete did it. I wondered if Momma would have been so gung ho to pray had Daddy been home. Everyone bowed their heads like I was automatically going to agree, so I started in with "God is great. God is good. Let us thank Him for our food." I was glad I had that little jewel stuck in the back of my mind and didn't have to make something up. Even so, the house seemed oddly silent as I heard my tongue-tied words float over the table spread with Momma's fancy supper.

Just as everyone began eating and Mrs. Brown said, "Anne, you must give me this salad recipe," Daddy turned onto the driveway, slinging gravel.

"Oh, good. There's Lee." Momma jumped to greet Daddy, but her face had turned as minty green as the pecan whip salad. Abby and I exchanged glances. Lucky raced to the back door and began barking and scratching near the doorknob.

I wanted to warn Brother Brown. I wanted to say to Mrs. Brown, "Now, get prepared for whatever mood walks through that door." But I sat there staring at my plate and counting inside my head. *One Mississippi...*

After twelve Mississippis, Daddy walked into the kitchen, took off his John Deere cap, and staggered into the dining room, giving a little nod to Brother Brown, who stood to shake his hand.

"Harold, he's filthy. Let him wash up first," Momma said. "Honey, go wash up. We just started, but you can catch up."

Harold? Brother Brown's name was Harold? And Honey? Since when did Momma call Daddy, "honey?" When Daddy passed behind my chair on the way to the bathroom, I caught a whiff of whiskey. Or maybe I imagined it, because the unpleasant smell was still inside my nose from pouring it down the drain.

Mrs. Brown looked like she was trying to chew each bite of food twenty-five times, not because the steak was tough, because it wasn't, but probably because she was trying to give Daddy time to join us before she cleaned her plate. A preacher's wife was required to be polite that way.

"So, Abby, I understand you went to church camp recently. I've already heard a little from Grace about it. What did you think?" Brother Brown asked.

"I liked it pretty good. Especially when we sneaked off and skipped preaching." Abby clasped her hand over her mouth the minute the words came out.

"Abby!" I yelled.

"Well, that sounds like an interesting story," Momma said. "Is there something you girls need to confess, Grace?" Momma smiled and looked from Abby to me. I knew if Brother Brown hadn't been sitting at our table, she wouldn't have been smiling at all. And like in the movies when a bell or a noise interrupts a tense scene, something happened to take the attention from Abby and me.

A gigantic crashing noise came from the direction of Daddy's bathroom. It was so loud that everyone's shoulders cringed at the same time, and Mrs. Brown said, "Mercy sakes, what was that?"

I reached the bathroom first, before anyone else moved. Daddy lay in a pile on the tile floor, partially tangled in the shower rod and curtain he had lugged down with him. He wasn't moving. Steam filled the room and fogged the mirror above the sink. Momma's can of hairspray lay on the floor. Water continued to spray from the shower and splatter on the wall and into the floor beside Daddy's wet head.

Momma shoved me from the doorway. At first, I thought Daddy was dead, but he wasn't. He had been knocked out cold. The goose egg on his forehead turned purple immediately. Brother Brown was the unfortunate person who had to assist with moving Daddy's naked drunken body.

Mrs. Brown herded Abby and me toward the bedroom, as though she might be able to protect us or distract us or help us not see. "Girls, why don't you show me your bedroom?"

"Well, it isn't very exciting," I said. I was glad we had cleaned our room, even though all we did was shove everything underneath our beds.

"Do you want to play Operation?" Abby asked, pulling Mrs. Brown toward the messy closet.

"Abby, Mrs. Brown doesn't want to play a board game with us," I said. "She only came for supper."

"Abby, why don't you show me your doll instead?" Mrs. Brown suggested, nodding toward Abby's bed, where Patti sat propped on a pillow, wearing my too-short church dress from last Sunday.

"Her name is Patti," Abby said. "We're twins."

I rolled my eyes and pinched the space between my eyes. There was no way Lisa Marie Presley had to deal with such craziness.

"I can certainly see the resemblance," Mrs. Brown said. She sat beside the silly doll, struck up a conversation with Patti like she was our real sister, and overall acted pretty nice, considering Daddy was sprawled out naked in the bathroom down the hallway. When Brother Brown peeked into our bedroom, the whole night began to seem unreal—Brother Brown standing in our house, Mrs. Brown talking to Patti—and the entire disaster was my fault.

Chapter Nineteen

The morning was cold. Twenty degrees colder than yesterday, Miss Lamb said. Even though Mr. Mooney had turned on the radiators, the school felt chilly inside, and the surface of my desk was cold to the touch. I pulled my sweater tighter around my neck. Beyond the window, the trees on the playground blazed with color. Past the playground, Mr. Barns's cotton field was beginning to turn white, as bolls had begun to split open. October was one of the best months of the year. "It's the one time of year I put money in the bank instead of taking it out," Daddy said during supper last night and almost even smiled. That was the case during good years anyway, and this year's crop was good.

I stared at the blank paper on my desk and held my pencil at the spot I would write the first word, but I couldn't think what that word might be. Not yet. While everyone around me scribbled, Miss Lamb began stapling construction paper pumpkins in the middle of the front bulletin board. Her stapler made a *ka-thunk ka-thunk ka-thunking* noise that bored into my head.

"What I Did on My Summer Vacation," that was the essay topic Miss Lamb had assigned. It would have been a better topic if she'd assigned it on the first day of school when our memories were fresh with trips to the library and riding bicycles until dusk. Summer seemed like forever ago, and mine ended with a disaster. I stared at the brilliant orange tree in the middle of the schoolyard and thought about Daddy's naked episode in front of Brother and Mrs. Brown.

At first, I had been sure Daddy was dead on the floor of the bathroom. Turned out he was drunk and dehydrated. Dr. Fairley made a house call and lectured him about the risks of combining whiskey with the strong medicine he was taking. I heard the whole conversation through the vent in our bedroom closet. Once Momma realized Daddy would live, she lit into him like a hornet. They yelled at each other for an entire night while Abby and I hid underneath her bed with blankets and pillows and a flashlight for seeing. We pretended to be camping while a booming thunderstorm moving overhead, the sort that brought hail and tornadoes.

Eventually Momma's yelling turned to crying. Niagara Falls crying. She cried so much, we skipped church on Sunday morning. I was relieved we didn't have to see Brother Brown anyway and wondered if we would be better off changing churches. By Sunday afternoon, Daddy was making promises. He promised to take better care of himself and take his medicine and not work so hard and cut back on his drinking and a whole bunch of other things I knew would never happen. By the time he discovered I had poured his whiskey and beer down the sink, I had completely forgotten about it.

"GROUNDED." I wrote the words across the top of my notebook paper in large block letters and underlined it twice. That's what I was. I'd been grounded since Labor Day when I was dragged into the kitchen and forced to sit at the table while Momma lectured me on not touching things that didn't belong to me. Daddy shouted at me and called me a lying thief. I may have been a thief in the strictest sense of the word, but I hadn't lied about anything. When he said, "Explain yourself young lady," my answer was easy.

"I want you to stop drinking so much."

For a split second, Daddy seemed sad, like he knew I was right, but he could never give up the whiskey he loved more than us. He kicked a chair into the wall and yanked a sheet of paper from his pocket. "This is what you owe me," he shouted, flipping the paper onto the table. The page, ripped from the small notepad Momma kept next to the phone, was a detailed bill totaling five dollars and thirty-five cents for the "damages" I had caused when I threw away his liquor. I picked at the scruffy torn edge and wondered if there was an official name for those tiny bits of frayed paper that bugged me so much, especially when they scattered inside my notebook.

Momma eventually said I was grounded which was no big surprise. Parents always threw grounding on top of a punishment like a final exclamation point. I asked for how long, and Daddy said, "Forever." No matter. A regular day living in the boring country was not much different than being grounded. When Momma and Daddy ran out of things to yell about, I was sent to my room to think about what I had done.

I pulled my savings envelope from inside my jewelry box and stared inside it. I didn't have much money, only a few dollar bills from my birthday money and loose change I had found underneath the couch cushions and floor mats in the back seat of the car. Although Daddy would have probably disagreed, found coins were not considered stolen because of the "finders keepers" rule we lived by in our house—even Momma, who kept all the coins she found in the bottom of the washing machine. I dumped the contents on my bed. There was barely enough.

I decided to make up my own bill—a list of all the damages Daddy had caused me in my ten years—drinking and yelling and being in a constant rotten mood and calling me bad names that no daughter should ever hear from her own Daddy. Assigning dollar amounts for each item stumped me though. Any amount sounded ridiculous, too much yet not enough. I left the total blank but knew it had to be a trillion times more than five dollars and thirty-five cents. When I folded it and placed it in my jewelry box, underneath my special Boon Chapel marble, I felt better. Like I had moved the problem somewhere else.

After everyone went to sleep, I grabbed the money I had counted out, tiptoed into the kitchen and wrote Daddy a note.

> Dear Daddy,
>   Here is the money I owe you. I'm sorry I made you
> so mad, but I stand by my reason.
> Your daughter,
> Gracie

It was short, simple, and written straight across the page with no erasing. I left it on the kitchen table so he would see it first thing when he ate his cereal. I stacked the money neatly, paying him back mostly in quarters, dimes, nickels, and a bunch of pennies.

***

So far, fourth grade had been good. First of all, my best friend, Janice, was wearing the same short, pixie haircut Lucille cursed me with at the first of summer. Hers was white blonde, because that was her natural hair color, but otherwise, we were like twins. In fact, most of the girls in my class got that haircut over the summer. Momma was right about it being the latest style.

The second most interesting thing about fourth grade was my teacher, Miss Lamb. She was not only brand new to our school, but it was her first year of ever being a teacher. Nothing about her fit at Savage Crossing Elementary School. She wore tight, black skirts that made it difficult for her to sit, so she usually leaned against the front of her desk most of the day. When she walked to the office to copy worksheets, her black patent high heels tapped and echoed along the hallway. Her short, wavy hair, styled like Elizabeth Taylor's, was much too glamorous for teaching school, but the oddest thing of all was her eyes. She had one green eye and one blue eye.

Having a new teacher came with definite benefits. On day one, when Miss Lamb did the first roll call of the school year, she announced our last names only and told us to sit wherever we liked. What a relief to not hear Eudora, my horrible middle name, even once. I tried to estimate how many hours I had wasted during the summer worrying about it. And not sitting in alphabetical order? I was certain this was some sort of first day of school miracle, or a sign that she had no idea what a teacher was supposed to do. Since that day, we had changed seats a lot. She was big on moving the desks around and rearranging the classroom. That was certainly nothing like third grade where I sat in the exact same desk and stared at the head of the exact same classmate the entire year.

When the final bell rang, Miss Lamb told us to finish our essays at home. Since I hadn't started mine, I'd have a lot to do. I waited for Abby by the big tree near the cafeteria like Momma told me to do. She strolled around the corner snail slow, swinging her book satchel as if she had all the time in the world. The buses were lined up, ready to go with engines roaring and smoke billowing from the tailpipes. Momma would be mad if we missed it. "Hurry up!" I yelled to her when she got within shouting distance. Finally, she got it in gear and ran the rest of the way.

Unfortunately, nothing had changed about the school bus since last year. Riding the school bus was one of the worst things about school. In the morning, Abby and I were picked up super early, before sunrise even. The bus route was long and spread along all the dirt roads in the county. By the time Mr. Jackson pulled into the schoolyard, we had been riding on the bus at least an hour. The end of the day was even worse. The same group of morning kids took up twice the bus space in the afternoon. After being contained all day inside a classroom, everyone expanded to the point of nearly bursting. Shirttails flapped untucked, shoe laces dragged untied, notebook pages flew into the aisle. And usually before Abby and I got home, someone threw a paper airplane into Mr. Jackson's head, or a fight broke out in the back, causing him to pull off the highway and lecture us.

***

I had a whole page of long math problems to do. Math was the only subject that didn't come easy to me. After ten minutes and a lot of erasing, I yelled, "I hate math!" then slammed my book shut and threw my pencil across the den, hitting the paneled wall above the television.

"Daddy can help you when he gets home," Momma yelled from the kitchen. "And stop throwing things."

"I don't want Daddy to help me!" I yelled. I didn't want his help, but I needed it. Daddy could solve confusing problems with the same ease as any schoolteacher. Maybe better. He was a numbers man. I was not a numbers girl. I hated word problems most of all and saw no use for such baloney.

I shoved my math worksheet back inside my notebook and began to work on my "What I Did on My Summer Vacation" assignment. Turning to a clean sheet of paper, I stared at the ceiling and thought about all the events of the past summer. How much should I tell? What should I leave out?

I began to write. One sentence turned into a paragraph. One paragraph turned into two. I didn't stop writing until I finished. When I proofread it, I decided it was at least worth a B+. Maybe even an A. My summer, filled with getting baptized, going to church camp, a possible suicide, and Daddy spending five days in the hospital with Elvis, turned out to be more interesting than I had remembered.

After supper, Daddy agreed to help me with math. We sat at the kitchen table with our heads so close together I could smell the cigarette smoke on his breath. He worked the first problem, writing each step on a separate line, pausing after each to ask if I understood. And so far, when Daddy explained it, I did.

Daddy was so smart and confident in his ability to get the correct answers that he didn't use a pencil or eraser. Instead, he used his fancy ballpoint pen, the same one he used every Friday to sign payroll checks. I bet if I lined all the pencil erasers I'd used up working math problems, they would stretch from our back door to the edge of the cotton field.

"Now you work the next one," he said.

I tried but got flustered, and the whole answer was wrong from step one. He made me nervous even though he wasn't trying to.

"This is easy. Why can't you understand it?" His hazel eyes stared at my hazel eyes, and I sensed his frustration. It was impossible for me to think around him. My brain was trained to be ready and on alert, in case he got mad about something.

I took a deep breath. "I just don't. I guess I take after Momma. Seriously, Daddy, why would I ever need to know the exact time two trains would meet if one left Chicago traveling sixty miles an hour and another left New York traveling eighty miles an hour?" Grown-ups designed ridiculous questions to torture us in school.

"Grace, it's an example. A way to make you think. You aren't trying. Break it down, and think about what the question is asking. It's common sense." He wrote it out a different way, his numbers drawn to scale like artwork. I watched the way his fingers moved and could almost see his mind work as he thought of other ways to explain it.

"I am trying, I promise." And I was. "Do you use math on the farm?"

"Every day. I calculate the amount of seed and chemicals to buy. Everything is based on acres. Expenses are allocated to different fields, different crops." He got excited talking about it so I asked him more questions, and he talked to me longer than ever. Daddy helped me finish the entire math assignment, and I was relieved to know I would get a good grade on it. I even understood it too.

Chapter Twenty

At exactly three thirty-seven p.m. on October third, my piano-playing future came to a screeching halt when Mrs. Allard rapped my knuckles with the ruler she kept in her lap. I yanked my hands from the keyboard and rubbed my fingers. Tears stung my eyes, but I kept quiet. "You showed such promise when you began on this musical journey, but your enthusiasm has waned."

No joke, I thought. I always have to keep one eye on that horrid ruler.

Every Tuesday after school, she and I sat thigh-to-thigh on the piano bench in the music room, while I stumbled through whichever song I'd been assigned, and she shook her head, grumbled, and usually whacked my fingers with a ruler at least once. "Did you practice at all since I saw you last week?" she asked. When she turned and stared at me, her pointy nose almost touched my ear. She always wore black as though she dressed for Halloween year round. Or a funeral. Someone always ready for a funeral was not someone I wanted to be around. She was skinny and stern and everything about her was severe from her chiseled cheekbones to the straight part in the center of her black hair.

"Yes, ma'am. I practiced a lot!"

"Let me play it for you so you can hear what it should sound like," she said as she moved closer to the center of the bench, and I scooted to the very edge. She played the song correctly while I tried to balance myself and not fall to the floor. The bench vibrated as she pounded the keys. "Are you watching my fingers, Grace?" I glanced at her hands. Her wedding ring sparkled, and I wondered what man would marry her and why.

"Yes, ma'am," I said again even though mostly I stared at the clock above the piano.

Abby snickered. She stood at the front of the room and drew a flower on the chalkboard while waiting her turn. I was certain Abby had no worries, because she had memorized last week's song in only a day or two. And I knew my song okay too, but no matter how well I played at home, I couldn't replicate it during official lesson time. Mrs. Allard made me nervous, and she smelled of *les oeufs*—that's eggs in French.

The clock must have been broken. Stuck at three thirty-seven. Time had frozen, and I was trapped at my evil piano lesson forever. Certainly more than seven minutes had passed since my lesson began. When Mrs. Allard caught me glancing at my Cinderella watch, she said in a calm voice, "This lesson is over. Trade places with your sister and stop wasting my time. I can only teach those who want to be taught."

That was fine by me. Anyone who used a ruler to get her point across was a terrible teacher in my opinion. I took a seat in the corner and pulled my new library book from my satchel. I seriously doubted Nancy Drew took piano lessons, but if she did, her teacher was lovely and encouraging and wore a flowered dress and probably offered a homemade treat beforehand, because Nancy was famished from spending all day in school.

I began reading. I tried to block out the sounds of the piano, but it was impossible not to hear. Abby played through her entire song without stopping, and even though she missed a few notes here and there, Mrs. Allard bragged and bragged and bragged on her effort until I wanted to puke.

While I sat and read, the clock hanging above the piano sped right up and Abby's lesson was over in five seconds. Time always worked against me, either dragging at church or during my piano lesson, yet blinking by when I was doing something fun like riding my bike or reading.

Mrs. Allard put five silver stars across the top of Abby's sheet music and hugged her stiffly around the shoulders, which was taking it a bit far. She'd never hugged either of us before. "You did a great job Miss Abby," she said.

Abby grinned and looked at me, and I knew she desperately wanted to stick her tongue out but held it inside. Nah-nah-na-nah-na. I heard her even though she didn't say it.

Mrs. Allard walked over to me, and I looked everywhere other than in her eyes. "Before your lesson next week, you need to do some serious soul searching, and try to determine why you want to continue with piano lessons. Piano playing is not for everyone. I think you should either put your whole heart into it, or concentrate on something more suitable. All right?"

"Yes, ma'am." I was ready to quit right then, leave my piano book on the bench and never look back, but I crammed the music and library book into my bag and left. I ran all the way to Momma's car parked beside the cafeteria.

"You're finished really early," Momma said as I opened the back door. She laid her magazine on the seat and glanced at the dashboard clock. I slumped into the back seat and shoved my bag into the floor at my feet.

"Yeah," I said.

Abby skipped along the sidewalk, swinging her bag. I wanted to trade places with her, just for five minutes, to know what it felt like to not have a single concern.

"Gracie got kicked out of piano," Abby announced before we had even backed from the parking lot.

"I did not!" I wanted to kill her and silence her blabbermouth forever.

Momma stared at me in the rearview mirror. "What happened?"

"Well, she—" Abby began, but Momma cut her off.

"I prefer to hear from Gracie, please."

"Mrs. Allard didn't like the way I played my song today and told me I needed to search my soul for the reason my piano playing is atrocious. Something like that, only she didn't use the word atrocious, I added that since it's one of my bonus spelling words this week."

"And why do you think that is?" Momma asked. She sounded sympathetic, at least, but a bit disappointed. Momma loved playing the piano. She was good at it and could play any song in any book without practicing.

135

"Because I'd rather do something else, like play outside or read or learn to speak French. Soon I'll be old enough to try out for the basketball team or the cheerleading squad. Piano playing is really a waste of Daddy's money if you think about it. And I can't afford to get another bill from him."

Momma gave me a look like she thought I was being a smart mouth but surprised me by agreeing I shouldn't waste Daddy's money. As we drove through town, nothing more was said about my piano playing. Even Abby was quiet and still with her head leaning against the window. The trees above Main Street touched in the center, forming a canopy, bright orange and red, and thick enough for squirrels to walk across without ever touching the ground. I wanted to be a squirrel or a bird, living in a nest high above town, seeing everything, but being involved in nothing. Maybe Mrs. Allard was right. Piano playing wasn't for me, and that was okay.

When we got home, Momma's plan became clear when she removed the chore chart from the refrigerator door and added another chore right below brush teeth. Practice piano one hour. One hour every day! Instead of wasting Daddy's money by going to my piano lesson unprepared, I would make good use of his money by becoming the grandest pianist ever.

"Every day? You've got to be kidding me."

She wasn't kidding. She was serious enough that she delayed cooking super while I wrote an apology letter to Mrs. Allard on Momma's best stationery. Momma hovered over my shoulder to make sure I said all the right things, mainly, I would try harder to do my best and not waste her time.

What about my time? My time meant nothing.

She handed me a matching envelope and told me to write "Mrs. Allard" on the front like I couldn't figure that out for myself. "Give it to her tomorrow before the first bell rings. Put it in her hand," Momma said.

Knowing I had years of piano playing ahead of me was a horrible, depressing feeling. Something to dread for the rest of my life. I would never make my kids take piano lessons, not that I would be having kids because of the whole never-getting-married thing. Right then, as I stuffed my letter into the fancy envelope, I vowed to always remember how bad it felt to be bossed around from sunup to sundown. I would not be that kind of adult, cross my heart and hope to die right in the kitchen.

Momma made pork chops, which I didn't much like. Of course, after the day I'd had, I wasn't expecting spaghetti or cheese pizza or anything delicious. And English peas from a can? Yuck. The perfect vegetable for a perfectly dreadful day. Daddy kicked off his boots on the back porch and didn't mess up the kitchen floor, which was a good thing given Momma's awful mood. Abby said since she wasn't hungry for pork chops, Patti could have hers. She plopped Patti in her chair and both eyes popped open. Then, I swear, she winked at me. Momma said a bad word and banished Patti to our bedroom for all future meals. Abby was told to sit and eat every bite of her pork chop and not say a word. I couldn't wait to go to bed and start over tomorrow, even if I had to apologize to Mrs. Allard.

Once we all gathered around the table, Momma began hinting about my piano lesson problem, saying things like, "You'll feel better once you give that letter to Mrs. Allard," and "Maybe she'll let you make up the time you missed today," until finally, Daddy asked her why she was talking in code.

"Just say whatever you're trying to say, Anne," he said.

"Maybe Grace should tell you," she said.

The one thing I didn't need was a fight with Daddy. I kept my mouth shut and picked at my food. I slipped a few peas onto the floor without anyone noticing. Lucky ate them in one noiseless lick.

"Well, someone needs to tell me," he said, flipping over the newspaper he'd been skimming. And then it began. Momma relayed every detail about how I wasn't doing well in piano, and how I had gotten into trouble during my lesson. She pulled the chore chart from the icebox door and announced I now had five extra hours of weekly piano practice to worry with, in addition to my Saturday practice. "Gracie will be apologizing to Mrs. Allard first thing in the morning," she said as she slammed the chart onto the kitchen table.

My eyes teared. I felt Daddy staring at me, but I concentrated on the pork chop on my plate. I wasn't used to Momma making me feel so bad.

137

Daddy leaned his chair onto its back legs, opened the icebox and reached inside. He grabbed the beer closest to him, and I noticed his shelf had been restocked with bottles. My hands clinched as I prepared for his tirade about wasting hard-earned money and being lazy and not obeying authority figures. Abby swallowed so loudly I heard her. Daddy opened the bottle and took a long drink. When he finally spoke, he sounded calm.

Eerily calm.

"So, Grace, you don't like piano?"

"No, sir."

He nodded his head as though he studied the situation. He pressed his full lips together, but he didn't look mad. His mad face had been burned into my memory, and this wasn't it. When he spooned a bite of peas into his mouth and swallowed, there were no throbbing veins or anything.

"Why don't you like it?" he asked, looking at me and waiting for my answer as though regular, normal conversations were typical for us.

He was torturing me. That was it. Instead of getting right on with my punishment, he was building me up to trap me in my own reasoning. Was it possible to be double grounded?

"Everything about it is hard for me. I can't keep all those notes in my mind, and once I learn one song, Mrs. Allard moves on to a harder song. And she expects me to memorize it the very next week. Nothing about it is fun. She makes me so nervous. When I mess up, she whacks me across the hands with her wooden ruler. And she smells weird too." I took a deep breath.

Daddy laughed.

Momma smacked him on the arm. "I really doubt she whacks you with a ruler," Momma said.

"Oh, yes, she does," Abby piped in.

"If you don't like it, then don't waste your time taking lessons," Daddy said. "Find something else you'd rather do. It doesn't matter to me."

What?

We were living in an alternate universe where Momma had turned into Daddy, and Daddy had turned into Momma. I once saw something similar on the *Twilight Zone*. Or maybe I had fallen and smacked my

138

head during P.E., and now I was in a coma and everything was a bizarre dream. Daddy's solution about quitting piano lessons was the easy one, the one I wanted to hear, but for some strange reason, I didn't think it was the right one.

Momma pushed back her chair and said, "Well, that's just fine!" Her ears turned red and she began clearing the table even though Daddy was still eating. She ranted on and on about how she does her best to teach us to be upstanding people, yet Daddy erases everything in one minute.

He shook his head and brushed her off with a wave of his hand. "I don't have time to listen to this," Daddy said.

The days were growing shorter and shorter, and darkness seemed to rush up and surprise us right after supper. With harvest coming on, Daddy had lots of work to do and went back to the fields. Momma, who was in a sick-of-everyone mood, disappeared into her bedroom to read. "Don't knock on my door unless the house is on fire," she said.

She didn't have to worry about me bothering her. I grabbed the flashlight and slipped out the back door. With Abby taking one of her famously long baths that always began with bubbles and ended with an ocean of water on the floor, it was the perfect time for me to do some exploring.

A bright moon lit the way as I ran along the yellow-dashed line in the center of the road. No cars. No sounds other than frogs. When I stepped onto the back porch of the gray house, the floor creaked, but I kept going. I opened the kitchen door and stepped inside.

With the flashlight beam pointed on the floor, I walked through the kitchen, into the hallway and to the front room I had observed so many times from the front porch windows. Someone had been there. The couch and chairs were now covered with white sheets. I moved the light along the bookshelf and scanned the titles. Mostly boring-looking books. History. Shakespeare. A leather bound *Atlas of the World* that was old and crumbly and took up half a shelf. Along the bottom, I saw an entire collection of *World Book Encyclopedias*. To be able to look something up whenever a question popped into my head—what must that be like? Near the bookshelves, a long sturdy desk was empty except for a lamp and a cup of pencils sharpened to perfect points. I became so wrapped up in the idea of having my very own library with a quiet place to sit and do my homework that I forgot where I was and what I was doing. When I saw someone across the room, I screamed at my ghostly reflection in the mirror. I looked like the thief Daddy accused me of being not that long ago.

Off the library, there was a bedroom not much bigger than the room Abby and I shared. I sat on the edge of the bed and moved the flashlight around the room from corner to corner. There was a trunk against the wall and a heavy dresser covered with black and white photos. I lay back on the bed. The bedspread was pale blue or white, I couldn't tell in the darkness, and the mattress felt lumpy. Or maybe a slat was broken like mine. I closed my eyes and pretended to be Goldilocks. This bed felt too soft. Outside the window, two cats began fighting, my cue to leave. I hated that noise worse than anything, those sickening mewing and hissing sounds like one might kill the other. I stood and smoothed away the imprint of my body. I made it home as Abby was draining the tub.

Chapter Twenty-One

I took a shortcut through the second-grade playground and headed straight to the music room. The wind was blowing hard, picking up leaves and twisting them all around my feet. I wished I'd worn a heavy coat like Momma said. Instead, I wore my windbreaker, which did nothing to keep me warm. Piano music drifted from Mrs. Allard's classroom and found me on the sidewalk well before I reached the door. It was a slow song that reminded me of the background music in a depressing movie. When I peeked through the square window in the center of the door, I saw her playing, her feet pumping the pedals and her wrists tilted in the graceful position I could never master. With the rhythm of the song, she moved her head side to side. She closed her eyes and smiled as though she had a special secret. Music didn't possess me like it possessed her. In the minute or two I watched, I came to understand I would never play music that way. But I decided I would try harder.

When the bell rang across the playground, Mrs. Allard shook her head as though waking from a trance. She looked sad, like the best part of her day had ended.

I knocked. She motioned me inside and didn't seem upset with me anymore. She even put her arm around my shoulder and walked me toward her desk. She smelled nice and fresh and clean.

"I wrote you this letter," I said pulling it from inside the pocket of my book bag. "It's an apology letter." I placed it in her hand like Momma said.

"Thank you, Grace." She unfolded it.

"It says I will try to do better and not waste your time, but I have to hurry to class or I'll be in trouble with Miss Lamb." She seemed grateful for the letter and placed it in the pocket of her black skirt.

As I ran back across the playground, I noticed Roy Henry riding his bicycle/horse on the sidewalk. I waved at him and he waved back. Seeing Roy Henry before Mr. Mooney chased him away from the schoolyard was lucky. Even though he wasn't right in his mind, he was the best sort of person, because he was nice inside where it mattered. I barely made it to my classroom before the tardy bell rang.

"Grace, can I have a word?" Miss Lamb called me up to her desk. The whole class turned to stare at me and snickered in unison as I walked to the front of the room. My face flamed. Only five minutes into the day, and I was in trouble.

"Yes, ma'am?"

"Students, quiet down now," she said, in a much too sweet voice to make anyone actually quiet down. While I appreciated Miss Lamb's pleasant attitude, if she expected to control us, she would have to be a little tougher and at least stop smiling all the time. We saw uncertainty behind those mismatched eyes, a disastrous thing for a schoolteacher. I thought she was more suited for a Sunday school classroom than my fourth grade.

As I stood in front of her desk, someone threw a paper airplane at my head. It sailed over my shoulder and hit the manila folder just as she pulled out my "What I Did on My Summer Vacation" essay.

"Students, I'm not going to tell you again," she said before turning her attention back to me to me. "Grace, dear, I wanted to talk with you about this homework assignment." She placed her perfectly groomed fingertips on the surface of my paper. Her skin was milky and unblemished, and she wore no rings.

"Okay." I stared at my report. She turned it around so I could see it. There were no red marks on it other than a checkmark in the corner.

"This was supposed to be a true story of your summer, not fiction."

Behind my back, classmates chattered, growing louder and more animated. Miss Lamb spoke in a low voice, and I had to strain to hear her.

"It is true," I said. I felt nervous even though I had no reason to be.

142

Her blue and green eyes had gold flecks around her black pupils. I wondered if she were some type of Martian sent to spy on us.

"Really? All of it?"

"Yes, ma'am, and there were other parts I didn't include. Things you really wouldn't believe." What would she think if she knew about Daddy running away to Vera's Bar and Momma throwing all his underwear outside and how Daddy passed out naked in front of Brother Brown?

"Oh, okay then." Her eyes widened as she slipped my report back into the folder.

At the end of class, Miss Lamb passed out information packets to be carried home to our parents. "Take one and pass them back," she said. Automatically, the first kid in each row took the packet on top, pressed his nose to the paper and breathed in the potent purple ink smell while passing the rest of the stack over his shoulder. The second student repeated the process, and so on until everyone received the paperwork. The passing and sniffing of mimeographed worksheets was the most well-orchestrated thing our class ever did. Sniff, pass. Sniff, pass.

When Janice handed the stack to me, the papers were still slightly damp. I took one and held it to my nose, inhaling the intoxicating smell before ever reading a word. I would have given up recess to work in the office and run off papers for any teacher who asked. There was nothing like that smell.

"Now don't forget. Give this to your mothers," she said. "It's very important information about the Halloween carnival." The instant she said "carnival," the bell blasted overhead, and Miss Lamb didn't have to deal with the wave of excitement that swept us from our desks and carried us to the school bus. That was good planning on her part.

As soon as I got on the bus, I pulled the packet from my book bag and showed it to Abby. She had one too. They were identical. Seven pages stapled together with a cover sheet that hardly counted because all it said was, "Savage Crossing Halloween Carnival – Come One, Come All." Dates and times for planning meetings were listed on a calendar, and a red star filled the space for Saturday, October twenty-first—the date of the big event. There was a page about fundraisers and a picture of a lawnmower donated by Savage Crossing Hardware to be raffled off. Daddy would like a new mower, I'd bet. Another sheet included suggestions of donation items for the big school rummage sale scheduled next weekend in the gym. Sign-up sheets listed five different committees. The whole fancy packet seemed like a sneaky way to get the parents to do all the carnival work. I showed it to Momma the minute I walked in the back door.

"Oh, I love the Halloween carnival!" Momma said. She was carrying an armful of towels but dropped them in a heap on the kitchen table to take the packet from me. She flipped through the pages. "October twenty-first. I was afraid they weren't having it this year. They're waiting so long to start planning." She pulled out a chair, sat down, and scanned each page, her finger moving along the lines. When she got to the last page, she started over, re-reading each page more slowly. Right away, she picked two committees to be on and called Mrs. Barns to see if she wanted to join the same ones. Right after supper, Momma gathered up junk for the rummage sale from every closet in our house.

That night, I couldn't sleep for worrying about the carnival. Tomorrow was the day each class would elect a representative to serve as king and queen. Then, on the night of the carnival, the Halloween king and queen for the whole school would be selected from the class representatives. Most of the girls were crazy-excited about the whole thing. But not me.

***

While we messed around on the monkey bars at recess, it was all anyone talked about. Gina, a smart but strange girl in my class who raised her hand twenty times a day and only ate vegetables for lunch, came over and passed out slips of paper to each of us that said, "Gina for Fourth Grade Queen of Halloween." I took one but told her I was undecided. I couldn't believe anyone would be nervy enough to ask for votes.

Janice refused to take one of her "vote for Gina" papers and said, "No offense, Gina, but why should we vote for you? You never talk to any of us."

144

"Because I'm most qualified," she said in a matter-of-fact way before walking off without another word. All the girls standing around the monkey bars laughed. Snootiness was not a popular trait.

"That hyena-Gina is one weird girl," Arlene said loud enough for Gina to hear. Everyone nodded and agreed.

Arlene Harris was weird too. And mean. She was two feet taller than anyone in my class and at least a year older, because she flunked fourth grade last year. Her skin was coal black, and she had a shifty look in her eyes and never brought pencils or paper to class. But she was good at rhyming, that was for sure. She had a rude nickname for everyone. I tried to avoid her, but when I couldn't, I acted cool and laughed at her jokes, because I was afraid not to. Everyone seemed to feel the same, even the boys.

"Who do you think should be Halloween queen?" I asked Janice.

"I don't know," she said. I thought Janice would make a great fourth-grade queen and planned to nominate her. But I decided to keep it a surprise.

"Paleface Grace, who are you gonna vote for?" Arlene asked me. She leaned against the monkey bars with her arms crossed over her huge chest. She'd probably been born wearing a bra.

"I don't know. What about you?" I ignored the paleface remark.

"I thought I'd nominate myself. Queen Arlene," she laughed and threw her head back. Everyone laughed. "Unless you want to be queen. I bet you've always dreamed about being the school queen." She grinned at me. This was one of those conversations that could turn bad fast. The other girls exchanged glances.

"Me? Oh, no," I shook my head. "I think the whole thing is stupid."

Arlene nodded as though she agreed. When she rushed off to talk to someone by the swing set, I felt relieved.

***

I sat at my desk, reviewing my spelling words one final time before the test. All morning, kids asked when we would pick our class king and queen. "As soon as the spelling test is over," Miss Lamb said. Finally, she told us to get a blank sheet of paper from our notebooks and number from one to twenty-one. She began calling out the words.

145

"Number one. Abundant. A-bun-dant." She used it in a sentence next, something she always did. "Pumpkins are abundant at the grocery store this time of year."

I wrote the word with no problem.

"Number two. Nutrients. Nu-tri-ents. Pumpkins are filled with good nutrients."

She was on a pumpkin kick. I wrote the word, almost forgetting the "s" at the end but adding it before she said number three. This went on until she called out our bonus word, number twenty-one. "Atrocious. A-tro-cious. Her piano playing was atrocious," Miss Lamb said.

What? I jerked my head up and looked at Miss Lamb walking back and forth in front of the chalkboard. Her skirt made its regular swishing sound. She held her spelling book open and wasn't looking in my direction even though that sentence seemed directed at me. Maybe atrocious piano playing was as common as pumpkins in October, but it seemed an odd coincidence.

We exchanged papers with a classmate and graded each other's tests. This time when Miss Lamb called out each word, she spelled it. The whole process was tedious and the worst part of Friday, because kids constantly asked her to re-spell a word. I graded Janice's paper, and she graded mine. We both made perfect scores plus five extra points for the bonus word.

The time had arrived to talk about the Halloween carnival. The girls could barely sit still in their seats. Some even took notes while Miss Lamb spoke. Based on the boys' willingness to be quiet, I thought they were strangely interested too. "First we need nominations for queen," Miss Lamb said. "Raise your hand if you would like to nominate someone."

Gina raised her hand and asked if it would be okay to nominate herself. Miss Lamb said she thought it would be better to nominate a friend. Mary, a quiet girl who always sat in the back row, raised her hand and nominated Gina. Gina sat up a little straighter, if that was possible, and clapped for herself, touching only the tips of her fingers together.

"Let's have two more nominees," Miss Lamb said as she wrote Gina's name on the board.

I raised my hand. "I nominate Janice." Janice bounced in her seat, turned around, and smiled at me. One of her sisters had been fifth-grade queen last year, and she had done a good job. Janice would be a natural. Miss Lamb wrote Janice underneath Gina and said her name, "Jaaanice," as she looped the letters together in one smooth movement.

"Yes, Arlene?" Miss Lamb said as Arlene's hand shot up.

"I nominate Grace to be Halloween queen," she said. She cocked her head to the side and stared at me with a challenging sort of look on her face. I felt my face burn and knew I certainly wasn't a paleface at that moment. I shook my head no. Janice turned and smiled toward Arlene, but she looked upset. I wanted to refuse, to say I wasn't interested, but when I opened my mouth only a gulp came out.

Maybe it would be an interesting thing.

Miss Lamb wrote my name below Janice and moved on to king nominations which turned out to be Bubba, Wilbur, and Mitchell, all nominated by various girls because boys never nominated anyone for anything. They preferred to sit on the sidelines and watch the day play out, which was probably the best way to be. When the lunch bell rang, we headed to the cafeteria. As Arlene walked past Janice and me she said, "So whose it gonna be? Paleface Grace or Jealous Janice?" She cackled and ran ahead, breaking in the lunch line to be first.

"I hate her," Janice said.

"Me too. I guess she couldn't think of a rhyme for your name," I said.

At the end of the day, our classroom election was held by secret ballot. I voted for Janice, and I was pretty sure she voted for me. Miss Lamb sat at her desk, unfolded each slip of paper, and made hash marks on a folder. The class watched every stroke of her red pen. When she finished, she cleared her throat and said "Can I have your attention?" even though everyone already stared at her. She made the king and queen announcement with great fanfare like it was a huge deal. Bubba was the class king and I was to be his queen.

Chapter Twenty-Two

The full attention of Savage Crossing Elementary—students, teachers, and PTA—turned to the Halloween carnival. Spelling words were forgotten. Any homework assigned was completed during the day, to allow time after school for classroom money raising. Momma and Mrs. Barns sent Bubba and me to school each morning with homemade chocolate chip cookies to sell at recess. After school, Momma set up a table in the parking lot and sold popcorn balls and chocolate cupcakes to all the hungry kids waiting to board the school buses. Mrs. Barns even donated Bubba's favorite board games to the school rummage sale. She said the fourth-grade class needed the money more than he needed to waste time playing games. The whole thing was ridiculous but exciting at the same time.

On the afternoon of the coronation, Momma took me to Lucille's Beauty Shop, the awful place responsible for my pixie haircut. "Do not let that woman pick up her scissors," I reminded Momma when we pulled up in front of her shop. She would style my hair, and that was all. Momma promised.

"Hello, Grace!" Lucille grinned and seemed happy to see me.

I gave her a fake smile. "I'm growing out my hair," I said firmly, so there would be no misunderstanding.

"I can see that. It looks nice," she said. Lucille washed and rolled my hair, but I never once took my eyes off her scissors, which sat soaking in a glass jar filled with bright blue water. She set the timer on the big hair dryer for twenty minutes, and I sat underneath it until my hair almost caught on fire. When she unrolled the curlers, each ringlet hung like a Shirley Temple curl until my entire head was one crazy mass of twists. She ratted and teased and lifted sections of my hair with her comb, then misted the roots with hairspray. When I left her beauty shop, she had transformed my shoulder-length hair into a stiff helmet sturdy enough to hold the Queen of England's crown.

All the way home, I stared at myself in the rearview mirror. The top was puffy and combed back, and the flipped out ends were so stiff I could lay a crayon in the curl and it wouldn't fall out. I knew because I tried it. The crayon stayed put even while I walked through the carport and into the kitchen.

Momma had arranged all my clothes across my bed like a fancy display at Goldsmith's in Memphis. New white tights, a new pair of black patent Mary Janes, and the purple velvet dress she had been sewing for two weeks. As Momma helped me pull the dress over my huge hairdo, I felt a little like Cinderella. "Go look at yourself in the entryway mirror," she said. "You look so pretty!" I ran to check. From the top of my poufy hair to the tips of my new shoes, other than the freckles on my nose, I didn't recognize myself at all.

***

Bubba and I stood with the other class kings and queens and peeked at the huge crowd filling the bleachers. The Halloween carnival was such a big deal that it rooted dirty farmers out of the fields during cotton harvest, even Daddy, who never came to anything. Since there was nothing much to do in a small town, everyone showed up for school events, even old people with no kids. It would have been the perfect time for a cat burglar to go from house to house, stealing everyone's stuff.

Miss Lamb helped with last-minute things—lining the classes up in order, re-tying the first-grade king's tie, and keeping all of us quiet as we waited beside the girls' locker room. The Savage Crossing teachers had disguised the gym with pumpkins and Indian corn and stalks of wheat, yet even with all the decorations, the gym still smelled like popcorn and sweat. A long, red carpet ran from the bleachers to center stage, and a spotlight shined on the thrones, which were someone's dining room chairs. Mrs. Allard's gigantic upright piano had been placed underneath the basketball goal. I bet Coach Greene was plenty upset about having a stage in the middle of his shiny gym floor—normally nobody was allowed to walk on the court without wearing high-top basketball shoes.

At last, Mr. Mooney walked onto the stage, welcomed everyone, and thanked the PTA moms for their hard work. It was one of the first times I'd ever seen Mr. Mooney not slinging his huge paddle. When Mrs. Allard began playing the piano, Mr. Mooney announced the first-grade representatives, and Miss Lamb motioned for them to walk. The audience clapped as two, cute, tow-headed kids walked to the stage like they were the flower girl and ring bearer in someone's Halloween wedding. Next, the second graders went—I knew the girl from Abby's class. For a few minutes, the program was disrupted when Roy Henry ambled up the red carpet, waving imaginary guns. The kids in the audience cheered for Roy Henry, but Mr. Mooney hobbled down the aisle and shooed him away.

Mrs. Allard pounded on the piano again, which was the cue for the third-grade king and queen to walk.

When my class was announced, Bubba grabbed my arm like Miss Lamb showed him in practice, but he set too fast a pace and I almost tripped. I looked straight ahead and noticed one of Papa Pete's old wagon wheels sat propped in the corner beside a hay bale. My hair felt heavy and the waistband of my new white tights dug into my belly. I hoped they wouldn't fall down.

When we reached the stage, instead of waiting for me to step onto the first stair, like we had practiced, Bubba jumped up the steps ahead of me, then turned and looked at me with a what-are-you-waiting-for expression on his face. We made it to our spots without embarrassing ourselves too much, but I felt flustered and my head hurt. As the fifth-grade nominees joined us, they seemed uncomfortable too.

And then my cousin Candi stepped onto the red carpet. Although she stood about a foot taller than her sixth-grade king, no one noticed him. She had a natural way of gliding across the gym floor, and her golden blonde hair moved like silk across her back. When she waved to the audience, her hand floated through the air like Miss Arkansas.

Lucky for me, this was no Miss America pageant. I knew I had no chance in a bathing suit or talent competition. Savage Crossing royalty were determined by only one thing—money. The class that sold the most cupcakes and cookies and ultimately raised the most money for the school won.

Once everyone made it to the stage and stood in a row on both sides of the throne chairs, Mr. Mooney announced what everyone had been waiting to hear. "Ladies and gentlemen, I present to you the 1972 Savage Crossing Halloween King and Queen, Bubba Ray Barns and Grace Lee Abbott."

Wow. Did I imagine hearing my name? I turned to look at Mr. Mooney, and he nodded and grinned. The clapping was thunderous in the gym, and near the front of the bleachers, I saw Momma jump to her feet and pump her arms overhead. Daddy was clapping and smiling too, and that made me feel happy and special all the way to my toes. But my toes wouldn't move and my feet were cemented in place. Bubba pulled me toward center stage where Mr. Mooney draped both of us in heavy, red velvet robes trimmed in white fur. He placed the glittery crown on my head, but since he didn't know anything about girl hair, his mammoth fingers scraped the bobby pins against my skull. Mrs. Allard overloaded me with an armful of giant white and yellow mums that smelled like the flower shop where Momma bought funeral arrangements. Bubba's neck completely vanished beneath the thick, fuzzy collar of his robe. It was cruel to load down a boy in fur and flowers, and Bubba looked startled by the whole thing.

***

The tall, pointy top of my crown touched the ceiling of the car, and the air smelled like yellow mums mixed with cigarette smoke. When Daddy cracked the window to flick his cigarette outside, I felt a rush of cool autumn air. My stiff hair didn't move, but I held tight to my crown with one hand and encircled the bouquet with my other. Abby buried her nose in an oversized mum and inhaled like she was about to hold her breathe for five minutes.

"Be careful! You'll sniff them all out." I said.

Daddy grumbled, "Yeah, don't mess up those damn flowers. They cost me fifty bucks."

I wasn't sure what he was talking about, but I didn't want the night to end in an argument. Being crowned queen had been neater than I expected, but I was tired and glad the event was over. I lay my head back and shut my eyes. That's when I smelled smoke. Smoke had begun to curl up between Abby and me.

"The car's on fire!" I yelled. Abby and I both scrunched our bodies closer to the windows, and I grabbed the door handle, preparing to jump and roll.

Momma draped her body over the front seat and began swatting in the direction of the smoke using her Halloween carnival program. Daddy cussed and swerved Momma's car into the gin lot. When we poured out of the car like circus clowns, me with an armful of mums and Abby dragging her plastic jack-o-lantern, I wanted to laugh and cry at the same time. Daddy yanked my velvet dress from the back seat and stomped on it right there in the dirt with his heavy cowboy boots. Momma found Daddy's cigarette butt in the back seat, smashed it out and kept saying, "Oh no, oh no, oh no." When the fire was out, she picked up my dress and held it the rest of the way home in her lap like a newborn baby.

After I brushed out all the hairspray from my hair and crawled into bed, Momma apologized over and over about my dress. "I'll make you a new one," she said. I really wasn't upset about it. She was the distraught one, probably because she'd sewed it with her own hands and wanted me to wear it at the next Boon Chapel Christmas program.

"It's okay, Momma. I don't think it's ruined. No one will notice the hole." I gave her hand a little pat like she sometimes did to me. From my bed, I could smell my beautiful queen flowers on the dresser. "Momma, why did Daddy say those flowers cost him fifty dollars?"

Momma explained that when Mr. Mooney counted the money to determine which class raised the most, Daddy and Mr. Barns each threw extra money into the PTA pot to push our class ahead. Something about that seemed wrong. I stayed up late into the night feeling bad about winning, like we cheated.

Chapter Twenty-Three

Since Halloween fell on Tuesday, the mayor of Savage Crossing moved trick-or-treating up to Saturday so kids wouldn't have to stay out late on a school night. I didn't see what difference it made since we had to get up and go to church on Sunday, but the whole town and the surrounding area went along with it. Mr. Mooney made an announcement about the change in school, and the *Savage Crossing Crier* ran a story in the paper so everyone would know.

When Saturday finally arrived, the night turned cold and blustery, and the moon became trapped behind clouds I couldn't see. Momma never let us go door to door with our friends in Savage Crossing. She preferred to drive us around in the country from farmhouse to farmhouse. Although her method took longer and we went to less houses, we ended up with more candy. People in the country without many visitors handed out gobs of candy instead of one or two pieces.

Nana had never been trick-or-treating in her life, not even as a kid, so she decided to go with us. She even pulled together a scary costume. By simply wearing an old stocking over her head, she became the witch from *Snow White* with a shriveled and misshapen face. Abby went as a hobo. Her look was easy enough to manage with a pair of old pants and dirt smudged on her cheeks. Patti, who according to Abby was dressed like a gypsy, went with us. Since she wasn't a real person, she stayed in the car. I dressed all in black, with a long, black wig, dark lipstick, and my silver crown, to get more use out of it. Even though it was cold, I didn't wear a coat because who ever heard of a witch wearing a coat? Between trick-or-treat stops, I was glad to warm up in the back seat of the car, but after hitting all the houses from Cottonwood Corner to Sugar Ditch, I couldn't feel my toes.

We always saved the best house for last and ended our night at the Carlocks. Their gingerbread-style house was wedged between looming trees and set back off the road. Momma drove slowly along their long, twisty drive. A carved pumpkin flickered from the porch, promising the best sort of candy. "This is the last stop, girls," she reminded us. Just before we reached the house, she turned off the lights and stopped the car. "They'll never figure out who you are if they can't see our car."

While Momma waited with the motor running, Nana walked with us up the unlit brick pathway. I held my crown to keep it from blowing away. My pumpkin felt heavy from lots of candy.

"Trick-or-treat!" Abby and I yelled when Mrs. Carlock came to the door. We thrust our plastic pumpkins toward her. The wind blew my stringy witch hair across my face into my eyes.

"Do you have candy for my starving children?" Nana pleaded in a scary voice, adding an evil cackle and rubbing her hands together like all witches did.

"Do we know you?" Mrs. Carlock asked with a smile. She held a bowl overflowing with assorted candy, including lots of chocolate.

"We are a poor family who needs lots of candy," Nana screeched, nearly scaring me.

Mrs. Carlock gave Abby and me homemade popcorn balls and big fistfuls of candy, more treats than any others had offered. In a way, I wished we weren't trying to be so sneaky. If they had known who we were, they might have invited us inside for hot chocolate. Beyond the front door, I saw Mr. Carlock warming his hands in front of a fire, and their plaid sofa looked deep and cozy. Instead, we thanked her and rushed back to the comfort of the car. My eyes teared from the cold wind.

"You were right, Momma," Abby said. "She didn't recognize us."

"She still has no idea who we are," Nana laughed and waved at Mrs. Carlock who watched us from the front porch. She waved back but wore a confused expression. The drapes around the dining room window moved aside as Mr. Carlock peeped out. I felt inside my pumpkin to determine the identity of the latest additions based on the size and shape of each small candy. Unwrapping a piece of toffee, I popped it into my mouth and dropped the wrapper back into the jack-o-lantern.

Momma left the lights off and inched backwards down the driveway. When she was a good ways from the house, she turned the lights on and flooded the trees with an eerie glow. When Nana yanked the stocking off her head, everyone laughed because her hair stood straight up, electrified by the cold, dry air. No one laughed when Momma rammed our car into a tree and jolted us forward.

She said a bad word and slammed on the brakes. I grabbed my candy to keep from losing it on the dark floorboard.

Nana cracked open the car door and peeped out toward the back. Mr. Carlock, who must have heard the crash, rushed from the porch and met Momma and Nana behind the car. They all talked and visited like smashing the car was no big deal. Abby and I stayed inside and stuffed candy in our mouths.

I heard Mr. Carlock tell Momma that her fender had a scratch and her taillight was broken. "You'll be okay to drive home. It's nothing major," he said.

"I bet Daddy won't see it that way," I mumbled to Abby through a sticky chew of caramel.

"He'll be mad for sure," Abby said. Patti said nothing, because she was mute.

Momma and Nana chatted all the way to Nana's house, but once Nana got out of the car, the drive home turned solid quiet. Halloween hadn't ended well.

"Momma, do you think Daddy will be mad at us?" Abby asked.

"Not too bad," she said.

I could tell by the tone of her voice that she was worried. Little things like a broken taillight or forgetting something at the store often caused gigantic fights. When we pulled into the driveway, I felt the nerves building in my stomach the same way as when I had a big test at school. "Momma don't tell him. He won't know," I said.

"Gracie, he'll find out sooner or later," she said.

Daddy was sitting at the kitchen table, reading the farm and business section of the newspaper while eating soup with crackers crumbled on top. "Anne, you didn't leave me with any candy, and we had a trick-or-treater," he said, but he was sort of laughing about it.

During all the years we'd lived on that road, we'd never had a single trick-or-treater.

"Who was it?" Momma asked. She was surprised too.

"One of the tractor drivers brought his son over. I had to give him crackers," Daddy said, shaking his head. He took another spoonful of soup.

"Daddy, we have some terrible news," I said.

Momma shifted her eyes toward me, and Abby echoed, "Yeah, bad," under her breath.

"What?" He looked at me, then Momma, then back to me. I felt my heart thump.

"We stopped at the Savage Crossing gas station to air up a tire because Momma's tire looked almost flat, and while Momma was fiddling with the air machine, some man smashed into her car. He just backed right into her and drove off, before Momma could even look up. He peeled down Main Street and almost ran over Roy Henry. I didn't get a very good look, but I think he was driving a blue truck." I gulped air and felt my face flush. Momma stared at me. Abby stared at Momma. "It wasn't Momma's fault," I added.

Daddy pushed his chair back and grabbed the flashlight from the back porch. The screen door slapped behind him.

"Gracie Lee, what on Earth? Have you lost your mind?" Momma said. She cleared dirty dishes from the kitchen countertop, placing everything in the sink and running the hot water. "I can't believe you," she said as she scrubbed the soup pot.

Daddy walked back into the kitchen and placed the flashlight on the countertop. "A blue truck you say, Gracie?" He stared at me. Right through my eyes and into my skull. My cheeks burned. I felt tears swim in my eyes. Somehow he knew.

"Yes, sir," I said in more of a question than a statement. "I might be wrong though. About the color," I stammered.

"Well, it could have been worse. Only a broken taillight and a scratch. The way you described it, I thought the whole back end was smashed. I better not find out who was driving that blue truck though," Daddy said. When he opened the icebox, I noticed there were only three beers lining his shelf. He grabbed one and popped the top with

156

more force than normal. Momma exhaled. I was afraid she would rat me out, but she didn't. She probably didn't feel up to a fight either.

Chapter Twenty-Four

I woke with a massive headache and thought there was a good chance my brain might explode in the car. I had begged to stay home from church, but Momma wouldn't let me. "You need to go to church, young lady, especially after your lie. We're all coming clean with Daddy as soon as we get home today," Momma said as she preached on the drive to Boon Chapel. The fields passed outside the window in an emerald smear. If I flung open the car door and rolled into Kochtitzki Ditch and broke my neck and croaked, I wouldn't have to come clean about anything.

"Why? I saved your hide, Momma." I kept my eyes on the cotton fields heavy with bolls. Daddy was already picking at the home place. The field at our house would be ready this week.

"Grace, don't sass me. My hide doesn't need saving."

I thought differently.

In Sunday school class, our lesson was about Joseph and how his jealous brothers stole his coat of many colors, rubbed goat blood on it, heaved him into a pit, and left him to be sold as an Egyptian slave. When the brothers returned home with Joseph's coat smeared in blood, his daddy, Jacob, who was way nicer than my daddy, thought a ferocious animal had killed his son. While Momma talked about the deceitful brothers, a squirrel watched me from the maple tree outside the window of our classroom. He had an acorn in his mouth and was twitching his tail as though daring me to chase him; only I was stuck behind the glass window, listening to Momma drone on about dishonesty. Since last Sunday, the tree had turned from bright and brilliant to dry brown. I wondered if the squirrel noticed the difference in leaf color, or saw color at all. Momma must have thought I wasn't paying attention, because she asked me to read the passage from Genesis. But I was paying attention, and I read it without stumbling over any words. I'd heard the story of Joseph's troubles a million times, so I could watch the trees and the squirrel and listen to Momma with different parts of my brain. Even with a headache.

"So what do you think about this story?" Momma asked the Sunday school class.

"I feel sorry for Joseph. His own brothers stole his favorite coat," Dian said.

"I feel sorry for Jacob, thinking his favorite son was killed," I said.

"Why do you think Joseph was the favorite?" Momma asked.

"The Bible doesn't talk much about the other brothers, so he must have been the only important one. Plus, the other ones were killers."

The squirrel bounded to another tree and disappeared from my sight.

"The brothers also lied," Momma said, staring at me.

"Yes. With no good reason," I said staring back.

Momma went on to point out that lying was bad no matter the reason, but I still believed there were degrees to lies. Momma told little white lies, as she called them, to her friend Maggie all the time. Last week, she went crazy for Maggie's new, striped dress, asking where she bought it, and saying it was perfect with her red hair, but as soon as Maggie backed down the gravel driveway with our bottle of vanilla extract, Momma said all those horrid stripes made her look like a jailbird. I almost reminded her of that during Sunday school class, but kept quiet.

During announcements, Mr. Davidson talked about Harvest Supper scheduled in two weeks. Two weeks! Harvest Supper, a heavenly buffet of homemade casseroles and pies and cakes spread from one end of the church to the other, was the reason I continued going to church. Well, that plus the fact Momma made me go. And, Hell, of course. I suspected Hell kept most people going back, except old people like Nana and Mrs. Sweet and Aunt Clara. They seemed to love going to church without being made to do so.

During preaching, I opened my Sunday school book back to today's lesson and began drawing a picture along the side in the white space. The drawing began as Joseph's coat of many colors. Even though I only had a stubby pencil and technically no "colors," I shaded the coat different degrees of dark and light so the stripes were obvious. By the time Brother Brown said, "Now, in closing...," I had filled the entire margin of the page with flowers and vines and a sun in the corner.

When the first stanza of "Just as I Am" started, I stood and began walking up the red carpet toward Brother Brown. Momma removed her glasses and let them fall and rest on her chest, suspended by a gold chain. She glared at me and shook her head, but I didn't care. I walked directly to the first pew and kneeled. Brother Brown met me there. He seemed a bit slow to bend, and I wondered if we should start sitting on the pew during our Sunday morning visits instead of kneeling at the pretend altar.

"Brother Brown, I told a lie last night to Daddy. I know it was a sin, but it was a necessary sin."

"Have you prayed for forgiveness?"

"No. It seems wrong to pray for forgiveness when I would do it again to save Momma."

"Save your Momma from what?" His tone of voice made me think he was afraid to know.

"From Daddy."

"Maybe you should tell me what happened." He leaned in so close I could see each pore on his nose, and the way he scrunched his forehead made me know he was worried about what I might say. After having supper at our house and seeing Daddy drunk, he took me more seriously.

"Well, last night when we were trick-or-treating at the Carlock house, Momma hit a tree and busted out the taillight. You can go outside and see for yourself if you don't believe me. I lied and told Daddy someone backed into her car at the gas station. That way, he didn't kill Momma over it."

I heard the congregation singing the fourth stanza, sounding flat and dragging a beat or two behind the music. My time with Brother Brown was almost done. He reminded me that it was wrong to lie, no matter what, and tried to assure me Daddy really wouldn't have killed Momma over a broken taillight. He didn't sound very convinced himself.

160

"But what about little lies? They can't be as bad as huge lies, are they? Adults tell little white lies all the time," I said.

"Grace, lies are untruths no matter the size. Even though it may be easier to tell a little white lie to avoid hurting someone's feelings, the truth is the best course of action. Lots of little white lies add up." He advised me to ask for forgiveness, and I told him I would think about it. That was the best I could do.

Momma began lecturing me the moment we got in the car. "Grace, I thought we agreed you would talk to me before you go up and speak to Brother Brown again." She gripped the steering wheel with both hands, and her gold dangle bracelets jangled around her arm as she turned onto the highway.

"*Je suis désolé*," I said.

Momma rolled her eyes in the rearview mirror.

"I forgot," I added, realizing immediately that two more lies had slipped between my lips before I'd even left the church grounds. I wasn't sorry, and I hadn't forgotten.

She sighed. "You know, Grace, we aren't Catholic. Brother Brown isn't a priest required to hear your weekly confessional."

"I can't help it if I have a lot of questions." I twirled Barbie's hair.

"There's the woods!" Abby announced.

"Slow down, Momma, so we can look for hobos," I asked, welcoming the change in subject.

Momma sped up. She shoved an eight-track in the player and turned the volume high. Linda Ronstadt blared all the way home.

Daddy was waiting in the front yard. As our car approached, he took a drag on his cigarette, then dropped it into a patch of clover and smashed it with his boot.

"Keep driving, Momma!" I yelled, but she ignored my warning and turned into the drive.

Daddy was some sort of warlock with evil powers. I was certain of it. One moment, he smashed his nasty cigarette butt in my favorite spot to find clover for necklaces, and then one blink later, he materialized in a rage at my car window. He banged on the glass, jerked open the door, grabbed my elbow, and yanked me into the cool autumn day. The strap of my purse broke, dumping its contents onto the floor of the carport. Barbie sprawled at his feet, still smiling.

"A blue truck, huh?" He didn't shout, which made it scarier.

Abby screamed and crawled onto the floorboard, trying to hide.

"Lee, leave her alone. We were going to explain as soon as we got home from church," Momma pleaded.

"Church!" He smirked. "A lot of good church does any of you. Bunch of hypocrites. I live with a bunch of damn liars."

"You're hurting my arm." I felt tears come, but would not allow them to spill.

Daddy crushed Barbie with one heavy boot, smashing and grinding her into the concrete. Then he dragged me into the kitchen and shoved me into a chair.

"Bar-bieeee!" I felt a tightness that would not break.

"So, what do you have to say? Talk, Baby-Grace."

Instead, I cried, and I hated it. I hated letting him get to me, but more than anything, I hated that my favorite Barbie lay in an oily spot on the carport floor with Daddy's boot mark scarring her perfect face. I bit the inside of my cheek and chewed on the edge of my tongue, trying to stop the flow of tears, but my stomach heaved. "Momma accidentally hit a tree at the Carlock house. That's it. She didn't mean to."

"Are you that stupid to think I wouldn't find out? Everyone was talking about it down at Vera's this morning. You are such a weak coward. Go to your room and don't move. Don't even breathe."

I fled.

Through the bedroom walls, I heard Momma's sobs and Daddy's yells. I couldn't make out the words, only the roar of one long rant. A crash. A fist slammed into the kitchen wall.

Then he came for me.

I sat on my bed and stared past his face to the window, trying to appear brave. When he removed his belt, I thought about other things.

Planting irises at Nana's house.

The smell of the soil.

The feel of the dirt between my fingers.

He made me bend over and grab my knees. I buried my face into the soft folds of my turtle quilt. It smelled fresh, like Momma's detergent, or an early summer morning when the sun barely glowed above the horizon. His strikes came steadily, one after another, burning my skin through my corduroy skirt. I thought about Mae's long, exotic fingernails and how the tips tickled my scalp when she braided my long hair. When I jerked to avoid the belt hitting my bare legs, the heavy brass belt buckle struck my lower back instead.

I collapsed on the floor. Someone should kill this man, I prayed.

Chapter Twenty-Five

Daddy was gone for four days. Every night before I went to sleep, I prayed that his sickness would come back and rot his whole body. I knew that was a bad thing to pray, but I prayed it anyway. I didn't go to school all week, because I felt sick inside and out. I didn't even have to ask to stay home. Momma suggested it. After the way Daddy hurt me with his belt, Momma seemed sick too. When Janice called to check on me, I told her I had the flu. But it was worse than the flu. There were no aspirins, no words, no thoughts to make me feel better. On Wednesday, Abby brought my homework from school along with a stack of get well cards handwritten by my classmates. Even Miss Lamb made one from red construction paper.

I changed Barbie's dress and brushed her hair. After Daddy smashed her on the carport, her arm had popped off, but Momma put it back on. I gave Barbie a bath, and most of the dirt washed away. The very tip of her nose would be skinned forever, but her hair looked the same—silky and golden. Momma offered to buy me a new Barbie, but I said no. I didn't want to trade her in just because she had a scar on her face.

Tomorrow, I would go back to school. I didn't want to miss my Friday spelling test. Plus, sitting around didn't make me feel better about anything. I didn't know how Momma lived each boring day without going crazy, but she seemed to enjoy doing chores around the house. She had some sort of special strength that kept our whole family from falling apart. If something changed and Momma was thrown into a different life in a different place, she would settle in and be okay. We all would be, as long as Momma was around.

I thought about writing another letter to the gray-house man but was starting to believe he would never write back to me. Instead, I wrote in my diary. I wrote about being home sick with the flu and how I went to the doctor and got a shot and how Dr. Fairley said it was the worst case of the flu he'd seen all fall and how I threw up for two days and how I accidentally dropped Barbie on the carport after my doctor appointment and her arm popped off and how she skinned her nose, but that she was still beautiful.

It was all fiction.

I couldn't write the truth about Daddy, even in my diary.

***

Friday night while we played Candy Land at the kitchen table, Daddy's truck turned into the driveway. Abby ran to the back porch and looked out. "Daddy's home. And there's a stranger with him." Momma drew another card and moved four spaces.

My heart hammered against the inside of my chest. A few Mississippis later he strolled into the kitchen, carrying a huge Sterling's sack and talking with a man we'd never seen. "I brought you girls a surprise," he said. The man beside him smiled but looked nervous, shifting from one foot to another like he had ants in his pants. I didn't move from my chair. Momma was silent and stared at him with ice blue eyes.

"What is it?" Abby whispered.

"Come see." He pulled a box from inside, letting the sack fall to the floor. It was Barbie's Country Camper, something we'd wanted since we'd first noticed it at the store. Abby ran over and looked at it, her eager eyes big and bright. I couldn't. "And this is my friend, Douglas Daggett," he said and pointed to his new buddy. Momma said hello but didn't stand or shake his hand or anything, which was not like her.

Mr. Daggett had beady eyes that flitted around the room like he was searching for something to steal. It didn't take us long to learn he had the most annoying laugh ever, an earsplitting cackle that made the invisible hairs on the back of my neck crawl. I immediately nicknamed him Hyena Man. I wondered if calling him a name behind his back was the same as telling a little white lie. I wondered if I was as bad a person as Arlene.

Hyena Man slept in the den on the couch that folded into a bed, and for several days and nights, he ate our food and watched his favorite shows on our television. Every day, when Abby and I got off the school bus, he would be standing on the carport, smoking Daddy's cigarettes and throwing the nasty butts on the ground like a big litterbug. I ignored him as best I could and waited for Momma to tire of playing hostess and maid. With each passing day, her words became curter, her smiles less frequent. Each night before I went to bed, I counted the number of beers in the icebox, but it was impossible to keep track with Hyena Man in the house. Finally, on Friday, one week after he arrived, it happened. As we stepped off the bus, Momma greeted us halfway up the driveway. I could tell she had been working hard because her cheeks were flushed bright red, and the yard was filled with mounds of raked leaves. A cold wind threatened to scatter the piles making the chore seem pointless.

"Is he still here?" I asked as we walked toward the house.

"Yes, but not for long." Momma said with steely eyes. She went to the kitchen sink to wash her hands, then swallowed two aspirin and rubbed her lower back. Hyena Man strolled into the kitchen, opened the icebox, and stuck his head inside like he had bought the food filling the shelves. Just at that moment, Daddy turned into the driveway. Abby and I sat at the dining room table, pretending to do our homework while watching the whole thing unfold.

Daddy grabbed a cooler from the back porch, set it on the kitchen table, and loaded beer into it. Momma wiped down the kitchen countertop and unloaded the dishwasher.

"Douglas, come ride on the farm with me this afternoon. I'm picking cotton over by the levee," Daddy said.

"I think it's time Douglas headed home. His vacation is over," Momma said as she stacked bowls into the cabinet. She spoke to Daddy as though Hyena Man wasn't standing in the middle of the kitchen, chewing a mouthful of leftover meatloaf. Pin-dropping silence filled the kitchen.

Daddy turned and glared at her, and I could see the veins throbbing in his neck. He slammed shut the cooler, swung it off the table, and faced Momma. "Don't you ever speak that way to one of my friends again," Daddy yelled. His body shuddered, and the muscles in his arms tensed. With his free hand, he formed a fist, and I worried he might punch Momma. "This is my house. I say who comes and goes. Douglas is welcome here anytime."

Hyena Man stood immobile in the middle of the kitchen. His eyes darted from Daddy to Momma, then down to his dirty tennis shoes. He rubbed his matted hair nervously, like he was looking for something to do with his hands.

"I'll tell you what, Lee. You can leave with him. I'm tired of cooking and cleaning up after you and your buddy without so much as a how-do-you-do," Momma said. Her voice was calm and composed.

Daddy stared at Momma. A volcano of anger grew in his eyes. *One Mississippi.* That was all the time it took before he spewed a bunch of bad words and called Momma an awful name. When he slammed his fist into the wall beside the back door, part of the paint crumbled and the imprint of his knuckles was left behind. The bean rooster picture Momma, Abby, and I made two summers ago crashed to the floor, and the corner of the frame broke. That made me gasp. We had worked hard on it, designing and gluing seeds and popcorn and dried beans to the rooster's chest. I remembered it clearly, because I had a huge splinter in the bottom of my heel, and my foot throbbed and throbbed while we worked on the rooster. When Momma finally got that splinter out, I was never so glad of anything in my life.

Momma stood firm, glaring at Daddy. She didn't apologize or say a word. I imagined her insides were shaky because mine were, but she didn't show it. Abby covered her eyes with her hands. I started across the kitchen to rescue the rooster picture, but Momma held her arm out and stopped me, the same way she kept a bag of groceries from falling from the car seat when she slammed on her brakes. Daddy banged the screen door so hard it broke off its hinges. Hyena Man chased after him. None of us spoke until we heard Daddy sling gravel on the driveway.

"Momma, you were so brave!" I said. Abby ran and hugged her legs, almost knocking her down. Momma shook her head and looked pale. She told us to please be good and to not make a mess while she took a nap. She spent the rest of the afternoon in her bedroom. I didn't bother her, and I didn't make a mess. I knew what it was like to be exhausted from arguing with Daddy.

A few hours later, Daddy returned home for supper without his sidekick. Momma must have assumed he wouldn't come home for a few days because she cooked hot dogs, which he hated. Daddy ate his food without complaining and acted as though nothing had happened. I still hoped he would apologize for beating me with his belt and for smashing Barbie's face, but he never said anything about it. He never said anything about the broken screen door, or the rooster, or the hole in our kitchen wall either.

Chapter Twenty-Six

On Monday afternoon, as soon as we got home from school and gobbled down our snack, Abby and I ran outside to play until sunset. Neither of us had homework, which was a nice surprise. The days were getting shorter and cooler, but we bundled up and never gave a thought to the brisk wind that stung our cheeks and numbed our fingers. Hidden high in the mimosa tree, Abby and I discussed our plans for a tree house. Yesterday after church, we had asked Momma to let us have some boards and nails and a hammer. She said it wasn't tree house season. I didn't think there was any such thing as tree house season and thought it was her way of saying no. We went ahead, drawing up a plan and climbing each tree in the yard to test limbs and observe views. It turned out that the view was the same from every tree—rows of white, fanning in every direction like fields of autumn snow. All over the county, farmers were picking cotton. The air smelled of harvest—an earthy, dusty, wonderful smell that I doubted regular, non-farmer kids appreciated.

"I don't think these limbs are strong enough for a tree house," I said. The middle branches were sagging underneath the weight of both of us. The mimosa, one of our favorite trees, was maybe better suited to summer shade picnics. "Hey, look!" I pointed. In the distance, Daddy's truck was coming up the road. Supper wasn't for several hours, and during cotton-picking time, Daddy usually ate well after we did and sometimes after we were in bed. I watched him pull into the driveway, not too fast or too slow, but at a normal speed, which provided no clues to his mood.

As he walked onto the back porch, we sat extra still so he wouldn't notice us sitting high in the tree. Before we could decide whether to go inside and snoop or wait to find out what was going on, he and Momma both walked out. Momma pointed to us in the tree, ratting us out.

"Come on, girls. I've got something to show you," Daddy smiled and motioned to us from the driveway, then slid into his truck. Something spectacular must have happened for Daddy to come home early during cotton harvest. Since his recent adventure with Hyena Man, Daddy had tried to be friendlier, but I was suspicious.

"Abby-Grace!" Momma yelled when we didn't rush right over. She had tied a scarf around her hair and carried her pocketbook.

"Crap," I whispered to the sky. Adults never gave any consideration to the important things kids were busy doing. When Momma climbed into the truck, Abby and I looked at each other, then jumped down from the tree and went to join her. We sat in the middle, straddling the dusty two-way radio.

"Daddy bought a new piece of land. You girls need to see it. It'll be yours someday." She smiled and looked over at Daddy who chewed on the end of a toothpick. There was plenty of time for that. We were busy thinking about the tree house we wanted to build. "And this isn't just any land, girls," Momma continued. "Johnny Cash grew up there." She said Johnny Cash extra slow and lifted her eyebrows like this was front page news.

"Johnny Cash? Isn't he in jail?" I asked, coughing and sputtering from the smell of Daddy's cigarette smoke mixed with farm truck dust.

"He sings about jail, but he lives in Nashville." Daddy's tone of voice changed back to annoyed. He gave me a sharp look, probably because it was a smart aleck thing for me to ask. It was hard to be pleasant when I was being forced to waste my after-school time going to look at dirt. When Daddy smashed his cigarette in the ashtray, a spray of gray embers swept across my legs. I listened as Daddy spoke into the two-way radio and asked Mr. Barns about picking cotton on his home place. Mr. Barns answered, but the sound was choppy and broken, and I couldn't make out what he said.

"Can I talk to Mr. Barns?" I asked Daddy.

He gave me a strange look but handed me the mouthpiece of his radio.

"Mr. Barns? This is Gracie. Is Bubba with you?"

"No. He had football practice today."

"Okay. Well tell him I said hi." I had forgotten that Bubba was on the pee-wee football team. I hung the radio mouthpiece back on the holder and thought it was pretty cool to talk to someone while riding in a truck.

Going anywhere with Daddy meant factoring in extra time. He drove slow enough to watch the crops grow from the side of the road. My mood began to sink with the sun as I realized it would be dark by the time we got back home. We rode past the cotton gin and through Savage Crossing. A man stood at the corner of the gas station as though he propped up the building. Daddy waved with one finger, and he nodded back. I looked for Roy Henry but didn't see him.

On the drive to our new land, Momma and Daddy talked about the price of cotton. Although I didn't understand everything about it, I knew Daddy sold most of his cotton before he even picked it, which explained why he studied the prices in the newspaper every day. I became more interested when Daddy talked about picking cotton at the field behind our house. Playing in the cotton was one of my favorite things.

"Even though we got a late start after that damn flood," Daddy said, "Our cotton is good this year," he told all of us. "The soybeans look good too," he said as he stared out the window. Momma nodded her head. I felt relieved.

Daddy's new land was past the high school, farther than all his other land. We turned onto a bumpy gravel road that was surrounded by ditches overgrown with weeds and tiny orange flowers. The plain gray sky stretched over the cotton fields. Daddy's truck rocked sideways, just slightly, in the gusty wind.

"Where are we?" I asked.

"Dyess. Well, the outskirts of Dyess. See the water tower over there?" Momma pointed to a white tower hovering like a mushroom over a stand of trees. Daddy stopped the truck, and we all filed out to see the land up close. The biting air whipped my hair around my face. I wished I had worn a hat.

"Our property is from that ditch, all the way around to that road," Daddy said, gesturing from one end of the field to another. Between rows, the dry ground was cracked and split, and the cotton was nothing like Daddy's regular lush and healthy crop. Instead, thin plants poked from the dirt and stringy cotton clung to the bolls as though the field had already been picked once. But somehow, I didn't think that was the case. Daddy always picked each field twice because some bolls weren't mature enough to pick the first go around. That second picking was like licking the icing from the bowl when Momma made cake frosting. It got the last little bit of cotton still clinging to the plants. This field looked different, though. The plants looked stunted like the cotton never had much of a chance.

Next to the field, a small, tired farmhouse settled into the gumbo. The porch railing sagged, and a missing shutter had left an outline on the siding a different shade of dingy. Momma pointed at it. "Johnny Cash lived in that house and went to high school in Dyess," she said.

"Right there? In that little house?" I asked and pointed. This gave me a lot to think about. I had watched Johnny Cash on television and, not that long ago, his picture had been on the cover of *TV Guide*. He always wore black. And he was rugged, with soulful eyes, not what I would call handsome, but exactly how someone who lived in that house surrounded by a dried-up cotton field would grow up to look. I stared at the dirt beneath my shoes and imagined Johnny Cash walking along that same road every day to school. If he could escape farm life, there was hope for me.

That night when I tried to sleep, I thought about how Johnny Cash started out as a farm boy not too far from our house. The whole growing up thing was interesting. It seemed that one little decision led to another little decision, and before long, all the little decisions added up to a gigantic life plan. How did someone like Johnny Cash become rich and famous and get to sing on the radio, yet someone else become so desperate he tried to commit suicide? I decided to write another letter to the man in the gray house, in case he was still depressed.

Dear Man Who Lives in the Pretty Gray House,

Even though you haven't answered any of my letters, I want to tell you that's okay. I believe you would write if you could. I don't think you are dead

172

because someone picked up all the sticks and limbs from your yard after the storm we had after Halloween. Also, when I rode my bicycle by your house last weekend, I noticed your mailbox only had two pieces of mail. I hope you don't mind that sometimes I look inside your mailbox. It's part of my clue gathering. I would never take anything, not even junk mail. By the way, your yellow mums are blooming around your birdbath, and they look really pretty.

If you come back home soon, you are invited to Harvest Supper at Boon Chapel a week from Sunday (at night). Believe me, it's the very best time to attend Boon Chapel because there is eating instead of preaching. The ladies bring their most delicious dishes, and you can even go back through the line and get seconds.

Write back soon.

Your neighbor,
Gracie Abbott

Chapter Twenty-Seven

The Boon Chapel church ladies spread long wooden tables with platters of every type food imaginable, including my favorites—fried chicken, mashed potatoes, and green beans with little bits of bacon floating in the juice. And the desserts? *Si magnifique!* Desserts had their own special table along the wall, arranged like a fancy display from one of Momma's magazines. There were fruit cobblers, pies of every sort—pecan, apple, chocolate, coconut cream—and of course, Nana's strawberry cake, with real strawberries mixed in the pink frosting. Nana's cake was my favorite.

Harvest Supper made all that squirming on rock-hard pews worth it. I loaded my plate with a spoonful of this, a taste of that. Momma had brought her best dish, chicken and dressing, along with a new creation, broccoli casserole made with orange cheese from a jar. The old people raved about the broccoli casserole and even went back for second helpings, but we kids passed it up in favor of Aunt Clara's macaroni and cheese. I kept an eye out for any guest who might possibly be our neighbor from the pretty gray house, but no one new appeared, only the regulars.

"What're you doing? You can't eat that," I whispered to Abby. She had spooned a hearty helping of Mrs. Sweet's dressing onto her plate. She gasped at her mistake and returned it back to the dish with a plop. At Boon Chapel, there was an unspoken competition concerning who made the best dressing. If your momma brought dressing, you better not sneak a taste of someone else's. I knew Mrs. Sweet's was *délicieux* too—I tasted it once just to see.

Dian and the Donaldson twins were sitting together at the end of a folding table, so Abby and I joined them. The noise level in the back room of the church was high as the entire congregation talked and visited like they hadn't seen each other in years. As I took a big bite of fried chicken, Mrs. Brown walked up to our group and sat in an empty chair right across from me. That was about as odd as anything.

"Do you mind if I sit here, girls?" she asked as she went right ahead and sat down. We traded glances like this was a church trick of some sort.

"Sure," I said while everyone else nodded.

"So how is everyone?" she smiled as she looked around, her eyes pausing for an instant on each of us. She began salting her food, probably two or three Mississippis worth.

Everyone said, "Fine," at the same time. I didn't know that much about Mrs. Brown, but if someone asked me to describe her, I'd say she loved salt. She used such a heavy hand with the shaker, I could see it sparkling like sugar from where I sat.

"Are you girls excited about Thanksgiving?" she asked.

"Yes, ma'am," Abby said. I nodded, because my mouth was full again. In a way, she was completely messing up Harvest Supper. I was eating faster than normal and being forced to talk about things I didn't want to talk about. It was then that I noticed she was wearing the same bright orange dress she had worn to our house last summer, only this time she wore a brown sweater with it. Could something as simple as an outfit change someone's mood from stuffy to friendly? Eventually, Mrs. Brown took her plate and moved to another spot. We must have been holding our breath, because we exhaled in unison.

While the adults gossiped, drank coffee, and ate second helpings of pie and cake, we kids ran outside to play Ghost Train, which was the scariest game ever. Lining up in single file, we walked slowly around the church to the edge of the cemetery and around the propane tank. Except for the dim, amber glow coming from the church windows, the night was cave-dark. Somewhere hidden among the shrubs, the person who was "it" lurked, waiting to creep up and grab the kid at the end of the line. No one was allowed to speak, although the person grabbed usually shrieked because it couldn't be helped. We all continued walking around and around, until only one person, the person at the head of the line, was left walking.

To be fair, we decided the lineup with a game of rock-paper-scissors. Just my luck, I had to be first in line, which I hated. Being first meant eventually I would be the last one walking, and there was nothing spookier than walking alone through a graveyard on a blustery night.

When the game began, I could hear Dian's footsteps crunch through the leaves a few feet behind me, but behind her, everyone else's footsteps were drowned out by the howling wind. I counted trips around the church until I lost track. As leader, there was no way for me to know how many people still walked behind me or how many had been captured. As long as I could still hear Dian walking behind me, I kept fairly calm and focused on what lay in front of me. When Dian got captured, she screamed like she was being murdered.

I was all alone. The scare factor intensified as I walked beneath the stand of dark cottonwoods. The temperature seemed to drop in those few lonely moments. The wind swirled around me, making chill bumps pop out on my neck. I couldn't turn and look behind me because it was against Ghost Train rules.

Shadows morphed into mysterious objects waiting to kill me and drag me under the ground with all the dead bodies buried beneath the tombstones. I continued walking and listening, alert to every sound and smell and gust through the black tree branches.

After another trip around the church, I was sure everyone had actually, truly, been captured by a murderer, a lunatic who hid in the cotton field, waiting for us to play this game, maybe even the man who lived in the gray house. I had invited him to come, but instead of eating chicken and dressing, he was eating the kids, one by one, and I was next. I took giant steps, like Momma does when she's shopping in town, rushing from store to store and checking things off her list. When I heard someone behind me, I tried to prepare myself for the grab. Get ready, get ready, get ready.... As the hand grabbed my shoulder, I cried into the night.

The ghost screamed too.

The ghost was Abby.

***

"Y'all are asking for trouble," Momma said, as we pulled out of the church parking lot and turned toward Sugar Ditch instead of home.

"What do you mean?" I asked. Since Daddy was working so late getting the cotton out of the fields before winter set in, Momma promised to bring him a plate of food. I held the paper plate in my lap and could tell by the mounded shape of the foil covering the top that Momma heaped a lot of food under there. Even with all the time that had passed, the bottom felt warm through my jeans.

"Playing scary games at church is not a good idea, especially games with ghosts," she said.

"Do you think ghosts are real, Momma?" Abby asked. The night was so black I couldn't see Abby's face until a car passed and illuminated the back seat. In a flash, darkness returned.

"You just never know," Momma said. I'd never known Momma to be afraid of ghosts or anything for that matter.

"You never know what?" I asked. Ghost Train was one of the most fun things we did at Boon Chapel and being scared crazy was what made it fun. I wasn't sure why that was.

"Grace, there are some things we don't understand, because we aren't meant to understand."

Since I didn't understand what she was really trying to say, I changed the subject. I had learned to do that pretty well, mainly by listening to Momma and Maggie. "Where is Daddy picking cotton tonight?"

"Sugar Ditch," she said. As we passed Vera's Bar, there weren't many trucks out front, probably because the farmers were picking cotton instead of drinking beer. Momma turned onto a dirt road that I couldn't see and found her way to Daddy's field. She knew how to get to each of Daddy's fields even though all the dirt roads and ditches looked the same. Especially at night.

In the distance, three pickers moved through the field like massive dinosaurs, churning up dust mixed with cotton lint. Momma parked on the turnrow, and we walked over to Daddy's truck. I carried the plate of food and wondered if he was looking forward to it. At first, he didn't notice us because he sat inside watching the pickers and talking on his two-way radio to someone. When he saw us, he stepped outside and grunted hello. His truck was his office, the dashboard was covered in papers, and his cooler sat in the middle of his seat. Momma took the plate from me, pulled the foil cover off, and pulled a plastic fork and knife from her coat pocket. Daddy sat on the tailgate of his truck and ate his Harvest Supper meal unhurriedly, probably too tired to muster excitement about chicken and dressing and creamed potatoes. Daddy put all his effort and energy into the crops he raised, leaving nothing for himself or anyone else. Momma always said he worked hard for us, but I thought there was something more to it, like maybe he was trying to prove something.

Momma pulled her coat tighter around her body. "It's chilly. We'll see you back at the house." Daddy nodded and said something I couldn't hear. Momma knew better than to ask what time he would be home or to say, "Don't work too late." As we backed down the dirt road, our headlights cast a dark outline around the bill of his cap. His face was unrecognizable.

Chapter Twenty-Eight

Next to summer vacation, our three-week Christmas break was the most wonderful time of the year. Teachers assigned no homework, I had no immediate worries other than regular life things, and if we were lucky, snow would fall for at least part of the holiday. Five days into our break, though, we still didn't have our Christmas tree.

"Can we go today?" Abby asked as she worked on her Christmas list. Since breakfast, we had been sitting at the kitchen table, studying the Sears Christmas catalog, turning down pages and circling items we couldn't live without. Christmas lists were not taken lightly. Santa saw us through to spring and summer birthdays. "Why do we have to wait so long?" she added when Momma didn't respond.

"Dian already has her tree," I said, folding my arms over my still-flat chest. I was prepared to debate, yet knew there was a delicate line between being persuasive and simply annoying Momma. Plus, with Santa watching our every move, we knew we were treading on delicate ground.

"Aunt Fannie is nicer than I am." Momma squirted dishwashing liquid over the dirty dishes in the sink, and a froth of fresh-scented bubbles grew. Aunt Fannie was usually nicer, but I didn't dare agree.

I read over my list to make sure it was complete and included exactly what I wanted—mainly a new bicycle with a banana seat and a few of my favorite Nancy Drew books—then signed my name at the bottom. At the top of Abby's list, she asked for a dump truck.

"Abby, are you sure about that? That's a boy present." Although we both had tomboy tendencies and loved to play in the dirt, I didn't think wasting her main Santa gift on a boy present made sense. At the mere mention of a slot car or a baseball bat, Papa Pete would buy it for us.

Abby took my advice. She erased and erased and erased until she almost ripped the notebook paper. With Momma's help, she then wrote baby doll in large block letters with a black marker at the top of her list. That was a much better choice. After rummaging through Momma's junk drawer, I found a roll of clear adhesive tape and raced into the living room with my Santa letter. Abby followed.

Our empty stockings were already hanging from the mantle. I taped our letters on the wall next to the rock fireplace, Santa's magical entryway into our house. Writing our lists well in advance of Christmas allowed plenty of time for toy building and sleigh packing. Santa needed as much time as possible. He was the second busiest man I knew, next to Daddy. I stared at Abby's letter. With all her erasing, the notebook paper looked crumpled and wrinkled, with stray pencil marks everywhere.

"Maybe you should write your list over. It's so messy," I said shaking my head.

"Don't worry, it's fine," Momma said as she walked into the living room without making a sound. She still wore her yellow rubber dishwashing gloves and seemed more concerned about her household chores than Christmas.

"It's fine," Abby repeated and stuck her tongue out at me when Momma wasn't looking. I would have started over with a clean sheet of paper.

After spending the entire morning pestering Momma about getting a tree, we finally gave up. Tree-buying was not on her list for the day. It was hard to imagine being an adult with complete control over an afternoon or a day or an entire life yet not wanting to rush out and buy a Christmas tree. Maybe if we made a paper chain to count down the days until Christmas, Momma would realize how close Christmas was and be more willing to tree shop. Some people had to see things before they really believed.

While Momma vacuumed all around us, moving furniture and making noise, we spread our chain-making supplies on the dining room table. With twelve days until Christmas, I divided a piece of red paper into six fairly even strips. While Abby cut out the strips along the mark I had drawn, I repeated the process with the green piece of paper. Once all twelve pieces were cut, we glued them into loops, alternating colors.

Red.

Green.

Red.

Green.

Red.

Green.

Red.

Green.

Red.

Green.

Red.

Green.

When our paper chain was finished and the glue had dried, Momma let us hang it from the nail in the kitchen where the bean rooster picture used to be. Since Daddy slammed his fist into the wall and broke the wooden frame, that portion of the wall had been bare. Momma said she was planning to fix the frame, but so far, the picture was safely stored in the back corner of her bedroom closet. Whenever her closet door stood open, it looked like a real rooster lived behind her clothes.

"Our chain looks good, don't you think, Momma?" I asked when she walked through the kitchen, dragging the vacuum cleaner toward the den.

"Yes, very nice," she said, but she didn't pay it much attention.

"It covers the ugly hole Daddy punched in the wall too," Abby said. Momma looked up again and nodded.

The next morning, we made a great production about removing the bottom link from our paper chain. "Time to take off a link, Abby," I said as though delivering a line in a play.

Abby, who knew what to do because we had practiced in our bedroom, jumped from her chair and scampered over to it but could barely touch the tail end with the tips of her fingers. I went over to help. Even though I could only lift her a couple of inches, it was enough that she could tear the last link off. "Yay!" she shouted as she held the ripped paper above her head like a prize. Momma smiled. Daddy stared at us like we were crazy.

"One day closer to Christmas. We should probably get our tree soon," Momma said. Our plan was working.

"Today?" Abby and I both asked at the same time.

"Soon," Momma said. Although "soon" meant not today, we were making progress.

***

Two days later, Daddy came home early so Momma could use his truck to fetch our tree. The back room of the hardware store had been transformed into an enchanted pine forest. Trees were propped against the wall, several rows thick, hiding all evidence of shovels, rakes, and sacks of giant dog food. I brushed at the tree limbs and stirred fresh balsa through the icy air. My frosty breath spread then disappeared into evergreen boughs.

Momma held tree after tree upright for us to consider.

Was the top straight enough for the star? Was the bottom the right size for our red metal stand? Was it the perfect shape to fill our large living room picture window?

"I love this one!" I said after walking around it twice. Abby chose a different one that basically looked identical to the one I chose. Momma preferred to shop, to consider lots of trees before selecting her favorite. I saw no need since every Christmas tree was beautiful. Even the small, scraggly ones looked cute, and I felt sad we couldn't adopt them all. Eventually, when Abby became distracted looking at a display of fake snowmen covered in fake snow, Momma agreed to buy my tree. Mr. Turpin, who had been hovering around waiting for us to decide, loaded it into the bed of Daddy's pickup truck and tied it down with rope from the big spool by the aisle where seed packets were sold in spring.

"You picked a fine tree," he said. He wore a furry hat with flaps covering his ears, and his fat cheeks were as pink as Santa himself. I nodded and felt happy about our decision since, after all, Mr. Turpin was an expert who'd had plenty of time to study all the trees.

"Momma, do you want me to ride back there with it?" On tiptoes, I reached over the side of Daddy's truck and strained to touch the top, where the gold star would go.

"Don't be ridiculous. It's twenty degrees outside." I kept a watchful eye on it all the way home, as though our tree were a new puppy that might jump out and run away.

At breakfast the next morning, Daddy ignored Momma when she said he looked tired. "Why don't you take the day off and rest?" she said. Daddy said farmers got no sick days. Even when the ground was too frozen for crops to grow, farmers had work to do. Abby and I stared at the tree sitting outside on the front patio. Its thick branches, lightly dusted with snow, filled the window and blocked the view of the highway and winter field beyond.

"When can we bring the tree in?" I asked.

"Not until after breakfast." Momma added a smear of butter to my grits, which pooled yellow against the white creaminess. Momma had hard and fast procedures about tree decorating. Her number one rule was the tree could never be allowed inside the house until the day after it was purchased. Waiting was agony, yet somehow Abby and I had managed to sleep through the night, knowing our tree stood alone outside in the bitter cold.

Now it watched us eat breakfast. "I'm not hungry," Abby sulked. She ran to the dining room and stared outside, her palms flattened against windows coated with dust that clung to everything long after fall harvest. "Look at it, Momma. It wants to come inside. What if it gets buried in snow?"

A gray bird landed on the patio and pecked around, his sharp yellow beak searching for anything to eat. "Why do we always have to wait a whole day to decorate?" I swallowed a spoonful of the hot grits, and it burned all the way down into my belly.

"I've told you before, the boughs have to fall. If we decorated the minute we untied it from the truck, the ornaments wouldn't hang right." Momma refilled her coffee cup and added a squirt of something sweet from a white bottle she stored in the overhead cabinet. She was moving through her routine as though it were a regular morning. Four stirs of her spoon to mix the powdery creamer. Scanning the newspaper for grocery sales. Filling in a line on the crossword puzzle with her yellow pencil. Even her blinking seemed snail slow.

"Did Nana teach you this rule?" I asked. I didn't think such a silly idea would come from Nana. "You know Momma, there's such a thing as gravity. The weight of the ornaments and the pull of the Earth's gravity will help the branches fall more quickly."

"You girls are wearing me out," she said. Momma didn't care anything about Isaac Newton. Daddy chuckled and headed out the door with his thermos of coffee.

After the breakfast dishes were washed, and every single thing Momma could think to do was done, she freed the box of ornaments from the top shelf in the utility closet. Even though it was only an old, yellowed Goldsmith's box reinforced with duct tape, inside hid Momma's impressive ornament collection—silver and gold balls, fragile globes, and trimmings of every color and size.

Digging around in the box, I became reacquainted with my favorites while Momma dragged the tree into the living room and began wrapping strings of lights around the "fallen" Christmas tree branches. Instantly, the room smelled of Christmas.

"Oh, I forgot about this one!" I said holding up a small red bell that made a tinkling sound when I moved it. I had received it last year at the school Christmas party when we drew names. This year, instead of exchanging gifts, my classmates and I brought socks to give to the starving kids in Africa. It was a school-wide project with each class bringing a different item. Abby's class was in charge of bringing new toothbrushes. As far as I knew, none of the classes brought actual food for those poor kids, so I wasn't sure how we were helping them not be hungry.

"I made this one when I was a little kid," Abby said, admiring an angel ornament she had cut from a picture in her coloring book and glued to a piece of red construction paper. Green flecks of glitter floated to the couch as she waved it overhead.

While Momma decorated all the high spots, Abby and I hung ornaments on the bottom section of the tree. When we finished, Momma pronounced it our most beautiful tree yet. She continued on with her daily chores, but Abby and I spent the remainder of the day playing and reading in the living room to be as close as possible to the tree.

Chapter Twenty-Nine

I removed another link on our paper chain, which no longer looked like a chain at all. There were only two links left. *Deux*! *Rouge*.

Vert.

The whole notion that Santa would soon load his sleigh and travel to every single kid's house—the ones on the good list anyway—consumed my waking hours and filled my dreams. I wondered about his last-minute preparations and whether or not he was like Momma, packing two or three days in advance.

"Momma, I'll wash the breakfast dishes," I said after we'd finished eating. Momma had made biscuits and gravy and a whole skillet full of bacon. Daddy dropped his newspaper onto the table and gave me a skeptical look. I jumped over and took the apron Momma was about to wrap around her waist and tied it around my own. The red ruffled hem hung to my shins.

"That would be really nice, Grace," she said. "Maybe I'll go take a nice, long bath." Momma refilled her coffee and took it with her saying, "I'll see y'all in an hour." When she practically floated around the corner into the hallway, I realized I should offer to do the Saturday breakfast dishes more often and not just when I was hoping for last-minute points with Santa Claus.

Once Momma was out of earshot, Daddy pulled his wallet from his pocket and began peeling off ten and twenty dollar bills. "Grace, here's some money. Get your Nana to take you to Sterling's after lunch. Buy your Momma something for Christmas from me." He counted the money into my hand like the lady at the bank did when Momma cashed a check. "Twenty, forty, sixty, eighty, ninety, one hundred. Don't lose it."

"I won't." I folded the money in my hand. The wad felt thick and substantial and important, and I wished I could keep it and walk around with that kind of money all the time. Even though I'd never tell anyone I was rich, just knowing I could buy anything I wanted at any time would be some kind of feeling.

Daddy had given us money for Momma's gift last Christmas too, so this year we'd been expecting it. Momma had even whispered to me last night before bed, "Daddy hasn't given you any money yet?" When I shook my head no, her eyes were flat and dull, the color of lake water on a cloudy day.

"He probably forgot to go to the bank. I bet he'll remember tomorrow," I said while rubbing my eyes. "Or, maybe he's already bought you something." For once, I was sleepy, but I knew if we talked much longer, the feeling would go away.

"Without help? Oh, I doubt it," she said. Before I fell asleep, I tried to file a reminder on a shelf in the front of my brain so I would remember to ask Daddy about it. Luckily, he remembered because by breakfast, all I could think about was Santa.

"What do you want us to get her?" I asked. Daddy poured the rest of the coffee into his thermos and pulled on his heavy coat.

"Something good. You and Abby decide," he said. "You know what she likes." In the few seconds it took him to open the back door and leave, a blast of cold air filled the kitchen and chilled my feet through my thick socks.

"Abby, go tell Momma that we got the money, but don't barge into the bathroom while she's taking a bath." I hated when Abby did that to me. She raced through the dining room and into the hallway. While I finished washing the last dish, I heard her jubilant cheer, "We got the money, Momma!"

Nana must have been on standby. As soon as I handed over the cash to Momma, Nana pulled into our driveway, and in no time we were headed to Goldsmith's in Memphis instead of Sterling's in Savage Crossing. What Daddy didn't realize was Momma had been planning this shopping spree for months. In late August when we did our back-to-school shopping, Momma picked out a fancy topaz ring and paid the man behind the jewelry counter ten dollars to hold it for her. For the past several months, Momma made small payments on the ring with grocery money she had squirrelled away in the hidden compartment of her billfold. What would she have done if Daddy had given her a new vacuum cleaner, and she couldn't bail out her layaway present?

Although snow covered our gravel driveway and the fields around our house, the interstate was clear. Momma was glad about that. During the drive to Memphis, Nana and Momma talked non-stop about our Christmas Eve dinner to be held at Nana and Papa Pete's house after the Boon Chapel Christmas program. The whole conversation was interesting to me, because they were planning to cook the exact meal they had just cooked a few weeks ago for Thanksgiving—turkey and dressing, creamed potatoes, green bean casserole, and sweet potatoes rolled in flaked coconut, which I didn't like but ate, because it was tradition. The before and after foods would all be the same too. Celery sticks spread with cream cheese, sweet pickles and green olives for snacking before dinner, and two kinds of pies for dessert. Instead of saying, "Why don't we make exactly what we made for Thanksgiving?" and moving on to a different topic, they rehashed it down to the meringue on top of the chocolate pie. And just like that, we were crossing over the Mississippi River and into Memphis.

Getting inside Goldsmith's was a bit complicated, but we'd done it enough to understand how it worked. After taking the stairs to the bottom floor of the parking garage, a tunnel underneath the street connected the garage to the store. It was no ordinary tunnel. That l-o-o-o-o-o-o-o-o-n-g passageway was one of the best parts of Goldsmith's. Inside, the air was fresh and clean—infused by a zillion shampoos and hair sprays that lined the shelves. Every shampoo ever invented could be found in that tunnel, even all the cool ones advertised in Candi's teen magazines. Every time we walked through, we begged Momma to let us buy a bottle of new shampoo, but she always said, "Maybe on the way out." On the way out, she was always in a hurry to get home to start supper.

Just beyond the tunnel, a bakery displayed trays with iced cookies and cakes and gingerbread men. Walking by without stopping was a torturous thing. The sugar sparkled underneath golden lights, and the sweet smell of cinnamon drifted to my nose. Sometimes Momma let us get a cookie, but only if she, too, was hungry, and not this time because she had only one thing on her mind—buying her ring. We walked quickly past and into another world filled with escalators and elevators and wide stairs and rails for swinging on when we could get away with it. Unlike Sterling's, there was a separate floor for each department.

While Nana went with Abby to the bathroom, Momma pulled me aside, unsnapped her purse, and pulled out her billfold. "Gracie, I'm giving you the money. You pay for my ring so when Daddy asks, you won't have to lie about it." This was another example of one of those little white lies that didn't seem so bad. She placed the wad of money into my palm and closed my fingers around it. "Tell the lady at the counter you need to pay for something in layaway. Give her this ticket. There's enough money here for the balance plus tax," she said as she handed a white slip of paper to me.

"Do I give her a tip?" I asked.

"No." Momma looked confused at first but then understood what I meant. Daddy always tipped the waitress when we ate at Bill's Grill, so it was a good question.

While Momma stood nearby pretending to look at a display of ladies hats, I walked ahead to the jewelry department, a large area enclosed by crystal-clear glass cases filled with all types of jewelry. Gold rings, watches with leather bands, and bracelets were draped over green velvet cloth. Necklaces hung from hanger-like displays. Fake white hands stuck straight up out of the velvet and showed off birthstone rings, one on every finger, even the thumb. An entire case contained earrings—milky pearls, tiny gold balls, small silver hearts. How did anyone ever choose?

"May I help you," a man peered over the case at me. I hadn't noticed him at all, and my stomach turned a flip for no reason. He wore a pinstriped suit with a vest that made him appear pencil thin. I stared at his spindly mustache and thought he looked more like a cartoon villain than a jewelry salesman.

"Yes, sir. I'm here to pay off my momma's ring. It's on layaway." I slid the white slip of paper across the countertop and accidentally left a smudge on the glass.

He picked up the paper, read the number and said, "Wait here, miss." When he walked away, I erased the smudge I had made on the countertop with the elbow of my wool coat. Standing still, I didn't touch the clean glass again even though I had the urge to run my hand along the top. When I looked back at Momma, she and Nana were talking. Abby was making silly faces in front of a full-length mirror.

"Here we go," the man said as he placed the small box on the countertop. It was a square satin box—something ideal for holding a treasure. "The balance is one hundred fifty-two dollars and eighty-five cents with tax."

"Can I look at it?" I asked. It wasn't that I didn't trust him. I wanted to be the first to see it.

"Certainly," he said. With a twist of his wiry wrist, he opened the lid with a snap.

The ring was pretty. Really, really, pretty, like something a lady would wear to an elegant ball. I wondered if Momma would wear it on her Saturday night dates with Daddy, or if she would save it for truly special occasions. The shiny gold band held a round, smoky blue stone almost the size of a penny, and there were two tiny diamonds on each side. When he slid it closer for me to see, the light caught the edge and the stone glinted, looking more silver than blue. But it was the box that intrigued me. The ring sat bolstered by a puff of gray velvet, like a tiny pillow. Like a dream.

I pulled the fistful of money from my purse and began counting it out the same way Daddy had counted the money to me earlier in the day. "Twenty, forty, sixty, eighty, one hundred, one hundred and twenty, one hundred and forty, one hundred and fifty, plus a five-dollar bill makes one hundred and fifty-five dollars."

The man took the bills and arranged them so that all the United States Presidents were facing the same way, then pressed numbers on the cash register and handed me two one-dollar bills, a dime, and a nickel in change. For fifty cents more, he offered to wrap Momma's gift in slick white paper with a silver ribbon. That sounded like a nice thing to do, but I asked him to please not put one of those Goldsmith's stickers on it. He looked at me strangely but said okay.

Chapter Thirty

On Christmas Eve morning, I spent a little more time trying to make my hair look decent for church. Momma spent more time on breakfast too. She made scrambled eggs and cinnamon toast. That sprinkle of cinnamon and sugar made a regular piece of white bread, more like dessert. After Momma placed all the food on the table, she rushed back into her bedroom to finish dressing.

"Did you get something for your Momma yesterday?" Daddy muttered.

"Yes, and she'll love it!" I said, flashing a knowing smile at Abby.

"Yes, she'll love it," Abby echoed.

"Good," he said as he continued reading his paper. "Did you have any change left?"

"Yes." I had been waiting for this question and handed him a nickel. He smirked and told me to keep it. The real story was we had used all the money Daddy gave us. The small amount left over from Momma's secret stash was used to buy cookies at the Goldsmith's bakery. Since I didn't want to be accused of stealing his hard-earned change, I had dug a nickel from the bottom of my jewelry box to give him. I didn't think he would really take it, but even if he had, five cents was a small price to pay.

Last night after our trip to Memphis, Mae had come to stay with us while Momma and Daddy went to a Christmas dance at the American Legion. Momma looked glamorous in a long, ruby-colored dress that showed off her waist with a silver belt. She wore a bunch of jangly silver bracelets on one arm, and I thought it was too bad she couldn't wear her new ring. Daddy even looked handsome in his dark, gray "funeral" suit. That's what he called it since he only wore it to weddings and funerals. According to Daddy, weddings were only a different type of funeral.

While they were out, Abby and I ate supper fast so that Mae could help us bake sugar cookies. All we had to do was slice and bake them, but since we weren't allowed to cook without an adult, Mae did the oven part. Afterward, Abby and I added red and green sprinkles on top and put the best looking cookies on a special plate to save them for Santa.

Later, when Mae fell asleep on the couch, which she sometimes did, Abby and I decided to make Christmas presents for Momma and Daddy. Although we didn't have much money, we had lots of art supplies, and I had a great idea for presents—gift certificates. With construction paper and markers, we made an IOU for Momma promising five Saturday morning dish washings. And for Daddy's certificate, we promised to clean and polish his cowboy boots five times. We put expiration dates of next Christmas on both, because having something like dishwashing and boot polishing hanging over our heads for the rest of our lives would have been a drag. After folding and decorating the outside of the certificates, I hid them under the tree.

***

"Daddy, our Christmas program is tonight," I said.

"Uh-huh," he said without looking up from his newspaper.

"You should come!" Abby cheered and bounced in her chair, jingling the bells on the red ribbon tied around her hair. That sound would annoy Momma before the end of church. Daddy didn't say anything or look up from his paper.

"Abby has a solo," I said. She beamed.

"Is that right?" he muttered.

"Yes! I get to sing a whole line of 'Silent Night' all by myself." Abby began singing as Momma walked through the kitchen in a tither.

"Girls, we're late. Hurry and brush your teeth. We need to go." Momma grabbed a piece of toast, took a big bite, and dropped the rest on the plate. She opened the door and let Lucky run outside while we brushed our teeth.

192

On the short drive to Boon Chapel, I stared at the winter fields passing by my window, a blur of straight rows crowned with snow. In winter, nothing grew. After the energy and excitement of picking cotton, the soil seemed to hibernate like a bear waiting for spring. Christmas was the best time to go to church, but Daddy had no interest in hearing Abby and me sing in the annual program. I didn't think he believed any part of Jesus's birthday story. He only believed in hard work and taking care of his fields. He might have been a little less grumpy, if he could find a way to believe God was the one in charge of growing those crops.

The parking lot was more crowded than normal, so Momma parked on the side of the road. Inside, the pews were filled. Nana waved us over to our regular spots while Momma raced up to the piano, apologizing for being late. Service started with holiday hymns instead of the same tired songs. Everyone sang with extra enthusiasm and even kept up to Momma's tempo. Her fingertips had a bit more pep to them.

Sunday school class was about the shepherd boy who visited baby Jesus. Even though we all knew the basic Christmas story by heart, it was one that never got old, and I learned something new each time I heard it. Later, when Mr. Nicholson read announcements, he reminded the congregation about the Christmas Eve program at five o'clock. Everyone nodded and looked around at those of us who would sing later. Nana gave me a little pat on the shoulder. She was wearing a Christmas tree pin on the collar of her jacket that sparkled every time she moved.

Brother Brown's morning sermon was about Mary and how she obeyed God and did what was asked of her and was overall a worthy and faithful servant. He said Mary was a young virgin who had never "lain with a man." Although the specific details were fuzzy to me, I thought he was talking about s-e-x. I had a vague idea of what that meant because we sometimes talked about it on the playground, mainly to see if anyone had figured it out. When the angel Gabriel said, "Fear not for behold I bring you tidings of great joy," Mary and her whole family went right along with everything.

When Brother Brown said, "God found favor with Mary. She was full of grace," Abby elbowed me as though he had called out my name. She wasn't paying attention at all.

193

Even though Jesus's birth happened a long time ago and Mary was dead and so were all the people who knew her, I couldn't help but feel sorry for her. She was forced to have a baby when she was only a young girl. I imagined her classmates teasing her and her parents yelling at her, at least in the beginning. She must have been scared crazy. I couldn't understand how Brother Brown and all the adults glossed over this important part of the story. What if Gabriel visited me in the night? There was no doubt in my mind that such tidings would not be well received by Lee Abbott. Not at all.

When it came time for the invitational hymn, I was hoping for a Christmas song, but we sang the same old one. Although I hadn't planned to go up and talk to Brother Brown, he looked over at me, so I decided it would be a good time to ask him a few things. Nana moved her knees to the side to give me more space to walk. I slipped right past Aunt Clara with no problem because she was a tiny bird. As I walked toward the pulpit, I noticed a bright green handkerchief poking from Brother Brown's suit coat pocket. He looked very Christmas-y.

"Good morning, Grace."

"Good morning, Brother Brown."

"What's on your mind?"

"Mostly, I'm thinking about Christmas."

"That's understandable. Anything specific?"

"Yes, three things actually," I said. "But if you don't have time for all three, I can spread them out into next year." Saying next year like it was a long time off was a fun thing to do when *next year* officially started next week.

He smiled and told me to go ahead. "I'll do my best to cover everything today," he said.

So I started with the easiest thing and explained how hard it was for me to remember the most exciting part of Christmas was baby Jesus's birthday and not all the new Barbies and board games on the shelves at Sterling's.

"Yes, the commercial side is difficult to ignore, isn't it?" he said. "There's no reason to feel guilty about wanting a new toy at Christmas. Just keep Jesus in your heart, and remember he's the real reason we celebrate."

I shook my head okay but worried I had been thinking more about the new bicycle on top of my Santa Claus list than I had been thinking about Jesus. Maybe that was understandable since there wasn't a single thing in Sterling's to remind me about Jesus. "The other thing I want to say, even though I know you can't do anything about it, is I wish Daddy would come to our program tonight. But he won't."

"Did you invite him?"

"Yes. Abby and I both did." He looked down at his brown shoes like he didn't know what to say, probably because there weren't any words to make it better. If I made a list of all the things I knew to be one thousand percent true, Daddy won't go to church, would be near the top. "Why do you think he won't ever come to church?" I asked.

"Grace, people don't go to church for a variety of reasons. Some are uncomfortable. Some simply are nonbelievers. Some find it unnecessary and have their own ways to worship. There's no way for me to know your dad's reason, but if you'd like, I could stop by and talk with him about it sometime."

"Oh, God, no." I said then clasped my hand over my mouth. "I'm sorry for saying 'God' that way, but definitely not. That would only make him angry. Like super-duper angry."

He averted his eyes like he knew I was right. "If you change your mind, I'd be happy to."

I shook my head and made him pinkie swear not to. When we joined little fingers, his felt stiff and cold like a twig that had fallen from the mimosa tree. I got the impression he had no idea what we were doing, but he did it anyway.

"You said you had three things?" He stared right in my eyes, and for the first time I felt like he was really listening to me.

"Yes. I don't want to have a baby." I pointed to my stomach. "I'm only ten years old, and if I'm forced to have a baby, my entire life will be ruined."

Brother Brown coughed and coughed until he pulled that swanky green handkerchief from his pocket and wiped his mouth with it. His eyes and nose turned candy apple red.

"Grace, why are you worried about that?" He whispered and glanced over at Momma, which meant I would probably get a lecture later. Momma began to play louder, or maybe I imagined it, but every

195

note seemed harsher and brasher as though she was sending me a message through her fingertips.

"I'm just saying, what's to keep Gabriel from visiting me in the night? I'm always awake anyway. If God was looking to have another son, it would be my luck to be chosen and forced into it. Plus, I have the perfect name for it."

Brother Brown walked me over to the front pew and we sat. "Grace, that sort of virgin birth won't happen again."

"How can you be so sure? Does the Bible say that?"

"Well, no, not in so many words. Maybe this is a topic better suited for your mother."

"Brother Brown, you're the preacher. She's just the piano player."

"Grace, do you remember John 3:16?"

"Yes." It was one of the first verses I learned when I was a little kid. I began to recite it to him so he wouldn't think I was lying. "For God so loved the world that he gave His only begotten son…Brother Brown, what exactly does begotten mean?"

"Grace, the point I'm trying to make are with the words 'only son,'" he said.

"Oh. So Jesus will always be an only child, like my cousin Dian?"

"Yes, I think so." He stood so I stood. When he draped his arm around my shoulder and walked me toward the red carpet, I knew our conversation was finished. I wasn't sure I got clear answers to any of my questions but went back to my pew. Everyone was sick of singing "Just As I Am." I could hear it in their voices.

On the way home, I asked Momma the meaning of "begotten."

"It's an old-fashioned word used in the Bible to show family generations."

"So like Daddy was begotten by Mamaw Pearl?"

"Sort of. But I think that word is only used to refer to men. Like Grandpa Abbott begat Daddy," she explained.

"Because God was a male chauvinist pig?"

"Grace. Don't say that."

I shrugged my shoulders, because that was how it sounded to me. "What would happen if the angel Gabriel appeared to me and forced me to have a baby? Would you be happy about it?" I asked.

196

"I'm sure I wouldn't, but you don't need to worry about things like that happening." Everyone seemed convinced Mary's troubles couldn't happen again, so I shoved the thought to the back of my mind and decided to think about Santa Claus again. Still, I was glad I had brought it up in case it did happen to me. Momma had been forewarned.

***

The Boon Chapel ladies seemed to live for the night of our Christmas Eve program. They beamed up at us as we stood in a semi-straight row, singing Christmas hymn after Christmas hymn with no harmony or variety. We sounded average, but the congregation seemed delighted, swaying their heads and applauding after each song. As the piano player, Momma always got stuck with the job of planning the whole thing for the youth group. I didn't think we could technically be considered a "group" since there were only five of us: my cousin Dian, the Donaldson twins, Abby, and me. Momma said anything over a pair was a group, so maybe so.

Nana sat in the third row with her hair piled higher than normal, because she wore her wiglet on special occasions. She looked calm and pulled together, even though I knew that she must have worked hard all afternoon to have our dinner ready to eat as soon as the program was over. Momma did the same. She whipped together a green bean casserole and a pecan pie just after lunch. When we dropped it off at Nana and Papa Pete's house on the way back to church, I smelled turkey roasting in the oven. Daddy disappeared all afternoon, so we never got another chance to invite him to the program—not that he would have come.

I was wearing my purple Halloween queen dress, the one Daddy burned with his cigarette. Momma sewed a row of rickrack above the spot where my waist would go someday, and that pale pink trim covered the hole well enough. As I stood between my sister and cousin, I thought about how much time we'd spent together in this ordinary building and how although I usually didn't want to go to church, lots of things happened here. Maybe songs sung and words spoken would someday turn out to be important instead of a waste of time.

Abby's voice sounded clear and steady, and she did a good job on her "Silent Night" solo, even the "sleep in heavenly peeeee-eeeeeece" part that was hard to sing. I played "We Three Kings" on the piano. Even though my nerves were in a tangle, I did an okay job and my fingers moved across the keys without having to think about it. The Donaldson girls, who got fancy hairdos for the occasion, sang a duet without music. Dian read the Christmas passage from Luke about the great tidings that I knew would have never been considered joyful at our house. The last song in our lineup was identical to last year's and every year before—"We Wish You a Merry Christmas"—with the entire congregation joining in for the final verse. The final verse was the same as the first verse. Momma said everyone expected it so we couldn't change it up.

The best thing about the night was the conclusion, because that's when Santa appeared in the back of the sanctuary, wearing a red suit lined in white fur. His fluffy beard hung to the middle of his belly. Over his shoulder, he lugged a large burlap bag. "Ho, Ho, Ho!" Santa said as he walked up to us first, because he knew we were the stars of the night. He spread good cheer to each of us in the form of plain paper sacks he pulled from his bag. The Boon Chapel Santa wasn't the real Santa. It was Mr. Donaldson.

I opened my sack and inhaled the smell of Christmas—an apple, a tangerine, assorted nuts, and individually wrapped chocolate and peppermints. I peeled off the tangerine skin in one section. The segments burst in my mouth, sweet and juicy. Abby started eating her chocolate right away, but I saved mine.

***

On the drive to Nana and Papa's house, I stared at the starless sky. It was too early to spot Santa, but I wondered where he was. Daddy met us at Nana and Papa's house after stopping to pick up Mamaw Pearl and Candi. It was a big family gathering, and one of the only nights of the year when Daddy was in a happy mood. He smiled, and talked, and as far as I could tell drank tea instead of whiskey. He even helped Nana put the extra leaf in the dining room table. By the time we sat down to eat, her table was crammed with so many bowls and platters that I could barely see her red Christmas tablecloth.

I tried not to eat too much, because I didn't want my stomach to hurt while I was opening presents. On Christmas Eve, after everyone ate and all the adults had eaten second helpings of dessert and drank a ton of coffee, we finally exchanged presents. These presents were usually clothes and shoes and gifts other than toys, since Santa was in charge of toys. But clothes were a good thing, especially since I was getting too tall for most of mine.

Nana and Papa gave Abby and me a snow-cone machine! I wanted to make one right then, but Momma said no, not until we got home, and probably not until after Santa Claus came. Nana got a bright orange pantsuit from Papa Pete that she seemed to love, probably because she picked it out herself. Momma unwrapped Daddy's present with great fanfare, carefully removing the fancy paper without ripping it.

"Oh, my goodness, Lee! You outdid yourself!" Momma oohed and aahed and made a giant fuss over the topaz ring she'd had in layaway for months.

"Does it fit?" Daddy asked, taking Momma's hand and seeing it for the first time. He gave me a skeptical look, but when Aunt Fannie bragged on his taste in jewelry, he grinned with his chest all puffed out. We stopped opening presents for five minutes while everyone took turns admiring Momma's ring. Candi almost got it stuck on her middle finger.

When we finally got back to the gifts, Daddy made an announcement. "I have jewelry for all the kids too. Grace, Abby, Dian, and Candi." We were all surprised, even Momma, when he pulled a plain grocery sack from beside the couch. Inside were four matching brown envelopes. "Go ahead, open them," he said as we all stared at him. He had never bought us real presents without Momma's involvement, and he'd certainly never gotten Christmas gifts for Dian and Candi. I reached into my envelope and pulled out a bracelet wrapped in tissue paper. It was a copper cuff with someone's name on it. At first, I thought it was a mistake because the name engraved on it was PFC James Tyler instead of Grace Abbott.

"P.O.W. bracelets!" Candi said as she slipped hers onto her wrist. Then I understood. We had read about these bracelets in the newspaper.

They were being sold as reminders of soldiers missing or held as prisoners of war.

"Wear your bracelets until your soldier returns from the war," he told us. I glided the cuff on my wrist and squeezed the sides to make it tighter. I wondered what PFC James Tyler was doing on this Christmas Eve and vowed I would never take off my bracelet until he was safe at home. Momma took a picture of the four of us wearing our bracelets. We stood in front of the Christmas tree with our arms touching.

***

I awoke on Christmas morning, wondering if I had been good enough. Unable to bear the thought of a cold, empty living room on Christmas morning, I sent Abby ahead to scout. "Be quiet and don't touch anything," I warned. Abby tiptoed off in her footie pajamas while I prayed that Santa, once again, had graciously overlooked my trespasses. Would Santa leave toys for the "good" child, while skipping the child who sometimes lied—with valid reasons—and caused trouble?

My new bracelet pinched my skin during the night. I repositioned it and rubbed the purple mark on my wrist. James Tyler. I squeezed shut my eyes and hoped if I concentrated hard enough about him, he would stay safe.

"He came!" Abby whispered, jumping on the edge of my bed. Her eyes gleamed in the gray morning light.

I exhaled, relieved. Since Santa never left a note behind in our stockings, no official warning, or hint as to a possible close call, there was no way to know how far down on the good list my name had appeared. But the simple fact that Santa's reindeer managed to locate our farmhouse chimney, year after year, astonished me.

"What did he bring?" I asked, flinging back the covers and popping my feet onto the floor in one fluid movement.

"Lots of stuff. I only peeped from the door, so it would be a surprise."

"Are you sure there are toys for both of us?"

"Yes, there were toys on both sides of the tree!" That was a good sign. Santa always arranged Abby's gifts on the left side of the

Christmas tree, near the piano. Mine were on the right side of the tree, closest to the fireplace. Joint gifts, like the Easy Bake Oven we had gotten last year, were placed right in the front of the tree as a clue that we were to share them. I imagined Santa put Abby's presents on the left side because she was left-handed.

I paused in the doorway and stared at the living room, not wanting to disturb the dreamlike scene. As I gazed at the multicolored tree lights, flickering and sparkling against the icicles, Abby scooted past me to grab her new doll. Since Santa never wrapped gifts, our living room looked like a toy store. I walked to the couch and sat across from the tree, continuing my survey of the room. Santa had brought me the new bicycle I wanted. It was exactly like the one at the store with a banana seat and long streamers coming from the handlebars and a basket in front for carrying things. On both sides of the Christmas tree, stacks of books had been arranged—Nancy Drew for me and assorted books for Abby. I felt bad about Abby's stack. Even though I was almost three years older, everyone, including Santa Claus, treated us like twins and assumed we liked the same things. Abby would never read her stack of books, so really I got a double stack, and she got shortchanged. A new board game sat front and center of the tree, but the biggest surprise of all was the Christmas miracle parked in front of the fireplace, below our stockings. We both stared when we saw it, shocked. Santa had left a dump truck for Abby. He really did know what she wanted, even after she'd erased it from her list.

A few minutes later, when Lucky tried to eat the chocolate in Abby's stocking and we both started yelling at him to stop, Momma and Daddy staggered into the living room still half-asleep. "What on Earth?" Momma asked.

"Lucky almost stole Abby's candy, but I got it from him," I explained.

"Look at all this junk," Daddy said as he stood surveying the room with his arms crossed across his bare chest. I was glad Santa didn't hear him say such a rude thing.

201

Chapter Thirty-One

Miss Lamb explained action verbs while I drew a picture of a cotton boll on the cover of my notebook. Slow, tiresome winter made me want to cry, especially after the thrill of Christmas. The only part of the day with any sunlight was wasted behind an uncomfortable desk at Savage Crossing Elementary. I dragged myself around, dull and glassy-eyed, shocked at how quickly Christmas vacation had slipped away.

As sluggish and dismal as the day had begun, everything turned in a blink, the way miraculous things sometimes did. It happened in the library. Janice and I were sitting together, working on our language assignment, when Mrs. Penny, the librarian, tapped me on the shoulder and said, "Come with me, Grace."

I was in trouble, even though I hadn't done anything wrong except maybe whispering. It had been over a year since we'd even looked at Michelangelo's naked statue picture. Janice gave me a worried look. In fourth grade, we were often in trouble for things we hadn't realized we had done.

I followed Mrs. Penny behind the checkout desk, where students weren't normally allowed. If I hadn't been nervous about being in trouble, the whole thing would have been cool. On the floor, a cardboard box held new books and magazines wrapped in plastic. Unexpected things hid beneath the counter, like paper towels, foam cleaner, and a bag of butterscotch candy. I twisted the P.O.W. bracelet on my wrist, moving it around and around, while waiting to hear what I had done wrong.

"Grace, I need a library helper and thought you might be a good candidate," Mrs. Penny told me.

"Really?"

"You would help me during your study hall. Miss Lamb said since you are an excellent student, you wouldn't miss that period of school." Mrs. Penny spoke in a serene voice, which made everything sound significant.

"How much will I get paid?" I was already imagining the money I could add to the meager savings in my jewelry box.

"It's only a volunteer job," Mrs. Penny said, but her tone was kind, and she didn't make me feel stupid for asking. Mrs. Penny always said the only bad questions were those not asked.

"I'll take it!" Even without getting a salary, I was eager to get started. Most of the teacher helper jobs went to fifth and sixth graders, so I knew it was special to be asked. Candi worked in the principal's office with Mr. Mooney's secretary, but being surrounded by books was the best job of all. The library was the nicest, quietest place at Savage Crossing Elementary. Even the air smelled clean and important.

I worked the last period of the day before the final bell rang. Right off, I could see why Mrs. Penny needed my help. By the time I showed up, lots of kids had filed through the library, leaving messy shelves behind. Mrs. Penny showed me how to re-shelve books so that all the spines were even and aligned on the bookshelf. I respected her organizational skills.

On the bus ride home, I thought about all those books and authors and their words neatly lining thousands and thousands of pages. I learned more in that one hour with Mrs. Penny than I did in a week with Miss Lamb, who spent half the time telling us stories about her college sorority, her most favorite thing in the world. I could tell by the faraway look in her blue and green eyes that Miss Lamb would have rather been back in college than spending her days trying to wrangle our fourth-grade class. She should have put more thought into her life's career.

***

"What are you doing?" Abby asked. She flopped across my bed holding her Barbie coloring book.

"Organizing." I had pulled all my books from the bookshelf in the hallway outside our bedroom door and placed them in four rows on the floor. Dusty cobwebs were strung along the back of the bookcase and onto the wall, and some had stretched across my books.

"Why?" She asked. Abby shoved most of her books underneath her bed, never to be read.

"So I'll know what books I have." I squirted white foamy dots of furniture polish along each shelf and used a washcloth to smear it into a glossy shine.

"Can't you just look up on the shelf and see your books?" Abby asked as she rolled over and hung upside down off the side of the bed. Patti, who had been lying next to her, fell onto the floor and stared at the ceiling.

"I want them in alphabetical order according to the author, like Mrs. Penny files the books at the library."

"Do you want to color?" Abby, who was a gigantic wiggle-worm, jumped to the floor and now lay on her belly, flipping through her coloring book.

"Maybe later."

The project took me the remainder of the night with a break for supper and another break to practice piano because Momma said it couldn't wait. No one seemed to understand the importance of organization. "You need to clean up this mess before bedtime," Momma said. Daddy yelled because he couldn't walk into the bathroom without stepping over a pile of crap. I ignored both of them.

When I finished, I counted and listed eighty-four books on a sheet of notebook paper. Sixty-one books were check-marked red, to show I had read them, including *The Lion, the Witch and the Wardrobe*, which I had just finished the previous weekend. I folded the list and stuck it in front of the first book on the shelf. I didn't pack the shelves too tight, to allow for new books.

Chapter Thirty-Two

Other than snow days, the only wintertime excitement was our class Valentine's Day party, and in fourth grade, we almost lost the privilege of even having the party because we were so bad. At least that's what Miss Lamb threatened all through the beginning of February.

The boys were particularly rowdy on rainy days, when we had to play inside during lunch. Yesterday, Bubba broke our world globe into two sections and wore half of it underneath his shirt all morning. Miss Lamb ignored him until after social studies, when he started moaning and grunting and flopping on the floor, pretending to have a baby. Then while she tried to deal with him, Mitchell climbed on top of the closet, grabbed the pendant lamp and swung from it. I was surprised the light fixture didn't fall, but our old schoolhouse had been built strong enough to survive earthquakes and fourth graders. Later that afternoon, during a science film, Wilbur slipped out the window and ran away from school for the fifth time. I watched him sprint across the football field and disappear into the weeds along the ditch by Bubba's house. Not being a tattletale, I kept my mouth shut, but Arlene, the meanest girl in class and maybe the whole school, alerted Miss Lamb when she said, "Wilbur's run away again! Look at him go!" Wilbur was roadrunner fast, with strong, short legs. I admired his dedication to escaping Savage Crossing Elementary School. It took Mr. Mooney two hours to find him drinking a Coke down at the gas station.

As I pretended to work on my spelling words, I gazed out at the cold, bright sky painted above the playground equipment. Staring at the sky could solve most riddles, and our class was definitely a riddle. The thing is, we weren't any worse than we were in third grade. Or second grade. Or any grade. We were always the same, just older and bigger. High above the trees, a flock of ducks flew in formation, heading east toward the Mississippi River. We were similar to those ducks, each blindly following the leader. Since my classmates and I had started school together in first grade, we were too comfortable, wild and rowdy like brothers and sisters. I reckoned the real problem rested with Miss Lamb. She had no control.

After lunch, when Miss Lamb had been worn to a frazzle, she let us finish our Valentine boxes since tomorrow was Valentine's Day. We girls sat quietly for hours, transforming our ordinary shoeboxes into pink and red works of art. I had brought in one of Momma's high heel shoeboxes. It was extra-large, almost the size of a boot box, with space enough to hold lots of Valentines. Since the boys didn't care one iota about using scissors and cutting out hearts or making Valentine boxes, they did the minimum required to satisfy Miss Lamb by covering their boxes in paper and writing their names on the outside in marker. She sat at her desk, graded papers, and didn't seem too concerned since at least they were keeping quiet. The boys could entertain themselves for hours by squirting globs of Elmer's glue on their fingertips and peeling it off like dried skin once it hardened.

At two o'clock when it was time for study hall, Miss Lamb told us to stack our boxes in a row on the back table and return the art supplies to the cabinet. "And try to do it without sounding like a herd of buffalo," she said.

I placed mine on top of two others so it wouldn't get squished. The boxes looked bright and festive, lining the back table like a pink and red brick wall. Even the boys' barely decorated boxes looked okay mixed in with the girls' pretty ones.

"Students, as long as you don't make any noise, I don't care if you spend your study hall hour working on homework, reading your library book, or writing notes to each other. I have a headache and don't want to hear a pin drop," she said.

Although I wouldn't have minded writing another letter to the man in the gray house, I didn't have time. Mrs. Penny needed me in the library.

I spent my entire library shift cleaning. I noticed the problem first, before Mrs. Penny even. Someone had scribbled over the top of the corner table with a black marker. Since the second graders had just been to the library, I wondered who among Abby's classmates would do such a thing to a library table. The ink marks eventually came off, but I had to use half a can of special foam cleaner and a whole roll of paper towels. Cleaning that table the way I did, Mrs. Penny knew I was serious and trustworthy. She left me alone in the library while she went down to the office to copy papers. That made me feel good inside. Most teachers didn't treat us like real people.

When the bell rang, I headed over to the music room for my piano lesson. Even though my lessons had been going better because I had been putting more effort into practice, I wasn't looking forward to it. I saw Abby walking across the playground and caught up to her, because she was walking turtle-slow even though the wind was brisk and cold.

"Why are you walking so slow?"

"I'm not. I'm walking normal."

"Race you!" I said. Abby kept walking at her same slow pace so I easily won, but little good it did me. When I got to the music room, I drew in a cold, deep breath and peeped inside. The room was dark and quiet. Afternoon shadows fell across the piano in a gray crisscross pattern. I tried to push open the door, but it wouldn't budge. I sat on the sidewalk and leaned against the brick building, wondering why Mrs. Allard wasn't waiting for us. Abby floated across the straw-like grass with no regard for the wind whipping her hair into her face.

"Why are you sitting out here?" Abby asked when she finally reached me.

"The room is locked. Maybe we won't have our lessons." That would have been a welcomed ending to the day. "Abby, I spent a whole hour cleaning marker from one of the library tables right after your class was there. Who do you think would mess up a table like that?" She shrugged and said she didn't think anyone would do it. "Well, I doubt Mrs. Penny did it," I said.

"Grace, Abigail," Mr. Mooney called from around the corner and motioned us toward him.

"Are we in trouble?" Abby whispered.

"Probably," I said, as I stood and brushed off my backside in case there was dust on my jeans. We walked toward him, slowly, dreading to hear what he had to say.

"No piano today. Your mother is on her way to pick you up. You can come sit in my office and wait for her," he said.

"Thanks, Mr. Mooney, but we'll wait outside. It isn't too cold." I would have rather frozen than spent time in Mr. Mooney's office. Bad kids went there when they were in trouble, and sitting in his office today could mean licks with his paddle tomorrow. Mr. Mooney towered over us and scowled, not liking my answer. With his giant arms, he encircled our shoulders and guided us toward the building. Fortunately, before we made it inside, Momma pulled around the circle drive and stopped only a few feet away.

"No lesson today!" Abby announced as she slid into the back seat and slung her book bag into the floor.

Momma turned to us. Her eyes looked small and solemn. "Mrs. Allard was in an accident this afternoon," she said.

"What kind of accident?" I asked.

"I don't know any of the details other than she was taken to Memphis. It doesn't sound good."

"Is she gonna die?" Abby asked.

"I don't know. Let's pray that she is okay." Momma pulled around the school and onto the road, then circled the square and parked in front of Savage Grocery. "I need to run into the grocery store. You girls can stay in the car," she added.

While Momma was inside, Abby and I didn't say much. I thought about Mrs. Allard and figured Abby was thinking about her too. Even though I felt relieved about not having to take piano lessons—maybe for a long time while she recovered in the hospital, and maybe forever if she lost a hand—I hoped she wasn't in pain. Mrs. Allard loved to whack my fingers with that wooden ruler, but I hated for anyone to be in pain. Plus, lately, she'd been nicer to me.

As we drove home, we saw the spot on the highway where her accident occurred. A highway department man made us stop while another car passed opposite us. Orange cones marked off part of the road. Broken glass littered the side of the road, and muddy ruts marked the ditch and into the field like deep scars.

At supper, Daddy said Mrs. Allard had run into the back of a tractor. Tractors always poked along, clogging up the road, but I couldn't imagine how she hadn't noticed it. Later when I went to bed, I wondered if Mrs. Allard was in the same hospital that Daddy and Elvis had been in. Before I fell asleep, I prayed that she would be okay even though I hoped I wouldn't have to take piano again. Things changed so fast, even in the boondocks where nothing much good happened.

Chapter Thirty-Three

Valentine's Day was sunny and warmer than normal, and the boundless blue sky reminded us that spring would arrive soon. It was more of a gazing-out-the-window sort of day, and even Miss Lamb had a hard time concentrating on fractions. When a cardinal landed on the tree just outside our classroom window, Miss Lamb pointed and told us the cardinal was a female. "Her colors aren't as bright," she said. "That's for protection." For a while, I forgot my math worksheet and considered what it would feel like to be that simple bird. During morning recess, Janice and I draped our jackets on the monkey bars and sat side-by-side on the swings, talking and laughing and feeling the sun's warmth on our face. The day was perfect for exchanging Valentine's cards and eating homemade cupcakes with thick pink icing. It was not the sort of day to discover our music teacher had died during the night, but she had.

After lunch, Mr. Mooney called everyone into the gym and made an announcement. Some of the teachers dabbed at their eyes with tissues while most of the kids sat silently stunned. Other than a few sighs and gasps, no one said anything. I wondered exactly how it felt to die, and if she was in Heaven looking down on us, watching our reactions, or if she had better things to do now. I rubbed my finger along James Tyler's name engraved on my P.O.W. bracelet. I couldn't get my thoughts around the idea that some people died for no real reason, and others, like me, sat around with nothing to do. Two nights ago, Daddy had called us into the den, and we watched a special news report of soldiers returning home from the war. Some had been prisoners for years. As each soldier stepped from the plane, his name was announced so the whole world would know he had survived. My soldier's name was never mentioned. Neither was Abby's. Momma said she would keep checking the newspaper for our soldiers' names. They might still come home, she had said.

When we filed out of the gym, Mr. Mooney's secretary handed an envelope to each kid. Inside was a paper, for our parents, explaining about Mrs. Allard's death. Miss Lamb told us to ask questions if we had any. "It's not good to keep things bottled up inside," she said. No one felt like doing anything the remainder of the afternoon, even Miss Lamb, so she let us read quietly at our desks or sit and reflect about Mrs. Allard. I stared out the window at the trees beginning to bud. I tried to find the cardinal again, but she was gone.

Boy, there was nothing like a death to ruin the mood of a Valentine's Day party. "Mrs. Allard would want us to enjoy our party," Miss Lamb said. I felt bad that Mrs. Allard missed Valentine's Day and thought it would be better to die on a regular boring Monday when there was no possibility of having strawberry cake. At two o'clock, Mrs. Barns showed up with a humongous platter of chocolate cupcakes, each topped with one of those hard, sugary heart candies that says something like "Be Mine" and tastes like chalk. Janice's mother brought three kinds of chips and onion dip. I had almost forgotten that Momma had sent me to school with pink plates and napkins and plastic forks. When Miss Lamb gave me a nod, I took them from the paper sack stored in the coat closet and placed everything neatly on the food table.

Miss Lamb told us to place our Valentine boxes on the edge of our desks, so that during the party, cards could be handed out. Janice and I quickly delivered our cards then filled up our plates to eat. We watched as some of the other kids handed out their cards. Most of the boys walked along and quickly popped cards into box after box, as though they'd given no thought to matching Valentine with friend. Wilbur's stack of envelopes didn't have names on them. What was the point if the message wasn't sincerely chosen? I had worked on my cards for several days, selecting each one carefully and writing something interesting on the back in my best handwriting.

The party ended as soon as the bell rang. Clutching my box during the bus ride home, I didn't peek inside or read any of the cards.

Sometimes the best part was the anticipation. Abby held her box tightly too. "Was your party fun?" I asked.

"Uh-huh, but it's so sad about Mrs. Allard."

"Yeah." Mrs. Allard's death came as a shock. She wasn't old enough to die and hadn't been sick, yet one day she taught music at school and the next day she was gone. I also felt relief at the prospect of not having to take piano lessons again. That made me feel guilty.

As soon as we got home, I sorted through my Valentine cards while Abby and Momma talked non-stop about Mrs. Allard. So far, Janice had given me the cutest card, and that wasn't surprising. Her Daddy was in the Air Force, so she shopped at the PX store where everything was cooler. Miss Lamb's card said, "You're a Deer" and had a picture of a cute deer on it. She signed it "Miss Lamb" with flawlessly joined cursive letters, probably to remind us how important it was to always write neatly.

Finally, Momma mentioned piano lessons, which caught my attention. "Until we find someone new, I'll teach you at home," she said. I didn't understand why we hadn't been doing that from the beginning.

The next card in my box was sealed with Cupid stickers and hand-drawn hearts, as though someone had taken extra time to make it special. Careful not to tear it, I opened the envelope and unfolded the heart-shaped Minnie Mouse card. Handwritten on the back were the words, "I really like you. Do you like me? – Your Secret Admirer."

My heart skipped in my chest. Secret Admirer? I stared at the handwriting hard, but didn't recognize it. I probably didn't want to know anyway, because there are twelve boys in my class, and I didn't like any of them. I re-folded the card and buried it deep inside my box.

Chapter Thirty-Four

Brother Brown only spread the word of Jesus when it was warm. In the wintertime, more often than not, we would arrive at Boon Chapel to find the church was too cold for Brother Brown. On the Sunday after Valentine's Day, another cold front plunged down from the North Pole, and we arrived at the church to see Brother Brown pacing and shaking his head. He and the important men like Mr. Donaldson congregated around the furnace, whispering to each other, knocking on it and fiddling with the knobs in the back. After a few minutes of this, Brother Brown walked out the front door, without so much as a word to the waiting congregation. Mrs. Brown popped up from her pew and followed after him, tap-tap-tapping along the red rug. She was clutching her umbrella and wearing the same curdled expression she wore most every Sunday.

"No preaching today," Mr. Donaldson announced from the pulpit. "Brother Brown thinks it's too cold." All the old ladies, including Nana, Mrs. Sweet, and Aunt Clara, sighed and exchanged glances. Other than the cold air streaming from the hole in the floor between my feet, it didn't seem cold to me, but I wasn't complaining. This turn of events extended my weekend by at least an hour. When I remembered the Valentine's card I had brought with me that morning, I grabbed my purse and raced out the front door. Brother Brown sat in his car, surrounded by a cloud of smoke as his engine raced, and I wondered if something was wrong with his engine. He was bundled inside his wool coat with a scarf wrapped around his neck. I waved. Mrs. Brown saw me and pointed, and Brother Brown cracked his window open.

"Brother Brown, I was going to give you this later, during the invitational hymn," I said, passing the Valentine card through the window. "It's a Valentine card."

"Thank you, Grace. That's very nice of you," he said. He looked flushed and nervous, like I had upset his quick getaway.

"Okay, that's all I wanted. *Au revoir*, and I hope you warm up. You too, Mrs. Brown." She nodded at me and partially smiled as she pulled on her leather gloves.

When I walked back inside, Momma's frown caught me and followed me back to my seat. I grinned big at her. I couldn't understand why she worried so much about me talking to Brother Brown. From the pulpit, Mr. Donaldson was talking to the congregation about important church things. He looked calm and comfortable, not in the slightest bit cold. If he hadn't been a farmer, Mr. Donaldson would have made a good preacher.

"Since we all got up so early and drove to church, we'll still have Sunday school class," he said. So we did. Those cold Sundays were exciting. No preaching, yet we all got credit for being there, and we got to go home early.

After lunch, Momma spent the afternoon sewing in her bedroom. Daddy worked on his farm books and mumbled about taxes, which always added tension. The afternoon had turned blustery, and the clouds hung low and full. I dressed in my warmest clothes, stuffed bits of toilet paper in my ears, and ran the whole way to the gray house without stopping. Still there was no sign of anyone, no car in the drive, no smoke drifting from the chimney. I poked a Valentine's Day card inside the mail slot and heard it fall to the floor on the other side of the front door. I considered sneaking back into the man's kitchen and doing some more exploring, but I was cold and knew I only had a few minutes. When I left, Abby had been setting up the Monopoly game on the dining room table. Soon, she would be searching for me to play with her. Walking back home, I watched my breath curl from my mouth and wondered if spring would ever find us. I made it back home before anyone missed me, but my throat felt raw from breathing such icy air.

Sunday afternoon turned into a long game of Monopoly that ended with me in the poorhouse and Abby owning the bank. I hated to lose at

Monopoly, especially after Daddy became interested in our game. He pulled up a chair, popped open another beer and began studying every move. "There's no hope for you Grace," he said. "You're strategy makes no sense." I looked at the board and couldn't imagine what he saw, but soon after, the whole game slid downhill as though he put a nasty hex on me.

Daddy began coaching Abby. She giggled and bounced her little dog game-piece around the board, never landing on my properties. Every Community Chest card Abby drew meant money in her stash. Usually from me. Daddy made a huge deal out of it and said he would start asking her opinion before betting on the horses at the horse track. Abby's face nearly separated from all the smiling. When I wasn't handing over money to my brilliant, rich sister, I was trying to roll doubles to get out of jail. Abby collected a bunch of monopolies—the best ones according to Lee Abbott—and when I landed on each of her hotels one after another, I was forced to mortgage my favorites. Even though the whole stupid thing was a game, I felt awful, like I was a big, fat loser in real life.

***

That gloomy feeling sat with me on the bus and followed me to school Monday morning. All traces of Valentine's Day had been removed from our classroom, and a goofy, green Leprechaun hung on the bulletin board. St. Patrick's Day was the only day we were allowed to pinch people without getting in trouble, but only if they forgot to wear something green. And having green eyes didn't count. Last year, Bubba claimed his green eyes were the same as wearing a green shirt, but no one fell for it.

Miss Lamb seemed extra quiet and told us right off we would be making sympathy cards for Mrs. Allard's husband. Although doing something crafty sounded better than math or history, a card for a dead person's husband didn't sound so fun. She went on to explain that since her funeral would be held in her hometown in Oregon, there would be no other way for us to say goodbye to her. Funerals were great mysteries to me. I'd never been to one, which was a lucky thing, really,

215

but the whole "saying goodbye" to a dead person seemed a strange notion.

While we worked on our cards, Miss Lamb played a record in the back of the room. The music was quiet and sounded like a flute, and I wondered if she did it as a tribute to Mrs. Allard or more to keep us calm. Whichever her reason, we worked quietly, folding construction paper and drawing pictures and writing words to a man we'd never met. I chose a pale blue piece of paper and colored a lilac flower on the front. Inside I wrote, "I'm sorry Mrs. Allard died. I hope you aren't sad forever. Love, Gracie Abbott." It turned out nice.

Chapter Thirty-Five

Daddy's sickness disappeared and stayed away during winter. As the days grew longer and warmer and greener, cottonwood seeds floated from trees and dusted the grass like snow. All around, farmers plowed fields, preparing for spring planting. I sat at the kitchen table, dumped cereal into a bowl, and counted down the last days of school. One more month.

"No need to rush this morning. Your bus won't be here until seven-thirty," Momma said. She was piddling around rinsing dishes and stacking them in the drain board, acting as though the words she'd spoken were as normal as, "I think I'll make cornbread for supper."

"What?" I said. I knew that adults planned our lives behind the scenes and caused change, but when I was sitting half-asleep at the breakfast table, eating a bowl of nearly stale cereal, and Momma made a huge announcement as though it were nothing, I needed more details.

"Yes, the bus route changed. You and Abby will be picked up later in the morning and dropped off earlier."

"Then why did you wake us up so early?" I asked. "And why would the route be changed so late in the year? That doesn't make sense."

"I don't know, Grace. Just be glad," Momma said. She never explained why she woke us so early, but this news was huge. Since the beginning of my school career, I'd been picked up before sunrise and dropped off late in the afternoon. Suddenly, with no warning, life had shifted. I would have more time to sleep, and in the afternoons, more television watching time.

Such a slight change made a vast impact, but not in the positive way I expected. Instead of boarding a quiet, dark bus that gradually filled with schoolmates as the sky brightened, Abby and I boarded that morning to find the bus already filthy and heaving with wild kids. Wadded notebook paper littered the aisle. Being thrust into the chaos right after brushing my teeth was more difficult than getting on the bus first and slowly adjusting to the noise. One of Abby's friends waved at her from the back of the bus, and she disappeared, leaving only one open seat next to Arlene.

Arlene.

The meanest girl in school.

I would have rather stood in the aisle than sit with Arlene, but that would have grabbed her attention, the opposite of what I wanted. So I eased into the seat beside her.

"Hi, Arlene," I smiled but looked down at my hands too quickly, so I pretended to pick at my fingernail.

"Hey, freckle-face Grace," she laughed. "Look, girls. The little rich girl decided to sit with us today." Her friends in the surrounding seats turned around and leaned into the aisle. Today would be my day to be picked on by Arlene. I knew it instantly. "Since we forgot our milk money, you can share with us." She yanked the small bag from my shoulder and rifled through my things as the others snickered. I felt my face and neck turn red. The bus heaved with noise and commotion, and anyone who might have noticed my dilemma, pretended not to see.

I jerked my purse from her grip. She smiled like it was a joke, but her smile was evil, her teeth too perfectly straight and pearly white for someone so mean. Although the whole thing happened fast, my money was gone, all of it—milk money and lunch money—along with my hairbrush. One of Arlene's friends, an older girl everyone called "Sugar" who could throw the dodge ball harder than any boy in school, punched the bottom of my notebook with her fist. Sheets of paper flew up and sailed into the aisle and underneath seats, including my English essay and math homework. As we turned into the schoolyard, I scrambled around on the floor, trying to gather my papers.

When Mr. Jackson stopped the bus in front of the school, kids bounded out the door and scattered onto the playground, leaving me to pick up my trampled papers. Jamie Bard, a quiet boy in my class who saw it happen, stopped to help. He handed me my English essay, which now had a dirty footprint in the middle. As Abby walked up the aisle to leave, she noticed me crawling around on the dirty bus floor. "What happened?" she asked.

"I tripped," I said. Jamie nodded sympathetically and continued helping me collect my dropped notebook papers. He had suffered Arlene's meanness and understood the importance of keeping quiet. Being a tattletale was worse than being a bully, and making a big deal out of something usually made things worse.

"Hurry, Abbott. Off the bus," Mr. Jackson said.

"Sorry, I dropped my notebook," I said.

Mr. Jackson sank back into his seat while I gathered my papers.

My bad day never improved. I felt Arlene's eyes on the back of my head during class. When I went to sharpen my pencil, she stuck her big foot into the aisle and tried to trip me, but I was too fast for that. At lunch, I felt extra hungry, just knowing I had no money. When I confessed to Janice what had happened on the bus, she shared her lunch with me so I wouldn't starve to death. She promised not to tell anyone, and I knew she wouldn't.

Later, we all filed back into the classroom and took our seats. Arlene raised her hand and asked to go to the bathroom. "I ate way too much at lunch," she said, being dramatic. I pretended not to hear her and wrote my name over and over on a piece of paper to look busy.

Even Miss Lamb, who was nice as cherry pie, became annoyed with Arlene. "You may be excused, but you've had plenty of time to use the restroom during recess," she said. Arlene rolled her eyes and muttered something as she walked out the door, but Miss Lamb didn't seem to notice.

After an entire day that felt pointless and as slow as preaching, it was finally time for my library shift with Mrs. Penny. When the bell rang to signal the last period of the day, I grabbed my homework assignments from my desk, along with my no longer organized notebook, and stood to leave. Arlene leaned next to the door with her arms crossed as though she waited for someone. She carried no books, no homework, nothing. I walked passed her, as though she were invisible, even though I could feel her smiling at me. She didn't say anything.

Free. I was almost free for the day. Working in the library was a highlight, an entire quiet hour with lots of books to re-shelve. As I walked along the hallway, I passed all my old classrooms—third, second, and first grade. Soon fourth grade would be over too. Just before I reached the library, I walked by the office and automatically glanced through the glass window to see if anyone was in trouble. Kids that got sent to the office often had to sit across from Mr. Mooney's desk and write lines—something like "I will behave in class"—a billion times. And yes, someone was sitting right in front of Mr. Mooney's desk.

It was Momma!

I blinked to make sure, and then stood outside the door, wondering what to do. My heart plunged. Why was I in trouble? I peeked at them again and tried to listen, but the door must have been soundproof because I couldn't hear a single word. Mr. Mooney looked serious but not mad. Momma was wearing a nice skirt and blouse, not her regular housework clothes. She nodded over and over. When the tardy bell rang, I ran the rest of the way to the library so I wouldn't be too late. Mrs. Penny looked up, said hello, and didn't seem to notice I was a tiny bit tardy. My rolling cart was filled, so I began working on it right away, putting away book after book while trying to figure out why Momma was at school.

I couldn't think of a single thing I had done wrong. This had to be about Arlene. Someone heard about my problem on the bus and reported it. But who? I felt nauseous. If Arlene got in trouble, she would do something worse to me. "Grace, did you hear me?" Mrs. Penny was standing at the door with a stack of folders.

"I'm sorry?"

"Where've you been? I've been talking to you for five minutes and you haven't heard a word." She chuckled.

"I just have a lot on my mind." I had been concentrating so hard, the entire rack of books was almost put away, and I didn't remember doing it.

Mrs. Penny told me about the upcoming book fair and how she might need extra help from me during recess. When she went to the office, I returned the empty book cart to its spot behind Mrs. Penny's counter. I decided to wipe down the tables, but the bell rang just as I got the foam cleaner out.

Momma met Abby and me in the hallway, and we rode home with her instead of riding the bus. Even though Arlene never rode the afternoon bus, and I had no idea why, anytime I could skip a bus ride was a treat.

"Why are you at school?" I asked the second I saw her.

Momma's lips were sewn shut. "I'll tell you when we get to the car," she said.

"Am I in trouble?" I asked.

"Should you be in trouble?" She herded Abby and me out the front door of the school and into the warm afternoon.

"No. But sometimes it happens anyway."

On the drive home, Momma explained that Mr. Mooney had asked her to be our new music teacher, at least until the end of the school year and maybe next year too. This was excellent news, not necessarily because Momma would be my teacher, but because I'd never have to ride the stupid bus again. As Momma talked, I could tell by her wide blue eyes and the way she moved her hands around that she was excited about the prospect. I didn't blame her. Cleaning house day in and day out had to be a dull job.

Later, when Momma cooked supper, she practically floated around the kitchen, humming and dancing. Even the way she stirred sugar in the pitcher of tea sounded different, more rhythmic, and cheerful. By the time Daddy came home, Momma's news was about to explode from her, but as we gathered around the table Daddy began mumbling about the new Johnny Cash land and how hard it was to plow. "The gumbo is like sticky black wax," he said shaking his head and taking a bite of beans.

"Daddy, Momma has some big news," Abby said as she wiggled in her chair, her ponytail bouncing from side to side in one loop. Daddy cut his eyes to Abby and then Momma.

"Well, hell, let's have your news," Daddy said, waving his hand in her direction. He dropped his spoon, crossed his arms over the chest, and leaned back.

"It's not that big of a deal, but it could be. Mr. Mooney called today and asked me to come meet with him. Don't worry, no one's in trouble." Momma's laugh sounded nervous.

"Who's Mr. Mooney?" Daddy mumbled.

"Our school principal!" I said in mid-swallow nearly choking on, not only my bite of food, but the mere idea that he didn't remember Mr. Mooney.

"He's real tall, like a giant," Abby added matter-of-factly, because it was true.

"Lee, for heaven's sake, you know him. He's been the principal for years. Mabel Mooney's son. He lives in that red brick house just past town, the one with all that white gravel in the flower beds." Momma pointed toward Mr. Mooney's red brick house, even though we couldn't see through the kitchen wall where she still hadn't rehung the rooster bean picture. At any given time, Momma could probably write a report on any Savage Crossing citizen, while sitting at the kitchen table, without doing any research other than digging out everything she already knew from her brain.

"Yeah, yeah, so what about him?" Daddy said.

"He talked to me about the piano teacher position. Since Mrs. Allard's passed, he's been using substitutes, but he hasn't found anyone regular. And don't tell us you don't remember Mrs. Allard," she paused, but Daddy only stared at her. "Since I play the piano at Boon Chapel, and I was a teacher before Grace was born, he thought I might be interested in finishing out the school year."

"*C'est brilliant*! You'd be perfect, Momma."

Abby nodded and agreed with me.

Daddy leaned back into the table, took another bite of food, and appeared to swallow without chewing.

"And the best part, if it works out this month, the job will be mine next year. What do you think, Lee? Isn't it great? I was so flattered that Mr. Mooney thought of me." Momma pressed her hand against her chest like her heart was about to burst from the thrill of it.

Daddy grabbed a beer from the icebox and popped the top. The foam rose to the top but didn't flow over. "I don't think it's a good idea."

Momma's face fell, and her eyes went from bright to pale in one puzzled blink. "But why? Don't you think the extra money would be nice? If you're worried about the house, the girls can do more to help out. Right, girls?"

"I think it's exciting!" I said. Momma was right. More money would mean Daddy wouldn't have to work so much, and maybe he wouldn't always be in such a bad mood.

Daddy guzzled his beer and didn't say much else about it. Momma's face wilted, but she said, "Lee, why don't we think it over and talk more about it later."

That night, after Abby fell asleep and I stared at the bedroom ceiling, Momma asked Daddy about the job again. From their bedroom across the hallway, I heard their voices becoming louder and louder. I twirled Barbie's hair and waited for Daddy's explosion. "We don't need any lousy extra money. I make plenty of money without you going to work every day." Momma said something I couldn't make out. "If you need more to do, I'll give you more work around here," he said.

When Momma slammed the bathroom door, Lucky bounded from Abby's bed and stood in the middle of our bedroom floor, He watched the door without moving. A low growl escaped him that seemed to come right from his belly. "Lucky! Come boy," I whispered. He jumped to my bed, and I stroked the velvety spot behind his ears to keep him from barking. Momma turned on the bathroom faucet and the pipes moaned inside our bedroom wall, but the rushing water couldn't disguise the sound of her crying.

Lucky burrowed underneath the covers and settled between my feet. I laid Barbie on the pillow beside me and pulled the sheet up to her waist. "Try to get some sleep, Barbie." I turned the fan on high. It hummed and made the nightstand vibrate, but still we heard.

***

For three days in a row, Arlene and her mean friends surrounded me in the bus aisle, snatched my purse, and stole my money. They were quick and vicious, and I didn't bother to put up a fight because it wasn't worth it. I held tight to my notebook and never dropped my papers again, which was at least something. After the second day, Abby figured out what was happening. When she quizzed me about it, I promised her a whole dollar from my jewelry box if she wouldn't tell Momma. Abby swore not to tell, but said I could keep my dollar.

"Momma, are we rich?" I asked.

Momma scrubbed the grimy collar of Daddy's work shirt with a toothbrush. When she was done, she stuffed it into the washing machine with the rest of the load. She sprayed the next collar and began scouring it. I added water to my second bowl of grits and stirred.

"Gracie, if we were rich I wouldn't be rubbing my hands raw on these shirts. We're regular people," she said. "Middle of the road farmers. Why do you ask?"

"Because Arlene called me a rich girl."

"Grace, your Daddy works hard every day to see to it that we are comfortable."

"I know." And I did know.

"Everything is relative. We are much better off than lots of folks, but there are plenty of people sitting high and mighty who have no idea where their food comes from. There's always someone worse off and always someone better off. Be happy with what you have." Momma had gotten riled up, and I was sorry I had opened my mouth about it. Ever since Daddy refused to allow Momma to take the music teacher job, she'd been grumpy. Last night, I had listened in on the telephone extension and heard her tell Maggie she might do it anyway. I knew she wouldn't, not without Daddy saying it was okay. It was unfair for one person to decide the future of another.

"Can I take my lunch to school today?" I asked for the second day this week.

"No. Stop asking. You know the rules." Momma was big on sticking to the rules, and the only day I was allowed to take my lunch was on meatloaf day.

"What if I make it myself?"

"Grace, the sun's barely up and you're getting on my nerves. All those poor people you were asking about would be thankful to eat cafeteria food."

Then an idea came to me. "Is it okay if I take my empty lunchbox to school? I need it for extra pencils and things."

224

Momma lobbed it at me, probably to make me hush. "Don't lose it." With only air inside, it felt hollow and light. Abby spotted the bus from the dining room window just as I rushed to the bathroom.

"Gracie, you better not miss that bus!" Momma yelled from the kitchen. Did she really think the bus would pull away without me? I didn't think Abby would let that happen, plus I could never be that lucky.

I stepped onto the bus and marched past Mr. Jackson. The bus was cram-packed and loud, and I saw the mean girls in a huddle three rows back. Abby passed with no problem and disappeared into the madness. As I approached, Arlene stuck her broad arm into the aisle. "Halt!" she demanded.

I slapped a quarter into her palm then pushed my way past the gang, swinging my lunch box. I didn't need milk with my lunch. I could drink free water from the fountain.

"Oh, rich girl's taking her lunch to school now," said Sugar, who always wore her fuzzy hair in two ponytails. I got to the back of the bus without anyone grabbing my purse or looking inside my empty lunch box. My lunch money was tucked safely inside my saddle oxford, beneath the arch of my foot.

Chapter Thirty-Six

Daddy invited all of us along with him for his spring Farm Bureau conference in Little Rock. Momma said we could take one friend, and since the only person Abby and I could both agree on was Dian, she got to go too. Momma and Daddy decided Mae should come to keep us from running wild. Plus with Mae along, Momma would be able to attend meetings and dinners with Daddy.

We were to leave Friday after school, but when we got home from school that day, Daddy was complaining that the motel rooms would be too expensive, food would cost an arm and a leg, and paying Mae for the entire weekend would be a waste of money. "When she gets here, I'll tell Mae we don't need her," he insisted, refusing to hear any of Momma's protests.

Our luggage sat by the back door. Momma was busy packing a grocery sack with snacks for the weekend and a cooler filled with cold drinks. I could tell by every movement of her hands and the way she latched the ice chest that she was upset about Mae being uninvited, and I agreed it was a rude thing to do. Nana always said you should follow through with things and keep your word. I hoped Daddy didn't un-invite Dian, who had ridden the bus home with us and was playing in the bedroom with Abby.

At four o'clock on the dot, Daddy carried the cooler out to the car, Momma grabbed the grocery sack she had packed, and we said goodbye to Lucky who wasn't going with us. Nana had agreed to stop by and pick him up Saturday morning on her way home from the beauty shop. Lucky would get to spend the weekend with Nana and Papa Pete. That was a good deal for him.

Just as Momma pulled the door shut and locked it, Mae's husband turned their battered car into the driveway. "I'll go tell her," Daddy said. My stomach sunk, and I dreaded hearing the conversation. A mosquito buzzed around my ankles. I swatted at it and hoped we left soon. The warm April afternoon felt more like June.

Mae's car smoked up the driveway as it came to a rolling stop just behind Momma's. Her husband, whose name I'd never known because she only called him "My Old Pair of Pants," or "Pants" for short, waved at us, his arm draped out the open window casual and easy. Mae shoved open the door as though it weighed five hundred pounds. It made a great noise like a moaning, rusty beast.

A movie star stepped out of the car and onto the gravel drive. Mae wore a red pantsuit, and her hair had been swirled and shellacked into a glamorous beehive. Red hoop earrings swung from her earlobes. Her cheeks glowed with circles of rouge.

She looked *très chic* and nothing like our regular Mae.

"Lee, we have to take her. She went to the beauty shop," Momma whispered to Daddy.

She slammed the car door and stood for a moment on the gravel drive as though giving us time to take in her new look. Abby whispered to me, "Is that Mae?"

I'd never heard such a whistling sound stream from Daddy's lips. "Damn. You ready to go, Miss America?" He offered Mae his arm and escorted her to Momma's car. She sashayed past me in a sweet-smelling cloud of perfume.

Somewhere in Daddy's grumpy body lay a sweet, soft spot for Mae.

Mae sat wedged in the front seat between Momma and Daddy, while Dian, Abby, and I sat in back. From my view in the back seat, she didn't look like Mae at all, but her buttery voice sounded the same as she talked about fishing at Sugar Ditch and the best place to dig nightcrawlers. When Daddy asked about her children, he sounded genuinely interested, and between them, they kept the conversation flowing all the way to our first bathroom break. As we drove along the interstate, her new hairdo bounced against the ceiling, and her laugh warmed the space in the car. If Daddy had made her stay at home, our drive would have been quiet, empty, and long.

With Dian and Abby's input, I made a list of things we planned to do during our exciting Little Rock weekend, things like staying up late, watching scary movies, and swimming in the motel pool no matter how cold the water was. At suppertime, we stopped at a rest area on the side of the highway. Momma chose one of the picnic tables away from the smelly garbage cans and spread a blue-checkered tablecloth I'd never seen before over the concrete top. She set out a platter of fried chicken she'd made at home, along with barbecue potato chips and a plastic container of green grapes. If I hadn't heard the trucks whizzing by, I would have thought we were at the shady picnic area at the Memphis Zoo. We all crowded around the table and ate until there was no chicken left.

***

It was exciting to check into our room, choose beds, and find the snack machines, but once we'd done that, we felt crowded and bored. The Little Rock television broadcast the same four channels we had at home. Down below us, the swimming pool held no water. "Closed for repairs," the sign said. Mae taught us to play poker with cards she pulled from her tote bag. Since we had no money for real gambling, we used chocolate-covered peanuts Momma had packed in the grocery sack. I ate my winnings, and my stomach felt queasy.

As twilight settled over the city, Dian and I stood on the balcony and counted all the red cars passing on the interstate. When that got old, we jumped on the beds in our room while Mae went to talk to Momma and Daddy.

"Mr. Lee, these girls needs a swimming pool." Mae was shaking her head and pacing in front of Momma and Daddy's television. Their room connected to ours with an open door.

"I can't help that the swimming pool is closed. They'll live." I couldn't see Daddy on the other side of the wall, but he sounded annoyed and distracted.

"Mr. Lee, there's another motel down the highway. It has a pool. I noticed it on the drive in." Mae stood in the doorway, wringing her hands. Her bright red fingernail polish matched her pantsuit. She looked too fancy for our motel.

"I don't have time to mess with it. We have a party tonight and meetings all day tomorrow beginning at breakfast." She came back into our room, plopped on the corner of the bed, and didn't say anything. But I could tell her mind was hard at work.

The next morning, Momma's eyes looked happy when she waved to us from the doorway. "See you tonight," she said. Her loopy gold earrings swung and nearly touched her shoulders when she walked away. Daddy told us to be good, and he checked the door twice to make sure it had locked behind him. While we watched cartoons and ate dry cereal in bed, Mae pulled the telephone book from inside the desk drawer. Compared to the Savage Crossing phone book, the enormous Little Rock one looked like the Sears Catalog, and I wondered what it would be like to live around so many people. She fanned through the pages, searching for a number, her long fingernails making flicking noises on the edges.

"Who're you calling?" I asked.

"The motel with a pool." We clapped and cheered, but not too loud, as Mae began talking to the reservation clerk and explaining our situation. "We'll be there within the hour," we heard her say.

As I surveyed our motel room, it appeared we had already been living in our small space forever. We began slinging our scattered clothes and shoes back into our suitcases. Mae gathered up all the little bottles of shampoo and crème rinse and added those to her bag. She said they were free to guests, and we were expected to take them. After Mae loaded herself down like a pack mule, we carried as much as we could and followed her single-file along the side of the interstate to the motel with the swimming pool.

I lugged the suitcase Abby and I shared. Abby's only job was to carry Momma's small makeup bag so she could concentrate on walking. Dian carried her suitcase with no problem that I could tell. The trek took longer than I thought it would. The plastic suitcase handle dug into my palm, and I stopped to switch hands several times. As traffic zoomed past, a few cars honked, but no one ran over us. At last, we stepped onto the parking lot, and I was glad of it. Mae wiped her forehead and said, "Praise be."

229

As soon as we checked in, we changed into our bathing suits and watched from the balcony as Mae went back to get the cooler, which had been too heavy to carry on the first trip.

***

Mae didn't like to swim, so she sat in a lounge chair while we jumped from the diving board, did cannonballs, and swam underwater from one end to the other. The water was cold and clear and smelled strong like someone had dumped too much chlorine in. We had the pool to ourselves the entire day and even ate our lunch out there. When dusk came and our lips turned purple and our teeth chattered uncontrollably, Mae wrapped us in soft, white towels. We raced back to our room, leaving wet footprints all along the concrete sidewalk.

"How will Momma and Daddy find us?" Abby asked as we piled into bed to watch a movie.

"I left a note for Mr. Lee at the front desk of the other place," Mae said.

A few hours later, they found us and seemed more than a little impressed we had managed to relocate ourselves. Mae had arranged Momma and Daddy's suitcases just as they had been in the other motel room. She had even turned down their beds nice and neat. "How did you move everything, Mae?" Daddy asked examining the room.

"Mr. Lee, we walked. These girls needed a swimming pool." Daddy shook his head, chuckled, and shut the door between our rooms.

Like most good things, our weekend was over in a blink. We had gotten in so much swimming that our skin looked permanently shriveled. We stayed up late watching movies and ordered pepperoni pizza Saturday night from a restaurant that brought it to our room. On Sunday, Daddy drained the empty cooler and re-packed the car with our bulging suitcases. Nothing seemed to fit as well in the trunk, even considering we no longer had the grocery sack of snacks or the picnic fried chicken.

Mae sat between Momma and Daddy again on the ride home, but she wore regular clothes and didn't look so fancy although her hair was still piled high. I slept almost the whole way home. An entire weekend of swimming had been tiring and even my legs and arms ached from all the fun.

I woke as the car bumped onto our gravel driveway. Instantly, I knew something was wrong, but I was too sleepy to know what. Daddy said a bad word and braked the car so abruptly I banged my head against the passenger seat in front of me. Abby fell onto the floorboard. Momma gasped, "Oh no," and then she and Mae both shot out of the car while I rubbed my eyes and tried to grasp what had happened. Abby and Dian looked confused too.

At some point while we had been swimming and having a grand time, a thief had robbed our house. The screen door stood wide open. While we hung back on the carport in case someone was still inside the house, Daddy walked through each room. "Look in the closets too!" Momma yelled at him. Her easy, relaxed weekend had been erased, and her blue eyes fogged over as she stared at the open door where Daddy disappeared. It didn't take him long to come back outside, shaking his head and cussing something horrible.

Every kitchen drawer had been dumped into a huge heap. The contents of Momma's junk drawer had been strewn across the linoleum. Daddy said he thought the thief had been searching for specific things. Along with the television, record player, and home movie projector, the robber had stolen Daddy's truck from the driveway, something none of us had immediately noticed. Momma sat at the dining room table with her head in her hands while Mae tried to comfort her. "I'll never go on vacation again," Momma said. I hoped that wasn't true.

Daddy called the cops, and a policeman from town showed up to make a robbery report, just like on television. He sat at the kitchen table and scribbled out a list of everything that was missing on a notepad he pulled from his shirt pocket. His pudgy fingers all looked the same stubby length. Watching him write, I wondered how quickly he'd be able to pull out the pistol strapped inside his holster if there was an emergency. I had never seen a policeman in real life, so I studied him closely, especially his black uniform.

Momma offered him a glass of iced tea. When he declined, she just stood at the sink, twisting a dishtowel in her hands.

Daddy paced back and forth. His face was dark and tense.

"You may notice more things missing after a few days," the policeman said. He tore a paper from his pad and handed it to Daddy.

I ran to my bedroom and checked my Cinderella jewelry box, but nothing was missing. My few dollars of savings were still in the envelope, and my special Boon Chapel marble sat undisturbed in the corner. I was grateful for that.

Later in bed, I couldn't calm my mind. I imagined the robber walking down our hallway, stepping into our bedroom, and breathing our same air. The hair on my arms tingled and stood straight out. If Lucky had been home instead of at Nana's house, I felt certain the robber would have been too afraid to come inside. Lucky's body shifted next to mine as though he knew I was thinking about him. I scratched his ears and tried to think of something other than the stranger who had been inside our house.

Eventually, I pulled out my diary and wrote about the whole creepy thing, then spent some time learning a few new French words from my French lesson book. I did all this writing and reading and learning underneath my quilt with a flashlight so Abby wouldn't wake up. Not that she would have.

Chapter Thirty-Seven

Miss Lamb surprised us with a field trip. We really didn't go anywhere, just down behind the football field to the location of the first schoolhouse in Savage Crossing. Only a few crumbled fieldstones remained from the site, so we used our imaginations to think about how the building would have looked a hundred years ago. The clover felt soft and spongy, and I raked my fingers through the patch of green, searching for a four-leaf clover but not finding one. A blur of words about Indians and history flowed from Miss Lamb's pink lips, but after a busy weekend and a robbery and not much sleep the night before, I felt drained and hollow, like I wasn't really sitting there. When she passed around a few real arrowheads, I handed them to Janice. Daddy found Indian artifacts all the time on the home place, but I was too tired to mention it, plus I didn't want to seem like a show off or interrupt Miss Lamb on the one day she'd managed to keep our class under control. Everyone was sitting quietly and when questions were asked, they were good ones. Wilbur, who could have easily run away, didn't. It was as though removing the confining school walls calmed him and kept him with the group. Arlene hadn't shown up for school. Her absence meant fewer class disruptions, and I could breathe without worry.

During lunch, I told my friends all about our trip to Little Rock, ending with the robbery. I usually didn't have any news whatsoever, so it was fun to be the one with something to report. They were interested, mostly about the robbery, and listened while I relayed every detail about the policeman and all the things that had been stolen from our house. We all agreed it was creepy to think a stranger walked around inside our house and touched our doorknobs and pulled out drawers. It wasn't often we had a real, live mystery to solve.

"What if it's someone we all know?" Janice said. "Like him!" Janice swung her head toward Mr. Mooney who had just walked behind our table.

"It wasn't Mr. Mooney. That's ridiculous!" I whispered almost too loud. We all glanced toward him as he walked between tables, patrolling the cafeteria and swinging his wooden paddle. Laughter exploded from Bubba and Mitchell. Janice should consider being an actress someday. She had a good imagination and a naturally expressive voice.

***

Momma's friend Maggie was at our house when Abby and I got home from school. Momma was pulling plates and cups from the cabinet, and her coffeemaker had just begun to drip into the pot. A chocolate sheet cake sat on the kitchen counter. As Maggie sliced it, I wondered how many of Momma's ingredients had been baked into it. "I want to hear all about your trip to Little Rock," Maggie said to Momma. "Do you girls want a piece of cake?" she added almost as an afterthought.

Abby shook her head yes, and Momma said it was okay as long as she promised to still eat supper later. I preferred my regular snack of peanut butter and crackers and ate at the dining room table with a mound of homework around me.

"The butcher at Savage Grocery said you were robbed. Is that true, Anne?" I glanced into the kitchen as Momma poured coffee into cups. Momma nodded but so far had said very little. The robbery was obviously the real reason for Maggie's visit.

"What did they take, Anne? They didn't take your jewelry, did they?" she asked, not waiting for the answer. "I think your whole house has an eerie vibe now, just knowing complete strangers walked around and touched all your things." She swept her arms around the kitchen, her whole body trembling like she had the heebie-jeebies.

I was attempting to ignore Maggie's loud voice so I could work on the sentence diagramming assignment Miss Lamb had given us.

Realizing the end of the school year was approaching, she had begun to double up on homework. Our class was lagging behind, because she had to spend too much time disciplining. At least, that's how Miss Lamb saw it.

Momma filled Maggie in on the theft, half-heartedly. She sounded tired of talking about it after having reported all the details to the policeman and telling Nana the story. The more excited Maggie became, the shriller her voice became.

I closed my notebook and listened. Momma sounded more enthusiastic when she talked about our weekend away. "Maggie, I'm ready for a big change," Momma said, after describing the shrimp cocktails served at the banquet in Little Rock.

"Oh, what kind of change, Anne? Are you planning to take that music job at school?"

This was the exact sort of conversation Maggie lived for, but I, too, was interested in knowing about this change.

"Oh, no. I've decided to pass on that job. I have my hands full as it is, with Lee and these kids."

I rolled my eyes. I didn't appreciate being lumped in with Daddy, and not only that, I knew the real reason Momma didn't take the job. It had nothing to do with having too much to do around the house.

"A new haircut. Something totally different. Lucille is so behind the times. All those Little Rock women had stylish hairdos, sleek and sophisticated. I felt completely frumpy the entire weekend. I'm going to make a hair appointment at a place I heard about in Memphis."

Momma showed Maggie a new style in her favorite magazine, and after Maggie approved it, they jawed a bit about some new barbeque restaurant across from the courthouse in Savage Crossing. Eventually, Maggie left, with a cup of brown sugar and two of Momma's magazines, but not the newest one.

The week went by fast even though each day felt the same as the one before. Every morning, I gave Arlene my milk money in exchange for a peaceful bus ride. During the day, I spent more time thinking about summer than schoolwork, and at night, I tried to gather clues about our robbery. So far, there were none. All week Momma studied the pictures of the models in her fashion magazines, sometimes even asking Abby and me what we thought of different hairstyles. The night before her fancy hair appointment in Memphis, I helped her narrow down the choices. She tore the page that showed her favorite style from the magazine, folded it, and put it in her purse. Momma said it was best to show the beauty operator a picture so there could be no misunderstanding. After my summer hair fiasco at Lucille's, I almost said, "No joke," but held my tongue.

On Friday, when we got back from school, I barely recognized Momma. Her brown hair was straighter and even seemed longer. She had a new bottle of shampoo and a big round hairbrush to style her look, which cupped under at her shoulders. Thick, blunt bangs hid her forehead. I touched the back, and it felt satiny smooth. Somehow, the perm Lucille had given her in January was gone. As she peeled potatoes and bent to pull a pot from a low cabinet, her hair moved in one soft wave. Although I needed to work on my homework, I stared at her hair for a good long time.

"You're home a little early," Momma said as Daddy walked through the kitchen door. The idea that I hadn't heard him drive up surprised me. For the past week since his truck had been stolen, Daddy had been forced to drive Papa Pete's truck, which was quieter on the gravel.

Daddy dropped his sweaty cap on the kitchen table and stared at Momma, his eyebrows crinkled together across his nose forming a deep line. The sleeve of his khaki work shirt was jagged and ripped as though he had gotten caught in a plow. "What the hell happened to your hair?" he said.

"I got a new haircut. What do you think?" Momma smoothed the sides with her fingertips and twirled in the center of the kitchen floor. A clean, fresh scent spread through the kitchen as her hair swung and fell back into place. She looked like a movie star.

"It makes the huge hump on your nose look even bigger. That's what I think."

"No, it doesn't! It's very fashionable." I slammed my glass on the kitchen table harder than I had intended, but I didn't care. "Momma looks stylish. Just like a fashion model," I said.

"Shit." Daddy shook his head and wandered off to take a shower.

Momma turned away from me, and her shoulders slumped. She held the wooden cutting board over the boiling pot of water and slid the potatoes in without splattering. How she kept from slinging the scalding water at Daddy, I didn't know. I hated Daddy as hard as I ever had and didn't understand why he could never say anything nice to anyone. "Your hair really does look beautiful, Momma. Daddy doesn't know anything about style," I said.

"Thanks, Gracie," she said. "Go ahead and pour the tea, please."

After Momma got all the food on the table, Daddy walked through the kitchen wearing clean jeans and a plain, white T-shirt. His hair was slicked back and looked oily, but it was only wet. When he opened the icebox to grab a beer, I counted six along the shelf. Without even a glance to the table, he told Momma he wasn't hungry and disappeared out the back door to the patio. I stared at all the bowls of Daddy's favorite foods and felt sick inside. "He's so mean!" I yelled.

Momma gave me a hard look and held a finger to her lips, which meant *Shhhh*. "Abby, why don't you invite Patti to sit with us," Momma said. Patti hadn't eaten with us in ages, so this thrilled Abby. I didn't want to look at that dreadful doll, especially now that one of her arms kept falling off, but I liked the way Momma filled Daddy's empty chair so easily. We ate a longer than normal supper and chatted about school and what we might do on Saturday. Momma told us about the beauty shop in Memphis and how the walls were filled with bright lights and big mirrors. She even agreed to help us make a paper chain to count down to summer.

***

On Saturday morning, the same policeman returned to our house. He removed his hat and lingered at the kitchen table, this time accepting the offered glass of tea and a refill even. He had come to report he had solved our crime. As he relayed details of the story, he sat taller and smiled bigger than the last time we saw him, and I thought his chest swelled inside his black policeman shirt. Daddy, who had been walking out the door when the officer arrived, came back inside, sat at the kitchen table, and tapped his hand impatiently. The police officer didn't understand how busy Daddy was. Instead of getting down to business, he built up the whole account as though he were writing an essay for Miss Lamb's class using lots of adjectives and adverbs.

Finally, Daddy said, "Could you just cut to the chase? I have somewhere to be." I knew "somewhere" was out in the field.

"Oh, sure, sure," he stumbled over his words and went to the end of his story. Daddy's truck had been discovered the night before when the thief had attempted to auction it off down the road at Cottonwood Corner. When the auctioneer opened the bidding, someone from the crowd recognized Daddy's truck.

How interesting! Daddy's truck had been parked right down the road while he sat on the patio drinking beer.

"Your robber wasn't too bright." The policeman shook his head and chuckled, taking a big swig of iced tea. "He left fingerprints smeared all along the dashboard and steering wheel." The officer went on to explain how our television and other items had been found too. Turned out the robber lived in an old farmhouse down close to the river. "He had your television all hooked up to a big antenna. When we knocked on his door, all his kids were sitting around watching it. Honestly, I was surprised he hadn't already sold it. That whole family lives like wild animals. It was a sight to see." He laughed like it was funny, but everything about it sounded sad to me.

When Daddy asked about the robber's name, the policeman said, "Harry." I didn't know anyone named Harry, but his kids had to go to school at Savage Crossing since it was the only school around. The policeman said Harry had a record a mile long, which must have been a bad thing based on the way Momma shook her head and sighed. "He'll be going away this time, I'd bet on it," he added as he wrote something on the bottom of a form he pulled from a folder labeled Lee Abbott.

That's when I figured everything out. Written across the top of the form in black marker was the name William Harris. Not Harry. Our robber was Arlene's daddy.

Chapter Thirty-Eight

Itook my regular spot on the third pew and asked Nana if she had any gum because I had a dry, horrible taste in my mouth for some unknown reason. While she scratched around in the bottom of her pocketbook, I glanced toward the hole in the floor for the first time that morning. And there, gazing right back at me was a plant. Sometime during the past two weeks, a single slender stem had grown right through the half-dollar sized hole and into the air-conditioned church. The pea green sprout on the tip looked like a baby soybean.

I poked Abby and pointed at this crazy church miracle. What a curious thing to happen. The sun never reached the dirt underneath the floor. And how would a seed get down there?

"Oh," she said. The "O" shape of her lips matched her round eyes.

I reached down and touched the tip of it. The sprout bent beneath my fingers then popped back to its original position, standing strong a half-inch or so above the floor. The plant felt tender and waxy and newly born.

I stared at it through the entire first hymn and was careful not to step on it when Mr. Donaldson dismissed us for Sunday school class.

Our Sunday school lesson was about loving our neighbors. When Abby reminded Momma that we had no neighbors, she said "neighbor" was defined in the Bible as anyone we come into contact with. When I asked Momma if she had chosen to teach on this specific topic because our house was robbed by our "neighbor"—I made little quotation marks with my fingers just like she did—she said, "No, Gracie, if you will notice, this subject happens to be the next lesson in our book."

She was right. Sunday's date was printed at the top of the page beside the lesson entitled "Love Thy Neighbor As Thyself." I still thought it was a strange coincidence and maybe even one of those "Jesus works in mysterious ways" sort of things. Like the magic soybean plant growing through the floor at Boon Chapel.

Momma said the most important thing to remember was to love God with all our hearts. The second thing was to love our neighbors. Momma passed around the coffee can filled with pencils and told us to take one and write down various ways we could love our neighbors. My entire mind was blank of nice ideas. All I could think about was mean Arlene and the way she had made me nervous every single day, and how, for the past several weeks, she had stolen my milk money. Then I considered her Daddy. Although we had never met Mr. Harris, according to the Bible's definition, he was our neighbor simply because we had come into contact with him when he broke the lock on our back door and helped himself to our television.

Everyone stared blankly at Momma. No one wrote a word. Dian popped her knuckles one at a time, making a cracking, bone-breaking sound. Outside the window, the low murmur of Boon Chapel men floated through the air.

"Maybe we should do this exercise together," Momma said. "Dian, what do you think?"

"I guess being a friend to someone who isn't very nice?"

"Yes. That's a good one." Momma wrote it on the chalkboard like a real teacher. "What else?"

"Treating people the way we want to be treated," one of the Davidson girls said. Momma said that was an excellent example and wrote that down too. Each time she turned to write on the board, her new haircut swung freshly around her shoulders.

"Grace? What can you add?" Momma asked me. I stared at the red pencil in my hand and twirled it between my fingers.

"Maybe forgive people who rob our house and steal our milk money?"

Momma, who didn't know about my milk money problem, frowned and said, "Why don't we just say 'forgive those who wrong us'?"

I shrugged. "Same difference."

Eventually, after reading a few Bible verses and talking more about not holding grudges and setting good examples, Mr. Davidson rang the bell and we returned to our pews for morning announcements. I positioned my Mary Janes on either side of the plant growing through the floor and kept an eye on it while listening. There wasn't much news to speak of other than we should all remember to pray for Sister Clara who was having an operation on her foot next week. "Sister" Clara, who was my Aunt Clara and Nana's older sister, sat in her regular spot on the end of our third-row pew. She nodded and waved at the congregation with her bird-like hand. I looked down at her foot, but nothing looked the matter with it to me. Mr. Davidson also reminded everyone about the Boon Chapel Mother's Day celebration coming up in two weeks. Even though the event wasn't nearly as big as Harvest Supper, we got to eat cake and ice cream after Sunday school and the mothers got a special treat. I looked up at Nana, and she smiled and patted me on the shoulder.

After we dragged through two hymns and Aunt Fannie sang a solo, Brother Brown preached about the Good Samaritan. His message, which I actually listened to while I folded a piece of blank paper into a Chinese fortuneteller, was almost identical to the lesson Momma talked about in Sunday school. I glanced up at the yellowed ceiling and wondered if God was trying to tell me something by repeating similar lessons in both Sunday school and preaching?

As soon as the invitational hymn began, I stood straight as a rod and marched to the front. Brother Brown closed his Bible and took a few steps in my direction. He wore a tan tie with his brown suit and his weak smile made me wonder if he was a little sick.

"Happy Sunday, Grace," he said with his thin lips but not with his eyes, which seemed to stare past me.

"Happy Sunday, Brother Brown. I need to talk to you about a few things."

"Okay," he said as he motioned toward the first pew, empty as usual, other than his brown hat, which lay in the corner. We walked over, sat side-by-side, and leaned our heads toward one another because the whole walking-up-during-the-invitational-hymn-experience was a quiet, private sort of thing.

"First off, this is a long story, so I hope you aren't too hungry or tired or anything." He smiled and said he had plenty of time. "There's a mean black girl in my class who's been stealing my milk money for a while. That's not what I really want to talk about, but it's part of the whole story."

"Okay, go on." He nodded, leaned in even closer, and I thought maybe he was wearing a new aftershave.

"If you haven't heard yet, last weekend our whole family went to Little Rock for a farmer meeting. It was pretty fun, because Mae went with us and we stayed in a motel and got to swim a lot. But the not-so-fun part happened when we got home and discovered our house had been robbed." Brother Brown's eyes popped wide open behind his smudged glasses, so I could tell he hadn't heard about our recent misfortune. Considering how fast gossip traveled in our county, this was yet another amazing thing about the morning so far. "Don't worry, though, the Savage Crossing policemen caught the thief. He lives down by the river with a whole bunch of wild kids. The thief, not the policeman—I don't know where the policeman lives." I paused to let Brother Brown catch up. Based on the way he cocked his head and blinked his eyes, the details of my story seemed to roll into his ears faster than his brain could take everything in. When he nodded, I continued. "The good news is we got our television back. The bad news is the robber's daughter is Arlene, the awful girl who has been stealing my milk money."

"I see," he said.

"Until today, I didn't realize we had any neighbors. The only house near us is empty, because the man who lived there shot himself and disappeared off the face of the Earth. Now you're saying everyone is our neighbor, even these thieving people whose house is too far away to see from our yard?"

"The Bible says it, not me. I'm just the mouthpiece for the word of God."

I wanted to roll my eyes but managed not to. "Exactly how are we supposed to forgive robbers who steal our only television? They must be the worst sort of neighbors."

242

"Gracie, God says to love your neighbor as yourself, and part of loving is forgiving. So, yes you need to find a way to forgive them and definitely pray for them. They need your prayers."

"I knew you would say that. It doesn't seem fair that we have to do all the loving and praying and forgiving while they steal and don't follow any rules. I'm not kidding, Brother Brown, Arlene is the meanest girl I've ever run across."

"As a Christian, you have a responsibility to be the bigger person."

"What does that mean? Should we let them keep our television? Pretty soon everyone would hear about it, and we'd be living in an empty house with no furniture or clothes or anything."

"Well, that's an extreme example. I suggest you pray about it. Answers come during prayerful consideration."

I decided right then and there that preachers were like weathermen. They liked to talk and make predictions, but everything boiled down to nothing more than a guess. No one knew what would happen tomorrow. If all the preachers and weathermen suddenly vanished, whatever was going to happen still would.

"Okay, well, I'll think about all this and pray too. Thanks Brother Brown." He shook my hand and his felt like a cold, limp fish.

***

Once we got home, the rest of the day and night went by quickly like Sundays always did. I went to bed, dreading school. I especially dreaded seeing Arlene now that I knew her dad would be going to jail. She would blame that on me, I felt certain. I did as Brother Brown suggested and prayed for some sort of answer to my problem with her. As I stared at the shadowy ceiling, I didn't feel like God heard me at all. If he was real, why would he let people like Arlene exist? If I ever met him outside the Pearly Gates or on my deathbed or wherever, that would be one of the first things I would ask him. Not in a smart aleck way, but in a regular, need-to-know way.

After tossing and turning and having a horrible nightmare about strangers inside our house, I woke to the sounds of Momma rattling around in the kitchen. I woke up, somehow knowing that I would no longer be chicken-hearted. Arlene could beat me up or kill me right on the school bus, but I wouldn't give her any more money.

The icebox door opened. Soon, the smell of bacon reached my nose. Daddy mumbled something to Momma. I heard the tinkling sound of a spoon against the side of Momma's coffee cup and thought it sounded much like the silver bell we hung on the Christmas tree every year. According to my Cinderella watch, it was not yet five a.m. Daddy usually ate cereal for breakfast, but sometimes he wanted bacon and eggs. On those mornings, Momma got up before the sun and cooked them for him. She never seemed to mind, but the other day I heard her tell Maggie, "I don't know when I became Lee Abbott's beck and call girl."

Later when I asked Mae exactly what a "beck and call girl" was, she said it was someone who did all the steppin' and fetchin'. "Like a maid?" I had asked. Mae nodded yes, and I could see why Momma felt that way.

Our bedroom was still midnight black. Lucky felt heavy draped over my feet at the bottom of my bed. I rolled over and tried to go back to sleep, but all I could think of was the milk money Arlene had stolen from me in the past two weeks. What made one person a hard worker and another person a thief? I must have fallen back asleep just as Momma flipped on the light and told Abby and me to get ready for school. That sort of annoying thing made for a bad way to start the day.

I rested my head on the kitchen table and ignored my bowl of grits. My brave, early morning feelings had evaporated through the pores of my skin, and now I only wanted to skip school and hide from my problems. The grandfather clock in the dining room played a few notes, which it did every fifteen minutes. Mr. Jackson would be pulling up to our house soon. I moaned and made a bunch of sick noises, but Momma ignored me. Finally, I announced, "I'm pretty sure I have the flu."

"You don't have the flu. Eat your grits." Momma cracked open an ice tray and emptied it into the plastic freezer container. One piece fell on the floor and sailed over the linoleum to my foot.

"I have a fever. I can tell."

She sighed, walked over, and placed her wet palm against my forehead to make her quick determination. "You don't have a fever."

"Your hand is wet and cold. How can you tell without the thermometer?"

"Eat. Your brain needs fuel."

I ate a few bites, swallowing without tasting while thinking about Arlene the whole time. I really was sick, but not with the flu. I was sick of Arlene, sick of giving her money, sick of being a scaredy cat. I swallowed a bit more breakfast then put my bowl in the sink. Momma gave me a hug, told me to have a good day, and I was out the back door.

"Grace, you forgot your lunch box!" Momma yelled after me. She held up the lunchbox I had been carrying to confuse Arlene.

"I don't need it anymore," I said. Momma nodded and went back inside the house.

Abby stood by the rosebush, swinging her book satchel, the outline of her hair illuminated by the fiery, early morning sun. In the distance, the bus appeared on the deserted highway. Abby raced off to meet it. From the mimosa tree, a lone bird chirped, his voice clear and steady. I took my time walking to the highway.

"Good morning, Abbott," Mr. Jackson said as I stood outside the doorway of the bus. He was the only person who called me by my last name.

"Hi, Mr. Jackson." I took a deep breath, grabbed the rail, and hoisted myself up the steps into the loud bus. Gripping my purse, I moved the strap over my still-flat chest and picked my way through the aisle toward the back. When Arlene stuck her dirty shoe into my path, I stepped over it without stumbling.

"You got any extra money today, rich girl?" Arlene shoved my shoulder. Multi-colored plastic barrettes, like those a young child might wear, adorned her plaited hair and poked in all directions.

"No. Why don't you ask your thieving daddy who robbed our house and stole my daddy's truck?" I stared into her black eyes without blinking or looking away, even though my knees quivered and the grits in my stomach roiled. The chaos of the bus vanished, and I didn't hear or notice anything beyond the two of us standing in the cramped aisle.

Mean Arlene and Paleface Grace.

This was it. There was no turning back. I felt my hands clinch, one around my notebook and the other on the edge of the closest seat. The bus rocked forward, but I planted my feet and stood stiff and straight.

"Don't you dare talk about my daddy," she growled in a low, gravelly voice, sounding more like a boy than a girl. Her cheeks bloomed ruddy through her dark skin.

"Well, it's the truth," I said, staring her square in the face.

"Ouch, that white girl done tole you a thing or two," Sugar jeered. Laughter spread among the gang. I pushed my way through to the back and sat beside Jamie Bard. He smiled and nodded at me. I almost felt sorry for Arlene. In an instant, her entire group of friends had turned on her, teasing and whooping it up all the way to school.

Chapter Thirty-Nine

On the second day of May, Abby turned eight years old. Since her birthday happened in the middle of the school week instead of during summer break like mine, Momma made up for it by dragging it out. On Wednesday, Abby's actual birthday, Momma baked chocolate cupcakes for her whole class. For supper that night, we met Nana, Papa Pete, Mamaw Pearl, and Candi at the Yellow Jacket Café for hamburgers and onion rings. Daddy was feeling sick, so he didn't go. Momma took him a piece of peanut butter pie wrapped in plastic wrap, and he ate it in bed. I never got to eat pie in bed when I was sick, but that was one of the benefits of being old. Later, on Friday night, Abby had a bunkin' party with three of her best friends plus Dian. I stayed over at Janice's house so Abby and her friends could have the bedroom to themselves. Abby had promised they would keep their hands off my things, and as far as I could tell, they had. Momma said they kept her up all night.

One week later, school let out for summer. Fourth grade, my most chaotic school year at Savage Crossing Elementary, ended calmly. After I had confronted Arlene on the bus, other than an occasional scowl sent my direction, she no longer bothered me. On the last day of school, Mrs. Penny gave me a special certificate for working in the library. I tacked it in the middle of my bulletin board above my bed.

There was nothing like the first Saturday morning of summer vacation when I cracked open my eyes and realized every day, for the next three months, would be like a string of carefree Saturdays—except for church days when we couldn't sleep late and had to look presentable.

On Mother's Day, which always fell on a Sunday, Abby and I awakened early enough to cook breakfast for Momma—cinnamon toast, with a bowl of strawberries, and whipped cream in a can. We made extra toast for Daddy too, because it would have been rude not to. When Momma walked into the kitchen, she wore her pale blue bathrobe cinched tight at the waist. Her new, thick bangs lay straight and severe against her forehead, held in place by some sort of stretchy pink tape.

"Happy Mother's Day!" Abby and I cheered.

"What a nice surprise!" Momma grinned and sat down in the chair Abby pulled out for her. I poured her orange juice. Daddy sat down too, but he pulled out his own chair.

"Daddy, you should come to church with us today," I said. "Mother's Day is a big deal at Boon Chapel."

Daddy grunted in my direction. I stared at him and tried to determine if his sickness had returned or if he was only grumpy. I had decided to invite him to church because I worried his chances were dwindling. For months, his sickness had disappeared and Momma told everyone he was well, but who really knew what was happening inside his body. In science class, we had been studying the human body and learning all about digestion and bones and muscles and cells. I found myself watching Daddy and wondering if his blood and cells looked the same as mine, or if they were diseased and misshapen. Last night, I heard Momma remind Daddy that he had a checkup at the end of the month.

"I don't feel right," he had said.

Momma reassured him that everything was probably fine, but she didn't sound so confident to me. When I asked Mae what she thought would happen to us if Daddy got sick again and died, she said I shouldn't worry about those sort of things. "Mr. Lee looks healthy to me." Mae was a lot of things, but she wasn't a doctor.

Just before we left for church, Momma pinned a corsage to the lapel of her Sunday dress. It was fancy—a scarlet rose, with a matching satin ribbon, and tiny white flowers like the ones growing near the turnrow. Pulling scissors from the junk drawer in the kitchen, she said, "Grace, run outside and snip off rose buds for you and your sister.

Don't get your shoes muddy." Abby and I weren't old enough to wear big, store-bought flowers.

An overnight shower had left puddles in the low spots along our gravel driveway. Being unable to splash through the middle of them seemed an unfair temptation and a waste of good rain. I hoped the water would still be there after church when I could get my play shoes as muddy as I liked. I headed for the fat rose bush near the edge of the field with Abby chasing after me. Despite avoiding the mud puddles, wet grass clung to our shoes and white socks.

This bush always bloomed pink on Mother's Day, as though it understood the importance of its job. Some roses were already tired and dying, but even those smelled fragrant, like Momma's expensive one. I selected a tight bud and cut the stem carefully, where there were no thorns. Abby walked around and around the bush, trying to make her decision. When she stopped in front of an open flower, I reminded her that it would be too big. Last year, I picked one of the roses already in full bloom. During Sunday school class, it was absolutely perfect, and I caught whiffs of its perfume while we read from the Bible, but by the invitational hymn most of the petals had fallen off, leaving me with an ugly safety pin and a thorny stem on my dress.

Once Abby chose a nice small bud, we picked our way back inside, and Momma pinned our rosebuds on our dresses. Daddy was reading the newspaper at the kitchen table. When it was time to go, he went to his alcohol cabinet and got something to pour into his orange juice. Momma told him to go easy, but he just grunted and poured a bit more.

I held Nana's corsage in my lap all the way to church. Like Momma's, it came from the flower shop in Savage Crossing, but instead of a pink or red rose, Nana's corsage was a giant, white gardenia with petals as soft as velvet. Momma said gardenias were the sweetest flower of all, and she was right. The smell filled my nose, and I knew I would remember it forever.

As we walked into the chapel, I raced to my third-row pew, anxious to check on my magic bean plant growing through the floor. I wondered how much taller it had grown during the past week. At first, I thought I had stepped into the wrong row, but I quickly counted one, two, three and looked down again.

My plant was gone.

249

I dropped to the floor and stared through the knothole at the dirt below. There was no evidence of any plant; nothing shriveled, no root pulled from the ground. Even though the plant had probably been a weed, it seemed unique and special, growing wild and free through the floor. For it to disappear as though it never existed? What an awful, disappointing thing to happen.

During the morning part of service, Mr. Davidson asked all the mothers to stand in a row in front of the pulpit so everyone could clap and smile at them. He gave a little talk about how important mothers were and how we'd be lost without them. I knew that was a fact and thought it might have been the truest thing ever said from the pulpit of Boon Chapel. When I looked around at the still seated congregation, I realized every Boon Chapel woman stood up at the front, leaving only the kids and men in the pews. I never knew until that moment that Mrs. Brown was a mother too.

Not surprisingly, our Sunday school lesson was about important mothers in the Bible like Jesus's mother, Mary, and Sarah, the wife of Abraham who'd had a baby when she was super old. I believed the bravest mother in the Bible must have been Moses's mother who set her baby adrift in the Nile River to save him from being murdered. She had a strange name I could never pronounce or remember.

When our lesson ended, we filed out of our classroom and back into the sanctuary. Mr. Davidson and Uncle Will stood near the side doors and handed red carnations to all the mothers. Aunt Fannie held her flower to her nose, smiled and passed it to Dian. Dian looked happy to have it and carried it carefully to her seat. I wondered what it would feel like to see my Daddy handing flowers out at church. As Mr. Davidson went over announcements, I stared at the vacant hole in the floor. Nana's gardenia, only inches from my nose, filled the air with a nearly overpowering aroma.

After a few hymns, Brother Brown began preaching about Martha and how busy she was and how she burned the candle at both ends like today's mothers. I didn't pay much attention since he seemed to be speaking to all the mothers anyway. I thought about my magic bean plant that had held no magic at all. I tried to imagine what had happened to it. I decided it must have died from lack of sun and water and eventually blew away or disappeared into the dust. Although I'd planned to walk up the red carpet and talk to Brother Brown during the invitational hymn, I no longer felt like it. I didn't have anything in particular to say, anyway. I stared at the empty hole until services ended.

**

The freshly planted fields flashed by the car window as we drove home from church. I stared without blinking as long as I could. The soil was dark from the recent rain. Wildflowers and grasses filled the ditch banks. Spring made me feel hopeful even when I didn't want to.

"Since it's Mother's Day, maybe Daddy will take us out to eat lunch. Maybe that barbeque place in town," Momma said. "I didn't put a roast in, so I'm counting on it." She laughed with her whole face and sounded extra happy.

I really wanted to look for tadpoles in the big ditch behind the field once we got home, but since it was her day, Momma should choose. Plus, going out to lunch was a rare thing I never wanted to miss.

Whatever plans Momma had made in her head changed the moment we pulled into the driveway and saw a strange truck parked there. "Whose truck is that?" I asked. It appeared to be built from different colored parts all held together with gray glue. Someone had scrawled, "Wash Me," on the dusty back window.

"I don't know." Momma's shoulders slumped. She sighed as she grabbed her pocketbook and Bible. I mentally prepared myself, taking a deep breath and swallowing hard before following Momma and Abby into the house.

Daddy and Hyena Man were sitting at the kitchen table, eating last night's leftovers. Momma's nostrils widened. Without officially greeting either of them, she said, "I need to get out of these clothes." Her new, swingy haircut swished back and forth as she disappeared around the corner.

"Daddy, it's Mother's Day," I said.

"Yeah?"

"We should take Momma out to lunch," Abby said.

"So, y'all take her to lunch. She's not my momma." Daddy returned to his conversation. Hyena Man's maddening screech filled the house.

Abby and I hid in our bedroom for several hours, listening to records and playing with the new paper dolls Abby had gotten for her birthday. Since we didn't have a lock on our door, I made a "DO NOT ENTER" sign from red construction paper. After I cut it into the shape of a stop sign, Abby drew a frowny face on it, and we taped it on the door. When we got hungry, I sneaked into the kitchen and made us bologna sandwiches with lots of mayonnaise. Daddy and Hyena Man had left the dirty bowl in the middle of the table. I washed it so Momma wouldn't have to.

Hours later, when I heard Momma in the bathroom, I tiptoed out and asked her, "Is Hyena Man still here?"

"Shhhh! Come in and shut the door," she said. That answered my question.

"How long is he staying?" I groaned. Momma didn't know. No one knew.

***

Three days later, Hyena Man was still hanging around with Daddy. During the day, they rode on the farm together, ate lunch and supper at our kitchen table, and stayed up late drinking beer. I found it amazing that Daddy could drink so much at night, yet still be a good farmer during the day. Both men treaded softly around Momma who spent most of her time with Abby and me. Momma announced it would be a great time to spring-clean the playhouse. Spring cleaning turned out to be a serious thing. We took down the eyelet curtains and washed them in Momma's washing machine and even cleaned the windows with newspapers and vinegar water.

On Thursday night, Daddy decided to grill ribs and invite a few friends over. He was trying to make up to Momma, I could tell, but inviting a bunch of wild friends over wasn't the best way to do that. Momma invited her friend Maggie, and they made potato salad and garlic bread while all the men hung out in the back yard. By the time the sun dropped behind the Savage Crossing water tower, most of

Daddy's friends had swarmed to our farm like locusts in the Bible, ready to devour Daddy's barbecue. As the night grew later, the music grew louder and the laughter more animated. Waiting and waiting for Daddy's ribs to roast, Abby and I chased lightning bugs in the front yard. We trapped and saved the ones we caught in an empty Mason jar, poking tiny holes in the lid so they could breathe.

"Go get me a platter," Daddy barked across the yard at us while he opened another beer. Hyena Man told a joke, and the men erupted, making my cheeks flush. I didn't understand the joke, but something about it seemed bad and dirty.

I went to find Momma who was sitting with Maggie in the den. They were drinking fancy drinks with cherries in them while Tom Jones crooned on the eight-track. "Momma, Daddy needs a platter."

"There's one on the kitchen counter." Momma pointed toward the kitchen. She and Maggie looked to be deep in conversation. Hugging the heavy platter against my chest, I carried it to the back door then stretched my arms toward Daddy, offering the platter without stepping outside.

Daddy snatched the tray and yanked me by the wrist into the smoke-filled night. "Come here. You need to be more social." The crowd of men standing on the back patio—some I knew, some I'd never seen before—were laughing and talking all at the same time, surrounding Daddy like his fan club.

"What's your momma doing?" His thick words sounded muddled and in slow motion.

"Drinking with Maggie," I said flatly. A bug light attached to the side of the house provided a muted glow around the barbecue grill. If I squinted, the brilliant orange dots of burning cigarettes, one for each of Daddy's friends, danced in the shadows, distant and festive. The odor of smoke and sour beer overwhelmed the space between our faces.

"Hey, guys. Seems Baby-Grace has a smart mouth just like Anne." Laughter exploded as he yanked me toward him, nearly pulling me off balance. His hand clamped around my arm, and I felt the squeeze of each individual finger. I looked past him toward the plum tree, averting my eyes from his crazed ones. Daddy's breath moved my hair. "Don't be a smart ass. Tell your Momma the ribs are done." He took a drag on his cigarette and blew smoke into my face. "You hear me?" He squeezed my arm even tighter. I pulled back. When he released his firm grip, he left behind the furious sting of his cigarette.

"Owwww!" I yelled. "You burned me!" I held my arm and slammed the door against the laughter. Fighting back tears, I ran through the den, past Momma and Maggie. "The ribs are done!" I yelled.

"What's wrong, Gracie?" Momma asked. I didn't answer. She continued chatting with Maggie.

I held a cold, wet washcloth over my arm while I searched the medicine cabinet for anything I could find that might ease the white fire. Toothpaste, face cream, aspirin, I shoved everything into the sink. Searching. Searching. When I removed the washcloth, the flaming circle just beneath my small pox vaccination had already blistered. Even the surrounding freckles appeared dark and angry.

I choked back tears.

Vaseline would have to do. I carefully dabbed a dot over the spot and hid the cigarette burn with my last Snoopy Band-Aid. I splashed cold water on my face and went back out to find Abby.

While the adults gathered around the picnic table, Abby and I filled our plates and ate alone at the kitchen table. I tried to put the incident from my mind, but the searing pain would not be ignored. I let the pain flow through my body until I felt no emotion. Daddy's ribs were tender, maybe his best yet. I pulled meat from the bones and mixed pieces into my baked potato. Abby talked non-stop about the cute boy who sat behind her in class. "He has bright blue eyes," she said. "He's real smart too." I wanted to remind her she was only a second grader and none of that mattered. Nothing mattered. But I didn't say anything. I ate and ate until my stomach ballooned like a ripe watermelon. Then I went to the bathroom and threw up.

Later, after everyone left, I walked through each dark room of the house, breathing the stale air. I hoped that if walls have memories, this night would be forgotten. Empty beer bottles, nasty overflowing ashtrays, and bowls with caked-on cheese dip cluttered every surface. I held an open whiskey bottle to my lips, turned it up and swallowed. The liquid slipped down my throat, leaving a slow scald, instantly making me lightheaded. I went to bed and lay there, waiting for sleep, still engulfed by the pain in my arm. I watched the jar of lights flicker from the dresser. By morning, the bugs were dead.

Chapter Forty

Brother Brown held a large, brass ring over the pulpit and swayed it back and forth like he was trying to hypnotize us. The key ring, more fitting for a school janitor than a preacher, was crammed with keys of all shapes and sizes. "Who among you would like a key that will unlock the future?" he asked.

For a minute, I almost raised my hand like I was at school. Then Momma's sneeze reverberated through the sanctuary and reminded me I was sitting in Boon Chapel.

"Keys are important in our everyday world," he told the congregation. "But they won't help us if we leave them at home on our kitchen table."

I wondered what Brother Brown's kitchen table looked like and what sort of food Mrs. Brown cooked for him. He had visited our house, but we'd never been invited over to his. I didn't blame him.

Brother Brown continued swinging his keys like he might do a magic trick. "God is the key. Seek what God wants for your life, not what you want," he explained. Brother Brown was getting a bit creative with his sermon. I'd never known him to use a prop.

Next, he asked, "Would you like the key to a happy life?" He paused, to build suspense, but I knew this was a trick question.

Without turning my head, I cut my eyes as far to the left as possible and saw Nana and Aunt Clara watching intently. They were nodding and smiling and appeared mesmerized, even though they already had perfectly happy lives. Miserable people who needed to learn about Brother Brown's keys weren't sitting inside Boon Chapel.

They were down the road at Vera's Bar, or at home, already drinking beer.

Brother Brown asked us to turn to Deuteronomy. I flipped through and pretended to find the right chapter, then listened as Brother Brown recited. "Children, obey your parents in the Lord, for this is right. Honor thy father and mother that it may be well and thou may live long on the Earth."

I frowned and stared hard at Brother Brown, hoping to send him the message that I had a big problem with the whole idea of that verse, especially the honoring my father part.

"The key is for us to obey God's law, and God said to obey your parents."

Brother Brown jangled his keys like sleigh bells and looked right over at Abby and me. Before I could roll my eyes or shake my head or anything, he looked to the other side of the aisle, at the Donaldson twins. I tuned Brother Brown out for much of the remainder of the sermon, choosing to look out the window at purple irises blooming near a tree stump in the corner of the churchyard. Nana called them bearded ladies because of the way the petals were arranged. Just staring out the window and thinking about them allowed me to imagine their sweet smell as vividly as sticking my nose in them.

I glanced down at Aunt Clara's foot. She'd had surgery a few weeks ago to remove a carbuncle from her heel, and this was her first Sunday back. Carbuncle sounded like a made up word to me. Aunt Clara wore a thick, white sock instead of a shoe on that foot, but otherwise, she walked with only a slight limp and smiled her same sweet smile. I wrote "carbuncle" on the palm of my hand. I'd look it up in the encyclopedia the next time Momma took us to the library.

Finally, Brother Brown wrapped up his sermon, and Momma played the first few measures of the invitational hymn. I stood and squeezed into the aisle, careful not to step on Aunt Clara's sore foot. Someone behind me yawned. I walked quickly to the front. Brother Brown, who was already expecting my visit, met me half way.

"I need to talk to you," I said, unsmiling.

"Well, good morning to you too, Grace," he replied, motioning me to the first pew where we sat instead of kneeled. Lately, Brother Brown seemed to be walking with a slight limp. I hoped he wasn't getting a carbuncle like Aunt Clara.

"God must be a practical joker if he expects me to honor my Daddy when he is mean as the devil himself. Isn't there anything in the Bible about parents honoring their children, or at least not hurting them?"

Brother Brown stared at the ceiling for a moment, opened his Bible to Psalms and read with a bland face. Even his voice sounded dull and brown as he droned like a robot. "Children are a heritage from the Lord, and fruit of the womb is a reward."

"Brother Brown, I don't know what that means. You need to explain it in regular, normal words. I'm just a kid."

"Grace, it means children are a gift from God. And yes, parents should take care of their children. That goes without saying." He covered my hand with his, and his face softened.

"Brother Brown, I've changed my mind."

"About what?"

"About praying for my Daddy. Don't waste any more of your prayers on Lee Abbott. Spend your time praying for someone else." When I jumped to my feet, my shoes made a clicking sound on the hardwood floor as though I wore taps on the soles. Brother Brown remained seated and stared at me like he wanted to say something more. The skin on his forehead folded into creases, and I could tell he was studying something serious. "Thanks for trying anyway. It's not your fault. Some people can't be saved," I added.

Brother Brown stood, draped his arm around my shoulder and accidentally touched the burned place on my arm.

"Ouch! That's my sore arm," I gasped.

"What happened to your arm?" he asked.

"I got burned." I looked up at him and for a split second knew that if Brother Brown dug just a little deeper and asked the right question, I would tell him everything. The music sounded distant. Brother Brown shifted from one foot to the other and stared at me without blinking.

Ask me.

Ask me.

The still fresh memory rushed back—the smell of stale smoke, the drunk laughter, the stabbing burn of the cigarette against my arm. The truth swirled on my tongue and nearly spewed from my mouth, yet something kept me from offering it to Brother Brown. I lightly pressed my palm into the burn spot on my arm. The pressure of my hand felt protective and oddly comforting. His eyes followed my hand.

"It really hurts too," I added.

He nodded and his face winced in sympathy, but he never asked.

Momma began dragging the lethargic congregation through the third stanza. I grew tired of talking to Brother Brown and found it hard to make eye contact with him.

"Why are you giving up on your Daddy?"

"He's never going to change. *Il est impossible.*"

***

I'd been waiting to hear Daddy's truck door slam. When it did, I grabbed Barbie and ran from the den. As the screen door slapped shut, I climbed into bed, slipped Barbie underneath my pillow, and tugged the sheet to my shoulders. Since the horrible night of Daddy's barbecue, one good thing had happened—Hyena Man had disappeared. No one mentioned him, but on Friday morning, Momma whistled a tune as she stripped the sheets from the couch-bed.

Ice cubes spilled into glasses and silverware clinked against plates. The aroma of fried chicken sent a grumble through my stomach. "Grace, supper!" Momma called. I focused on a leggy spider that was dangling over my dresser by an invisible thread. She climbed up toward the ceiling then propelled herself back toward the mirror before repeating the process all over again. Since I had read *Charlotte's Web*, I considered all spiders to be girls and tried not to kill them.

Momma pushed open the bedroom door. "It's supper time, Gracie. What's wrong with you?"

"I don't feel good. My stomach hurts."

Momma pressed a palm to my forehead. "You haven't felt like eating supper for two nights, but you don't have a fever. You aren't on some kind of starvation diet, are you?"

"No, I just don't feel like eating supper."

"Well, I'll check on you later." She flipped off the overhead light and Charlotte disappeared into darkness. As soon as I heard everyone in the kitchen, I turned on my bedside lamp and pulled my diary from underneath the mattress. On the top of a clean page, I wrote "DADDY" and added a big question mark.

I couldn't figure him out. Was he a bad person, or did he have a disease that made him mean? Or maybe the simple truth was he hated me.

Page after page, I spilled out the whole story about my burned arm, everything I could remember about that terrible night—how Abby and I trapped lightning bugs in a jar, how dusk smelled of honeysuckle mixed with barbecue smoke, how my stomach still feels sick and my arm throbs as though it has a fever. I stared at Barbie's skinned nose and even wrote about the time Daddy smashed her face on the carport.

I wrote the truth.

Chapter Forty-One

After a few days, my Snoopy Band-Aid was beginning to look nasty and no longer stuck around the edges. I figured I had to do something about it and went to find Momma weeding the flowerbed beside the carport. She pulled a red bandana from her pocket and wiped her forehead. Although it was early, the sun was yellow and hot and the air felt thick enough to see.

"Do we have any more Band-Aids?" I asked.

"In the bathroom. Why do you need a Band-Aid?" She stood and rubbed her lower back.

"For the sore on my arm," I said. I had been wearing long-sleeved shirts and keeping my arm hidden, but today Janice and her two sisters had invited me to go swimming. I needed a fresh Band-Aid.

"How did you get a sore?" she asked as we walked to the bathroom together.

"I don't remember."

Momma scrubbed her hands as though she might do surgery then rummaged through the cabinet underneath the sink. Like magic, she pulled out a box containing Band-Aids in a variety of shapes and sizes. I took a round one the size of the cigarette burn.

"Let me see." Momma removed the old bandage barely clinging to my skin and stared at my arm. Red streaks pointed to the place Daddy left his mark. "Grace, that looks infected. Is that a burn mark?" She looked more closely, her face near my arm.

"It's fine. I have to hurry. Janice's mother will be here soon," I tried to turn away, but she wouldn't let me.

"Grace. How did this happen? It looks like a cigarette burn." Momma opened a tube of medicine and applied a bit around the spot. I expected it to burn, but it didn't.

I didn't say anything.

"You aren't going anywhere until you tell me." Her eyes turned a stormy shade of blue, and she pressed her lips together until little lines formed all around.

"It happened Thursday night when all those awful people came to eat Daddy's barbecue."

"Who did this to you?" she asked in almost a whisper, and I wondered if somewhere deep inside she knew the answer.

I stared at Momma, letting silence build between us in the small bathroom. The sticky air smelled of hairspray. I remembered the time I had chicken pox and Momma had swabbed pink lotion on every blister after I took a bath.

"Grace, you won't get in trouble. You didn't do anything wrong. But I need to know."

Looking away from Momma, to the ceiling, I noticed a dead moth lying at the bottom of the globe light fixture. I imagined floating and hovering up there too. "Hyena Man," I said. My eyes filled with tears. His name had come to me with no warning.

"Douglas did this to you?" Her eyes widened and her arms dropped limp to her sides.

"Yes. Hyena Man burned my arm with a cigarette. And it wasn't an accident either."

Momma slammed the cabinet door and began ranting about how he was a monster, and how she'd never trusted him in the first place. "When I get through with him, he'll wish he'd never stepped foot in our house," she said.

A hard, violent wail exploded from deep inside me, and I couldn't stop the sobs that racked my body. Momma pulled me toward her and held me to her chest. She reminded me over and over that it wasn't my fault, and she almost cried too. "I'm not upset with you, Gracie. You didn't do anything wrong. Remember that."

I nodded into her blouse that smelled faintly of perfume. My stomach seized as I swallowed back memories of that night, wondering why I lied to protect Daddy. I'd pictured Daddy's clothes piled in the

262

driveway again, his jeans wet and dirty, his T-shirts covered with leaves.

"Try to calm down. You're going to make yourself sick, Grace," Momma said as she stroked my hair. I stayed there, enfolded in her arms, even though my body wanted to pull away and run.

"Okay," I choked out two syllables that sounded like someone else's voice. The fresh Band-Aid felt taut and scratchy against my skin. The feel of Daddy's grip on my arm stayed with me, and I smelled his cigarette smoke as though he stood in the tiny bathroom with us.

***

Janice's mother had packed ham sandwiches for lunch. I only ate a few bites of mine. Later, I threw up in the bathroom, which made me feel a little better. When Janice, who was in the next stall, heard me puking, I told her I had swallowed too much water when we were practicing our underwater somersaults. We spent most of the remaining afternoon lying on beach towels, trying to get a suntan. Janice's sisters lay on either side of us, and her mother, who sat underneath an umbrella most of the day, rubbed our backs down with lotion. Every fifteen minutes, Janice's oldest sister reminded us to turn over. We were shish kabobs on a grill, rolling in unison. The sun felt warm and delicious, and lying there doing nothing gave me time to think about why I had blamed the terrible thing Daddy did on someone else.

I lied not to save Daddy, but to save our family. The truth would have brought an awful fight, the last fight, because Momma would have thrown Daddy out for good. And as Nana always said, I did kill two birds with one stone. Never having to see Hyena Man again would be a humongous relief.

Since four o'clock was the time kids had to get out of the pool so old people could swim laps, Janice's mother decided we should leave. On the drive home, the guilt of the lie I told returned to me, and I felt sick at my stomach. I tried to take slow, even breaths, but when I saw Daddy's truck parked beside the plum tree, earlier than normal, my heart ballooned into my throat. I glanced across the cotton field to the pretty gray house and considered running away and hiding there forever. But I didn't. I waved goodbye to Janice and her family as they backed down the driveway.

The kitchen smelled of pot roast, even though it was a regular day. A strawberry cake cooled on the stove. "We're having an early supper tonight," Momma said. "Not for another hour, but earlier than normal." Momma's feet were bare. She had toilet paper threaded around each of her toes and freshly applied bright, red polish on her toenails.

"Why?" I asked, suspicious of every smell in the kitchen and every word that passed from Momma's lips. "Where's Daddy?" I asked.

"He's outside working in the pump house. Something broke today, and water spewed everywhere. He's been out there all afternoon." Momma placed clean dishes in the cabinet and put away the flour and sugar. She hobbled on her heels because of her drying toes.

"Why are we eating early?" I asked.

"I just thought it would be nice since Daddy's home early. Go change out of those wet clothes. Hang your bathing suit in the bathroom. Don't throw it on the floor." Momma said.

I went to my room, lay on my bed, and stared at the ceiling. Everyone in the entire world was nuts. Momma seemed cheerful, as though she had completely forgotten our morning conversation. She made no mention of the burn on my arm. When I got up to put on clean clothes, my bedspread held a wet outline of my body, almost like the chalk outline of a dead person, something I once saw on television.

Now that I knew where the Band-Aids were stored, I fished out a new one and stuck it to my arm. All that swimming seemed to have helped my sore heal a bit. The skin around it was no longer angry or marked with red streaks. I wore a tank top with my fresh Band-Aid in full view. I was ready for whatever would happen at the supper table.

Despite Momma's merry mood, I had a bad feeling. It was Abby's turn to set the table, so I filled the glasses with ice. When Daddy sat down, he looked tired and worn, and maybe even a little guilty. At least in my mind.

"Did you girls have a good day today?" he asked.

In all my days, Daddy had never once showed interest in anything we'd done except on report card day when he went over our grades with an eagle eye and complained if we made anything less than an A+.

"Yes!" Abby cheered. "Momma took me to Sterling's and we made a strawberry cake while Gracie was swimming."

Daddy grinned. I even saw some of his front teeth.

"What about you, Grace? How was your day swimming?" He looked at me and waited. He didn't look mad or grumpy at all.

I stared at the whiskers already beginning to poke out around his jaw and wanted to yell at him. *It was just groovy! I lied to Momma and puked at the swimming pool and, in case you were wondering, after a week of throbbing, the burn you gave me finally began to heal, so hopefully, my arm won't have to be cut off.* "It was okay." My words sounded feeble and pale and not from my own mouth.

After Momma filled our plates and sat down with us, her face turned solemn. "Grace, I want to talk about what you told me this morning," she said.

Oh, boy. Here we go, I thought.

"What?" Abby asked.

"Abby, you may as well know since this is a family meeting," Momma said.

I wanted to leave the table. I counted in my head. *One Mississippi...* I sat on my hands to keep them from shaking. Lucky, who was curled in a heavy ball on my feet, kept me from drifting away.

"I don't really want to talk about it," I said, refusing to look at Daddy. "Momma, why do you have to make such a big deal about everything?"

"You aren't in trouble, Grace. I told Daddy about what happened," Momma said. I felt my eyes blur, but blinked hard to drive back the tears. "And Daddy agreed Douglas won't be welcome here anymore."

"Good! Hyena Man laughed too loud and ate all our food," Abby said, doing a little jig in her chair. When she saw I wasn't smiling, she realized there was a serious reason behind the announcement. "What happened?" she whispered.

"He burned your sister's arm with a cigarette," Momma said.

Abby gasped and reached toward my arm, stopping an inch short of touching the Band-Aid.

"Did you cry, Grace?" Abby asked.

"No," I said, while watching for Daddy's reaction. He glanced at me above the rim of the tea glass he held to his mouth. As he swallowed, his eyes moved to my sister.

"I would have...." Abby said, her voice trailing off.

"Abby, your sister is very brave," he said as he reached for the salt and pepper. His voice sounded low and steady, and he spoke slowly.

I stared at Daddy and shook my head and wiped the tears that threatened to spill down my cheeks. "No. I'm not," I whispered. *I'm a coward. And a liar.*

No one ate much of the supper Momma prepared. I smashed a roasted potato, pushing soft ridges through the fork tongs.

"Grace, we want you to know that Daddy talked to Douglas today. Douglas drank too much and didn't remember anything about it. But he feels really bad," Momma said.

I kept watching Daddy. He stared back at me with vacant eyes, letting Momma do all the talking. "You did?" I asked.

"He won't be coming back over," Daddy finally said. His eyelid had one of those slight twitches like I sometimes got when I stayed up too late reading underneath the quilt with my flashlight. Only I didn't think reading had caused Daddy's problem.

"We should call the police," Abby said. "He should go to jail for doing something like that."

Daddy shifted in his chair and wiped his hands on his napkin. "No, I took care of it. We don't want to ruin his life because of something he regrets doing. He's sorry. He really is," Daddy said.

"Did he say he was sorry?" I asked.

"He said to tell you he was sorry for hurting you. He never meant that to happen. He's going to stop drinking so much too." Daddy reached out and touched my wrist, which felt as odd as anything. His eyelids looked heavy, and he spoke from a rare place I was unfamiliar with. I knew by the eye twitch and the way he was pulling strings of beef from his pot roast that this was the closest thing to an apology I would get. He and I both knew he hadn't confronted Hyena Man about something he didn't do.

"Well, when you talk to him again, you can tell him it was something I will never forget, but that I will pray for him and maybe try

266

to forgive him someday. That's what Brother Brown would tell me to do, anyway," I said, staring at Daddy the whole time.

"I'll tell him," Daddy murmured.

"Oh, I don't think either of us will be talking to Douglas again," Momma said, looking swiftly at Daddy for confirmation. He nodded. His face looked greenish, and I even felt a little sorry for him.

Chapter Forty-Two

On the first day of June, Momma and Daddy went to Memphis for Daddy's doctor appointment. Mae came to keep an eye on us. Even though I would be eleven in August, Momma said I was still too young to babysit Abby. When I asked Momma exactly how old I needed to be, she told me to stop worrying about it. "Enjoy your time with Mae," she said as she tied a scarf around her hair. It wasn't that I didn't want to see Mae, because I did. I just deserved to know.

We spent most of the afternoon in the back corner of the cotton field, Mae included. Thin white clouds crisscrossed the sky like ribbons, and my eyes were constantly drawn upward into the lazy day. While Abby and I messed around on the ditch bank, Mae rested on a tree stump and fanned her face with the straw fishing hat she had worn on her head. She said she didn't know why we were so fascinated with digging in the dirt when we had a perfectly nice, clean sandbox right beside the playhouse. I didn't know either, but it was the truth. Every so often, she stood up, placed the hat back on her head, and walked a few slow paces along the turnrow. Mae always wore the same old tennis shoes, once white but now the color of dust, the back of the shoes permanently smashed down by her wide paddle-like feet.

"My old legs get stove up if I don't walk every few minutes," she said.

"Mae, how old are you," Abby asked. I poked her in the arm, and she screamed like I had stabbed her with Momma's butcher knife.

"Don't you know it's rude to ask a lady how old she is?" I whispered to my sister. Abby didn't know those rules, and honestly, I was curious and a little glad she had asked. I waited to hear Mae's answer.

Mae laughed and said she didn't mind. "I'll be forty-five on my next birthday."

"When's that?" I asked.

"November one," she said and looked off into the distance like she was thinking about something far away. As long as we'd known Mae, we'd never thought about her birthday before.

"She's old." Abby cupped her grimy hand around my ear and spoke in a slow, quiet drawl. I nodded and agreed. She was older than Momma and younger than Nana, yet her face had less wrinkles than both of them.

"Mae, Abby and I decided a while back that if something ever happens to Momma and Nana and Mamaw Pearl, we would come live with you. If that's okay with you and your Old Pair of Pants," I said as I poked a stick into a hole in the side of the ditch bank and then stood back to see if a snake or some other creature might come out. Nothing did.

She laughed so hard she bobbed up and down and nearly fell off her stump. "Honey, I don't think that's gonna happen, all those people dying off at the same time, but if it do, you and Abby would be mighty welcome. My Old Pair of Pants wouldn't mind one bit." Abby and I smiled at each other, glad to have that matter resolved, but I didn't see anything so funny about it.

Mae knew exactly when the mosquitoes would come out, and so she rushed us back into the house before they feasted on our arms and legs. When I asked her where the mosquitoes went during the hot part of the day, she said she didn't know or care so long as they stayed hidden while we were playing. "Why don't you girls get your baths, and we'll be all nice and clean when Ms. Anne and Mr. Lee gets home?" she suggested. She said "we" as though she was planning to take a bath too, but she didn't. While Abby and I got cleaned up, Mae stirred up supper smells in the kitchen, aromas that reminded me it had been hours since we had eaten anything. Mae was the best sort of cook. Without planning or making out a shopping list, she could whip up something delicious with whatever was in the icebox by adding a little flour and a scoop of lard.

269

Abby and I sat at the kitchen table coloring when Momma and Daddy walked through the back door. Lucky greeted them, jumping and barking, but they both walked by without even giving him a pat on the head. Momma thanked Mae and pulled a few bills from her purse. Daddy didn't say a single word but went into the den and turned on the news. His recliner, which I never sat in because I felt sure it would dump me upside down, groaned and jerked as he pulled the side lever and collapsed backward. I pretended to color, yet kept an eye on Momma's every move, the way she rubbed her forehead and the way she shook her head, providing a sort of unspoken message to Mae. When Mae enfolded Momma into one of her vast hugs, the sort that makes everything better, Momma clung to her like she might fall down if she let go. But no words were spoken between them.

I glanced back into the den where Daddy lay motionless, probably sleeping already, his head pressed against the built-in pillow of his chair. Across his lap, his hands rested, clasped as though in prayer. I had a clear shot of the crown of his head, the thick swirl of his cowlick. On the television, the weatherman predicted scattered showers. Eventually, Mae disappeared out the back door where Old Pair of Pants was waiting in the driveway. I wondered how long he had been out there.

Momma motioned Abby and me into the living room, where nothing ever happened except Christmas. She spoke like a librarian, in a quiet, steady voice, using all her concentration not to cry. Daddy's cancer had returned. We asked a few questions but mostly we listened and didn't know what to say. According to the paleness of Momma's face and weepy look of her eyes, I thought she might be dying of cancer too.

"Now, let's try to enjoy the nice supper Mae cooked for us before it gets cold," Momma said in a flat voice as she stood to signal our meeting was over.

It was a delicious meal. Mae had made johnny cakes and fried okra and string beans with bits of bacon in it. I felt guilty for cleaning my plate while Momma only pushed her food around like I did when forced to eat mushy asparagus from a can. Daddy, still sleeping in his chair, missed the whole meal. Momma never woke him or nagged him about eating something. When Momma asked what we did all

270

afternoon, I said, "Nothing much" even though we had done lots of things.

Chapter Forty-Three

It seemed to me that when someone got sick, they should take care of themselves, doing the best, most healthy things possible to get well. Daddy did the opposite. He went through a period of blazing anger kicked off with a particularly bad drinking binge. When he vanished for an entire week, Momma called the police and reported him missing. I heard her tell Nana he had been so upset and out of his head, she worried he might do something stupid. Papa Pete kept an eye on the farm, and Bubba's daddy helped out too. Momma told Maggie it was probably Daddy's last fling. I wasn't sure what she meant until I heard her say, "The cancer is everywhere." Then she cried.

When Daddy came home, he and Momma spent a lot of time in their bedroom with the door closed. Wild arguing, words that flew mostly from Momma's mouth, turned to talking and then sobbing. I dug out a space in the bottom of our messy closet and sat with my ear to the vent trying to understand. Momma pleaded with Daddy to get treatment. Daddy said he would rather die at home than in a hospital. I wrote their entire conversation in my diary to re-read and think about later.

The air inside our house felt gloomy and diseased, worse than after our house had been robbed. Abby and I began to spend more time outside than inside, riding our bicycles and playing down at the ditch behind the cotton field. Papa Pete even brought over a load of old boards from an outbuilding he tore down so we could start on our tree house. We decided the cottonwood in the far corner was the best tree, and so far, we'd nailed the smallest pieces along the trunk to make a ladder.

***

We had a perfectly good dryer in the kitchen, but Momma was a believer in sundried sheets. "They smell better," she said when I quizzed her about it.

"Can me and Gracie stay at Nana and Papa Pete's house until school starts?" Abby asked as she handed a pillowcase to Momma. Since Abby was too short to reach the clothesline, she did the squatty jobs.

Momma stopped pinning sheets, kneeled down to Abby's level, and pushed the summer-streaked hair away from her wide eyes. "May Gracie and I," Momma corrected. "But why would you want to do that? I'd be so sad if you weren't here."

"Because I don't want to catch cancer and die," Abby said.

And just like that, Momma abandoned the basket of damp laundry and called a special family meeting at the picnic table. "Cancer isn't like the flu. You can't catch it. It didn't happen because someone sneezed on him, or because he forgot to wash his hands," she explained.

"Then how did he get it?" I asked.

"The cells in Daddy's body aren't growing right," she said, which really didn't explain it.

"Isn't there some sort of treatment he could get, maybe at that hospital in Memphis?" I asked trying to find answers without letting Momma know about my eavesdropping.

"He's taking medicine. And, yes, there are treatments in Memphis, but nothing is foolproof. And the treatments might make him sicker," Momma said.

"He probably wouldn't go anyway," I said, knowing that to be true.

When we returned to the clothesline, Momma made a little speech about how we needed to band together and be supportive for Daddy's sake. "Just act normal," she said, but for our family, I had no idea what that meant. Momma reminded us to pray for him every night. I told her I would, yet I worried my prayers wouldn't be very honest. Although I tried to forget how Daddy burned my arm, once something was done, it was hard to un-remember it. If God could do all those things the Bible said, he would recognize the difference between a true prayer and one prayed because Momma told me to.

"When we get finished with chores, can we go to the library?" I asked. In the back of my diary, I had begun making a list of words to look up in the encyclopedia. Words like cancer and treatment and carbuncle and other words I couldn't remember while hanging laundry out to dry.

"Not today. I have too much to do. Maybe later in the week," she said.

I said okay and tried not to sulk even though it wouldn't take any time for Momma to drive us to Savage Crossing. As I glanced toward town where I knew the library hid among the trees, my eyes stopped at the gray house just across the field. The gray house was my answer.

***

Daddy had been asleep for hours, and Abby fell asleep instantly, but Momma piddled around in the kitchen forever. Once she went into her bedroom and the sliver of orange light beneath the door went dark, I waited a few more minutes until there were no sounds in the house. I pulled on my shorts, grabbed my diary, and tiptoed out the back door. Lucky followed me without making a sound.

A fat moon hung above the tree in the back yard of the gray house and lit the back porch. The kitchen door creaked as I pushed it open and pressed it shut it behind me. I pointed my flashlight low to the dusty floor and followed its cone-shaped light into the front room, the one with the fireplace and shelves filled with books.

My own private library.

The room smelled like mildew and mushrooms, a dank, dark cave. When I closed the heavy drapes, air that had been trapped for months swirled around the windows. I clicked on the brass lamp in the center of the desk, and a shaft of light brightened the space and illuminated the high ceiling above my head. A man with a personal library wouldn't mind if I used his books for research. I felt sure of it. As I settled back into the soft, leather chair, I opened my diary to the list of words and selected an ink pen from a wooden cup because I forgot to bring my own.

274

Carbuncle. I'd look that word up first.

I pulled the encyclopedia labeled "C-Ch" from the shelf. Since I expected it to be a made-up Arkansas thing, I was surprised to find Carbuncle printed right between Carborundum and Carburetor. *A severe infection of the skin and tissues just under the skin. It is hard and painful and shiny dark red in color. It looks like a group of boils.* Gross! I didn't need to know anything more about that and was glad Aunt Clara had gotten rid of hers. Instead of writing the definition beside the word in my diary, I just wrote disgusting skin problem and left it at that.

Next, in the same volume, I looked up Cancer. Unlike Carbuncle which took up only one paragraph, Cancer took up two entire pages. I wrote down the sentences I considered most important. *Cancer is one of man's most dreaded diseases. It attacks persons of all ages, spreading by disorderly growth of cells. No one knows what causes cancer. A person's work or the place where he lives may contribute to the disease. Working conditions can cause cancer. Cigarette smoking is the principal cause of lung cancer. Cancer is often the silent killer.*

Eventually, I stopped writing and read the entire section from beginning to end. According to whoever wrote the encyclopedia, cancer could be treated by surgery, radiation, and chemotherapy. Those must have been the treatments Daddy refused to get.

Sitting in the gray house with an entire set of encyclopedias at my disposal, I lost track of time. Lucky curled underneath the desk and slept. Eventually I felt tired and my dry throat needed a drink of water. I looked twice at my Cinderella watch and even held it to my ear to make sure it was ticking right. Four o'clock? I couldn't believe how much time has passed. Quickly-quickly-quickly, I slid the books back onto the shelf, turned off the desk lamp, and opened the drapes. Lucky and I went out the same way we came in.

The sky was still dark. Morning had not yet come, even though night had slipped away. The air felt moist on my face as I gripped my diary and ran home. I barely tumbled into bed before I smelled coffee brewing in the kitchen. I slept half of the next day. Momma worried that I had "mono." I didn't know what mono was but wrote the word in my diary to look up next time I visited the gray house.

Chapter Forty-Four

Even sick with cancer, Daddy continued to wake before sunrise. He tried to keep the same work schedule, yet most everything had changed. After riding the farm until lunch, he slept during the afternoons, sometimes not waking until morning. Seeing Daddy lay wrapped in a quilt on the couch or under a mound of bedcovers before dark was as odd a thing as seeing Momma plowing the fields, not that she'd ever done such a thing. Nana said every storm cloud had a silver lining, and the fact that Daddy had almost completely stopped drinking was one of those silver linings. Eight bottles of beer had gone untouched for weeks.

Along with Daddy's change in drinking, Momma began cleaning like a crazy woman. Although she always kept our house tidy—and saw to it that Abby and I helped—her new cleaning obsession was bizarre, the air so heavy with kitchen cleaner my eyes burned. Everything except Momma's coffeepot had been removed from the kitchen countertops, the surface so spotless I could see my reflection. Even the wicker bowl containing apples and oranges and sometimes chocolate candy had been put away. Finally, after months of sitting in Momma's bedroom closet, the bean rooster picture had reclaimed its rightful spot on the kitchen wall covering Daddy's fist mark.

One particularly hot afternoon when the air stuck to our skin and even the most lightweight of clothes felt scratchy, Maggie came to visit. She wore her wiry, red hair knotted on the tip of her head like a ball, and her minty eye shadow had melted into a crease on her lids. "Anne, I brought you a book," she said, pulling a library book from her shoulder bag and placing it on the kitchen table. "It's not due back until next week. I thought you might want to read it. There's a wait list." Momma nodded as she plugged a box fan into the corner of the room. I grabbed the book—it was called *Jonathan Livingston Seagull*—and turned to the first page. I only read the first few sentences when Momma told me to go clean my room. The book was about a bird. Momma never read animal books so I didn't think she'd like it.

I pretended to wander off toward my bedroom, but really, I sat around the corner outside their field of vision. As they sipped iced tea with lemon because it was much too hot for coffee, Maggie remarked on the extra clean status of our kitchen. The ice made a tinkling sound against the glasses, and at first Momma didn't say anything. Then she said, "If I don't get out of this house, I'm gonna pull out my hair."

"Why don't we go to town for pie? That'll make you feel better." Maggie spoke in a low voice, more pathetic than sympathetic, and I imagined her patting Momma on the arm.

"No, I'm thinking of something more in the lines of a vacation," Momma said sounding a bit more upbeat. "Maybe to the lake." I went straight to find Abby to tell her what I had overheard.

Later at supper, Momma set the table extra nice with bright, flowery placemats and used all three utensils even though there was no reason for us to have knives or spoons. With Maggie hanging around all afternoon, I didn't know when she had found time to make such a big supper, but she had made fried chicken legs and homemade macaroni and cheese—not from a box. When she told Daddy she had made Boston cream pie for dessert, his eyes brightened for the first time in a long while. I stared at the rooster picture and wondered if it was happy to be back in the kitchen with us.

After Daddy started eating and bragged it was the best thing he'd tasted in weeks, Momma announced we were going on vacation. She said it like Daddy had no say in the matter. "A fam-i-leee vacation," she said drawing out the syllables long and slow. "The Fourth of July is just around the corner, and everything's planned. We can use the lake cabin. I've already checked with Nana and Papa."

Abby cheered and shot out of her chair like a rocket. I spewed questions asking when we would leave and how long we would stay. Last summer, we hadn't spent any time at Nana and Papa's lake cabin, so this was the best sort of news. Momma told us to calm down and finish eating supper.

"I'm not going to the lake," Daddy said as he swallowed macaroni and cheese like it hurt his throat. "Not only am I sick, there's too much to do on the farm."

Momma touched his arm and left her hand there right above his watch. "This is exactly what you need. We all need it. I have everything arranged, and you're going with us."

Daddy murmured about how it was too hot, but eventually he nodded. "I'm too tired to argue," he said. Abby and I began packing that very night even though our trip was three days away.

***

One of the best things about going on vacation was the "getting there" part of the trip, the anticipation of the fun to come, the stops and sights along the way. Daddy tried to ruin it. Before we headed out, he argued with Momma about every little thing from how he couldn't afford to be gone from the farm for even a few days to how she'd packed the car trunk wrong. Momma didn't fall for it. She kept a smile on her face and said, "Yes, Lee," and "You're right, Lee." I stared inside the trunk of our car that was crammed with life vests and suitcases and bath towels and grocery sacks filled with potato chips. Instead of complaining, he should have been more grateful to Momma for packing the car at all. That was a job normally reserved for him.

The drive took four to five hours, depending on traffic, bathroom breaks, and how long we had to wait for the ferry. Abby and I sat in the back seat, coloring, with a big box of crayons between us. To avoid becoming carsick, I took frequent breaks. Looking out the window, I studied the trees and signs along the way to calculate how much longer the drive would be.

At the halfway spot, we passed through Glory City, a bend-in-the-road sort of place that was no city at all. Since Momma didn't seem to be in a huge hurry, she pulled off the highway at the Dream Kastle and said we could get something to drink to go with the ham sandwiches she had packed for lunch. Daddy grumbled about stopping, but we ignored him and didn't let him spoil our good moods. While we waited in line to order, Daddy leaned against the car. Momma yelled over and asked if he wanted anything, but he only shook his head, puffed on his cigarette, and stared off down the highway. Dust floated from the gravel parking lot. The sun warmed my bare shoulders. I wished we were already at the lake, but I also knew that once we got there, the trip would be over in a snap, so I tried to enjoy every second of not being at home.

The couple in front of us couldn't make up their minds and asked questions about common sense things like if cheese came on their cheeseburgers. They were wrapped together like the Siamese twins I had read about in the encyclopedia, his arm around her shoulder and her whole body leaning into him, both moving as one. I tried to make out the words tattooed onto the guy's arm but couldn't get a clear shot and decided it probably wasn't worth seeing anyway.

Finally, the couple paid, walked arm-in-arm to a picnic table, and it was our turn. The smell of grease escaped from the partially opened window and inside the small box of a building, a man flipped burgers and pulled a basket of fries from sizzling oil. The woman behind the dusty glass wore a Cardinals baseball cap. She smiled and called me honey when she asked me what I wanted to order. I got a butterscotch malt, and Abby ordered chocolate, which was no big surprise. Momma stared hard at all the ice cream options on the menu but ordered a diet soda. She said she didn't need to gain weight before putting on her bathing suit.

Off to the side, a picnic area with tables and umbrellas offered circles of shade. Abby and I ran to claim a table, even though there were no other customers besides lovey-dovey couple. We thought it would be fun to eat our ham sandwiches and enjoy our drinks like regular picnickers, but Momma said we should hurry and get back on the road. "Daddy's ready to go," she said.

In the short time it took for us to get our order, the inside of our car had turned into an oven. The crayon I'd left on top of my coloring book had begun to soften, and the air smelled of fresh wax. Momma turned the air conditioner on full-blast because, at first, she could only grip the steering wheel with two fingers. "Gonna be a hot week at the lake," she said. Daddy nodded and stubbed out his cigarette butt in the ashtray.

Because my malt was too thick to slurp through a straw, the lady behind the glass had given me a long-handled plastic spoon. I drank in tiny swallows to make it last longer and not freeze my brain. Like most good things, it still disappeared quickly.

***

After a black, bottomless sleep, I woke to a dove cooing outside our bedroom window. It took me a few seconds to remember I was at the lake and not in my regular bed on the farm. I pushed aside the curtain and stared at the jumble of trees. A busy squirrel jumped from one branch to another, rustling the leaves. Pink sunlight filtered through the window. Through the thin, paneled walls, I heard Momma's breakfast sounds—the sizzle of bacon, the rattling of pots and pans. Momma believed a hearty breakfast before a day on the water was essential. With the lake calling, breakfast was a waste of time.

My P.O.W. bracelet had begun to leave a dirty, green circle around my wrist, but I'd not taken it off since Daddy gave it to me on Christmas Eve. Yesterday, Abby had asked if I planned to swim in my bracelet. What choice did we have, I told her. It was our duty. Even though President Nixon said the United States was finished with the Vietnam War, lots of soldiers were still missing.

I poked my sister.

"What?" Abby rolled over and yawned, then rubbed her eyes open. The expression on her sleepy face changed as she too realized we were at the lake.

"Let's go exploring before breakfast." She nodded and brushed the hair from her face. We pulled on our tennis shoes and disappeared out the back door into a fresh, cool morning.

It was too early for talking, so we walked without saying much to each other. The forest sounds seemed different at such an early hour, as though even the trees were yawning and stretching awake. I found a handful of shiny rocks and weighted down my pockets with them. Somehow, I knew the rocks would lose their gleam once taken home to the farm, but I took them anyway.

From the very beginning, I could tell this vacation would be different than our normal lake trip. Yesterday, as soon as we had unloaded the car and unpacked the groceries, Abby and I had changed into our bathing suits, eager to race down to the dock and jump in the water. Momma and Daddy's plans were different. They wanted to sit on the front porch and stare at the lake in the distance, which was a crazy thing to me. "In a few minutes," Momma kept saying. A few minutes had turned into what remained of the afternoon, and since Abby and I weren't allowed to swim without an adult, we were stuck. We stretched out side-by-side in the woven hammock and just lay, staring at the treed canopy. Her arm felt warm and alive beside me, and I was thankful to have a sister, someone who made me feel not so alone. The branches above us became darker and thicker in the growing purple shadows. The smell of charcoal had drifted our way as Momma started a fire in the barbecue pit.

As Abby and I continued our morning walk, the mountainside grew steeper, the further we traveled from the cabin. "We should probably start back," I said.

"Gracie, do you think Daddy's gonna die?" Abby asked as we both turned to retrace our steps through the woods.

"Yes." This time I didn't try to avoid the question. There was no other answer. I wondered what life would be like when he was gone. The thought made me feel hollow and a bit numb, but not really sad.

Abby nodded but said nothing more.

Even though it seemed we had walked a great distance, when Momma yelled, "Abby-Grace," we heard the clear echo of her voice and made our way back to the house for breakfast before she called us a second time.

Finally, after eating, washing the breakfast dishes, and putting everything away spic and span, we hiked down to the lake. Tiny violet flowers and black-eyed Susans grew wild along the gravel road leading to the water's edge. The sun blazed overhead and glared off the water. While Abby and I swam and practiced our dives from the dock, Momma floated on a pink plastic raft. Daddy napped in a lounge chair in the shade with a book spread open on his lap. It was the same Eudora Welty book he always kept by his bedside table.

When the sun moved straight overhead, Momma smoothed a beach towel on the picnic table and unpacked the lunch she brought in the cooler—turkey and cheese sandwiches, two kinds of potato chips,

French onion dip, and a plastic container filled with sliced watermelon. Daddy wasn't hungry. He drank a few sips of beer and poured the rest between the cracks of the dock.

The remainder of our lake trip passed much too quickly. Abby and I spent most of our time exploring the woods and shoreline while Momma and Daddy sat on the porch together. In the afternoons when Daddy napped, Momma walked down to the dock with us so we could swim. We went on short boat rides around the cove but not to the island or cliffs. She never wanted to be too far from the cabin.

On the day we returned home, Abby and I stood against the railing of the ferry, watching the shore come into view, but Momma and Daddy stayed inside the car. The sun felt hot on my sunburned nose, and heat rose from the wooden platform beneath my feet. Hiking and lakeside exploring had turned my white tennis shoes a dingy color, and my laces were filled with sticky hitchhiker seeds I couldn't pick out. I stared at the churning water. Although it looked the same, shimmery blue, nothing else about our trip had felt the same. It had likely been Daddy's last trip to the lake. I wondered whether or not he was sad about it. He had never much liked the lake, but sometimes the thought of losing something made it more important.

Chapter Forty-Five

A breeze swept across the backyard, making the afternoon feel more like early April than mid-July. I pulled a lounge chair over to the shade of the plum tree and pretended to read my Nancy Drew library book. Abby had been so engrossed in a television show that she didn't follow me outside. That suited me fine, because my real plan was to eavesdrop on Momma and Maggie who sat on the back patio, drinking iced tea with sprigs of mint from the flowerbed.

"Doesn't the sun feel nice?" Maggie said as she dropped her head back and presented her pale face to the sky. "Too bad we don't have more July days like this."

Momma nodded, copied Maggie's body movements, and they both sat relaxed with their chins pointed upward for at least five Mississippis. It was the quietest I'd ever known Maggie to be.

"So tell me all about your lake trip," Maggie finally said as she continued to lean back in her chair with her eyes closed. "Unless it's too hard to talk about," she added, looking up at Momma. Her thin palm shielded her eyes from the sun's glare.

"Oh, no, it was as good as could be expected, I guess," Momma said. She straightened back up in her chair and took a sip of tea. Maggie sat upright again too. My eyes focused on page twenty-four of my book, but my ears were tuned to their conversation.

"Basically, Lee slept a lot, and when he wasn't sleeping, he felt terrible. It's shocking to see him go from tough and strong to that weak. And it all happened so fast." Momma's voice trailed off as she looked toward the cotton field growing green and thick and blowing in the breeze. Maggie didn't say anything. "The girls were disappointed we missed the fireworks show at the marina, but he just wasn't up to it. Nights are the worst," she added.

Momma was right. Instead of driving over to the marina to see the huge fireworks, Abby and I lit sparklers from the front porch of the cabin. Sparklers were lame compared to what we had missed. Plus, since Daddy had already fallen asleep, we could have gone without him. Daddy didn't like fireworks, anyway.

Momma and Maggie continued yakking about stuff I already knew, but somehow it was more fascinating coming from their lipsticked mouths. When a gust of wind scattered their napkins and knocked over the can of bug spray from the picnic table, I expected them to go inside. But they didn't. They continued talking and I continued listening.

"Doctor Fairley said chemo would give him anywhere from a few more months to a year, but he won't agree. He says he'd rather die tomorrow at home than six months from now in the hospital." Momma rubbed her arms as though she had a chill.

"What are you going to do?" Maggie reached out and touched Momma on the arm.

"Take it day by day," Momma said with a weak smile. "That's all we can do."

That's what we'd been doing forever, I thought.

"And now Lee's mother knows. Bless her heart, she's beside herself," Momma added.

Although Daddy never told Mamaw Pearl about his cancer, she eventually found out about it from someone at the grocery store. As soon as we returned from the lake, she pulled into the driveway and parked right behind our bumper so close Momma could barely open the trunk. When Abby announced, "Mamaw Pearl's here," Daddy's face turned three shades of sick, and he exhaled what little energy he had left through his lungs.

From the moment her wide foot stepped onto the gravel, she wept and moaned as though Daddy had already died. Her swollen eyes and streaked face had the appearance of someone who'd been crying for hours or days even. Mamaw Pearl and Daddy disappeared into the kitchen while Abby and I helped Momma hang still damp towels on the clothesline. Momma didn't say much other than, "It was bound to happen sooner or later." I didn't blame Mamaw for being so upset. Not telling her was a rotten thing to do.

When Momma and Maggie began talking about the new issue of *Good Housekeeping* and a dessert recipe made with pineapple, I decided to go for a bike ride. The afternoon was perfect for it, and I wanted to check on the gray house. Instead of riding on the highway, I rode along the edge of the turnrow. The dirt had been baked smooth and concrete hard by the summer heat. Lucky, darting in and out of the field, chased birds and butterflies. The shallow ditch made only a small bump in my ride, as there was no water standing in the bottom. Waist-high cotton rustled in the wind, giving the afternoon a green, fresh smell.

I propped my bicycle underneath the massive backyard tree and sat leaning against the trunk, feeling its firmness, its strength. Lucky lay beside me with his head on my leg. He looked up at me with black, round eyes, and the angle of his face gave him a sad expression even though he had no reason to feel sad.

Chapter Forty-Six

Momma began talking about Daddy in terms of good days and bad days. "Oh, today was a good day," she would tell Nana when Nana called to check each morning. By mid-August, there were more bad days than good. Dr. Fairley ordered a hospital bed so Daddy would be more comfortable at home. Momma acted brave and tried to smile, but she was sad inside where the truth was. I could tell. "I hate the idea of a hospital bed," I heard Momma say to Maggie. "I need him to sleep in our bed." Then she cried into the phone and hung up when she couldn't talk anymore.

On the day the bed was to arrive, Abby and I helped Momma move Daddy's desk into the corner. The desk was bulky and hard to budge even an inch. Finally, we shoved it across the room, leaving behind two deep scars on the hardwood floor. Momma shrugged her shoulders and didn't seem to care. When the delivery truck turned into our driveway, I watched the men unload Daddy's new bed. It looked serious with rails on the side, like a baby bed. Momma asked them to set the bed up so he could see the cotton field from the big window. When they finished, she lay on the bed, looked out the window, and asked them to move it a foot to the right.

Mamaw Pearl started sitting with Daddy almost every morning. Momma encouraged her to be positive and upbeat, but her one-sided conversations always turned to Jesus and the Bible. That only made Daddy overly aggravated, and he would yell at her until he ran out of energy and collapsed on his feather pillow. Although his face still looked tan and healthy, it was so strange to see a white sheet pulled to Daddy's chin.

Mae came three afternoons a week to give Momma a break. Simply having her around made things a little better. She did laundry and helped change Daddy's sheets. On the really bad days, she helped Daddy walk to the bathroom. I usually went outside when that happened.

I began counting down the days to my birthday, the days until school started in the fall, the days until anything new would happen. Only there didn't seem to be anything good on the horizon.

Days.

Hours.

Minutes.

Seconds.

Time meant nothing. Each day dragged along, with Abby and me trying to stay out of the way. Daddy's moans filled the darkness each night.

One particularly hot Wednesday night, Abby and I went to bed talking about church camp and the things we did there last year. This year, Momma said we needed to stick closer to home. I wasn't disappointed about missing all that preaching and singing, but Abby wanted to go, especially since Dian was going back.

"Do you think Devil's Bathtub is still there?" she asked me in a drowsy voice.

"Of course, it's still there. It's been there forever, probably even as far back as the dinosaurs," I said. "Do you really think it could dry up and disappear in one year?"

Abby didn't answer me. Maybe she had fallen asleep. Or maybe she simply didn't want to talk anymore.

***

Thursday morning, we awoke to different scenery. Overnight, a carnival set up rides and food booths on an empty field across from the Cottonwood Corner auction house. The idea that such magic could appear with no warning, and while we slept, made me feel excited and hopeful, yet I knew the carnival would disappear as quickly as it had come. Abby and I needed to act quickly if we were to enjoy this turn of events.

287

"Can we please go today?" I whined to Momma while she ironed sheets she had pulled off the line. Now that Daddy didn't drive around all day on the farm getting his clothes dirty, her stack of ironing was much less.

"We'll see."

That meant no.

I plopped down on her bed and watched as Momma poured water into the iron. A cloud of steam billowed from the hole in the top. Behind her, the closet door stood open. Daddy's work shirts hung evenly spaced on hangers.

"Momma, has Daddy been saved?" I asked.

"He was baptized when he was a boy," she said. I watched as the iron glided across the thin cotton sheet, erasing the wrinkles. She draped the smooth section off the edge of the ironing board and repeated the process with another wrinkled section. I wondered if cotton from one of Daddy's fields was woven inside that sheet.

"At Mamaw Pearl's church?"

She nodded.

That made me feel better for him. I stared out the window into the vast sky. Were there really pearly gates up there? The whole idea seemed about as far-fetched as Jack's beanstalk. I twisted my P.O.W. bracelet and rubbed the green stain from my wrist.

"Momma, is Jesus real?" I asked. Lately, I felt suspicious of ideas that fell into gray areas, especially people I couldn't see and places that seemed more make believe than concrete.

"Goodness, Gracie, you sure have a lot of questions this morning." She stopped moving the iron and almost scorched the sheet. When she yanked it away, steam shot across the ironing board. "Just because you can't see him, doesn't mean he isn't real. He knows your heart and what you're thinking."

"Like Santa Claus?" I asked. Santa Claus seemed like a fairy tale too. Candi said Abby and I were smart to go along with the whole Santa story just to keep getting presents, but she said he was something parents made up to keep us acting good during Christmas.

"Well..." Momma paused and moved her eyes to the center of the bedroom ceiling as though she looked for an answer in the light fixture. "Sort of. No, not really. Well, he's more important. Jesus is much more important than Santa Claus." Momma stuttered a bit. Maybe she didn't know all the answers.

***

After lunch while Daddy napped, we went to town for milk and bread. "Go really slow through Cottonwood Corner," I said as we approached the carnival. She drove a little slower, but not much. People filled the place, and lines of folks waited their turns on spinning rides. Yellow globe lights outlined the midway.

"Can we stop and get hot dogs?" I asked as I cracked my window. The air smelled of spun sugar and freshly mowed grass. I wanted to be out there more than anything.

"No, that's ridiculous. You just ate lunch." Momma said. I watched the carnival pass by, so close, yet completely out of reach.

After supper, Abby and I played outside, swinging higher and higher until our swings bumped at the top and threatened to toss us into the air. The chains bit into my hands as I held tighter, tighter, and pumped my legs harder, harder. While dusk settled over the backyard, we continued to swing, facing the Ferris wheel lights that glowed red and yellow across the cotton field and blurred orange when I smashed my eyelids together. And there was music. Odd music that seemed to grow louder as the night grew darker. Music that sounded scary yet fun at the same time.

Later that night, I crawled into bed and fell asleep to the imagined taste of cotton candy on my tongue. I dreamed of games of skill and stuffed teddy bear prizes. In the night, thunder woke me. I lay in my bed until sunrise, listening to the sounds of the storm rolling across the farm, rocking the house like a train.

By Friday morning, the thunderstorm had moved over the Mississippi River, leaving a clean, new sky behind. The overnight winds had cracked two limbs on the cherry trees that were loaded with plump fruit. As Abby and I picked all the wet cherries and piled them into a bowl, I worried about the trees and whether we would ever have cherries again. In the distance, jutting from the field like a mirage, the carnival sat still and quiet. It was too early for rides and music and eating hot dogs, but soon the area would come alive again.

"Abby, I have an idea." She looked up at me with cherry-stained lips.

"Yeah?"

"Tonight, if it doesn't rain, we should sneak out and go to the carnival." Her eyes got big and bright, and she nodded her head up and down and up and down. "I bet we have enough money to ride a few rides and maybe get something to eat."

"Okay," she whispered even though no one was outside with us.

"Don't say a word. Swear?"

She stuck out her pinkie, and we both swore.

It was the longest day. Abby and I spent most of it planning and plotting. Even though we were already pretty good at walking down the hall without making a sound, we practiced. We counted out our meager savings and decided how much we could spare. In the end, we stuffed all of it into our pockets. "We can always bring home what we don't need," I said.

Finally, Momma finished cleaning the kitchen and went to bed to read. In no time, we heard the click her lamp made when she turned it off. Daddy had been sleeping for hours—his medicine saw to that. Our biggest complication was Lucky. He would want to go with us, and if we left him at home, he might whine at the door and give us away. So we took him along to his first carnival.

The glow of lights grew brighter with each step along the highway. Cars filled the lot, parked at every angle and along the side of the road. Music drifted through the warm air, and the loose change jingled through my pocket against my leg. I kept a tight hold on Lucky's leash, which he didn't much appreciate, and he pulled me quickly toward the carnival as though he knew where we were going. After walking beneath the arched entranceway, I stood flat-footed and took in the fantastic world so close to our house. What to do first?

"Let's get something to eat," Abby said pointing to a trailer painted with wide red and white stripes. A sign overhead advertised popcorn, cotton candy, fried dough, and something called elephant ears that I hoped weren't real elephant ears. We decided to pool our money and buy a paper cone of pink cotton candy to share.

Tickets for the merry-go-round cost ten cents, but the greasy man in charge wouldn't let Lucky ride even if we paid extra for him. "He's a good dog and he won't cause any problems," I assured him, but still he said no in a gruff voice.

At first, Abby didn't want to ride by herself, but since it was the only way, she eventually handed over a dime and pointed to a pretty blue horse. I winced when the man's germy hands hoisted her up and onto the horse's saddle. Lucky and I stood to the side, watching. Each time she passed us, she waved like she didn't expect to see us again.

After we each rode two rides, we walked around the grounds looking at the games lining the midway. The people working the booths tried to lure us over with promises of prizes, but we didn't play. "We can't afford to win," I told Abby. "Momma would be suspicious for sure."

I bought an admission ticket for the sideshow, mainly because I really, really, really wanted to see the Sword Swallower. According to the picture outside, he could stretch his neck long and skinny and swallow a sharp sword without dying. Twenty cents was a small price to pay to see such a thing. Abby had no interest, so she agreed to wait by the garbage can with Lucky.

As I handed my money to the man out front, he gave me a strange smile, and I walked inside the tent, feeling nervous like maybe I was entering a place of no return. The sideshow people each had a roped off section and a place to sit if they got tired. Those of us with tickets walked slowly along a straw-lined pathway and watched their unusual tricks. Although I expected the Sword Swallower to perform some sort of illusion, he threw his head back and really did stick a long sword down his mouth. I gasped when he did it, but he pulled it straight back up with no blood or anything. I clapped because it was a pretty neat thing he had learned to do.

The Fattest Man Alive sat on a shabby-looking brown couch and didn't seem to be wearing any clothes other than a much too small T-shirt that said "Keep on Truckin." His massive fat rolls covered his private parts, and I was glad about that. Next to the fat man, the Mermaid Girl looked like a regular person who had something wrong with her feet. The Lobster Boy had pincher-like hands or maybe he was missing a few fingers. Neither one of them—the mermaid or the lobster—had any sort of talent, so I just stared at them. The Tattooed Woman was an old, shriveled up lady who looked to be wearing some sort of body stocking. Overall, I got about a nickel's worth of entertainment.

As I left the tent, I pulled the coins from my pocket to count what remained. I had enough to ride one more ride and possibly get another snack. Maybe we'd ride the one by the midway next. It had looked fun. But…

I glanced left and right and quickly scanned the crowd. Abby and Lucky weren't standing by the garbage can where I had left them. Panic surged through my arms and legs, and in that split second I was sure Abby had been kidnapped and murdered and her body was now floating in the Mississippi River toward New Orleans.

Pink shirt. Pink shirt. Pink shirt.

I looked for Abby's hot pink T-shirt in the mass of carnival colors.

When I heard Abby call my name, I exhaled for the first time since stepping from the strange tent. As she waved a limp wave, I realized Abby was standing next to Mae and her Old Pair of Pants. No one was smiling.

We were in huge trouble. The worst sort of trouble. Mae was fit to be tied as she marched both of us over to her car in the dimly lit parking lot. She paced back and forth while Mr. Pants watched like he didn't want to be there.

"Now, I don't know what sort of craziness has taken hold of your brains, but I know you girls has better sense than to sneak out in the dark without your momma's permission. And her with all those worries about Mr. Lee. What was you thinking, Gracie Lee Eudora? Are you even listening to me?"

"Yes, ma'am." I couldn't stand to see the disappointment in her eyes so I stared at my tennis shoes and wished I could turn back the clock.

She pointed her long, fuchsia fingernail so close to my nose I could tell she had eaten popcorn recently. "Grace, you should be taking care of your little sister and not leaving her all alone while you pay good money to look at wicked people behind a circus tent. Lawsy, lawsy, lawsy…" I thought she might start drawing a crowd to preach. A couple walked by and stopped to listen for a minute before getting in their truck to pull away.

"Mae, are you gonna tell on us?" I whispered.

"Now, I know you just didn't ask me that." She spit the words between her teeth. I twisted my bracelet. "Get on in the car." Mae shoved us into the back seat where Abby and I sat huddled in the dark beside Lucky. I had no thoughts in my mind other than the trouble waiting for us. Especially me. As Mae drove us the few yards home, she kept saying things like, "As I live and breathe."

"As. I. Live. And. Breathe."

Because our driveway was nearly impossible to see without the carport light on, Mae almost stopped in the middle of the road before turning in. Fortunately for us, her car made no sound on the gravel. A dark house meant Momma was still sleeping. "No sense upsetting your Momma tonight. I'll talk to her tomorrow. You girls know better. As I live and breathe." She shook her head one final time, and I never felt so bad about anything.

Chapter Forty-Seven

Instead of waiting for Mae to show up and tell Momma about finding us at the carnival, Abby and I made a full confession at the breakfast table. I spent most of the night thinking about the madness of the carnival—the strange people who worked there, the flashing lights, and loud music. When I finally fell asleep, the man with the dirty hands visited me in my dreams. He chased me through the cotton field as my feet sunk deeper and deeper in mud, and I could hear Abby calling my name but couldn't see her. I woke before he caught me. I stared at our bedroom window until daybreak, wondering where the carnival people slept each night.

When I first began explaining what we had done, Momma's cheeks flared as though she'd painted beet juice on her face. She sat frozen in her chair, didn't say a single word and pursed her lips hard. Abby didn't say anything either. Since the whole thing had been my idea, I had agreed to do all the talking.

"We really are sorry for sneaking away to the carnival. It wasn't even that great because we couldn't ride any of the rides together, and I wasted almost a whole quarter to look at people who only got to be in the sideshow because they were born with deformed feet and stuff."

Momma drummed her fingernails on the table and slowly shook her head from side to side. I told her about the cotton candy and how Lucky didn't like his leash and how the man with filthy fingernails helped Abby onto the merry-go-round.

That's when she started yelling. "You could have both been kidnapped. Or murdered! Did you ever think of that?"

"Actually, I did. When I couldn't find Abby."

"It might surprise you to know there are bad people in this world. Crazy, insane, horrible people who do nasty things for no reason. You can't go sneaking around in the dark. You'll end up floating in the Mississippi River!"

I had already thought of that too, but I didn't admit it. Abby covered her ears with her hands.

"We won't ever do it again," I said. And I meant it.

"Are you gonna tell Daddy?" Abby asked as she dropped her hands to her lap.

Momma shook her head and began to tear up. "If something happened to you girls, I don't know what I would have done. We have to stick together. You know that, right?" She stared at me, and her eyes looked as flat as the buttons sewed onto my old Raggedy Ann doll. Momma hugged both of us tight. Soon we were all crying and nodding and making promises to always be together forever, even though I knew that wasn't very likely.

At first, it seemed that we wouldn't be punished, that maybe Momma was so thankful we hadn't been murdered that she would let us "think about our mistake."

I was wrong.

As we ate our now soggy cereal, Momma laid out a whole bunch of punishments. We were grounded until school started. There would be no television for two weeks. We both had to go to our room and write *I will not go anywhere without permission*—five hundred times for me and two hundred times for Abby since she was younger and a slow writer.

We went to our room and began writing lines immediately. I had written to the bottom of one page when I heard talking in the kitchen. It was Mrs. Barns. She had a low, distinctive voice that always sounded serious even when she wasn't upset. Bubba was with her too. I heard Momma say, "Gracie can't play with you, Bubba. The girls are grounded."

Abby shrugged her shoulder at me and asked, "How many lines have you written?"

"Barely any," I said.

With Daddy stuck in bed, our house had become a popular place. Not only did Mae come each afternoon, but Bubba's momma took on the role of Daddy's regular nurse. Since Daddy refused to go to the hospital, she visited several mornings a week. She had offered to do it one morning after dropping off important farm papers for Momma to read. "It'll be nice to have a real patient again after all these years of being the school nurse," she said. "Well, I shouldn't say nice because I hate that Lee's so sick. Oh, you know what I mean." And they laughed, but it wasn't a happy laugh.

Just outside our bedroom window, Lucky barked. He seemed extra excited, like maybe there was a squirrel in the tree. I hoisted myself onto the headboard and looked out the window. Bubba tossed Lucky's red rubber ball into the air. When he threw it toward the cotton field, Lucky sprinted after it, caught it in his mouth, and fetched it back to him. Bubba patted him on the head and said something I couldn't hear from my jail cell. Lucky offered a tail wag normally reserved for Abby and me.

"That's not fair," I said jumping from the headboard onto my mattress. The bed slat beneath me cracked a bit more. I couldn't believe I traded a fun afternoon playing with Bubba and Lucky for the stupid carnival.

By the time Momma called us to lunch, I was reading a book. I had written over one hundred lines but had put my notebook away, deciding I had the rest of the summer to write lines.

"Bubba had fun playing with Lucky today," Momma said as she smiled extra big and scooped tuna fish onto our plates. Since she knew tuna was not our favorite of the lunch choices, I knew she was still punishing us a little.

"That's nice," I said.

About that time, Daddy staggered into the kitchen and leaned against the counter. "Lee, you shouldn't be up!" Momma grabbed his arm and helped him to a kitchen chair. It had been several days since I'd seen Daddy out of bed. He looked skinny and hollow-eyed, and he needed a shave.

"I've been calling for you for thirty minutes," he mumbled. "I need something to drink." Momma helped him back to bed, while I poured him a glass of ice water. He had become so weak that I had to help him hold the glass in his hand. He drank only a few sips, and I placed the glass on the file cabinet next to his bed in case he wanted it later.

From the window of the den, I watched as Mae pulled into the driveway. I was relieved we'd already confessed everything to Momma. Otherwise, our bad day would just be starting.

Mae was glad to learn of our confession too. "I don't want to be no tattletale any more than you do," she said as she plopped her heavy bag in the corner of the kitchen and slipped off her shoes. "I tell you, I thought I might blow my top, seeing these girls out there amongst all that craziness." She handed Momma the newspaper. "I brought your paper in. It was out in the driveway."

I shoved aside my bland tuna and filled up on plain crackers instead. I wondered how long Abby and I would have to hear about last night.

"Well, thank God you were there to bring them home, Mae. I can't imagine what they were thinking." She took a sip of tea and opened the newspaper.

"They weren't thinking. That's the thing. The devil took hold of their brains," Mae said. They both talked like we weren't in the room.

"Girls, this is what we're talking about, right here!" Momma waved the newspaper above her head then poked her finger right into the face of that crazed lunatic Charles Manson. "See, Grace? Insane monsters like this are everywhere, killing innocent people for no reason." Momma read the article while Mae rushed around gathering dirty dishes to wash. "Oh my goodness, today marks the fourth anniversary of the day he killed all those poor people in California. I can't believe it's been four years already," Momma said. I couldn't believe our bad timing.

Chapter Forty-Eight

On Monday while Mae cleaned the bathroom and watched after Daddy, Abby and I went to the grocery store with Momma. "I need to get out of this house," Momma said. There were no cars parked out front and no people shopping. The whole store seemed closed, but it wasn't. A lady stood at the checkout counter doing nothing but waiting for someone to buy something. She nodded when we walked in.

Momma let me push the shopping cart. When Abby jumped on the end and began riding, Momma didn't make her get off even though I had trouble steering and turning corners. Abby climbed inside the basket, which made it more balanced and easier to push. She sat bunched together with her knees drawn to her chin and her fingers woven through the wire on each side.

"What are we buying?" I asked as we walked up and down several aisles without putting anything in our basket.

"I don't know," Momma said, staring straight ahead like she wasn't looking to buy anything. Usually she had a list, a pencil, and the whole thing was very organized.

I continued pushing Abby down every aisle except the one on the end with gigantic bags of dog food and charcoal. Momma walked over to the magazine display and took in everything with one slow, smooth sweep of her head. She didn't pick up a single one. We left without spending a penny.

"Why don't we go to the Yellow Jacket?" Momma said. Even though we had already eaten lunch, the Yellow Jacket Café was always a good place to spend time even if only to get a cold drink. As we walked past the bank, a lady watered pink-ruffled flowers that spilled over the edge of concrete pots. Momma said hello to her, and the lady said hello back, but there was no real conversation. Mr. Turpin swept the sidewalk in front of the hardware store, but before I could wave, he looked down at his feet.

The Yellow Jacket was filled with customers. A group of old ladies laughed and lingered over coffee, taking up a long table near the window. Workmen wearing matching shirts gobbled hamburgers like they had no time to spare. People perched on red stools along the counter, and all the tables were taken. Momma guided us to the only open booth in the corner. When I plopped down into the worn seat, I felt the springs bounce beneath me. Surrounding us, old timey photos filled nearly every inch of wall space from floor to ceiling. One of the faded pictures above our table was of a farm worker picking cotton by hand. He dragged a long burlap bag between rows, and I wondered if he had lived in Savage Crossing.

The man sitting alone at the table next to us looked familiar. He gave us a guilty-like glance as though he had played a part in our family troubles. Momma said hi to him. He nodded and eventually spoke. "How's Lee?"

"Not very good," Momma said.

"I was afraid of that," he said. Then he shook his head and looked away quickly, as though his words had dried up. When he took another bite of fried eggs, I realized he was having breakfast for lunch.

"Who's that?" I whispered to Momma.

"No one, just a man who works at the parts store," Momma said.

The lady who baked all the homemade desserts at the Yellow Jacket patted Momma on the shoulder and even left her hand there when she asked about Daddy. Her skin looked soft and her fingernails were trimmed and unpainted. Without asking, she poured coffee into Momma's cup. Swirls of steam rose and the familiar, rich smell filled the space around us. Abby and I ordered soft drinks, and Momma agreed we could order pie, which was a special treat for a non-holiday. Abby ordered chocolate. I decided on lemon meringue, but really, I only wanted the lemon part. The white part always felt weird on my tongue. Since Daddy's sickness had returned, Momma didn't seem worried about her diet and ordered onion rings to go with her coffee.

As we ate pie, we talked about normal stuff, and for a few minutes, I almost forgot we were beginning a strange journey to a place we'd never been. Momma asked if we were looking forward to school starting and reminded us to dig out our school bags from wherever they'd spent the summer. "Clean them up and see if you need any new supplies," she said. Even though my birthday was less than a week away, Momma never mentioned it. She was too busy worrying about Daddy and the farm to plan a party. Balloons and strawberry cake seemed unimportant when Daddy was dying at home in the den, so I never mentioned it either.

Momma placed money on the table, and we left without a word to anyone. As we walked back to the car, the man who always stood against the corner of the gas station waved from across the street, but even he wore a look that seemed to say, "Shoot, they saw me, and I don't know what to say or do."

I wanted to run into the middle of the street, like Roy Henry, and yell, "Even though Daddy has cancer, there's nothing wrong with the rest of us!" I got in the car with Momma and Abby, slamming the door shut.

"Why does everyone act like we're lepers? People who always waved at us before act like we're gonna spread cancer all over town!" I yelled as tears burned my eyes.

"Sickness and death make people uncomfortable. They don't know what to say," Momma said. "But not everyone acts that way. Mrs. Edith acted normal when she brought your pie and filled my coffee cup."

I wiped the tears and stared at the cotton growing along the highway.

Chapter Forty-Nine

Momma didn't forget my birthday, but instead of planning a regular party or a trip to Memphis, she pawned it off on Aunt Fannie, which was fine by me. Momma did find the energy to make my favorite strawberry cake. Still warm from the oven, she wrapped the pan tight in aluminum foil and trusted me to hold it on the short drive to Dian's house.

"We should have eaten some before we left," I said. I slipped my finger underneath the foil, releasing the sugary aroma. Scraping creamy icing from along the edge of the cake, I let it linger on my tongue until it melted. Then I scraped more icing. By the time we got to Dian's house, a channel the size of my index finger had been carved into one entire side of the cake.

It wasn't a real sitting-around-the-dining-room-table-blowing-out-candles sort of birthday affair. Instead, it was more of a regular sleepover during which I happened to turn another year older. And that was cool. Aunt Fannie hung crepe paper streamers over the kitchen table in my honor. They were probably leftover from Dian's last birthday party, but even so, it was a nice touch. While we ate large slices of cake, Aunt Fannie apologized for not having pin-the-tail-on-the-donkey or those horns that unravel when you blow into them.

"That's okay, Aunt Fannie," I told her. "I've outgrown that stuff anyway."

I opened two presents—a square leather purse from Dian and a bead kit from Abby. I liked them both.

Despite the near one-hundred-degree temperature, playing all afternoon in the washed-away gullies along Little River was better than any real party, anyway. The heat bore down on our heads and rose from the ground in waves. We dug tunnels for our Matchbox cars in the secret places we had found along the sand dunes while our Barbies sunned themselves on their own private beach. We built pretend houses using driftwood and old pieces of tin we found buried in the dirt. At dusk, when mosquitoes and sunburn drove us inside, we made mayonnaise sandwiches and ate more strawberry cake.

After supper, we played board games in Dian's bedroom. She had lots of good games that kept us busy for quite some time. When nightfall came, Dian suggested we have a séance. Dian was a natural at séances, not only because she was a good actress with a dramatic voice, but also because her house was perfect for summoning the departed. If we sat in the floor at the end of the hallway and shut all the bedroom doors, the hallway was pitch black, like a cave.

Dian asked Aunt Fannie for a candle, and she gave us a squatty orange one that she'd used in her jack o' lantern last Halloween. "I hope you realize you girls are messing with the devil," she said sounding a bit disgusted with our activity.

"We're only trying to reach Grandma Johnson," Dian explained.

Dian's grandma—who would have been mine and Abby's great-grandma—died before Dian was born. Abby and I still had Nana and Mamaw Pearl, so it seemed only right she should try contacting hers, even if it was from beyond the grave. We waited until nighttime when the spirits were more available. We waited until Uncle Will was snoring in his recliner beside the television.

Placing our fingertips on the plastic pointer contraption that came with the Ouija board, Dian reviewed the rules. Even though we already knew the séance routine, we always began the same way, to make it more serious and formal. "Concentrate on how Grandma Johnson looked," Dian said, nodding to the picture at the end of the hallway above Aunt Fannie's sewing machine.

Grandma Johnson had a round face and dark eyes that stared straight ahead, serious-like, and seemed to follow me when I walked down the hall. "Now close your eyes and think about her," Dian said. "Let's begin with a prayer."

We said the Lord's Prayer in a low voice to keep the devil away from our séance, and because it was the only prayer we all knew by heart.

"Grandma Johnson, we invite you to visit us tonight, on this twenty-first day of August in the year of our Lord, 1973," Dian said in her most theatrical voice.

"Ask her a question," I said.

"Shhhh! I'm getting to that! Grandma Johnson, are you with us?"

The plastic thingamajig felt cool to my touch. I cracked open an eye and watched it resting between the letters G and H. There was no movement.

"Grandma Johnson, this is your granddaughter Dian speaking. Are you with us tonight?"

A mosquito buzzed near my ear, but I resisted smacking it. Maybe Grandma Johnson was a mosquito now? Dian hummed. Abby didn't move or make a peep. In the distance, I heard canned laughter from the television and Uncle Will's snuffling snore. My legs, folded Indian-style, felt cramped and sweaty behind my knees, but I didn't move.

"Grandma, is Grandpa Johnson with you?" Dian continued. "Send us a sign, Grandma Johnson."

"You girls will be up all night if you don't stop that nonsense." Aunt Fannie appeared in the hallway, interrupting us just when the air was starting to feel solemn and different.

"Momma, you ruined it!" Dian's head fell backward against the wall, her whole body deflated as she kicked the Ouija board down the hallway and across the furnace floor grate.

"It's time for bed anyway, you crazy girls." Aunt Fannie staggered and stomped with arms outstretched like Frankenstein, making us laugh.

We unrolled our matching sleeping bags on the dining room floor, safe from everything bad. The window unit whirred and blew icy air across our faces.

"What do y'all want to do tomorrow?" Dian asked, her words soft and sleepy.

"Play on the river bank again," Abby said, yawning through her words. She turned to her side and tucked her hands underneath her cheek, the way she always slept, and closed her eyes.

"Do y'all really believe in séances?" I asked.

303

"Yes," Dian said." Don't you?"

"I don't know," I said. I didn't know what I believed anymore, but I doubted a toy company had invented some magic way to speak with dead people. Even if the Ouija board did work, when Daddy died, I doubted I would try to contact him. The way I saw it, he'd had eleven years to talk to me.

Chapter Fifty

"Brother Brown, Daddy's cancer is bad. Could you pray for Momma? She's sad and isn't even worried about her diet anymore."

"I will, Grace. How are you doing?"

"Fine. I turned a year older since last Sunday."

"Happy birthday, Grace."

"Thank you."

Chapter Fifty-One

My fifth-grade teacher, Mrs. Sinclair, wore long, flowy skirts and black, lace-up boots and circled her brown eyes in different colored, smudgy eyeliner every day. So far, we were having an easy as pie year, with more painting and drawing than long division. Art was her favorite subject. "And now we must awaken the soul," she declared each afternoon after our required studies had been completed for the day. She saw to it that time was reserved for tempera painting or free dance or pairing up to outline our bodies like dead people as we lay on giant lengths of white paper. Even though there were no new kids in my class, everyone seemed different now that our souls had been awakened. More mature even.

Wednesday afternoon, when Abby and I got home from school, Mae was helping Momma with Daddy. In a short time, he had become weak and tired and slept more than he didn't. Still, there was nothing wrong with his brain. If a math question stumped me, on one of his good days he could solve the problem in his head. On a bad day, he cried and yelled for Momma, unable to get comfortable or sleep. Dr. Fairley gave him strong medicine to help with the pain, but it didn't always work. When I wasn't at school, to avoid hearing his moans, I spent lots of time looking for interesting shells and rocks down at the ditch behind the cotton field. Sometimes I climbed a tree or hid in the playhouse and spent the whole afternoon writing in my diary. If he wasn't going to get well and be normal, I wanted him to die already. The whole thing seemed cruel even for someone like Daddy.

"Grace, where are you?" Mae called for me from Daddy's makeshift hospital room. I had just come inside from running all the way to the gray house and back without stopping. I was out of breath and parched. It had been some time since I had left a letter for our missing neighbor, so during library time that day I'd made him a birthday card, even though I didn't know when his birthday was. Filling a glass of water from the tap, I quickly drank it, and refilled the glass before going to see what she wanted. I stood in the doorway, not looking in Daddy's direction.

"Your daddy wants someone to read to him. I'm not a good reader." And she held out the book to me.

"Me?" I shook my head, ignoring the book in her outstretched hand.

"Please, Grace," Daddy said, with a broken and scratchy voice. His hazel eyes looked colorless and dazed, and his face was soft and swollen, distorting his normally strong jawline.

"Go on, Grace." Mae stabbed the air with the book, the one that had sat on Daddy's bedside table as long as I could remember, the Eudora Welty book responsible for my ugly middle name.

I took the heavy volume and stared at the front cover, then settled into the desk chair where Momma did payroll every Friday night. A bookmark held the place of his favorite short story, "Death of a Traveling Salesman." As I opened to it, I wondered how many times Daddy had read the story. Pages were puckered from having been turned again and again. Certain words had been faintly underlined in pencil.

I held my finger on the page but felt distracted and unable to read, so I watched Mae somehow fluff Daddy's pillow without bothering his head. She tied an apron around her wide waist and began tidying up around the room—straightening a stack of clean washcloths, scooping up cotton balls that had spilled and scattered across his desk. Until recently, none of those items would have been found in Daddy's office. I remembered a silly kindergarten game, a game played back when everything was fun and we had a good chance of getting the right answer. Our teacher, who had soft gray hair and a kind voice, placed things in a row on the table for us to consider—a pair of scissors, a ruler, a pencil, an orange. "Now kids, tell me which thing doesn't belong?"

"Grace. Read," Mae said.

I had been so far away, her voice made me jump. Opening the book, I began to read the story aloud. There was no way around it.

I could see right off why Daddy was interested in the story. From the very first sentence, the main character, a man named R. J. Bowman, drove his Ford on a dirt road in Mississippi. That sounded just like something Daddy would do, but the man in the story was a shoe salesman and not a farmer. And the man in the story was sick, too. I couldn't imagine why Daddy wanted me to read about a sick man.

Some of Mrs. Welty's phrases made no sense to me, but I continued reading, sounding out the hardest words. Daddy's slight breathing barely moved the blanket covering his chest, but each time I paused, he opened his eyes and smiled a wilted smile. So I kept reading.

At six o'clock, I took a break while Mae measured out Daddy's medicine. "This is some mighty strong stuff," she said. "Only a smidge will control Mr. Lee's pain, for a little while, anyway." I watched her slow, steady hands tipped with blood-colored fingernails and wondered how she had learned all the things she knew. The plastic syringe was not as scary as most, since there was no needle on the end. When she squirted the drops of liquid into Daddy's mouth, he seemed to swallow without even knowing.

"You're reading so good, Gracie," Mae said, straightening the blanket around Daddy's feet.

"I don't think he hears me." I picked up the book and returned to my chair.

"Oh, I bet he does. People hear all kinds of things when you don't think they can."

After Mae went home, I read a little more out loud. At some point, Momma poked her head in and smiled, grabbed a stack of papers off the desk, and tiptoed back out. Papa Pete came to go over the farm books, and I could hear them talking quietly in the kitchen. Even though I wanted to go see him, something about the story held my attention and kept me reading. When Daddy fell asleep, I turned down the corner of the page to remember where we were in the book.

In the middle of the night, Daddy woke us up, yelling and thrashing against the rails of his bed. We all ran to his bedside. It was a scary thing to see, the way his body rolled back and forth as though he had no control over his arms and legs. Momma couldn't calm him down and yelled for me to call Mrs. Barns. Since I knew Bubba's phone number by heart, I did it fast, my fingers automatically spinning the dial. The phone rang a million times in my ear before she finally answered, sounding confused and annoyed at such a late call.

"Mrs. Barns, this is Gracie Abbott. Momma asked if you could please come to our house quick. Daddy's lost his mind and we don't know what to do."

It seemed like the minute I hung up the phone, Mrs. Barns was standing at our back door, wearing her nightgown and loafers. She moved calmly around the room and kept saying, "Lee. Listen to me, Lee. Take a breath. You're okay."

Mrs. Barns held his arm and swabbed it with alcohol. When the long needle disappeared beneath Daddy's skin, he didn't flinch. I automatically grabbed the pink spot below my shoulder where Daddy had burned my arm not that long ago. His head sank into the soft pillow, and his body collapsed onto the mattress. He slept silently the rest of the night. Momma sat by his side until sunrise.

Chapter Fifty-Two

Momma no longer went to church, because Daddy couldn't stay home alone. Abby and I were still required to go, which didn't seem fair. As we sat at the kitchen table, waiting for Nana to pick us up, Abby and I ate plain corn flakes, because we were out of our favorite cereal. Momma heaved a big sigh like it had taken all of her effort to simply get the box of cereal down from the cabinet. "Why don't you start leaving it down lower so we can reach it ourselves?" I suggested. She said that was a good idea. Momma refilled her coffee cup, poured in a stream of creamer, and stirred it long after it turned from black to caramel-colored. Those Saturday nights when Momma got dressed up and Daddy took her out to eat seemed like forever ago.

On the drive to church, we told Nana all about how Daddy had been out of his mind on Friday night and how Mrs. Barns came over in her nightgown to help. "She gave Daddy a huge shot with a needle this long," Abby said as she held her hands at least six inches apart. Although the needle hadn't been quite that long, it had probably felt that way when it disappeared into Daddy's skin. Nana shook her head and reminded us to be extra helpful to Momma. As far as I knew, Nana still didn't know about our carnival trouble, and I was glad about that. So far, I had kept my promise to Momma too. Now that school started, I could look my words up in the school encyclopedias most any afternoon instead of sneaking over to the gray house in the middle of the night.

We got to church before anyone. Abby and I helped straighten the hymnals and made sure offering envelopes were available at each pew.

Most people seemed to arrive at church in a big clump, all rushing through the doors, talking and laughing and hugging like it had been ages since they had seen one another. Soon, all the regular seats were taken. All the normally empty pews were still empty. Like Daddy, Papa Pete never attended church. For as long as I could remember, he'd always had emphysema on Sundays. Now that Daddy was sick, Papa Pete was taking care of the farm full time, even on Sundays when his emphysema was normally at its worst.

With Momma absent, Aunt Fannie agreed to be our substitute Sunday school teacher. For some reason, with Momma not there, we all sat in different seats around the table. It happened automatically, and once we realized it, we were all surprised even though it wasn't that big of a thing. My view of the back wall was totally different, and although I could still see out the window, I watched the empty highway in front instead of the tree out back.

Our lesson was called "Bad Times for Good People," and I considered it interesting how, so often, our Sunday school book followed the ideas spinning around in my head. We took turns reading examples about Bible people who went through the worst experiences ever, even people who prayed all the time like Noah and Job. Aunt Fannie said that no one could escape hard times. She pointed out if God would let his own son go through the pain of dying on the cross with nails hammered into his hands, why shouldn't we regular folks have problems from time to time?

She had made a good point. I hoped I could remember to share her example later with Momma.

Brother Brown's sermon was about Moses and the tabernacle. When he read from Exodus, the bland words dribbled from his mouth so slow I thought even Nana nodded off for a second. "…and Moses brought in the table, and brought in the candlestick, and set the altar of gold, and hung the door, and set the laver—whatever that was—and anointed oil…" And on and on, with every single tiny thing Moses did except using the bathroom. Brother Brown had a way of choosing the most boring verses in the whole Bible.

I drew pictures in the margin of my Sunday school lesson book. Pictures of flowers, grass, and anything I could think of. Nana handed

Talya Tate Boerner

Abby and me pieces of gum. I said, "Thank you," with my lips and not out loud.

Being a preacher's wife and substitute piano player was not a suitable career choice for Mrs. Brown. I remembered the words of Mrs. Allard, my piano teacher who had died last year. She once said the piano should be treated with respect, the ivory stroked and coaxed into offering the most pleasing sound. Mrs. Brown lifted her thick wrists and banged at the keys, producing the same brash sound no matter the song. I felt certain she had no idea what pianissimo meant. I stared at her sensible shoes and winced as she pounded the pedals into the floor with the force of an uphill bicycle rider. Abby elbowed me and I snort-laughed. Mrs. Brown glowered at us. I wondered if she had forgotten about eating pepper steak at our supper table and being so nice to Abby and Patti.

When Mrs. Brown began playing "Just As I Am," I considered going up to talk to Brother Brown but decided I didn't much feel like it. He looked over at me as though he expected a visit. I shook my head no. It was only a slight shake, but Brother Brown cut the invitational hymn short after the third stanza. That was something.

Chapter Fifty-Three

The cotton field spread from our backyard to the horizon where the Earth seemed to curve. The plants stood chest high. Bolls had begun to dry and ripen. Soon the field would be snowy white. I walked between the rows and studied the leaves and the way they moved in the breeze. A bird darted in my path and flitted away, almost flirting. Lucky barked. My tennis shoes sank into the soft soil. The October air felt refreshing after the hot summer.

Nana believed in miracles and the power of prayer, but so far, I had seen no evidence of either. Or maybe my prayers canceled each other out. How many times had I prayed for Daddy to leave and never come back? And now I found myself praying he wouldn't be in pain.

In the distance, Mae's car puttered toward our house, leaving a faint, smoky trail on the straight, flat highway. When she pulled into the drive, I ran to greet her. She hugged me, and I felt better without a word being spoken between us. While Mae sat with Daddy, Momma ran errands in town. Abby and I went along, hoping for a trip to Sterling's or the record store on Main Street, but it wasn't that sort of trip. I wished we could go back in time, back to the point when Momma smiled more often than not, and Daddy's sickness was only from drinking too much beer. Now everything revolved around cancer. The very air in the house smelled stale and diseased. Every day was on hold.

At the drugstore, Momma picked up a refill of Daddy's pain medicine without stopping to sample the cosmetics or sniff the candles or anything. Then we ran quickly through the grocery store to get eggs, milk, and other regular ingredients, nothing extra or exciting. She did buy a carton of plain, vanilla ice cream, but only because Daddy basically survived on thin milkshakes. As we drove past the auction house at Cottonwood Corner, I shook off the recent bad memory of getting in trouble outside the sideshow tent and thought instead of last fall's Halloween carnival. Bubba and I had sold six cupcakes to the auctioneer. "I'll take them home to my kids," he had told us, as he placed them inside an empty, wooden soda crate. Soon, Savage Crossing would gear up for the next carnival, classroom kings and queens would be selected, mothers would be baking and selling homemade goodies to anyone with a quarter to spare. I wondered who would represent the fifth grade.

"Momma, did you know that since I was last year's Halloween queen, I'll get to crown the new queen?"

"That's true. I had forgotten about that," she said. "I hope your dress still fits."

It would probably still fit, but I knew it would be shorter. According to the marks on the side of our closet door, I had grown three inches taller since last year.

"Hey, look!" Abby yelled and pointed. "We left Lucky outside." Lucky jumped through the cotton field, scaring up flocks of blackbirds.

We never left Lucky outside.

When we pulled into the driveway, Momma's face grew pale, and her breath caught in her throat. Dr. Fairley's long gold Lincoln was parked in her spot in the carport. "Oh no," she whispered and brought the car to a quick stop, jarring my insides and dumping the groceries into the floor. Momma rushed to the back door. I grabbed Daddy's ice cream and followed with Lucky nipping my heels. The motor of Dr. Fairley's car made a ticking sound, as though it had only begun to cool down after the trip from town.

Mae met us at the door. "Mr. Lee was agitated and talking out of his head, so I called Doc Fairley." She was twisting a wet cloth in her thick hands, yet spoke in an unruffled voice. Mae knew how to stay calm even during times of crisis.

Momma rushed past her to Daddy's bedside. Abby and I stood in the doorway and stared at him. He barely made a rumple underneath the blanket and the hair along his brow was damp and pushed away from his face. Although he had spent much of the summer inside the house, his tan had not faded.

"He's resting now," Dr. Fairley said. He carried his doctor bag but was wearing regular clothes. "I gave him a shot. This is all part of the process, Anne." He touched Momma on the shoulder.

She nodded.

I ran and hid underneath my bed where nothing ever changed. The cracked slat was the same as before, split but no worse. The springs underneath my mattress had not loosened or corroded. I did find Barbie's missing pink shoe wedged in a tiny space between the baseboard and wall. I had been searching for it forever.

***

The next morning, Daddy seemed more alert and in less pain, but Momma didn't sound very optimistic when she talked on the telephone with Nana. "It was a bad night. I don't think he'll last much longer. A few weeks, maybe." Not wanting to hear any more, I placed the extension down and went to see if Daddy needed a drink of water or anything. He shook his head no.

In the afternoon, Mrs. Barns brought a chocolate cake over, and she and Momma sat together at the kitchen table drinking coffee. Momma picked at her piece of cake. Mrs. Barns spoke in her glum tone, the one she used in grim situations, like when Bubba got in big trouble at school or when she preached to the PTA ladies about the dangers of earthquakes. I heard her say, "Lee's pain level will intensify near the end. You may want to consider admitting him into the hospital if he lingers." For most of the day, I hung around the house, feeling headachy and uninspired. I spent part of the afternoon resting on my bed, watching shadows move along the ceiling.

While Momma heated up mini-ravioli on the stove, I flipped on the television. At six o'clock, there was nothing to watch, other than the news. And the only thing Walter Cronkite had to talk about was President Nixon and Watergate and crooked things going on in Washington, D.C. I watched for a few minutes because, based on the way Mr. Cronkite removed his black glasses and talked to me like he was sitting inside our den, something important must have happened.

"Mom-maaaaaa!" I yelled as loud as I could so she could hear me in the kitchen.

Momma materialized in front of the television almost as though she had twitched her nose like a witch and appeared. She waved a spatula around the room and practically growled at me.

"Momma?" I said in a whisper, questioning if she was really Momma.

"Grace! If you want to talk to me, come in the kitchen and speak in a civilized tone of voice. Don't yell at me from the den like a wild banshee." She stomped off without giving me time to tell her the Vice President of the United States resigned and everyone wanted Nixon to do the same.

I turned off the television and walked into the kitchen, trying not to make a sound. Momma stood against the countertop, dabbing her eyes with a tissue.

"I'm sorry, Momma."

"It's not you, Gracie," she said and gave me a hug. "I shouldn't have yelled like that. I just have a lot on my mind."

"I know. Me too," I said.

Momma tried to change her expression from sad to cheerful. "Tell your sister supper's ready." I came a heartbeat away from screaming her name, but stopped myself and walked into the bedroom to get her.

Abby dragged Patti into Daddy's empty seat and pretended to spoon ravioli into her permanently shut lips. I told Momma about the Vice President resigning. She didn't seem all that worried about it and said, "I didn't much like him anyway." I didn't think Momma much liked mini-ravioli from a can either, because she barely ate her bowl full. "Gracie, you're in charge of the dishes," she said. "I'm going to bed early."

When supper is ravioli, dishwashing doesn't involve much work. I wrote my name over the dirty bowls and spoons with a green stream of dishwashing soap, and then scrubbed off tomato sauce. I washed out the pot Momma used to heat it up and threw the empty can in the trash too. Abby washed Patti's face with a dishrag and dragged her back to the bedroom, leaving a faint mark on the floor through the dining room.

While Abby played with Patti in the bedroom, I had the television to myself. I flipped through every channel twice and settled on a movie about animals that seemed pretty good. When it was over, I decided to get a bowl of ice cream and eat it in bed. When I walked into the kitchen, I heard Daddy call my name.

"Grace..." I barely heard his ragged voice, but went to see what he needed. He nodded toward the book. I looked at the clock. It was late, but Daddy no longer had much awareness of time. Lately, our daily reading consisted of a paragraph or two before he slept. I counted the few remaining pages in the story and wondered if we would finish it. I placed my bowl of ice cream on the desk and began reading.

The next few paragraphs were confusing. While I read each word slowly, I couldn't quite understand the meaning other than Mr. R. J. Bowman seemed to realize he had an empty heart. And he was sad about it.

I stopped and reread one long sentence again, pausing with each comma and feeling bad for Mr. Bowman. I wondered if he was a real person and if he was still alive.

I looked to see if Daddy was listening.

Tears squeezed from the corners of his closed eyes onto the side of his face. He groaned and pressed his hands against his belly like I sometimes did when I needed to throw up. I didn't know if Daddy's tears came from pain or sadness or from the story I was reading to him. Or maybe the medication he took every four hours turned him into a different person altogether, someone I would learn to like in another time.

"Grace." He held out a shaking hand then let it drop back to the bed.

"Momma!" I shouted.

She didn't come.

I wanted to drop the book and hide underneath my bed until life returned to normal, or began again, but Daddy was staring into my eyes, appearing lucid. He reached for me again. His lips moved, but no words came out. This time he didn't drop his arm but held it steady.

I walked toward the side of Daddy's bed. Even in his sick condition, I felt afraid and worried—afraid I would say or do the wrong thing, worried he would become well and return to his old hurtful ways, terrified he would say nothing at all.

Daddy clutched my wrist, his grip still solid. "Gracie, you're the only strong one," he muttered. I stared at his face, trying to understand his words. "I can't...you know what to do."

"What?" I whispered and shook my head, not understanding. I was not strong. I was weak, the weakest of all. He'd said it before.

"You're the only one who can do it." A film glazed his eyes. He stared out the dark window beyond me, to something or someone not there. The wind blew and scattered the leaves from the tree next to the window, yet the room seemed peaceful, the house calm and ready.

"I'll get Momma," I said. He shook his head no and gripped my arm tighter, a few inches below the burn scar, which was only just beginning to fade.

"The medicine," he said. "The med-i-cine."

I glanced toward his desk and a tray filled with vials and bottles and a plastic sack of syringes. When I looked back at Daddy his furrowed forehead reflected his suffering, but he nodded, one slow up and down movement of his head. And then I understood what he wanted me to do.

"Okay," I whispered. He released my arm.

***

While Momma and Abby slept, I memorized every night sound, so I wouldn't forget—the fan as it whirred back and forth, the rhythmic tap of the shade against the bedroom window, Lucky's heavy breathing as he dozed at the foot of my bed. Outside, tree frogs croaked in darkness and trucks traveled down the interstate in one continuous drone. With my head against my wrist, I counted each second as it ticked off on my Cinderella watch. I waited as late as possible. Mae always said nothing good ever happened in the middle of the night.

One Mississippi, Two Mississippi...

I listened for the grandfather clock in the dining room and slipped from bed when the chime struck one.

Daddy's breathing was shallow and slight. I turned my ear to his chest and felt his tired heartbeat. I had never been so close to him. Or so close to death. Daddy had worn out his body and used up his life doing everything to excess. Farming. Always farming. And drinking. How often had I prayed for him to die? Now I felt empty.

I walked to Daddy's desk. Ledger books and farm reports had been replaced with rubbing alcohol and cotton swabs and a plastic pan for those times Daddy puked with little warning. When Lucky appeared at my bare feet, I jolted. "Shhhh," I said. He sat on his haunches and watched. My only witness.

I repeated the steps I'd observed over the past weeks when Mae gave Daddy his medicine. Insert the dropper into the glass bottle. Pull the plunger. Clear liquid poured into the tube, temporary pain relief. Instead of stopping at Mae's line on the tube, a splash of a dose the size of the tip of my little finger, I filled the dropper to capacity, ten times the normal amount.

A thread of broken moonlight filtered through the window, outlining the shape of Daddy's thin body underneath a pile of quilts. Although he slept, his hand twitched. I held the dropper into the ray of light and stared at it for a moment before pushing the tip of the plunger into Daddy's mouth. My hand quivered as the liquid disappeared into his throat without a sound. He swallowed automatically.

By daybreak, Daddy's body was cold.

Chapter Fifty-Four

Before the service started, Abby and I stood with Momma beside Daddy's casket. We stared at him while Momma whispered, "He looks good."

I didn't think so. Daddy's skin looked dull and plastic like the fake people at the Wax Museum in Hot Springs. I thought if I poked his cheek, the indentation of my finger would stay on his face forever.

I stared at Daddy's nose. His chest. I watched for any movement, an accidental jerk, a final breath. There was nothing. His heartbeat was gone. Momma said his body no longer had any blood inside it, but I wondered where all that blood went.

Two days ago, we took Daddy's black suit to the funeral home in town. Abby and I watched as Momma handed the plastic hanging bag over to the man in charge. "This is for Lee Abbott," she said as though he worked in the back room and had forgotten his sack lunch. Now Daddy lay stiff and straight, wearing that same suit, with a white shirt buttoned to his neck and a maroon tie knotted tight. I wondered if he wore shoes.

I wondered if he knew how uncomfortable he looked.

I expected him to sit straight up and say, "Anne, what the hell am I wearing?"

All morning Momma fussed around, worried about how to dress for Daddy's funeral, as though he might have one final chance to say, "That dress makes you look fat," or "I hate that color," or "You paid what for that?"

She finally chose a navy blue dress—dark, but not funeral black. "He never liked me in black," she said.

When Mrs. Brown began playing the piano, Momma and Abby and I took our reserved spots on the first pew. We were surrounded by family. Everyone looked sadder than I'd ever seen them. Mamaw Pearl wailed and held her head in her hands like she was in great pain. Sitting behind us, cousins and aunts and uncles from Tennessee I didn't know filled three entire pews.

Momma held a tissue to her eyes and dabbed at her face. I stared at the topaz ring on her finger and wondered if Daddy knew the truth about last year's Christmas gift now. A spray of white roses draped the end of Daddy's wooden casket, a casket so shiny and slick it looked freshly shellacked. Odd stands of spikey, purple flowers stood on both sides of the sanctuary, lined up like bridesmaids at a strange wedding.

Even though Brother Brown barely knew Daddy, he spoke as though they were best friends. He said things like, "He was a hard worker," and, "There was no better farmer in the county." Those were true statements.

While Brother Brown read from Deuteronomy, I stared at the baptismal font, the place my sins had been erased not that long ago. Since then, no one else had been baptized at Boon Chapel.

How many new sins had I racked up since my baptism? Lots. The worst sort of sins.

Brother Brown talked about life having seasons. He said no one from the youngest to the oldest is immune from death. Momma made a sobbing sound. Abby was crying too. He went on to say something about secret things belonging unto the Lord and how those things would be revealed. "Death is never easy to accept," he said.

What about murder, I wondered.

Eventually Brother Brown stopped talking, and Mrs. Brown led the Boon Chapel congregation in singing the drabbest, slowest version anyone ever heard of "Amazing Grace." It was a poor choice for Daddy, who would have preferred a country song. Also, he would have been happier buried in a pine box in the cotton field behind our house without all this big to-do. But that part wasn't up to me. Or him.

Glancing at the ceiling, I wondered if he was watching us. I didn't feel his presence.

I didn't cry.

Nothing about the afternoon seemed real.

321

At the end of the funeral, I planned to go up and talk to Brother Brown. To confess my crime. I was prepare to spend the rest of my days in the Savage Crossing jailhouse. But for the first time at Boon Chapel, there was no invitational hymn. Instead, Uncle Will and some of Daddy's friends carried the casket out the front door and into the clear fall afternoon.

Until Mae explained it to me, I hadn't understood the correlation of death to food, but during the previous few days, a steady stream of platters and crockpots had flowed into our kitchen from the ladies of Boon Chapel. Mae said southern women always cooked in times of trial. "Taking food to the bereaved makes everyone feel better, not only the grieving souls who don't have no energy to cook, but the neighbors doing the cooking as well."

More food covered our kitchen counters and dining room table than I'd ever seen in our house at one time. There was chicken and dressing, piles of spaghetti with meatballs, macaroni and cheese, buttermilk biscuits with fresh pear preserves, every type of pie, jugs of sweet tea, and a rainbow of gelatin salads, some with pecans and some with fruit cocktail suspended inside. Daddy's cotton choppers from Texas brought homemade pork tamales wrapped in cornhusks with a fiery sauce that burned my tongue. Someone from First Baptist Savage Crossing brought over a tray filled with lunchmeat and cheese, even Daddy's favorite olive loaf. For a minute, I forgot he wasn't there to eat it.

The smorgasbord of food turned out to be a convenient thing. After Daddy's coffin had been lowered into a grave near the big cottonwood tree, everyone had driven to our house in a follow-the-leader line of cars from Boon Chapel to our driveway. Maggie sliced cake and served sandwiches, and Mae poured iced tea and cleared the plates that piled up on the dining room table. Brother and Mrs. Brown talked to people in low, serious voices, nodding their heads a lot. Daddy's funeral turned into a strange sort of party. People seemed relieved with food in their bellies.

I sat on the end of the living room couch, nibbled an oatmeal cookie, and waited to talk to Brother Brown.

"How are you handling everything, Gracie?" he asked when he finally walked over to talk to me. He held a paper plate that contained the last few bites of a sandwich. I had a feeling he had grown tired of mingling with the adults. In some ways, being a preacher was worse than being a farmer.

"I need to ask you an important question, Brother Brown." I paused and waited until he looked into my eyes and gave me his full attention.

"Okay," he said. He placed the plate on the table next to me and waited for me to talk.

I swallowed the last of my cookie, then stood and faced him. "Are you like a doctor?"

"I'm not sure I follow you." He squinted his eyes and never moved them from mine.

"Do you keep secrets the way a doctor does? A doctor takes an oath and swears on the Bible he won't blab the things his patients tell him. I saw it on a television show," I added. My stomach felt sick, and I twisted my hands together. If I didn't talk to him soon, my insides would burst.

"Oh, I see what you mean. Yes, I suppose so." He nodded, with his hand on his chin.

I wasn't sure I believed him when it came to breaking the commandments and life or death issues, but I decided he was the only person I could tell. "Come with me," I said. I took his hand and pulled him down the hallway toward my bedroom. When I shut the door behind us, Brother Brown startled visibly at the life-sized poster of Donny Osmond covering the closet door. "Don't worry, it's just a poster," I said.

"Why don't you tell me what's bothering you," Brother Brown said. He sat down on the edge of my bed and crossed his arms like he was preparing to think hard and thoughtfully. His forehead crinkled, and his glasses shifted up before settling back on his nose.

As I paced back and forth in the small space between my bed and Abby's, I stared at the ceiling, trying to find the right words. Brother Brown didn't say anything for a few seconds.

"Grace?" He patted the bed next to him, but I shook my head and kept walking and turning and walking and turning. Finally, I stopped and sat beside him.

"I killed Daddy. That's what I need to tell you. I killed my daddy." My upper lip trembled and tears started from my eyes. I felt a jag in my throat as I pictured Daddy lying in that awful, cold box in the dark ground at Boon Chapel Cemetery. He was stuck there forever, wedged between dead people he didn't know and probably would never have liked.

"What on Earth do you mean?" Brother Brown moved in closer.

"I couldn't stand it. He was moaning something awful and in terrible pain. Mrs. Barns said he might linger or have to go to the hospital. Daddy told me to do it. At least, I think he did. He said I was strong, that I would know what to do. So I gave him a whole huge dose of pain medicine, enough that he never woke up again. Now I'm an eleven-year-old murderer."

The truth spilled from my lips in one spindly breath. Brother Brown took my spot between the beds and paced the small floor space while I sobbed. I cried and cried and couldn't stop even when my chest heaved and my heart clenched. I cried for what I'd done and what I'd thought, and for all those times I'd wanted Daddy to die and leave me in peace. I cried because I didn't want to go to jail.

"Grace, listen to me." Brother Brown held my shoulders and stared into my eyes that felt sore and too swollen for my eye sockets. Even hearing the worst of all confessions, he seemed composed and in control. "Your Daddy was near death. It was probably a matter of weeks or days. You actually helped him by giving him a compassionate way out."

"But..." I shook my head as the tears came again. My stomach seized and I thought I might throw up on his brown shoes.

"Grace, does anyone else know?"

I shook my head.

"Okay, good. I want you to understand that you helped your father. He's no longer suffering, and there's no need for you to suffer either." Brother Brown seemed sincere, like he really didn't think I was a killer. He prayed for me and said God would understand and forgive, which made me feel a bit better. Simply having told him gradually loosened the tight knot in my chest.

Yet still I worried.

I stayed awake all night, waiting for the police to come and take me to jail. I replayed my conversation with Brother Brown. He'd said I didn't do anything wrong, but I wasn't sure I believed him. I finished reading "Death of a Traveling Salesman." Then I re-read the entire story.

The police never showed up. When the sky brightened and morning slipped through the crack in our pale pink curtains, I pulled my diary from beneath my mattress and wrote out a full confession. It was my last diary entry.

Chapter Fifty-Five

Clutching Barbie around her thin waist, I grabbed my diary and disappeared into chest-high cotton. Lucky followed on my heels, nipping at my ankles. Eventually, he tired of my unhurried walk and bounded ahead, barking and biting at the wind, the tip of his white tail blending into the landscape. During the three days it took to plan Daddy's funeral, dry bolls split and burst like white cotton candy. Daddy never saw his last cotton crop. I wondered if he knew how extraordinary it had turned out.

Near the edge of the field, I closed my eyes and listened to the high-pitched, noisy call of birds flying overhead. They sounded restless and shrill, or maybe they were mocking the new day. Mocking me. The fall sun warmed my face, and the breeze made the fine hairs on my arms tingle. I scanned the ditch bank for the perfect spot, a private place hidden by brush and flowers. I found it beneath the shade of the tallest oak tree, an area as familiar to me as my own bedroom.

"Right here, Lucky," I said, plopping down on my knees. Lucky swiped half my face with a wet lick before I could stop him.

I scooped up heavy handfuls of rich, soft soil and piled the loose dirt nearby. Lucky sniffed and pawed at the hole, almost helping me dig. Barbie watched from a safe distance, dressed in her best ball gown.

When the hole was deep to my elbow, I settled my diary in the bottom, facing up. The bright pink cover looked bizarre against the dark earth. It was still locked tight, the tiny gold key in my pocket. On top of the diary, I laid Barbie flat on her back, facing the sun, with her sheer, tulle skirt spread all around. I lifted a fistful of dirt and held it above the hole. "Dust to dust," I said. Lucky cocked his head to one side and watched as dirt filtered through my fingers. Barbie's blonde hair, her painted-on smile, the skinned mark on her upturned nose—I buried everything beneath the soil of Daddy's farm. Standing on the mound, I pressed my tennis shoes into the freshly turned dirt until the land felt level again. Then I transplanted a yellow wildflower beside it.

"There's only one more thing to do," I said to Lucky. I walked to the edge of the ditch bank, took the gold key from my pocket, and slung it, hard. It disappeared beneath the murky surface of standing water without a ripple. Lucky barked and wagged his tail, but didn't chase after it.

On my way home, I stopped to rest and think. I lay back between two furrows, with my head touching the cool soil. Lucky gave me a curious look then lay down beside me. The earth's freshness held me, protected me. Overhead, fluffy clouds drifted, the sort more typical of June than October. "Our sky is filled with cotton too," I said. Pulling a clump from the boll nearest my face, I stretched the fibers, blocking the sun's glare with silky threads. The clean scent reminded me of sheets, sundried on Momma's clothesline. Nearby, on the interstate, trucks hummed, driving someplace else. As the sun moved higher overhead, Lucky and I walked back home through the cotton field.

***

Momma met me in the backyard. She stood with one hand on her hip and the other shading the sun from her eyes. "Grace, there's someone in the kitchen who wants to talk to you. For goodness sakes, where have you been? You've been gone all morning."

"Is it the police?" I asked, straining to see beyond the shrubs to the front driveway. My mind raced, and I considered darting through the field and escaping to the gray house. I wondered if he would be the same policeman who had helped us when our house was robbed and Daddy's truck was stolen.

"No, are you expecting the police?" Momma chuckled, but I didn't. She looked at me strangely.

"Who is it?" I felt relief, even though a part of me wanted to get it over with. Waiting for jail was maddening.

"Come see for yourself," Momma said. She draped an arm around my shoulder and pulled me toward the back porch. "What have you been doing? You're filthy." She picked a leaf from my hair and dropped it on the grass.

"Digging in the dirt."

A man sat at our kitchen table, drinking black coffee and eating funeral cake. Based on the crumbs spread across his dessert plate, it was probably Mrs. Penny's apple cake.

He stood, smiled, and reached out his hand. "Grace? It's so very nice to finally make your acquaintance. I'm Winn Berton. I live in the gray house down the way."

It took a minute for his words to register.

My breath caught in my throat.

"Really?" I rubbed my dirty palms against the front of my jeans then put my hand in his. Instead of shaking, he clasped it. He was tall and beanpole thin, with a shock of dark hair that stuck up in every direction. He looked unusual in a movie star sort of way.

"I saw your father's obituary in the newspaper and wanted to pay my respects. Of course, I wanted to meet you too." He grinned bright and wide, and he had very straight teeth.

I felt empty of words.

"Your letters really helped me during the past few months, Grace."

I glanced at Momma.

"Mr. Berton told me you'd been writing to him. Grace, I had no idea," Momma said, smiling as big and proud as if I'd entered a secret contest and won a fancy prize. She didn't seem upset at all, which I found odd. After all, I had been writing to a complete stranger.

"Yes, she sent me several letters and cards on special occasions. I wanted to thank you in person, Grace," Mr. Berton added.

"What happened to you?" I asked, immediately wondering if his truth was none of my business, but my words were already floating around the kitchen.

As he began to explain, we all sat together at the table. I found it difficult to concentrate and couldn't believe the man in the gray house was sitting in our house. In the flesh and blood, as Mae always said.

"It was a bad time for me," he began. "I was having lots of problems and trying to figure things out about my life and my future. I had just returned from Vietnam and was deeply depressed. I began taking pills. Too many pills. I thought they made me feel better, but really they made me sicker."

"Did you really shoot yourself?" I asked. Momma gave me a look but didn't say anything.

"Unfortunately, I did. Combat can do crazy things to people, Grace. I wasn't thinking straight." He paused and looked down at his hands. "My grandfather had an impressive collection of hunting rifles and shotguns, and I couldn't stand to see them in the house. I had decided to clean them up and sell them in Memphis. Like I said, I wasn't right in my head, and I don't remember much about what happened. If not for your mother's phone call, I wouldn't be here now," he said.

I glanced at Momma who was watching me. I remembered the gun case in his fancy library, and I wanted to tell him I'd been inside his house but thought better of it.

"Are you back for good?" I asked, finally thinking of something worthwhile to say.

"No, I'm here for a few days, packing up the house, preparing to sell it. Hopefully, you'll get new neighbors soon. Normal ones who won't cause so much trouble." His laugh was easy and genuine, and his mind seemed okay now.

"Oh." I felt let down and wanted to ask him not to go since he'd just come back, but I didn't. He and Momma discussed the gray house and how, after he'd inherited it from his dead uncle, he had planned to move in and fix it up. But he said something about college and the war and moving to New York, and that was the point when I noticed the package sitting in the middle of the table.

While Momma refilled his coffee, I scrubbed my grimy hands at the kitchen sink and rubbed the green mark from my wrist left by my copper bracelet. "Mr. Berton, I have a P.O.W. bracelet, see?" I extended my arm toward him.

"I like that, Grace. There are still lots of missing soldiers that need our thoughts. And you can call me Winn," he added.

I asked him if he knew my P.O.W., James Tyler, but he didn't. "Mr. Winn, maybe you should get a bracelet too," I said. "It might make you feel better."

"Maybe I will. And, Grace, I have a favor to ask you."

329

"You do?"

"Since I'll be cleaning out the house and selling most everything, I wondered if you might take some books off my hands? I seem to remember you mentioning in one of your letters how much you would enjoy having your own set of encyclopedias?" He cocked his eyebrows and his dark eyes glinted.

My face flushed. I'd never written anything about encyclopedias in my letters to him. I slowly nodded, and Momma said, "Isn't that nice."

"Good. I'll bring them by in the next few days."

He sat up square in his chair, brushed his hands together, and made the motions of someone about to leave. Momma tried to get him to stay for lunch or to at least eat more cake. He patted his board-flat stomach and declined. "Oh, I almost forgot, Grace, I brought you something." He reached for the package in the center of the table and handed it to me. It was wrapped in brown paper and tied with a silver ribbon. Right off, I knew it was a book.

Instead of ripping into the paper, I unwrapped the gift in a sophisticated manner, pulling off the tape and trying not to appear overly eager.

"Oh, wow." It was a journal. A fancy diary, covered in soft beige leather, with gold-tipped pages. In the center, in elegant script, my name had been engraved—not my whole name, just Grace L. Abbott.

"I assumed by your letters that you must enjoy writing. I hope it suits you."

"*Merci*," I said. Somehow I knew he spoke French too. "I have something for you too. I'll go get it." Momma gave me a curious look as I ran down the hall to my bedroom.

"Hold out your hand," I said. I placed my special marble in the center of Mr. Berton's palm. "I found this marble in a secret place beneath the floor at Boon Chapel. It will keep you safe, even when you don't realize it."

"Thank you, Grace. I'll treasure it." He squeezed his palm tight around it and smiled. I knew he was grateful to have such a gift.

After Mr. Berton left, I lay on my bed, stared at the ceiling, and thought about how complicated and far from perfect life could be. But it could be good too. Thumbing through the gold-tipped pages of my new journal, I inhaled the smell of fresh, clean paper. I placed my new

330

journal on the bedside table and realized it would be a long time before I thought of something important enough to write.

Talya Tate Boerner

About the Author

Talya is a Delta girl who grew up making mud pies on her family's cotton farm in Northeast Arkansas. After thirty years as a commercial banker in Dallas, she returned to the state she loves and now lives in Fayetteville with her husband, John, and two miniature schnauzers, Lucy and Annabelle. Talya is a regular contributor to *Delta Crossroads* and *Front Porch Magazine*. Her work has been published in *Arkansas Review*, Postcard Shorts, and The Write Life. Talya's love of food, farming, and nature is evident on her personal lifestyle blog, "Grace, Grits and Gardening." She loves to cook and believes most any dish can be improved with a side of collard greens. *The Accidental Salvation of Gracie Lee* is her debut novel.